THE Room ON Rue Amélie

THE Room ON Rue Amélie

KRISTIN HARMEL

GALLERY BOOKS

New York   London   Toronto   Sydney   New Delhi

G

Gallery Books
An Imprint of Simon & Schuster, Inc.
1230 Avenue of the Americas
New York, NY 10020

This Gallery Books export edition March 2018

GALLERY BOOKS and colophon are registered trademarks of Simon & Schuster, Inc.

For information about special discounts for bulk purchases, please contact Simon & Schuster Special Sales at 1-866-506-1949 or business@simonandschuster.com.

The Simon & Schuster Speakers Bureau can bring authors to your live event. For more information or to book an event, contact the Simon & Schuster Speakers Bureau at 1-866-248-3049 or visit our website at www.simonspeakers.com.

Interior design by Bryden Spevak

Manufactured in the United States of America

10 9 8 7 6 5 4 3 2 1

ISBN 978-1-5011-9302-6
ISBN 978-1-5011-7141-3 (ebook)

To Holly Root, Abby Zidle, and Kristin Dwyer.

All three of you recently made big career decisions and took on new challenges. I'm so proud of you—and so grateful for your professional support and wonderful friendship.
I'm so lucky to have you in my life.

And to all of you who have been strong enough to stand up for what you believe in—in the small moments and the large ones. Making the world a better place begins with even the tiniest acts of personal bravery. May you forever hold fast to the courage to follow your heart.

THE Room ON Rue Amélie

CHAPTER ONE

March 2002

She sleeps beside me, her narrow chest rising and falling, and already I miss her.

The sand in the hourglass is running out, flowing relentlessly toward the end. There's never enough time, not when a person has become a part of you. We were lucky to survive the war, my wife and I, and not a day passes that I don't think of those we lost. I know it's greedy to want just one more week, one more month, one more year with her when we were already given so much time. The last half century has been a gift we never expected, perhaps a gift we never deserved.

Still, I can't let go. I can't imagine my world without her, for my life didn't really begin until the day we met. But I'm as powerless to protect her in this moment as I was all those years ago in Paris, though both then and now I tried to fool myself into believing I had some control.

I rise quietly, careful not to disturb her. When she awakens, the pain will return, so while I yearn for her company, I'm grateful that for now, she's at peace.

I shuffle into the kitchen, boil water in our electric kettle, steep some Earl Grey tea, and make my way to the front porch. It's March, so the air is crisp, as crisp as it gets here in Antelope Valley, some sixty miles north of Los Angeles. I stare into the misty morning, and my breath catches in my throat when I see it: the first bloom of the season. In the coming weeks, the fields will turn brilliant shades of yellow, orange, and red. My wife will almost certainly be gone by then, but at least she'll have this, one last dawn to the poppy season.

"Thank you," I say, looking upward to where I imagine God must be. "Thank you for this."

I've been talking to God a lot lately, which is strange because during the war I might have argued that He didn't exist. But in the years since, I've surprised myself by slowly wending my way back to faith. It began with our daughter, Nadia, for there's no denying that she was a miracle. And when she had three healthy children of her own, I believed a little more. When our grandchildren gave us great-grandchildren, and my wife and I were still here, I had no choice but to acknowledge a higher power.

Then again, perhaps I'd known on some level that He was there all along, because what other explanation could there have been for my wife and me finding each other in the midst of such chaos all those years ago?

As I gaze out at the rolling fields, I can see our lives unfolding here, our daughter twirling in the sunlight, our grandchildren chasing each other through the blooms. I sip my tea and blink a few times to clear my vision. It's embarrassing how emotional I've grown lately. Men aren't supposed to cry, especially men of my generation. But when it comes to the love of my life, I'm powerless against the tide.

I finish my tea and head back into the house to check on her. She should still be sleeping, but I find her in bed with her eyes open, her head tilted toward the door. She's still beautiful, even in old age, even as she succumbs to the cancer we caught too late. "Good morning, my love," she says.

"Good morning, my darling girl." I force a smile.

"Have the poppies bloomed yet?"

I nod, and her eyes fill with tears. I know they're tears of happiness, and I share her joy. "Just one for now," I reply. "But the others won't be far behind."

"What color, my love? What color is the first one?"

"Red. The first poppy of the season is red."

"Of course." She lies back and smiles. "Of course it is."

When she focuses on me again, we gaze at each other for a long time. Looking into her eyes always washes the decades away and takes me back to the day I first saw her.

"I must ask something of you," she says softly.

"Yes." I know what it is before she says the words.

"I want to go to the top of the hill just once more. Please."

"I will take you." My strength has waned with time; I had a heart attack last year, and I haven't felt like myself since. But I knew this would be my darling girl's last wish, and I will make it come true, whatever it takes. "We can go when you're ready. But let's wait a few more days until the poppies are fully in bloom." Of course, the request is partially a selfish one; I want to give her a reason to hang on a little longer, to stay with me.

She smiles. "Yes, you're right." She's already fading, her eyelids heavy, her gaze growing unfocused. "She should be here, though, not me," she whispers after a moment. "It always should have been her." I know exactly who she's talking about: her best friend, the one who was like a sister to her, the one we lost so senselessly all those years ago.

"God had a plan, my darling." I can't say what I really want to, which is that I'm grateful it was my wife who survived. That's a selfish, terrible thing to think, isn't it? No one should have died at all. But fate doesn't always play fair.

"I'll see her again soon." Her voice is so faint I can hardly hear her as she adds, "On the other side. Don't you think I will?"

"Don't go yet," I say. "Please." And as she drifts back to sleep, I sink down into the chair beside her and begin to cry. I don't know how I'll live without her. The truth is, since the day I met her, it's all been for her. My whole life. My whole existence. I don't know how I'll say good-bye.

CHAPTER TWO

December 1938

The first time Ruby Henderson saw Marcel Benoit, she knew her life was about to change.

When she wandered into Café Claude on the west side of Central Park on a damp and frigid Thursday afternoon, she'd merely been trying to get warm. It was three days before Christmas, and she still wasn't accustomed to the Northeast's icy winters. The penetrating chill wasn't helping with her homesickness either. She hadn't been able to afford a ticket back to Southern California for the school break, but perhaps seeing her parents would have made the loneliness worse anyhow. Besides, it had been Ruby herself who had insisted, nearly four years earlier, that leaving her small desert town to study in Manhattan was a good idea. *I'm in search of a big life*, she had announced with all the confidence she could muster. *And I won't find it in the middle of nowhere.*

But now, surrounded by mothers holding the hands of cheerful children in thick coats, and with Christmas carols and the smell of roasting chestnuts in the air, she found herself wishing that she wasn't so alone. As a few snowflakes began to drift from the graying sky, she looked away from the window, sighed, and turned back to Fitzgerald's *The Beautiful and Damned*. She could always find comfort in a good book.

She had just taken a sip of her black coffee when the café door opened, letting in both a great gust of wind and a man in a black woolen coat. He removed his hat, revealing a thick shock of dark hair and chiseled features that reminded her a bit of Cary Grant. Ruby's breath caught in her throat as she stared at him. There was something about him, something mysterious and magnetic, that made it impossible to look away.

The man's gaze landed on her, and he smiled, a slow, perfect smile. He made his way, limping slightly, to the table directly opposite hers and sat down, removing his overcoat to reveal a perfectly cut navy suit. "Well, hello," he said, as if they were sharing a table, as if he'd come there just to meet her. She thought she detected the hint of an accent. He was young, no more than four or five years older than she.

"Hello." She was trying to sound casual, as if this sort of thing happened to her all the time, but she feared her burning cheeks were giving her away.

"I'm Marcel Benoit." The way he was looking at her made her feel as if they were the only two people on earth.

"Ruby Henderson."

"Are you waiting for someone?" Yes, he definitely had an accent, refined and exotic. British, maybe? No, that wasn't it.

Ruby took a deep breath and said the bravest thing she'd ever said to a man. It was, after all, Christmastime, and she had nothing to lose. "I think perhaps I was waiting for you."

His smile spread slowly, like syrup. "Well, in that case, may I join you?"

Ruby nodded and he stood, grabbing his coat and hat and taking the seat opposite hers. He smelled like pipe tobacco, sweet and spicy, and up close, she could see two tiny freckles just under his right eye. His eyebrows were thick and dark, and his nose and cheekbones looked as if they'd been cut from marble.

"I was just cursing my luck at being stranded so far from home during the holidays," he said, holding her gaze. "But now, I think, perhaps it is not so bad."

"Where are you from?"

"Paris."

But of course he was. She recognized the accent now, the way he carried himself, the way he was dressed. He was far too stylish to be from anywhere else.

"You're reading Fitzgerald, I see," he added. "He is a great fan of my city."

"Oh, so am I. Not that I've ever been. I've always dreamed of it, though. All of my favorite writers spent time there, you see. Hemingway. Gertrude Stein. Fitzgerald, of course. What I wouldn't have given to be a part of their Saturday salons!" She felt suddenly silly; she hadn't intended to sound so young, so naïve.

But he didn't seem to notice. "Ah yes, on the rue de Fleurus. I know it well. My father was a patron of Matisse."

"Henri Matisse? The painter?"

"Yes. He and my father knew each other before the Great War. In fact, he brought my father to Madame Stein's salon a few times."

"Is your father an artist?"

"Just an art dealer, I'm afraid. He died a few years ago."

"I'm very sorry." A heavy silence settled over them, and Ruby was glad when the waitress interrupted to ask Marcel if there was something he would like. He ordered a cup of black coffee and asked Ruby if she'd like to split a slice of apple pie. As the waitress walked away, Ruby wondered how they had advanced so quickly to the intimacy of sharing a dessert. Not that she minded.

"What are you doing here in New York?" she asked him.

He studied her for a moment. "I thought I was here for business. But now I realize I might be here for another reason entirely."

"And what is that?"

He leaned forward, locking eyes with her once again. "Perhaps to meet the woman of my dreams."

THEY WERE MARRIED THAT JUNE in a ceremony at her family's church in California, just after Ruby completed her degree, and by July, she was living in Paris. Marcel hadn't mentioned, at first, that his spacious apartment on the rue Amélie, inherited from his parents, had a view of the tip of the Eiffel Tower, or that it was located in the same building as a tiny art gallery called La Ballerine, whose narrow windows were filled with a changing array of beautiful ballet-themed paintings and sculptures made by local artists. He hadn't told her about the half-blind and entirely deaf Madame Lefèvre, who served rather inefficiently as the building's concierge, or about the way one could hear church bells echoing through the streets on Sunday mornings, a concerto of beautiful sounds. But these were the details that brought her new world alive.

Her parents hadn't wanted her to go, but Ruby had already made up her mind. She loved Marcel, and she would make a life with him. That life would be in Paris, at least for now, and though she would miss her parents terribly, she was eager for an adventure, something to stretch the boundaries of the small world she'd known.

"It's not the size of your world I'm worried about," her father had said, his face gray, when she told him this a few days before the wedding. "Europe is a powder keg, my dear. I was there for the Great War. The Continent has a short fuse, and all it takes is someone to light it. Hitler, it seems, is holding a match."

Ruby had shaken her head. After all, she read *The New York Times*; she understood the politics of Europe. "No, Father. Germany has been appeased. Now that they've received the Sudetenland—"

Her father had cut her off. "It won't be enough."

She was sure he was being overly cautious. "Don't worry, Father. I'll come back to visit very soon."

He had looked at her for a long time before nodding. "God willing."

And now Ruby was here, proving her point by living a life of gaiety in the city she'd always dreamed of. She and Marcel drank champagne at the finest cafés, attended the finest parties, wore the finest fashions. His job as an art dealer for the company his father had founded was lucrative and placed them in Paris's most elite circles. Admittedly, Ruby wasn't using her education degree, but she was confident she was doing something better: she was soaking up life. When she became a teacher one day, she'd be a better one because of all she was experiencing. Or maybe she was meant to do something else, something extraordinary, here in France. The future was wide open.

Paris certainly didn't feel like a city on the cusp of war, the way her father had warned, but as the months passed, there was a growing sense that Germany was only playing possum. It made Ruby increasingly uneasy. Could there be some truth to her father's words after all?

"We are fine," Marcel said firmly each time Ruby broached the subject. "You should not spend so much time worrying." He refused to discuss politics with her, which bothered her. Hadn't he known from the start that she was interested in world affairs? He had said once that it was one of the things he loved about her. But now he seemed to prefer taking her to grand parties and balls, where it had become her role to sparkle quietly on his arm. And though she enjoyed the revelry, she began to feel as if they were merely keeping up a façade. Sometimes, it felt as if the whole city was doing the same.

"I think war is coming whether we want to admit it or not, Marcel," she said as they made their way home late one waning August night from a ball at the Hôtel Salé on the Right Bank. The elaborate fete had been thrown by an American heiress, and Ruby felt emboldened, having just spent the evening among fellow expatriates who had actually been interested in hearing her opinion. "We can't just hide our heads in the sand anymore."

"I would never put you in harm's way, my darling." Marcel didn't look at her.

"But aren't you concerned? A war would change everything. What if Hitler wants Paris as a feather in his cap?"

Their car pulled down the rue de Grenelle, bringing the shadow of the Eiffel Tower into view. "And what a lovely feather it would be," Marcel murmured, gazing for a moment at the tower, a ghost against the moonlit sky. "But we won't let that happen, my dear."

"*Who* won't let it happen? It seems the French government is doing nothing but acquiescing, and the army isn't ready." The car turned onto the rue Amélie and drew to a stop.

Marcel got out and opened Ruby's door for her. "You shouldn't read so much of things you don't understand. Don't you trust me?"

She pressed her lips together. She wanted to tell him that she *did* understand, that she was smarter than he gave her credit for these days. When had he stopped listening to her? But it was late, her head was spinning from the champagne, and suddenly, she was exhausted. "Of course I trust you," she said as Marcel held open the grand red door to their building and led the way up the stairs to their first-floor apartment. "It's Hitler I don't trust."

"Well, fortunately," Marcel said, unlocking their front door, "you are not married to him."

LESS THAN A MONTH LATER, on the first of September, news arrived that Hitler's armies had invaded Poland, and that the French army was being mobilized. Two days later, France and their British allies found themselves officially at war with Germany. And though life went on in Paris, the theaters and cafés swelling with people desperate to escape the encroaching reality, there was no longer any denying that darkness was at the gates.

"The Maginot Line will hold," Parisians repeated again and again, desperation shining in their eyes. Ruby wanted to believe that the fortified borders were safe too. But she'd arrived here having pulled the wool over her own eyes. And now, she knew she had no choice but to stare straight ahead into the future, whether she liked the look of it or not.

CHAPTER THREE

December 1939

Hanukkah came early that year, and it seemed to Charlotte Dacher that perhaps the holiday itself was scrambling to happen faster than it was supposed to. Maybe it, too, was plagued with a dark sense of foreboding about the future.

Papa, of course, called that sort of thinking ridiculous. Hanukkah only seemed early because the twenty-fifth day of Kislev on the Hebrew calendar fell sooner than usual on the calendar the rest of the world used. "Hanukkah never changes," he said firmly, and Charlotte resisted the urge to make a face, for Papa never seemed to believe that *anything* changed. In fact, even with the dire news reports about the treatment of Jews in Germany and Poland, the ones Charlotte's friends whispered about at school, he simply pursed his lips and said, "But this is France. We are French now. Nothing will alter that."

But was that true? Most of the time, Charlotte didn't think much about religion at all. Lately, however, some of the other children had been calling her names, even saying that she had a big nose, which was ridiculous, because her nose was the exact same size as Thérèse Petit's, and everyone knew Thérèse Petit was the most beautiful girl in school, and a Catholic at that. Still, Jean-Marc Thibodaux in particular always seemed to have an insult ready for her. He called her "Dirty Yid" or told her to go back to where she came from. His friends had laughed when she'd looked at him blankly the first time and said she'd been born right here in Paris, just like him. "But your parents weren't," he'd sneered. "My papa says you don't belong here."

So that was it; the words were coming from her schoolmates' parents. It made Charlotte feel a bit better and a bit worse at the same time. Better because this wasn't really about her. Worse because it wasn't fair that she had to be the face of a religion she barely practiced. It wasn't as if she went around thinking about the Torah all the time.

"Ignore them," Micheline whispered when it was clear Charlotte was on the verge of tears. "They're just pigs. You know that. *Groin groin.*" Her friend's oinking always made Charlotte laugh, and she knew Micheline was right. Still, it didn't remove the sting.

"Why do we have to be Jewish anyhow?" she asked her parents over dinner on the first night of Hanukkah. She knew her question would upset them, but it would be so much easier to be Christian. Why couldn't they see that?

"Hush, Charlotte," Papa said. "Don't speak of things you don't understand."

Charlotte felt the familiar burn that she experienced every time her father treated her like a child. "How can I understand if you never talk to me?"

Her father stared at her and then seemed to soften. "You should be playing with dolls, not worrying about politics and religion."

"I haven't played with a doll in years. I'm almost eleven."

"Reuven," Maman said sharply. "Talk to her."

Papa sighed, took off his glasses, and pinched the bridge of his nose. It was his look of defeat, Charlotte knew, the one he sometimes wore after arguments with Maman. "Charlotte, being Jewish is something to be proud of, not something to be ashamed of."

"Then why do my classmates mock me?"

Charlotte could see him flinch, but he answered calmly. "Because they are ignorant. And cruelty is the weapon of the ignorant."

"But what if I don't want to be Jewish?" Charlotte persisted.

Her parents exchanged glances filled with sadness. "My dear," Papa said at last, "your mother is Jewish, and so according to our faith, you are Jewish too. It's a beautiful part of you. It will forever be."

Charlotte opened her mouth to protest, but she was out of words. She didn't want to change who she was, not really. It was just that she hated to be different. If only she could have blond ringlets and parents who invited the local priest over for supper, like Thérèse Petit.

After she helped wash the dishes and lit the first candle on the menorah with Maman and Papa, Charlotte stepped out onto the small terrace of their apartment, which offered a sliver of a view of the top of the Eiffel Tower. It was her favorite place in the world, for when she drew the curtains closed behind her, she found some privacy. Besides, she liked to imagine that the tip of the tower was actually the highest turret of a castle and that she was a princess who would one day return to her rightful place on the throne. Not that she would ever breathe a word of that daydream; she realized how childish it would make her sound.

"Good evening."

Charlotte jumped, startled by the voice that came from the next terrace over. She was always alone out here, so it hadn't occurred to her to look around. She blinked into the darkness until she saw a young woman with pin-curled auburn hair and crimson lips standing against the railing outside the apartment next door.

"Hello?" Charlotte answered tentatively. She'd seen the woman before; she was beautiful and very fashionable. She was perhaps twenty or twenty-five, and she was always wearing pretty, tailored dresses that showed off her narrow waist and high-heeled shoes that Charlotte would undoubtedly trip in. She had an accent, but when Charlotte had asked her parents about it, her father had said that it didn't matter where the woman was from, because she was French now, just like them.

"It's a lovely night," the woman said. She wasn't looking at Charlotte; she was gazing at the Eiffel Tower. "It's a bit cold, of course. But there's something bracing about the fresh air, isn't there? It snaps you out of a feeling of malaise."

How had the woman known that Charlotte was out here feeling sorry for herself?

After a moment, the woman spoke again. "I'm Ruby. I live next door to you. But then, you can probably see that."

"I'm Charlotte," Charlotte replied, feeling suddenly grown-up. "It's a pleasure to meet you."

"It's a pleasure to meet you, as well." There was a pause, and then the woman asked gently in her strange accent, "Is there something you'd like to talk about?"

"Pardon?"

"It's just that I couldn't help noticing that you seem upset. Unless you're sniffling because you've caught a cold. In which case, excuse me for intruding."

Charlotte was grateful that the darkness would hide her embarrassment. "No. I'm fine. Thank you."

"Well, then, perhaps you can help me with something."

"But I'm only ten," Charlotte blurted out. "Well, almost eleven." An adult had never asked for her help before.

Ruby laughed. "That's all right. What I need most of all is advice. You see, I'm American."

"American?" Charlotte was momentarily dazzled. She'd never met an American before; the immigrants she knew were from eastern Europe. "But America is so far away."

"Indeed it is. I fell in love with a Frenchman and followed him across the ocean to live here. He has lived in this building for a long time. Perhaps you know him?"

"Yes, of course, Monsieur Benoit. Well, my maman and papa know him."

"I see. Well, Charlotte, this is my problem, and it makes me rather sad: sometimes, people treat me differently because I'm American. They judge me before they know me."

It was almost exactly what Charlotte had been trying to explain to Papa! To think that the glamorous woman next door had the same sort of problem! "I suppose that's rather silly of them," she said slowly.

"How so?"

"Well," Charlotte said, struggling to put her thoughts into words. "The fact that you are American doesn't change who you are on the inside. It is just one piece of you."

"Hmm. That's quite a good point. But what do you think I should do about the way I'm feeling?"

Charlotte thought about this. "You can't always change other people's minds. But you can change whether or not you listen to them, can't you?"

"Why, yes," Ruby said. "You know, Charlotte, I think I was right. You are very wise indeed. I will think about what you said."

"Okay," Charlotte said, suddenly shy again. She wanted to ask Ruby many more questions. What was America like? Where had she learned to speak French so well? What did she think of Paris? Was she worried about the war that everyone said was coming to France? But Ruby was already moving toward the door of her terrace, and Charlotte realized with a great swell of disappointment that she had missed her chance.

"Thank you, Charlotte," Ruby said. "I hope we talk again soon." And then she was gone, leaving Charlotte alone to overlook the moonlit courtyard.

Only later did Charlotte realize that her kitchen window was open a crack, and that if Ruby had already been on her terrace, she would have heard Charlotte's whole conversation with her parents. The thought made Charlotte feel a bit silly at first, but by the time she went to sleep that night, she felt a little less alone.

CHAPTER FOUR

January 1940

It was icy cold and rainy when Thomas Clarke arrived at the Little Rissington airfield in the Cotswolds for the first time. *Not a very good welcome,* he thought. The conditions at Desford, where he'd learned to fly DH 82 Tiger Moths, hadn't been much better, but Little Rissi was supposed to be the real deal, the place where he would earn his RAF wings, where he would learn to fly fighters. He had imagined, somehow, wide-open, verdant fields and babbling blue streams. Instead, the world here seemed to be a study in all the shades of brown and gray, with the wind turning the raindrops into vicious projectiles. By the time he and Harry Cormack made it inside the brick building at the front of the complex, their brand-new RAF blues were drenched straight through.

"If Marcie could see me now," Harry muttered, glancing down at his sopping uniform as they waited for the station commander.

"You're lucky you don't have a sweetheart, Thomas. There's no one to see you in this state."

"Yes, lucky me." Thomas rolled his eyes at the man who'd become his closest friend at Desford, where they'd survived the harrowing first weeks of make-or-break flight training together. He refrained from mentioning that Harry likely wouldn't be seeing his love anytime soon anyhow. The world was at war, and there was a rush to get the newest recruits into the skies. Besides, Harry seemed to have a new girl every few weeks. Where did he find the time? And how could he worry about wooing the young ladies who hung around the pub they frequented when there was battle to be waged? Surely that sort of thinking was a distraction they couldn't afford.

"Attention!" a warrant officer bellowed to the soaked RAF hopefuls. Thomas and Harry sprang to ramrod straightness and turned their eyes toward the door.

A beak-nosed man with close-cropped white hair strode in, fixing them all with a steely gaze. "Welcome to RAF Little Rissington," he barked after the warrant officer had introduced him as the station commander. "You may have thought that your early training days were easy, but things are about to change. This is where we separate the men from the boys. It's up to you to decide which you'll be. Your studies here will be tough, your training relentless. Remember: the planes cost a bloody fortune. You, on the other hand, are easily replaceable. Act accordingly." He strode off without another word.

"Cheerful chap," Harry muttered.

"He was just trying to scare us," Thomas replied. But it had worked. As he and Harry trudged through the downpour toward the mess hall a few minutes later, Thomas's heart was in his throat, and he wondered, not for the first time, whether he actually belonged here.

Thomas was assigned to bunk with Oliver Smith, who'd also come from Desford, and Harry was four doors down. The next morning, they all made their way to stores to collect their assigned flying kits, parachutes, and huge piles of textbooks.

"Are we meant to read all of these?" Harry asked, feigning distress under the weight of the books.

"The planes cost a bloody fortune, chaps," Thomas deadpanned. "You are replaceable."

Harry and Oliver laughed, and soon, they were all choosing lockers in the crew room of Number 2 Hangar. As Thomas extracted his new helmet, his leather gloves, his Sidcot suit, and his pristine flying boots, he felt a surge of pride and trepidation. He was ready to be a man, for there was no room for anything else. He had to do all he could to protect England.

"WHY DID YOU JOIN UP, sir?"

The question came from Jonathan Wilkes, Thomas's flight sergeant, as they took off from the airfield at Kidlington, just east of Little Rissi, in a Harvard training aircraft. The low-wing monoplane was nothing like the Tiger Moths that Thomas had learned to fly at Desford, and he was still a bit overwhelmed by the sheer number of controls on the squat beast.

"It felt like the right thing to do, Flight," Thomas replied, guiding the trainer up through a sharp gust of wind. The stick shuddered, but Thomas kept his grip steady. "Helping the cause, and such."

"How so?" Wilkes persisted. His tone wasn't combative, merely curious. "You could have joined the army and been on the ground already."

"But I can do more here."

"Even if it's dangerous?"

"Danger is a part of war, isn't it?"

"Indeed," Wilkes replied, and Thomas had the feeling he'd passed some sort of test. "Well, then, I'm going to show you now, sir, what it feels like to stall in this aircraft. You're going to bring us out of it."

"Yes, all right." He'd gotten accustomed to stalls in Tiger Moths, after all. How different could this be? "Ready when you are."

The words were barely out of his mouth when the Harvard choked and whipped nearly to a dead stop in midair. An instant later, they were plummeting nose-first toward the ground.

"Dear God!" Thomas shouted, but the words were lost in the sudden shrieking of the plane's descent, the air outside biting at the wings.

"Easy on the stick, sir." Wilkes sounded calm, but his tone didn't do much to slow Thomas's racing pulse. The aircraft shuddered and whined, and though Thomas knew the cabin was sealed, he felt as if there were sharp gusts pulling at his flight suit. The air screamed as the barracks on the ground below came into focus. Thomas pulled back sharply, following his instinct to raise the nose of the plane, but it shook and stalled again and continued its plunge toward the earth.

"You increased the wing load too severely." Wilkes's tone was only slightly panicked. "Slow and steady, bring us out of it. Do it now."

Thomas took a deep breath and eased back on the stick, finally guiding the nose upward until they were once again parallel to the ground. "Christ, Flight! Are you trying to kill me before the Germans get around to it?"

The hint of a smile crossed Wilkes's lips. "Now we're going to climb back up and do it again, because you're going to need to be able to do that in an instant. The skies are unforgiving, and your sharp reactions will mean the difference between life and death." He paused and waited for Thomas to catch his breath. "The fate of England is in your hands, sir. You must proceed as if it is your destiny to save us all."

CHAPTER FIVE

June 1940

The exodus had begun in earnest by the time June arrived.

Paris was in bloom, the chestnut trees lush and fragrant. Flowers in blue, pale green, and deep red spilled from window boxes and inched across the public gardens, painting the silent streets. But to Ruby, it felt as if nature itself was taunting the city. Soon, the world she knew would be swallowed by the coming Nazi invasion.

Ruby could feel their approach like a storm on the horizon, the air pregnant with something sinister. Though the French had collectively closed their eyes to the truth for months, ignoring German aggressions near the border, the jig was up. The Germans had simply gone around the Maginot Line, steamrolling their way through the forests and into France. They would be here any day now with their stiff marching, their too-polished uniforms, their strange Nazi emblem, a colorless pinwheel warped by the wind.

French generals were already declaring the Battle of France finished as bedraggled troops retreated hastily south. Air raid sirens pierced the nights. Cars moved in stealthy darkness, their headlights painted dark blue. Shops closed, apartments were shuttered, and Parisians fled in droves, clogging the roads as German bombs splintered the countryside. Paris was deserted, and without the laughter of the neighborhood children, a curtain of quiet had descended. Even the Eiffel Tower, a dagger against the crisp sky, seemed preternaturally still, as if it, too, was holding its breath.

"For God's sake," Marcel said to Ruby as they huddled alone in the *abri* beneath their building, taking shelter as bombs fell somewhere to the southwest—the Renault and Citroën factories on the edge of the city, Ruby guessed. The Germans were pounding Paris, which had seemed impossible just a few weeks earlier. "You're being foolish."

The circles under his eyes were pronounced, his shoulders stiff, reminding Ruby of a tightly wound children's toy.

"I knew what I was getting into," she replied, not meeting his gaze. It wasn't quite true; she'd been lulled into a false sense of security at first. But then she had chosen to stay because he had. "I'm here with you."

"But that's the problem, isn't it, darling?" The endearment was sarcastic, not loving, and they both knew it. He was different lately, a far cry from the man she'd followed across the Atlantic the year before. His rejection from the French army—due to the marked limp in his right leg from the polio he'd battled as a child—now seemed to define his every waking moment.

"How so?" She fought to keep her tone even.

"You seem to believe you're invulnerable. I didn't ask you to stay."

"I'm well aware." In fact, he had tried to force her to leave, even writing to her parents to request their support in changing her mind. But she wouldn't run at the first sign of trouble. She wouldn't leave Marcel to face the invasion alone. She had cast her lot with him, for better or worse—and when he'd begun to try to get rid of her, it had only made her dig her heels in. "I still believe that we're safe here for now."

"Yes, well, it's very American to go around believing in pipe dreams, isn't it?"

She turned away as another blast rattled the building. Somewhere along the line, being American had become something to be ashamed of, in Marcel's eyes anyhow. He resented President Roosevelt for staying out of Europe's war, and as the months ticked by, and the Americans refused to engage, Marcel seemed more and more apt to hold Ruby herself responsible for the policies of her government.

"I'm sorry," he said, his tone softening. He placed a hand on her shoulder. "It's only that I don't know how I'd forgive myself if anything happened to you."

"I know." Ruby relaxed slightly, reminding herself that every marriage was bound to hit some snags. And really, who could blame Marcel for his sense of powerlessness? "But I feel that I'm meant to be here, Marcel. Here with you."

She expected him to make a face, but instead, he just stared at her for a long time. "Oh, Ruby. I've ruined everything for you. I pretended to be the man I wanted to be, but now you've seen the real me, a man whose pathetic injury has taken away his ability to protect you."

She took a step closer, putting a hand on his stubbled jaw. "I see you, Marcel," she said. "I have always seen you. Do you think the French soldiers retreating from the front feel any more in control than you do? We are all powerless for now."

"I suppose I should be thankful that you still see the world through rose-colored glasses. Perhaps it's helpful not to see the coming storm so plainly."

She wanted to protest, to tell him that she saw things as clearly as he did, but then he pulled her toward him, folding her in, and she held her tongue. Being in his arms again for the first time in weeks felt like coming home, even if it had turned out not to be the home she expected.

An hour later, when the three tones of the all-clear siren sounded, she led him upstairs, back into their apartment in the nearly deserted building, to the bedroom that had once been a sanctuary. It felt like a battleground now, and she knew they had to change that if they were to survive.

"You can't possibly want me," he whispered as she kissed him. "I'm nothing."

"You're my husband, and I stand by you," she said firmly, covering his mouth with hers.

He made love to her quickly, almost violently. She tried to hold on, to focus on his eyes, to make him come back to her, but he was somewhere else entirely until he collapsed on her, spent and panting, his skin damp. "I'm sorry," he murmured into her breasts. "I love you, you know. I do."

She waited until his chest was rising and falling against her before she replied, "I love you too."

Yes, Ruby would stay. Storms were meant to be weathered, after all.

"MADAME BENOIT?" A SMALL, TIMID voice jolted Ruby out of her fog later that night. She had been unable to sleep, and after tossing and turning for an hour, she had stepped onto the terrace. The air still carried the scent of burning rubber and smoldering metal; the German bombs had found their mark. She looked over to see Charlotte silhouetted in the moonlight next door.

"Charlotte," she said warmly, relieved to see her. The girl and her parents hadn't appeared in the shelter during the air raid, and Ruby thought perhaps they had fled. There were reports coming in of cars bombed to pieces while snarled in traffic on country roads, and Ruby had had the terrible feeling that something had happened to the Dachers. Even with Charlotte in front of her now, Ruby couldn't erase her sense of foreboding.

"Good evening, Madame Benoit," Charlotte said formally.

"Please. Call me Ruby, or you'll make me feel old."

"That is an American thing, I think," Charlotte said after a long pause. "Calling adults by their first names."

Ruby smiled into the darkness. "Yes, perhaps it is. Or perhaps it's simply a neighbor thing. Times are too dark now for us to be anything but friends, don't you think?"

"Well . . . all right." Charlotte hesitated. "Can I ask you a question, Madame? Er, Ruby?"

"Anything."

"Why are you still here?"

Ruby laughed at the girl's bluntness.

"Here in France, I mean," Charlotte clarified, a hint of embarrassment in her tone now. "Since you're American. Maman and Papa said you should have left months ago. Why didn't you?"

Ruby sighed. "Maybe because I'm stubborn. Or maybe because I don't feel that anyone—German or otherwise—should force me into fleeing. I think that's part of it, Charlotte. But I also think it's because once I make a decision, I try to stick to it. I made Marcel a promise to be his wife, to join my life to his. And so here I will stay."

"You're loyal. And brave."

Ruby thought of Marcel's words, hating how much they wounded her. "Some would say foolish."

"But staying makes you French, doesn't it? All of those people who would judge you, they didn't have a choice. But you did. And you chose Paris."

"I chose Paris," Ruby repeated slowly. "Well, maybe I am French after all. Thank you, Charlotte. You've just made me feel lots better."

Charlotte went inside soon after, but Ruby stayed on the terrace, lost in thought. When she finally stepped back inside, shutting the doors softly behind her, Marcel was sitting in the darkness of the kitchen, staring at her.

"What were you doing out there?" he asked her, an edge to his voice.

"Just getting some air," she said, feeling suddenly guilty, though she'd done nothing wrong.

"I heard you talking."

"Yes, to the Dacher girl."

Marcel lit a cigarette, the match flaring for a second in the darkness. Ruby watched as he exhaled a mouthful of smoke, obscuring her view of him. "You talk too much, I think."

Ruby's heart sank. An hour ago, she'd felt that things between them might be changing for the better, but now he was in another one of his moods. "She's a nice girl, Marcel. I think she feels very alone right now. I'm just trying to help."

"There are lots of nice people who are alone in the world." He took another long draw from his cigarette. "It's very American, you know, this need to talk to anyone and everyone. If you were truly as French as you'd like to be, you'd know when to keep to yourself."

"MARCEL, MON AMI!"

Marcel's old friend Aubert—a short, bespectacled man around forty with a receding hairline, hooded eyes, and a flat, wide nose—approached the table outside the Café Ciel where Ruby and Marcel sat. It was a Tuesday afternoon, and they were playing at being normal, pretending that Paris wasn't about to be occupied, that life could still go on as it had before. The Germans hadn't reached the capital yet, but they would be here any day now. The French government had departed for Vichy the day before, and the streets were filled with injured soldiers telling tales of horrors at the front.

Aubert embraced Marcel and leaned down to kiss Ruby on both cheeks. "You are looking radiant, my dear." He sat and beckoned to a waiter. "Champagne, my boy! Champagne for my friends!"

Marcel looked amused, but Ruby was troubled. The café—one of the few in their arrondissement that had actually stayed open—was nearly deserted, but the other customers were staring at them. "What is there to celebrate, Aubert?" she whispered. "Life as we know it is about to end."

"Ah, but it's not over yet, is it?" Aubert lit a cigarette and took a long drag. "Paris is still ours. And if you want to know, Ruby, I'm toasting to the future. I can see it already. We'll defeat them yet."

"Surely you're joking. Things couldn't possibly be bleaker right now."

Aubert smiled. "But it's only a matter of time. The Huns may be here for a little while, but with the help of the Brits, we'll push them out. Isn't that right, Marcel?"

Ruby glanced at her husband, expecting him to share her doubt, but he was staring at Aubert, his eyes gleaming. "Do you two know something about the invasion that I don't?" Ruby asked.

The waiter arrived then, popping the cork on their champagne and pouring the bubbly for them. Aubert didn't reply until they'd clinked glasses. "No, Ruby, of course not. I'm only saying there's hope if we band together. But it's nothing for you to worry about, dear. Things like this are better left to the men, don't you think?"

Ruby drew herself up a bit taller in her chair. "Aubert, I follow the news too. You can't think I'm not aware of what's going on."

"Of course," Aubert said, and Ruby could hear his amusement as he added, "Our university girl." He and Marcel exchanged smiles.

"Excuse me," Ruby said stiffly, rising from her chair. Aubert and Marcel half-stood too, but she ignored them as she made her way inside to find the *toilette*.

It wasn't supposed to be like this, she thought as she descended the spiral staircase at the back of the café. Especially with Marcel, and especially in Paris. Hadn't Gertrude Stein commanded respect here? Zelda Fitzgerald had run the town in the twenties, and now, it was common knowledge that a woman—the Comtesse Hélène de Portes—was pulling the strings of Reynaud's government. Ruby had met her; she was a shrill, irascible person known as much for her temper tantrums as for her extravagant parties. If someone like that could wield such power, what was Ruby doing wrong? Should she be speaking up more? Standing up for herself when Marcel intimated that she was incapable of grasping the truth? Or would that only drive him further away?

She touched up her lipstick and stared into the mirror. There were dark circles under her eyes, evidence of her lack of sleep. Her curls were loose and frizzy from the heat, something she would have fixed if she cared more. But it was impossible to think about things like that with the invasion on the horizon. What horrors would come with it? What would happen to the people she loved? To her?

She splashed water on her face and pinched her cheeks to restore some color. She smoothed her hair, gave her reflection one last resolute look, and headed back upstairs.

When she returned to the table, Marcel and Aubert were whispering, their heads bent together. As she approached, they pulled back and flashed her identical smiles. Was it her imagination that they looked almost guilty?

"What is it?" she asked.

"Just discussing the Germans," Marcel said. "Those bastards."

Unease crawled under Ruby's skin. "You two mustn't do anything foolish."

"Foolish?" Marcel's eyes locked on hers.

"It's best to keep our heads down until we figure out what the occupation will mean for us."

Marcel's face darkened. "We should just lie down like dogs?" he demanded. Aubert was smirking, as if she was proving him right.

"I just don't want you to do anything reckless."

"So you *do* think I'm powerless to fight for my country." Marcel looked triumphant and wounded at the same time.

"No!"

His eyes blazed, and they stared at each other until the silence became uncomfortable.

"Well, we are certainly not going to solve the problems of France this afternoon," Aubert said, cutting through the discomfort. He raised his glass and glanced from Ruby to Marcel. "To France. And what is to come."

"To France," Marcel and Ruby muttered in unison, raising their glasses.

But the tension lingered, and as they drank their champagne, no one spoke again. Ruby stared down the deserted Avenue Rapp toward the river. Though the Germans were still miles from Paris, she could already see them coming. She could feel the city changing. And though he was just inches away, she could feel Marcel drifting further from her by the day. All the champagne in the world couldn't turn back the clock.

CHAPTER SIX

October 1940

By October, it was clear that Paris had forever changed. The Germans had gotten comfortable, their officers settling into swanky accommodations at the Crillon, the Meurice, the George V, the Ritz. The French government had long ago decamped to Vichy, replacing the proud French motto of *Liberté, egalité, fraternité* with the Germanic *Travail, famille, patrie*: Work, family, fatherland. Huge German street signs had been erected, directing traffic to the *Zentra-Kraft* on the Champs-Élysées or the local village hospital in the *Orts Lazarett Suresnes*. German soldiers relaxed in cafés, dined at restaurants, and toured the monuments and museums as if they were on holiday.

The colder weather moved in, accompanied by a growing sense of unease. Ruby queued each morning to receive rationed portions of foods and supplies. She learned, along with the rest of Paris, to make fuel from wood and charcoal, oil from grape seeds, and cigarettes for Marcel from a strange mixture of Jerusalem artichokes, sunflowers, maize, and a small amount of tobacco. At first, it had seemed that food would still be readily available during the Occupation, but now that winter was approaching, it was clear that had been a clever mirage, affected by the Nazis to lull Parisians into a false feeling of normalcy.

There was a sense throughout the city that there might be a light at the end of the tunnel, though. A little-known general named Charles de Gaulle had emerged as a leader over the summer, stirring the pot of Resistance through a series of radio broadcasts from England. "Somewhere must shine and burn the flame of French resistance," he said, and so it began, simply at first, with Vs for victory appearing throughout Paris, scrawled in lipstick or crayon or coal on German cars, German flyers, and visible spots throughout the city.

Early one autumn afternoon, Ruby was returning to the apartment after waiting in line for more than two hours for bread when she encountered Charlotte's mother standing in the first-floor hallway crying. Her dress was wrinkled, as if she'd given up on ironing, and there were dark circles under her eyes.

"Madame Dacher?" Ruby asked hesitantly, approaching the older woman and putting a hand on her shoulder.

Madame Dacher whirled around, her eyes wild and wet. She blinked a few times, and her expression softened. "Oh, I'm very sorry, Madame Benoit. I'm terribly embarrassed. I thought I was alone. I didn't hear you approach."

"There's nothing to be embarrassed about, Madame Dacher. Are you all right?"

"Yes, yes. I just don't want to upset Charlotte. I was trying to calm myself before going inside."

"What's happened?"

Madame Dacher sighed. "Have you heard about the Jewish statutes?"

Ruby nodded, her heart heavy. The Statut des Juifs, passed two weeks earlier, banned Jews from positions in academia, medicine, law, and government. Jews were to ride in the last car on the Métro, relinquish their radios and bicycles, and stay out of cinemas, museums, libraries, and cafés. It was appalling. Ruby had tried to talk to Marcel about what might be done to fight the new rules, but he'd laughed at her, accusing her of coming to her senses about the Germans far too late. "You were the one who wanted me to keep my head down," he'd snapped, as if the oppressive new restrictions were her fault.

"We had to register, you see," Madame Dacher went on, tears coursing down her face now. "Just after Rosh Hashanah. We obeyed, of course. But my husband believes that something terrible is going to happen now. There is talk of Jews losing their businesses too."

"Surely that won't happen to you," Ruby said. Monsieur Dacher was a successful and well-respected furrier, a pillar of the community. "The French government won't allow things to go that far."

"But you see, it isn't the France we know anymore. As the weeks pass, I feel less and less in control of my own life."

"We've all lost control to the Germans, Madame Dacher," Ruby said, trying to reassure her.

Madame Dacher's expression was dazed as she looked up. "It's different for us, Madame Benoit. Surely you see that."

Ruby felt a strange gnawing in the pit of her stomach. "Yes, of course. I'm sorry."

"You must make me a promise," Madame Dacher said, suddenly reaching for Ruby's hands and squeezing so tightly that Ruby's fingers felt like bones in a sack. "If something happens to my husband and myself, you will look after Charlotte."

"But surely nothing will happen."

"Please. Give me your word."

Ruby felt a surge of hope, a sense that perhaps she could do something to help after all, even if only to assuage her neighbor's fears. "Of course. You have my word."

"Thank you," Madame Dacher said, releasing Ruby's hands and stepping away. She turned and disappeared into her own apartment, leaving Ruby alone in the hallway, breathless and uneasy.

RUBY WAS SITTING IN THE darkness that night, just past eight o'clock, turning Madame Dacher's words over in her head, when Marcel's key clicked in the lock.

"Hello, darling," he said, his words slightly slurred as he stepped inside and closed the door behind him. "How are you?"

"Marcel?" He was so uncharacteristically cheerful that Ruby was confused for a moment. "Are you all right?"

"All right?" he repeated with a grin. He lit a candle and sat down across from her in the kitchen. "Of course, my dear. And you?"

"I'm fine," she answered cautiously. "Where have you been?" She hated that it sounded like an accusation, for she hadn't meant it that way. She braced herself for one of his moods, but he merely smiled at her.

"I've had some drinks with a few friends at the Ritz, you see. Right under the noses of the Germans! They even bought us a round, with no idea that we are their enemies!"

"Marcel! How could you take such a risk?"

"You think *that* is risky? Toasting with the enemy? Oh, Ruby, how little you understand."

She clenched her fists. "I hate this occupation as much as you do, Marcel. You have to stop speaking to me as if I'm an uneducated fool."

"I know you're educated." He raked a hand through his thick, dark hair and gave her a perplexed look. "But you must admit that as an American, you lack a certain perspective."

"It's always about me being an American, isn't it? My God, Marcel, why did you marry me if you felt I was so inferior?"

"Inferior?" The confusion on his face deepened. "I've never thought you inferior, Ruby. I admire you. I admire your intelligence, your wit."

"But you talk down to me all the time."

"I don't." He was silent for a moment and then looked away as he swayed once more. "I don't mean to, in any case. I just wasn't prepared for someone who wanted to argue with me the way you do."

She could feel herself softening slightly. "I don't want to argue either, Marcel. I just want you to talk to me. To trust me."

"Ruby, I—" He looked at her for a long time, his gaze focused and unwavering. She resisted the urge to wilt and instead stared back, telling herself that whatever he had to say, she would withstand it.

But then he surprised her by leaning in and pressing his lips to hers, so softly and gently that at first she wondered if she was dreaming. She was so startled that she didn't kiss back, so he pulled away. "Ruby?" he murmured.

"I was so sure you didn't love me anymore," she whispered.

His eyes filled with tears. "Of course I love you," he said. "It's myself I cannot live with." And then his lips were on hers again, more insistent this time, and her body responded. He loved her after all, and she could feel it in the way he touched her, the way he pulled her to him, the way he drank her in like a man who'd just crossed a desert. Soon, his hands were beneath her skirt, tugging at her undergarments, sliding toward places they hadn't been since that late spring night after the bombs had fallen, before the Nazis took Paris.

She moaned, despite herself, as he lifted her dress over her head and peeled his own shirt off. His chest was just as solid as she remembered, but there was no time to think about that as his hands, and then his mouth, began to travel over her body. He led her to the bedroom, and as they fell into bed, she wasn't thinking about the Dachers or the Germans or the way the world was falling apart around them. She was thinking about the fact that here, in this moment, her marriage wasn't crumbling. Perhaps there was a life in front of them after all.

TEN WEEKS LATER, RUBY SAT on her terrace, watching the sky tumble into darkness, her head in her hands. It was Christmas Eve, and she was bundled up against the cold in one of Marcel's old sweaters. She still felt the chill in her blood, in her bones. She knew she should go inside, where there was a small fire burning, but she couldn't make herself move. The fear of what was to come paralyzed her.

Ruby was pregnant. She was sure of it. She was ravenously hungry all the time, though she could hardly keep food down, and she had twice missed her time of the month. There was no other explanation.

She was filled with both terror and joy at the prospect of a baby. Paris was dark and lonely, and as the fighting raged on across Europe, it seemed that things were growing tenser by the day. Bringing a child into a world at war seemed foolish, but perhaps bringing a child into a home like hers was even more so. After that night ten weeks ago, Marcel had returned to vanishing for days at a time. And when he was home, he hardly looked at her anymore. He hadn't noticed the swelling in her breasts, the way she moved like she was in possession of a special secret.

"Ruby?" Charlotte's timid voice wafted over from the next terrace, and Ruby sat up with a start. She hadn't heard the girl emerge from her apartment. "Is something wrong?"

"Oh, I'm all right." Ruby forced a smile. "What are you doing out here without a coat? You'll catch your death of cold."

"I just wanted to say Merry Christmas."

"Oh! Thank you, Charlotte. And a Merry Christmas to you too." She realized immediately that it was the wrong thing to say. "I'm sorry. I mean Happy Hanukkah. Has Hanukkah started yet?"

"It is just beginning." Charlotte hesitated. "Perhaps it's a sign, our holidays falling at the same time. Perhaps this is the year we will all come together."

"God willing," Ruby murmured. She knew that Charlotte had

absorbed her parents' worries in the last few months. Throughout the city, shops owned by Jewish people had been taken over by what the Germans were calling provisional managers; businessmen ousted from their own businesses. Monsieur Dacher, Ruby knew, had been forced to comply last week, and though he still went into his fur shop, he was treated as an employee rather than as the man who'd built the lucrative business from the ground up. It must have been demoralizing, humiliating.

"Are you sure there's nothing wrong, Ruby?" Charlotte asked after a long pause. "You don't seem yourself."

"Nothing you need to worry about, Charlotte."

"But maybe I can help. I *want* to help."

Ruby smiled into the darkness. Maybe it wouldn't hurt to share her news. "Can you keep a secret?"

"Of course."

Ruby got up and walked to the edge of her terrace so that she was just a few feet away from the girl. "I'm going to have a baby."

Charlotte's eyes widened. "A baby? Oh, Ruby! This is the best Hanukkah gift I could have asked for!"

Ruby laughed. "Well, the baby won't arrive until the summer."

"That's okay! It will just be so exciting, don't you think? Oh, this is such wonderful news! Is Monsieur Benoit very happy?"

"I haven't told him yet. I'm not quite sure how he will feel."

Charlotte looked confused. "Surely he will be overjoyed."

Ruby looked away. "Surely."

"Well, you must tell him as soon as possible. He's going to be a father! It will be the perfect Christmas gift!"

Perhaps Charlotte was right. There was no reason to keep the news from Marcel any longer. He was bound to notice soon enough, and perhaps telling him now would bring about a Christmas miracle. Maybe the Marcel she'd fallen in love with would finally come back. Maybe his focus would shift to planning a family with her. She would make sure that he knew from the start how much she needed him, and he would feel useful again.

That night, just past midnight, Marcel crept quietly through the front door. Before he'd had a chance to hang up his coat and hat, Ruby lit a candle. "Merry Christmas," she said, eager to get the words out before she changed her mind. "We're going to have a baby, Marcel. Isn't it wonderful?"

He stared at her before replying. "A baby?"

"I'll need your help of course," she said brightly, hoping her enthusiasm would be contagious. "There's so much to be done before the baby arrives."

"You're having a baby," he repeated flatly.

"*We're* having a baby."

For a moment, neither of them moved. Then, slowly, deliberately, Marcel strode toward the doorway, where he put his hat and his coat back on. When he turned around, Ruby was so surprised by the sadness in his eyes that she sat back in her chair, breathless.

"Oh, Ruby, what have we done?" he asked in a strangled voice.

"But—"

"This is a huge mistake." And then he was gone, slamming the door so hard that a glass perched on the edge of their curio cabinet plunged to the floor and shattered.

For a long time, Ruby sat motionless, staring at the broken shards.

CHAPTER SEVEN

January 1941

A baby! It was nearly all that Charlotte could think about. What a lucky child to be born into a home with a loving mother and father, where the parents were allowed to work. Her own home life had been greatly disrupted by her father's recent situation.

"Those Nazi bastards," Papa said on a snowy night in January as Charlotte sat huddled with her parents around the kitchen furnace. Fuel was scarce, and they were burning an old dining room chair. It had been stored in the closet near the front door for occasions when they might have guests, but Charlotte supposed that wouldn't be happening for a while.

"Reuven, your language," Maman said, casting a glance at Charlotte.

"It's okay," Charlotte said. "I know many bad words."

Her father fixed her with a glare. "Well, you should not. You are a lady."

"And yet you curse in front of her all the time," Maman pointed out.

Papa sighed and looked away. "It is the time we are living in. One cannot help but become emotional."

"This is not the first time we've endured desperate circumstances," Maman said.

Maman and Papa exchanged looks, and Charlotte knew they were thinking about the Great War. Maman had lost two brothers. Papa had lost his twin, Michel. All had fought for the French army.

"I know," Papa murmured softly, squeezing Maman's hand.

Charlotte knew she had promised Ruby that she wouldn't reveal her secret, but in the heavy silence, something made her blurt it out. "Madame Benoit is having a baby!"

Maman and Papa both turned to stare at her. "Madame Benoit?" Maman asked.

Charlotte knew she'd made a mistake by saying something, but there was a sparkle in her mother's eyes now that hadn't been there before. "Yes," she mumbled. "But it is supposed to be a secret."

"Oh my." Papa looked worried. "But how will a baby survive in the midst of all this?"

"They are not Jewish," Maman reminded him.

"I suppose. But still, to bring a child into a war . . ."

"It will end soon," Maman said.

Papa shook his head. "It will not end until all of France has become German. And when that happens, we will not be here to witness it."

"Why?" Charlotte interjected. "Where are we going?"

Her father turned to her, an almost dazed expression on his

face. "We are not going anywhere, my dear Charlotte." He wouldn't meet her eye. "Of course we are not going anywhere."

CHARLOTTE WORRIED CONSTANTLY THAT RUBY would know her confidence had been betrayed, so when she saw her standing on the terrace on a frigid morning in late January, she rushed outside to confess.

"I told Maman and Papa about the baby," she said, her words tumbling out. "I'm so sorry. I know it was meant to be a secret."

Ruby turned to her with a weary smile. Her cheeks were sunken, her face drawn, and she was too tightly bundled in sweaters and overcoats for Charlotte to see whether her belly had grown. "Oh, Charlotte, it's fine. I would have told them myself whenever I next saw them." Ruby took a sip from a steaming mug. "How are your parents? I haven't seen them in more than a month."

Charlotte looked down. "They are fine, thank you." The truth was that they were anything but. Papa was barely sleeping. At night, he pored over his account books and slammed his fists on the table. And Maman had slipped deeper into a depression that Charlotte didn't understand. Maybe when Ruby's baby came, it would bring Maman back to life. Ruby's own mother was all the way back in America, so surely Ruby would need Maman's help.

Ruby studied Charlotte for a long time, giving Charlotte the distinct feeling that she could see right through her. After a while, she smiled sadly. "And how are you, Charlotte? Is school going well?"

"I suppose. Although my only friend, Micheline, left for the south with her family three weeks ago. Papa says that even if I feel lonely now, I must hold my head high and pretend I don't hear the things the others are saying about Jews." Before Ruby could begin to feel sorry for her, though, Charlotte changed the subject, blurting out the question that had been weighing on her mind. "And Monsieur Benoit? He is very happy about the baby too?"

Something flickered across Ruby's face. "Oh, yes. I think he will make a wonderful father."

Charlotte nodded, but before she could say anything else, she heard her mother calling for her from inside. "I'm sorry," she said. "I must go to school now."

"Of course. I'll see you later, then. And, Charlotte? Whenever you feel lonely, remember you have me for a friend."

Charlotte couldn't shake the conversation with Ruby all morning. She sat through her teachers' lectures with her mind whirling as she replayed the look on Ruby's face again and again. Her words about Monsieur Benoit making a wonderful father had sounded like a lie, but how could they be?

Then again, Monsieur Benoit was a bit of a mystery. Charlotte sometimes felt guilty, because Ruby had made a point of calling Charlotte her friend, but Charlotte hadn't been completely honest with her. Wouldn't a friend tell another friend that her husband was keeping secrets? She knew only that late at night when she couldn't sleep, she sometimes heard Ruby's husband whispering to people in the hall outside her door. Once in a while, there were movements too, shuffling, scraping, clicking sounds that didn't make sense.

Now that Ruby was going to have a baby, Charlotte knew that she must find out what Monsieur Benoit was up to. It was the least she could do. Ruby had called her a friend, after all. So that night, after her parents were asleep, Charlotte crept out of bed and into the parlor. She felt fiercely protective of her neighbor all of a sudden, and as she sat in the darkness, waiting, she realized it was because of the look in Ruby's eyes when she'd talked of Monsieur Benoit that morning. Charlotte didn't understand what it was, exactly, but she knew something was wrong.

The hours ticked by, and Charlotte fought off the urge to fall asleep. By two-thirty in the morning, she began to think that she was being a fool. She had just gotten up to return to bed when there was a noise in the hall. She gasped and tiptoed to the door to look through the small peephole.

It was Monsieur Benoit! He was dressed in a dark overcoat that glistened with snowflakes. He had just come in from the cold, long past the curfew, and now he was standing in the hallway— crouching, really—and breathing hard. Charlotte stood as still as she could, but she had to stop herself from inhaling sharply a few seconds later when the front door to the building opened a crack. There was a noise on the stairs, and then there was a shadowy figure standing just outside Charlotte's door.

"The bird flies at night," the person said softly, and Charlotte was startled to realize that the voice belonged to a woman. Had Monsieur Benoit taken a mistress? While Ruby was pregnant? Icy anger coursed through Charlotte's veins.

"Only through the storm," Monsieur Benoit murmured back. It made no sense at all, but at least it wasn't the amorous reply of a man to his paramour.

"Here," the woman said, producing a small parcel from beneath her cloak and thrusting it at him. "Be careful." And then she was gone again, down the stairs and out into the snowy night.

Charlotte remained as still as a statue in the silence that followed. For a long time, Monsieur Benoit just stood there, clutching the parcel and staring at the front door. It was almost as if he was expecting someone else. Then, finally, he seemed to snap out of his trance. All at once, he was a flurry of motion, unwinding the strings of the package and pulling out its contents, which, in the darkness, Charlotte could barely see. But it seemed to be a collection of men's clothing, a tin of something, and a few fat sausages. *What on earth?*

Just when Charlotte thought the night couldn't get any stranger, Monsieur Benoit stepped to the blank wall opposite his apartment, looked around, and pressed on one of the panels on the lower right side. This time, Charlotte couldn't contain her gasp as a small door slid open and Marcel slipped inside. There was a hidden compartment in the hall large enough for a man? A moment later, he re-emerged, his arms empty, and touched the wall again. The door slid closed and Monsieur Benoit looked furtively around once more before entering his own apartment, which Charlotte could see clearly because her doorway sat in the corner of the building, overlooking the whole hall.

Charlotte wanted to venture out to test the hidden door for herself, but if Monsieur Benoit heard her, she would certainly be in trouble. So she resolved to wait until the next time she saw him leave at night. She would learn then what secrets he was hiding, and she'd tell Ruby when the time was right. That's what a true friend would do.

CHAPTER EIGHT

January 1941

By the start of the new year, death was everywhere. Oliver had been shot down over the outskirts of London just after the first of January, and John Stephens had plunged into the English Channel after taking down three enemy Messerschmitt Bf 109s. Still, Thomas kept fighting. He was feeling more and more at home in the cockpit; the Spit had become almost like an extension of himself. He didn't even have to think about how to get it to do his bidding anymore; it bobbed and wove with the slightest tick of the column. And even though the logical part of his brain reminded him that he could die at any moment, he felt invincible soaring through the heavens, at one with the bright blue sky.

The condolence letter home to Oliver's mother would be difficult, and as Thomas sat down to write it late one night at the base in South Wales where they had been stationed since late summer, he couldn't help but think of his own mother. He owed her a visit, but he hadn't been granted leave in quite a while. It was an all-men-on-deck situation. Nearly every night since early September, the Luftwaffe had bombed London. The city was burning, people were dying, and it was up to the RAF to put a stop to it. Some nights, it felt impossible. Other times, Thomas looked down at London below and marveled at the way the churches and monuments still stood tall, thumbing their noses at the Germans.

Thomas's mother still lived there, not far from St. Paul's Cathedral, and despite the fact that the bombings were continuous, she was insistent upon staying put. *This is my home, Thomas,* she'd written in her last letter. *If I let the Germans force me to leave, they've won, haven't they?*

He had replied right away, reminding her that the Germans would also win if they managed to take her life. *Won't you consider departing for a time, Mother?* he'd asked. *Harry's aunt Cecilia in Loughton would love to have you stay for as long as you'd like. I'm certain I can take a few days' leave to help you get settled.* But he hadn't received a reply, and now, as he began to write the letter honoring Oliver's life, he tried not to think about what it would be like for his own mother to receive such a note one day. After all, they had only each other; his father had died when Thomas was a boy, and there was no other family to speak of.

Dear Mrs. Smith, he began. *As you may know, Oliver and I were friends since the first day we met at Desford. He had a special way about him, a talent for making the fellows double over with laughter. Now, though we still try to maintain some sort of levity, if only to save ourselves from succumbing to fear and sadness, it's simply not the same. Oliver died a hero. As you must know by now, he shot down two German planes near London on the very night he died. Your son saved dozens, if not hundreds, of lives. It's little consolation, but—*

Thomas had just paused, considering exactly how to frame his words of comfort, when there was a loud knocking. He checked his watch. Nearly midnight. A knot in his stomach, he set down the pen and walked to the door.

"Clarke." It was Thomas's CO, his expression weary.

"Sir? Has something happened?"

The CO hesitated for a moment. "It's your mother, Clarke."

Thomas's vision went blurry for an instant. "My mother, sir?"

"Her home was hit," the CO said, not quite meeting Thomas's eye. "She didn't make it. I've just received confirmation."

Thomas's mouth went dry. "Sir, you're saying—"

"She died, Clarke. I'm very sorry."

"No, no, that can't be." How many flights had he flown over London? How many plots had he chased off, how many planes had he downed? He had fooled himself into thinking that he could keep his mother safe. After all, there were signs that the RAF was regaining control of the British skies. And every time he soared over the city where he'd been born and raised, every time he saw the dome of St. Paul's, he imagined that he could see his childhood home below the smoke and clouds. "When?" he asked. "I thought there hadn't been a major attack since the twenty-ninth of December."

That was the night the Nazis had dropped more than one hundred thousand bombs on London, pummeling the city's heart.

His CO hesitated. "She was injured that very night, Clarke. Apparently, her home was hit directly. It took rescuers a long time to sift through the rubble, and she was barely alive when they found her. She never woke up, and it took some time to identify her."

Thomas wanted to scream, but he was paralyzed. "Do you know—" He took a deep, shuddering breath. "Do you know exactly when she died, sir?" What good was he doing in the cockpit if he was powerless to save the person he cared most about in the world?

"Six days ago. I'm very sorry."

Six days. Six days when he'd been worrying about Oliver's family. Six days when he'd smiled and laughed and believed everything was normal. She'd been gone that whole time, and he hadn't felt it. Somehow, this was as hard to bear as the death itself.

"Clarke, you'll need to take care of arrangements," the CO said after the silence grew heavy and thick. "I will plan for you to have a few days' leave."

"But I should be here. Who will stop the Nazis?"

The CO cracked a tired smile. "There's a whole squadron of men out there trying to do just that. And many other squadrons across Britain, Clarke. We'll make it without you for a day or two."

"I—I can't."

"You must." The CO's smile faded. "I'm led to believe you're her only kin."

"Yes, sir." It wasn't until that moment that Thomas realized how very true those words were. He was alone in the world now.

"Is there anything I can do?"

"No, sir." Thomas could barely hear his own voice over the rushing sound in his ears. He longed to look into his mother's eyes, to see her bright smile, to feel her thin, fragile arms around him once more. He could remember her patiently teaching him to read, walking him to his first day of school, smiling as she proudly served a roast for just the two of them nearly every Sunday afternoon of his boyhood. He could see the worry in her eyes the day he told her he was joining the RAF, but also the pride. *Be well and safe, Thomas,* she had said, cupping her small, worn hands on either side of his face. *Just come home to me.*

As his CO bid him good night and Thomas closed the door, he realized there was no one else in the world to wait for him now.

CHAPTER NINE

April 1941

When Ruby awoke on an April morning with dawn filtering through the curtains, she was alone for the second day in a row. Marcel had disappeared more than forty-eight hours ago with no indication of when he'd be back.

"One day," she said to the baby, "this war will be over, and we'll have a good life, you and I. Your papa will be there too," she added as an afterthought. "He's going to love you very much."

She smiled at the sharp kick that she could see through the wall of her belly, and then, with her stomach rumbling, she got out of bed to begin her day. Ruby often awoke with a drumbeat of movement deep in her womb now, making her feel less alone. She had decided that the baby was a boy, that he would look very much like Marcel, and that when Marcel first laid eyes upon him, it would change everything. Perhaps she was as naïve as he accused her of being, but she preferred to think of it as hopeful.

She had just put on her dress—one of three empire-waist cotton maternity dresses she'd sewed from a pattern—when there was a knock at the door. She answered and found a small, bald, middle-aged man with thick glasses standing there, clutching his hat to his chest. He stared at her for a moment, and she at him. His clothes were rumpled, but there was something about his posture and bearing that hinted at a dignified station in life. "Can I help you?" she asked.

He glanced from her face to her belly and back again before clearing his throat. "I'm looking for the man of the house," he said, his flawless French inflected by an accent that Ruby couldn't quite place.

"He's not here right now," Ruby said. "Perhaps I can assist you with something."

The man hesitated. "I hadn't realized Monsieur Benoit had a wife."

"May I ask how you know him?" The man's repeated glances at her belly were making her uneasy.

"You are expecting a child, I see?"

"You are quite observant," Ruby said.

When the man looked up, apparently startled by her tone, she thought she saw something like kindness in his eyes for an instant, but then it was gone. "He should have informed us."

"Who *are* you?" Ruby demanded. When the man didn't answer, she added, "You are not French."

"Of course I am." The man was already backing away.

"Wait! Won't you tell me who you are?"

But the man had already turned and was hurrying down the

stairs. The last thing she saw before he disappeared out the front door was one final concerned glance at her belly, as if she was concealing a bomb that could explode at any moment, destroying them all.

BY THE TIME MARCEL RETURNED, late that night, Ruby had gone over the strange encounter again and again in her head, and with each repetition, she'd felt more unsettled. The man's accent had been hard on the consonants, a bit like the way Nazi soldiers spoke when they were barking orders. *My God*, she thought, her stomach turning. *What if Marcel is helping the Germans?*

And suddenly, the pieces were falling into place, and Ruby felt ill. His long absences. His lack of regard for the German regulations, as if they didn't apply to him. The war of morals she could see going on inside him. It all made sense. But how could he do such a thing? To collaborate would be unconscionable.

"You had a visitor today," she said when he slipped in the door. He visibly startled; he hadn't expected to find her glaring at him from the dining table.

"What are you doing out of bed?" It wasn't the reply of an innocent man.

"Waiting for you."

He stared at her across the flickering darkness. "What do you mean I had a visitor?"

"A man," she said slowly. "A man who seemed stunned to realize I existed."

As Marcel opened and closed his mouth like a fish, she could feel her heart hardening. He had put them in danger, Ruby and the baby, and he had the gall to stand there looking affronted.

"Well, who was it?"

Ruby looked him straight in the eye. "Your handler, I assume."

"What?"

"Or perhaps that's not the right term. *Der Meister*, is it? Is that not how they say it in German?"

His face turned white. "*Der* . . . what? The man who came here was German?"

Ruby stood slowly, her hands cradling her belly. "You're going to deny it, Marcel?"

He blinked rapidly. "How do you know he was German, Ruby? What did you tell him?"

"What did I *tell* him? Nothing. He just seemed appalled that you had a pregnant wife. I'm sorry if I'm getting in the way of your Nazi scheming. How inconvenient."

Marcel stared for another moment before moving toward her. She took a step back, putting her hand protectively on her belly, and he halted. "I'm not going to hurt you, Ruby." He sounded suddenly weary. He took a seat at the table and gestured to the chair she'd just vacated. "I would never, ever hurt you. Sit. Please."

Ruby moved the chair away from the table, putting some distance between them. "What could you possibly have to say that would make this all right?"

"I'm not helping the Germans. I would sooner die, Ruby."

"Don't lie to me. He certainly wasn't French."

He bit his lip. "You must take me at my word. I need to leave you out of this. For your own safety."

"It's hard to feel safe with Germans at our door."

"*He wasn't German*. For the love of God, Ruby!"

"Then who was he? What was he doing here?"

Marcel didn't answer right away. He stood and began to pace. "You're speaking of a man who's a little shorter than I? Bald? Glasses?"

"Yes."

He was silent for a long time. "He goes by Neville, although I assume that's not his real name. He's British intelligence."

"What?"

"I've been working with him. *For* him."

"But—" Was he telling the truth? And if he was, how had she read him so wrong?

"He shouldn't have come here. But now you know."

"I don't understand. You're working for the Allies? Why didn't you tell me?"

"Because you're in danger now, don't you see that? You weren't supposed to be involved in any of this, ever. It's my risk, not yours."

"But I'm your wife. And if you get caught—"

"I'm not *going* to get caught!"

Ruby took a few deep breaths to calm herself. The baby was kicking again. "I understand the stakes, Marcel."

"Do you?" His face twisted into a sneer. "As far as I know, you'll be telling the neighbor's girl in no time."

"I would never do that! You don't think I know how important this is? How dangerous?"

He looked balefully at her belly. "You don't understand things the way I do, Ruby. That much is clear."

"How can you say that, Marcel? I'm not the fool you've decided I am! I'm your wife, and I'm carrying your child. We're all in this together, whether you like it or not!"

He looked at her for a long time before his expression darkened. He smashed his fist against the wall with such force that he left a mark.

"I'm—" Marcel began, looking down at her. She was sure he was about to apologize for his temper, but then he stopped. "You will stay out of this," he said once more firmly. "That isn't a request." And then he strode across the apartment, slamming the front door behind him.

BY THE TIME RUBY MANAGED to fall asleep a few hours later, she knew in her gut that Marcel was telling the truth; she had played and replayed the visit from the bald man in her head, and she had to admit, his accent *had* sounded British. But wasn't Marcel's decision to work for the Allies—without telling Ruby—a betrayal too?

She awoke just before dawn with an intense pain in her lower back. She cried out and rolled to her left, looking for her husband. But his side of the bed was cold and empty, as it so often was these days. She struggled to sit upright, a hand on her belly, as if she could protect the baby from whatever was happening. "It's okay," she murmured, as much to the child as to herself. "Everything's going to be all right."

But then there was a searing pain in her abdomen, and she doubled over, nearly falling out of bed. She grabbed the edge of the mattress to steady herself and pushed herself onto the floor. She needed help. She needed to make it to the Dachers' apartment. They would know what to do. She collapsed at the bedroom door as her body was racked by another wave of agony.

Her cotton nightgown was soaked with sweat by the time she made it down the hall. She cried out and fell to her knees at the Dachers' doorway, but she managed to knock once and then again more insistently until she heard hurried footsteps approaching. The door swung open, and she looked up to see Monsieur Dacher standing there, white-faced, a candlestick hefted like a weapon. His fierce expression softened when he saw her.

"Madame Benoit, what has happened?" He put a hand under her elbow to help her up.

She was startled to realize she was crying. "I don't . . ." she attempted, trailing off. "I can't . . ."

"Sarah!" Monsieur Dacher called into the darkness of his apartment. "Come quickly! It's Madame Benoit!"

A moment later, Ruby looked up to see a bathrobe-clad Madame Dacher rushing down the hall, tailed by a stricken-looking Charlotte.

"I'm okay, Charlotte," Ruby managed. "Don't worry. Go back to bed."

Madame Dacher turned and said something to the girl, and although Charlotte looked worried, she retreated into the apartment, leaving the three adults alone.

"Madame Benoit?" As Madame Dacher bent down beside

Ruby and placed a cool hand on her cheek, her voice was soft and comforting, the way Ruby imagined a mother would speak to a child. She would speak to her own child that way, Ruby decided. Reassuring, gentle, firm. It was perfect. "What is it? Are you all right?"

"I don't know," Ruby managed. "It's just . . . Something is wrong with my belly."

Another sharp pain crackled through her, radiating out from the center of her body, and she moaned again. When she looked up, something had changed in Madame Dacher's face. "Oh, my dear," her neighbor said in that same soothing tone. "Let's get you up, shall we? Yes, that's right. Hold on."

Ruby couldn't seem to feel her legs, so she wasn't quite sure how she got to the couch, the ornate, gold-legged one in the Dachers' living room that she'd admired on the one occasion she'd been invited inside. But there was Madame Dacher beside her, placing a cool, damp washcloth on her forehead and murmuring for her to lie back. "What's wrong with me?" Ruby managed. "Is the baby all right?"

"Oh, dear," Madame Dacher said, kneeling beside Ruby and squeezing her hand. "I'm afraid your baby might be coming just now. My husband has gone for a doctor."

"Coming now?" Ruby repeated in disbelief, struggling to sit up. "No, no, it's too early. Far too early. I'm only six months along. And what about Marcel? Marcel should be here."

"Shhhh," Madame Dacher whispered, her voice soft and song-like. "We'll find Monsieur Benoit, dear. Everything is going to be all right. You just relax."

Ruby was about to answer, but this time, when the pain in her belly returned, it was so blinding that she lost consciousness, slipping into a silent, jagged darkness.

WHEN RUBY AWOKE, THERE WAS sunlight streaming through the window. It took her a few seconds to get her bearings, to remember the terror and the pain that had brought her here. The baby!

"Madame Dacher!" she cried out, sitting up with great effort. Her whole body ached, and she was still on the couch, covered in a white sheet and a faded blue blanket someone had knitted. "Madame Dacher?"

It was Charlotte who emerged from the kitchen instead, her face pale. "Ruby! Are you all right?"

"I—I don't know. What happened?"

"I—" Charlotte seemed at a loss for words. "I'm going to go get my mother, okay?"

"Charlotte?" Ruby felt suddenly shaky, unsure. "Is everything okay with the baby?" She began to reach for her belly, but Charlotte thrust a cup of tea into her hands instead.

"Here, drink this. I'll go get Maman."

By the time Charlotte returned with her mother in tow, Ruby already knew. She had felt the contours of her deflated belly through the blanket, sensed the emptiness in the space where life had grown. "I lost the baby, didn't I?" she asked in a whisper, her vision blurred by tears.

Madame Dacher waved Charlotte away, and as the girl disappeared down the hall, Madame Dacher sat down beside Ruby and took her hands. "My dear, I am so sorry. The baby was stillborn."

"No," Ruby whispered.

"The doctor arrived soon after you lost consciousness and gave you something for the pain. The baby was already coming. He—he never breathed. He didn't cry. He didn't feel a thing."

"It was a boy," Ruby said dully. It was just like she'd imagined, a boy in Marcel's image. He was gone before he'd ever lived.

Madame Dacher nodded, squeezing Ruby's hand. "I'm so sorry."

"May I see him?"

Madame Dacher looked surprised. "Oh, I'm sure you don't want to—"

Ruby cut her off. "Please. I must see my baby."

Madame Dacher looked at her before nodding slowly and rising. She returned clutching something swaddled that looked far too small to be a baby. When she put the bundle in Ruby's arms, Ruby gasped. Here, no larger than a child's doll, was her own son, his tiny face blue-tinged and still.

"No," she breathed. She bent to kiss his forehead, startled, despite herself, to find it so cold. "No," she whispered again. "You must come back." The baby had Marcel's nose, the shape of his mouth. Ruby wondered what his eyes looked like, but they were already closed forever. His ears were tiny and freezing; his hair was downy, his chin no wider than the tip of Ruby's thumb. "How did I let you die?"

"My dear," Madame Dacher said, gently taking the baby from Ruby's grasp when her tears had finally stopped falling. "It is not your fault. Sometimes all the love in the world can't protect a person against his fate."

CHAPTER TEN

April 1941

Marcel didn't come home the night of the stillbirth or the next. Ruby couldn't get out of bed; she knew she would never forgive herself for not protecting her child, though the Dachers' kindly doctor friend had told her she wasn't to blame, that these things sometimes simply happen for no reason at all.

Charlotte checked on her thrice a day, each time bringing food, which Ruby had no appetite for. "You mustn't worry, Ruby," Charlotte said on the second night, when she delivered a watery soup of potatoes and beef. "You will have another baby one day. I know you will."

And though Ruby nodded and tried to smile, her heart was breaking. She knew with a dull certainty that there would be no more babies. She'd been deluding herself into thinking that a child would have fixed what was broken in her marriage. Even if Marcel was working for a good cause, he had abandoned her long ago.

On the third night, Marcel came home just before midnight and found Ruby propped up on pillows on the living room sofa, staring at the wall. "What are you doing awake?" he asked.

"Where have you been?" she asked, instead of replying.

"I had work to do. I told you, Ruby, this isn't something I can talk about."

"Were you out with your British friend? Feeling that you were making some sort of difference in this goddamned war?"

He looked startled. "I *am* making a difference, Ruby. What are you going on about?"

She stared at him for a long time. What had she seen in him when their eyes first met across that café in New York? What had made her so sure that he was worth giving up her life for? She could hardly remember anymore. "I lost the baby," she said.

"What?" But she knew he had heard her, for there was suddenly a storm of emotions playing out across his face. Sadness. Surprise. Guilt. "Well. I'm very sorry," he said finally.

"Are you?"

"Ruby, maybe it's for the best."

"The *best*?" He might as well have ripped her heart out with his bare hands. "Our child is *dead*, Marcel."

"A baby is a liability in times like this."

"A liability? You believe he would have been a liability?"

Something flickered in his eyes. "The baby was a boy?"

"He looked just like you," she whispered. And then, before he could say anything else, she stood, cradling her empty belly, and walked into the bedroom, slamming the door behind her. She knew he wouldn't follow, even if a small part of her hoped he would. A few moments later, the front door of the apartment opened and closed. He was gone.

AS SPRING ROLLED INTO SUMMER, and the baby's due date came and went without anyone remembering but Ruby, Marcel became more elusive, more absent, and Ruby found herself worrying less and less about him. Was it because she didn't care anymore, or because she knew he'd always resurface eventually?

And while she resented the fact that he wouldn't give her the chance to understand what he was doing, she felt proud of him on some level. He was doing something to help, but what for? Nothing seemed to loosen the Nazis' stranglehold on the city, and people were being executed now for crimes as small as distributing anti-Nazi newsletters. Was that the kind of work Marcel was doing?

Paris had gone dark, even in the midst of a vibrant summer. Electricity had become unreliable—most nights, the city was lit only by moonlight. With so many Parisians still in the countryside, and the ones who stayed muzzled by uncertainty and fear, the quiet felt strange and sinister. Police sirens wailed more loudly than usual, and every time the growl of an airplane engine materialized in the distance, people tensed, ready for the worst.

In late July, Ruby finally received a letter from her mother, dated mid-May. *Dearest Ruby*, it said in neat, familiar script.

Your father and I are fine. We've received your letters and gather that ours aren't making it to you. We are trying again, in hopes that one of our messages will get through. We're overjoyed to hear that you are having a baby, and we implore you again to consider coming home—if not for your own safety, then for your child's. We've spoken with our congressman's office, and they might be able to arrange safe passage for you. The news reports from Europe are terrifying, sweetheart. I'm sure Marcel would not only understand, but would agree that this decision is for the best. Perhaps he can even come with you! Please keep writing, and we will do the same. We know we will see you—and our grandchild—very soon. Your father sends his love.

Ruby folded the note carefully and slipped it back into the envelope, marveling that it had reached her at all. She didn't realize until her address smeared that she was crying. Her parents were expecting her to come home—and to bring her baby with her. Receiving this letter now, months after it had been sent, was like a window to a past that she could never get back. There was no baby anymore, no chance for escape. Getting out of Paris would take an act of God, and Ruby had begun to wonder if He, like the French government, had deserted the city.

Ruby dutifully wrote back, telling her mother about the loss of the baby. She sobbed as she wrote, once again seeing her son's tiny, silent body, feeling the chill of him deep in her heart. She knew she wouldn't be returning to the States, not while the war still raged, and she told her mother this. Each time she thought of boarding a ship back to America, she thought of the Dachers, and especially Charlotte. Abandoning them now, when they'd been there for her in her greatest hour of need, felt unthinkable.

Ruby posted the letter and spent the rest of the day wandering the city with no real purpose in mind. It was self-destructive, she knew. If a Nazi soldier questioned her, she wouldn't be able to explain where she was going, for the truth was, she was going nowhere. She should have been one of the mothers pushing a pram occupied by a cooing infant. Instead, she was alone and as empty as she'd ever been in her life.

Paris was still Paris, with the lovely flowers of summer and the fresh, sun-drenched air. But the city was a shadow of its former self, and the blossoms and scents that had once been a comfort seemed merely like window dressing. Ruby, too, had become a shadow of the person she used to be. How had she ever giggled with her friends in a dormitory room, swooned over Clark Gable on the big screen, agonized about which dress she'd wear to a party? Now, she couldn't remember the last time she'd laughed; she hadn't seen a movie in years; she wouldn't know how to behave at a social event if she somehow found herself at one.

"You seem very sad," Charlotte said that evening when she appeared at Ruby's door to invite her over for coffee. One of her father's former customers had managed to get his hands on some real coffee beans, an incredible treat.

"Oh, I'm all right," Ruby reassured her. "But you're very kind to worry, Charlotte."

"You know," the girl said after a moment, "things are never quite as dark as they seem."

Ruby smiled. "Is that right?"

Charlotte nodded confidently. "You see, when you look back on things later in life, it's sometimes easier to see the purpose. So perhaps for now, it's best to try your hardest to focus on what lies ahead. The future is still something that can be changed, isn't it?"

"It seems to me that that's very good advice," Ruby said, her eyes damp. "Thank you."

Charlotte looked pleased. "So you will come for coffee? There's something my parents would like to discuss with you."

Curious, Ruby followed Charlotte next door to their corner apartment, where she found Madame and Monsieur Dacher at their table, a beautiful silver coffeepot and three ornate china cups before them. "We had hoped you would join us," Madame Dacher said, rising to kiss Ruby on both cheeks. "We wanted to share this with you."

"How very kind." As Ruby sat down, Monsieur Dacher began to pour. The heavenly aroma of coffee, so familiar yet so foreign these days, seemed to wrap the room in warmth.

Madame Dacher emerged from the kitchen a moment later with chocolates and a small bowl of sugar. "Charlotte, dear, go get ready for bed."

"But I'd like some coffee too! And I'd like to visit with Madame Benoit."

"We need to have a grown-up conversation," Madame Dacher said firmly. "Please, my dear. You can visit with her tomorrow."

"I'm not a child anymore, you know." But Charlotte said a terse good night to Ruby and her parents and headed toward the back of the apartment.

"There is a favor we would like to ask you," Monsieur Dacher said after all three of them had taken a first sip of coffee and delighted in how wonderful it tasted.

"Yes, anything."

"After this summer, we think that perhaps Charlotte will not return to school. There are—" Monsieur Dacher paused and began again. "There are circumstances that make it difficult now."

"I'm very sorry," Ruby said. The words were woefully inadequate.

"We are sorry too." Madame Dacher took over, glancing at her husband. "This is not the France we knew."

Ruby nodded, and the three of them shared a moment of silent understanding before Madame Dacher went on. "I will take over her schooling here at home. But we would like for her to learn English, and we were wondering whether we might impose upon you to help."

"Of course!" Ruby responded immediately. Not only did she owe the Dachers a debt, but she would actually enjoy the opportunity to spend more time with the girl.

"We feel that it will be an important language for her to know in the future," Madame Dacher continued.

"Britain will help us win this war," Monsieur Dacher added. "And we would like to know that Charlotte's future might include working with them."

"Also," Madame Dacher said, locking eyes with her husband, "we do not know what this war will bring for Jews. There are terrible rumors of things happening in the east."

The Dachers exchanged looks. "As you may know, Sarah is from Poland," Monsieur Dacher said. "She came to France as a small child with her parents, but she still has many family members who, until recently, were living near Krakow. We do not know what has become of them. As for me, my father is French, but my mother is from Poland too, and in fact, I was born there when she was on a journey to visit her parents."

"I assumed you were both born in France."

Monsieur Dacher shook his head. "Some of the reports from Poland in the last months . . ." He trailed off.

"The Germans are sending Jews to work camps," Madame Dacher said bluntly, her gaze far away. "And there are rumors that some of them are dying."

"But you see, it's impossible to know the truth, because things are often greatly exaggerated," Monsieur Dacher said quickly. "In any case, we feel strongly that such a thing would never happen here. The French will not turn on their own. We must endure the restrictions that have been placed upon us, but we will survive this."

"Still, we feel that Charlotte knowing English will give her an advantage, whatever the future should bring," Madame Dacher said. When she looked up, Ruby could see in her eyes that she didn't share her husband's optimism.

The coffee on the table between them was going cold, but Ruby was no longer thinking of what a rare treat it was. What must it be like to fear for your child's future this way? She had been powerless to protect her own child, but she could be there for Charlotte if it came to that. And that was something.

There were a thousand things Ruby wanted to say, a hundred promises she wanted to make. But the Dachers were proud, and Ruby knew they weren't looking for platitudes. They were looking for hope. "It would be my pleasure to help Charlotte learn English," she said. "When shall we begin?"

✦ ✦ ✦

BY MID-AUGUST, THE HEAT WAS sweltering, and the air in Paris seemed strangely still, as if the city itself was holding its breath. Ruby had been working with Charlotte for three weeks, meeting with her every Thursday afternoon. Ruby had never taught a language before, but she had begun to study French when she was just a bit younger than Charlotte was now, so she tried to remember how she had learned. Small words first, the kind you'd teach a young child, followed by pronouns and basic verb conjugations. English seemed more difficult than French, for it drew from so many different languages, but Ruby found Charlotte an apt pupil.

"Do you miss Monsieur Benoit?" Charlotte asked late one afternoon as their lesson was concluding. Ruby had taught her the numbers that day, all the way up to one hundred, and Charlotte had managed to conjugate a few simple verbs.

"Miss him?" Ruby was puzzled. "He hasn't gone anywhere."

Charlotte shrugged. "I only mean that he's often away. I wonder if it's hard for you being alone."

Ruby took a deep breath. Charlotte didn't miss a thing. "In truth, I think it is easier to be by myself than to be with someone who doesn't seem to trust me."

She worried that it was the wrong thing to say to a child, but Charlotte nodded in immediate understanding. "You wish he would not keep secrets from you."

Ruby blinked. "Yes."

"I wish that too."

Later, after Charlotte had gone, Ruby was left wondering what the girl had meant. How had she guessed that Marcel was keeping secrets?

Marcel surprised Ruby by arriving home at six that evening, toting a fresh chicken wrapped in newspaper. "I've brought dinner," he said.

"But where did you get it?" Certainly this wasn't the sort of thing that was easy to come by anymore. Her mouth watered, but she could also feel her stomach twisting with concern.

He frowned. "Does it matter? I've done nothing wrong, if that's what you're suggesting. I had hoped you would be as excited as I am about the prospect of a good meal."

"I'm sorry."

Marcel studied her for a minute, then seemed to deflate. "No, I suppose I don't blame you."

He walked into the bedroom without another word, and Ruby began to prepare the chicken to roast. She would use the carcass for broth later and would share some soup with the Dachers.

She had just slid the chicken into the oven when Marcel reappeared in the kitchen, his tie gone and his shirt loosened at the collar. He looked more relaxed than she'd seen him in months. Handsome, even. "It smells wonderful in here," he said.

"Thank you for bringing the chicken." She felt oddly formal with him, like he was a guest in her home.

"Thank you for cooking it." He was being just as proper with her. They had become strangers. "You've been well?"

She nodded and moved across the kitchen to uncork one of the two dozen remaining bottles of wine they had. Marcel had kept a small collection before the war. She poured a glass for him and one for her, and they toasted. "To peace," she said.

"To victory." His reply was immediate. "Peace without victory means nothing."

She nodded and turned away, sure he was scolding her.

"I'm sorry," he said. "I didn't mean that as a criticism. I— Sometimes things come out wrong."

"It's all right." She was surprised to realize she meant it.

"And I'm sorry, too, about the baby, Ruby. I really am." The words hung between them, and he waited until she looked up before continuing. "I feel very sorry that he died. You needed me, and I wasn't there for you. I haven't been there for you much at all, in fact. But things will be different soon. I promise."

"Does that mean you'll be able to tell me what's going on? Maybe let me help?"

His smile faded. "We've discussed this, Ruby. It would put you in danger." He raised his glass again. "But I want to become once again the man you married. I will, Ruby. I will."

They toasted, looking into each other's eyes. And for a long time afterward, as she sipped her wine, Ruby could see the hazy possibility of a different future.

MARCEL LEFT AFTER DINNER, THANKING Ruby politely for the meal and promising to be back soon.

Two hours later, Ruby had delivered some soup to the Dachers and was just finishing scrubbing dishes when there was a knock at the door, so tentative that at first she wondered if she'd imagined it. But then she heard it again, stronger this time. Ruby's eyes went to the clock. It was past curfew. A chill ran down her spine as she considered the possibility that it was a Nazi soldier, here to arrest Marcel for whatever he was doing. But when she peered out the peephole, it wasn't a German uniform she saw; it was what appeared to be a greenish-gray jumpsuit. And the man wearing it—dark blond hair, six feet tall or so—was bent down on one knee in the hall, breathing heavily.

Ruby backed away from the door, puzzled. A moment later, he knocked again, and when she didn't answer, there was a pause, and then she heard a series of strange noises from the hall. It took her a few seconds to recognize the sounds as sobs. The man began to mumble to himself, and she inched closer to the door, hoping she could catch a few words. She nearly fell back when she realized he wasn't speaking French or even German. He was speaking English. "Have to get to . . ." he was muttering. "They said it was here . . ."

Before she could second-guess herself, she pulled the door open. The man nearly lost his balance, tripping into her apartment before scrambling to his feet and backing away. "Oh, I'm so sorry, miss. I'm sorry. I mean, er, *Je suis déso . . .*" He trailed off, apparently unable to remember the final syllable in the French apology. "I'm, um, just really sorry, miss. I don't speak much French."

"Who are you?" she asked in English, which seemed to startle him.

"You—you speak English? Oh, thank heavens. Dexter. My name is Dexter. And, um, forgive me, but I've been walking for two days, and I haven't had anything to eat at all, and I'm afraid that the small wound I have on my shoulder has perhaps gotten a bit infected, so—"

"You're British?"

He nodded again. "And you? You're not French, are you?"

She didn't reply. "What are you doing here, Dexter?"

He hesitated, which was just long enough to make up her mind. She didn't know how he had arrived at her front door, but she had the feeling it had something to do with Marcel. And in the time that Dexter had been babbling, she had spotted the RAF patches on his chest. He was a British pilot, or at least he was dressed as one. And that meant that both of them would be in danger if anyone saw them together.

"Well, miss, you see, I was flying over northeast France, or at least I thought I was, when—"

"Come in," she interrupted. "Quickly. Before someone spots you."

He blinked a few times. "Thank you. Thank you so much, miss. I—"

She grabbed his right arm and pulled him inside, but as she began to hurriedly close the door behind him, she realized she was already too late.

Charlotte was down the hall, in the sliver of her own open doorway, staring at Ruby and the British pilot, her mouth open in an O of surprise.

Ruby could feel the blood draining from her face, but she managed to put a finger to her lips. *Tell no one,* she mouthed to Charlotte. *Please.*

Silently, Charlotte nodded and slipped back into her own apartment, closing the heavy door behind her.

CHAPTER ELEVEN

August 1941

Ruby was helping Allied airmen?

Charlotte stood with her back to the door for a long time. Her apartment was silent, her parents in bed. She'd heard a commotion in the hall and had gone to the door to investigate. *Perhaps it was Monsieur Benoit, up to no good again,* she'd thought. If she could see what he was doing, she would have something to share with Ruby. But instead, when she peered out, she realized there was a strange man in the shadows outside Ruby's apartment, knocking insistently. She had opened the door a crack, intending to tell him, in her firmest possible voice, to go away, for Ruby already had so much to deal with. But then Ruby's door had opened and the light spilling into the hall had revealed his uniform. Charlotte had frozen, terrified.

At first, she'd thought the man was German. After all, she'd gotten accustomed to seeing German uniforms spreading across her city like a growing mold. But his voice sounded different, and as

he spoke in low tones to Ruby, she made out a few familiar words—
Sorry. Flying. Thank you—and she'd realized he was speaking English. So he was British, then, or perhaps even American. He had to
be. And he must be a pilot too. There was no other reason an Allied
soldier would be in Paris.

Before she'd stopped going to school, Charlotte had overheard
gossip from her classmates that there were Resistance networks
sprinkled throughout Paris, French citizens who smiled to the Germans' faces and behind their backs helped pilots who'd been shot
down. She knew, too, that the penalties were stiff for those who
were caught working against the Nazis. The men were most often
executed, the women shipped off to prison camps in Germany.

But Ruby was helping? Why hadn't she said anything? Charlotte had thought she and Ruby were friends, but friends confided
in each other. Friends trusted each other. The only explanation was
that Ruby saw her as merely a child. But Charlotte was twelve and
a half now, old enough to help out, old enough to make a difference.
Besides, she could keep a secret. Even from her parents. Ruby could
trust her. Charlotte was determined to prove it.

She snuck into the kitchen, where she packed a small bundle
for the airman: a little cheese, some stale bread, sardines in a can.
Ruby's rations weren't any more plentiful than hers, and though
she knew her parents would probably notice the missing items, she
vowed she'd simply eat less over the next week to even the scales. If
she arrived at Ruby's door with food for the fugitive, surely Ruby
would see how serious she was about joining her secret mission.

Charlotte checked on her parents before she left to make sure
they were sleeping soundly. Maman was curled on her side, her

shoulder rising and falling, and Papa was on his back, snoring loudly. They were both deep sleepers; there was no way that she would wake them now as she slipped out of the apartment.

A moment later, she knocked on Ruby's door. She heard shuffling inside, but no one answered. She knocked again, but there was still no answer, only silence from within. Finally, she rapped for a third time and said quietly through the door, "Ruby, open up! It's Charlotte! I know about your airman."

There was a moment of quiet, and then Charlotte could hear footsteps. The door swung upon to reveal Ruby, red-faced, staring down at her.

"Charlotte!" she exclaimed. "What are you doing up?"

"I know about your airman," Charlotte repeated, presenting her carefully assembled bundle. "That's what he is, right? I've brought him some food."

Ruby's face went blank, though Charlotte noticed her cheeks were still flaming. "I don't know what you're talking about. There's no airman here."

"Ruby," Charlotte said slowly, her feelings hurt, "I saw him."

"Charlotte—"

"No! I'm tired of everyone treating me like a child! Maman and Papa act like I have no idea what's happening, but I see it every day. I understand way more than they think I do. And you! I thought we were friends. But friends don't keep secrets like this."

Ruby blinked a few times. "Come in." She put a hand on Charlotte's shoulder. "But you must be quiet. And you mustn't breathe a word of this. It could get us all killed."

Her heart thudding, Charlotte stepped into the apartment and looked around as Ruby closed the door. The pilot was nowhere to be seen. "Where is he?" Charlotte asked.

Ruby sighed. "Charlotte, dear, I'm not keeping things from you because I believe you're a child. I know you're not; this war has forced us all to grow up. And I feel that we're friends too. But some things are better not to discuss."

"Why?"

"Because if you're ever questioned by the police or by the Germans, you could be in danger. I'm American, so they might be more careful in the way they treat me. But you're—" She stopped speaking.

"I'm Jewish," Charlotte filled in. "That's what you were going to say."

"Yes. Yes, Charlotte. And if there's ever a problem, I want you to be able to say you haven't seen anything."

"But I *have* seen something. I saw the airman!"

Ruby turned away, placing her hands on the kitchen counter and staring out the window into the darkness beyond. Finally, she turned back around. "Honey, if the Germans come asking, you need to be able to deny having any involvement in anything illegal."

Charlotte held up the care package. "I'm already involved. See, I'm feeding your airman."

Ruby eyed the bundle. "Your parents will notice."

"I'll tell them I ate the food myself. They'll be angry, but it will be okay. It's better than him starving, isn't it? I know you don't have enough food."

"I have some."

"And now you have more. If he's injured, he'll need his strength back, right?" Charlotte could see Ruby wavering, so she pressed on.

"Ruby, I hate being helpless. There's not much someone my age can do to assist the Allies."

"It's not just people your age, Charlotte. I feel helpless too."

"Then let's help together."

Charlotte was certain Ruby was about to say no. But then there was a mighty crash from the back of the apartment. Ruby ran toward it, and Charlotte ran after her.

In the bedroom, they found a scene that would have been laughable if they weren't both so on edge. The airman was half-buried in a mound of clothes on the floor outside Ruby's wardrobe. Charlotte realized in an instant that Ruby must have hidden him there when she heard a knock at the door, and he'd somehow managed to fall out.

"Dexter?" Ruby said loudly, rushing to the airman's side. "Dexter, are you all right?"

To Charlotte's relief, the airman was awake, and he struggled to sit up, his face red. He mumbled something that Charlotte couldn't understand. Ruby replied in English, and it was then that he noticed Charlotte. His eyes widened.

"He said he was feeling a bit weak," Ruby said, turning to Charlotte. "I think he may have lost more blood than he realized."

"How did he come to be here?"

"I was just about to ask him that when you knocked on the door," Ruby said. "Now let me explain to him who you are and that you don't mean him any harm."

She turned back to the man and said something in rapid English. He glanced up at Charlotte once more and smiled, almost shyly. "*Merci*," he said with an awful accent. "*Merci beaucoup*."

Ruby turned back to Charlotte. "I explained that you brought him a bit of food and that you're a friend who can be trusted. Now, do you think you can help me get him up?"

Charlotte moved quickly to the airman's side. Up close, he smelled of grease and grass. He was breathing shallowly, there were beads of sweat on his tanned forehead, and his eyes were glassy.

"Just grab him under his left arm there and help me lift," Ruby said. "We'll take him to the dining table, all right?"

Charlotte nodded, and on the count of three, they hoisted the man, who was heavier than he looked, and helped him into the other room, where he collapsed into a chair. He looked terrible, but he was sitting upright, his eyes open, which was an improvement from a few minutes earlier.

Ruby said something to the airman again, and he smiled, first at her and then at Charlotte. Charlotte found herself blushing; he wasn't so very many years older than she was.

"I thank you helping me," he said in broken French, turning to Charlotte. "I know it is danger."

Charlotte smiled and said carefully in English, "You're welcome," just like Ruby had taught her. Then she turned to Ruby and said, "Perhaps it is better for him to speak in English. You can tell me what he says."

Ruby translated this to the airman, who nodded and began to talk. They went back and forth for a few minutes, and Charlotte caught familiar words here and there, but not enough to piece together the story.

"He says he's a pilot in the British air force," Ruby finally said, turning to Charlotte. "He was on a mission over the eastern part of

France when he was shot down. He managed to parachute out, and then he hid in a barn while the Germans searched the woods for him. At night, he found a river and followed it west using a compass in his flight kit. He just knew he had to make it to Paris."

"Why?" Charlotte whispered. "Paris is crawling with Germans."

"One of the other pilots in his squadron had been shot down before. And he'd been saved by a network who helped him to escape through a pass in the eastern Pyrenees mountains into Spain. He knew that if he came to Paris, he'd have a chance of returning to England."

"But why here?" Charlotte asked. "Why your door?"

"Because," Ruby said, swallowing hard and then hesitating, casting another glance at the pilot, "he says the man who lives in this apartment helped the other pilot."

Charlotte stared at Ruby. "Monsieur Benoit?"

Ruby hesitated. "I shouldn't be discussing this with you, Charlotte. I don't want you to—"

"I saw him," Charlotte interrupted, cutting her off.

"What do you mean?"

"He was in the hallway at night. He placed some sort of parcel into the closet in the hall."

Ruby went still. "What closet in the hall?"

"It's hidden. It's just across from your doorway. I can show you, if you'd like."

"Wait." Ruby glanced at the airman, who was looking back and forth between the two of them with a blank expression on his face. "You're telling me that you saw Marcel placing a parcel in a hidden closet? Why didn't you tell me?"

Charlotte averted her eyes. "I thought perhaps you knew. I thought you were in on it."

"No," Ruby said softly. "No. It seems I'm the only one who's been living in the dark here."

The pilot interrupted, saying something rapid in English and gesturing to the bundle of food on the table. Ruby pushed it toward him, then she jumped up from the table to retrieve a can opener, a fork, and a glass of water. "He says he hasn't eaten since his plane crashed," she told Charlotte. "He's starving."

"*Merci*," the pilot said again, nodding at Charlotte and pointing at the food. "Um, very hunger." He dug in, wolfing down the bread first, then the cheese, and finally the sardines. He sighed when he was done and leaned back, closing his eyes.

"I think he is badly injured," Charlotte said softly. She'd been studying him while he ate. Though the kitchen wasn't warm, his skin was pale and clammy.

"Yes, I think so too." Ruby sounded calm but concerned. She spoke to the pilot, and he shook his head and said something quickly. Ruby spoke again, her tone gentler this time, and finally the pilot glanced at Charlotte and then back at Ruby before nodding reluctantly. He unzipped his suit and winced as he wriggled out of the top half, exposing a torn and bloodied undershirt. He peeled that off too, and Charlotte and Ruby gasped in unison as they saw the giant, oozing gash across his right shoulder. Dried blood was caked all the way down his chest.

"What happened?" Charlotte breathed. It looked like the kind of wound a man could die from.

Ruby exchanged a few sentences with the pilot and turned

back to Charlotte with a grim expression. "He thinks a bullet went through his shoulder. He was shot before he bailed out." She glanced at the pilot once more, then leaned in to add in a whisper to Charlotte, "I'm very concerned that it is infected, but I don't know how to treat it. And it's too dangerous to call for a doctor."

"Monsieur Benoit will know what to do." Charlotte nodded decisively.

"But I don't know when he will be home. He has no way of knowing that this pilot is here. If he doesn't make it back for a few days . . ."

"The pilot could die." Charlotte glanced at the man, who looked back at her blankly. She was glad he hadn't understood. "Do you know where Monsieur Benoit goes? Or who he's working with?"

"I didn't even know he was doing any of this, Charlotte. You know more about it than I do, it seems."

"No, I don't." Charlotte's reply was instant, but then she felt guilty, for she *had* known more than Ruby and she hadn't bothered to tell her. It seemed that she, not Ruby, was the bad friend. "My parents are friends with the doctor who helped you when—" She stopped abruptly. "You've met him," she concluded instead.

"Yes. But we can't involve him in this. We don't know if he can be trusted, and even if he can, I'm not willing to put more people in danger."

"Then what do we do?"

Ruby was silent for a long time. The airman was trying to follow their conversation, but from the look on his face, Charlotte was almost certain that he didn't understand.

"We wait," Ruby said at last. "We hide him, and we wait for Marcel to come home."

"But what if he dies first?" Charlotte whispered.

"I'll do everything I can to reach Marcel," Ruby said. "And I'll clean the airman's wound and care for him to the best of my ability. Beyond that, we'll just have to pray."

"Okay. But you promise you'll tell me if I can help at all?"

Ruby smiled. "You *can* help. You can show me this secret closet."

CHAPTER TWELVE

August 1941

In January, just after Thomas had buried his mother, his squadron had begun missions over France, which was exactly the distraction he needed. Defending England's coast was important, of course, but playing defense wasn't the way to win a war. By bringing the fight to the Huns, the RAF was finally on the offense, which meant they actually had a chance.

Before their first trip across the Channel in late January, the CO stopped Thomas, Harry, and the others on their way to a Nissen hut for a briefing. "Don't even think about bailing out over France," he warned. "The place is crawling with Krauts, understand? May as well go down with your plane if you can't make it out."

The warning should have made Thomas's blood run cold, but it was cold already. Now that his mother was gone, no one—except maybe Harry—cared whether he lived or died. He was acutely aware of that every time he went skyward.

A huge map of the English coast and northwestern France was slung across the back wall of the hut, crisscrossed with red string. As he and Harry took seats facing the platform, Thomas noted that many of the airfields around London had string paths to a central meeting point in Canterbury, the launching point for a route across the Channel.

"Listen up, chaps," the station commander began, and a hush fell across the room. "We're bringing the war to the Germans now. It'll be dangerous, but this is a crucial step on the road to victory."

The CO spoke next, briefing the men on their flight positions, their target speeds, the enemy aircraft, and their mission goal—to keep German 109s from shooting down the British bombers that would drop their loads around Boulogne, a coastal area crawling with Nazis.

"What do you think, then?" Harry asked later as he and Thomas walked briskly through a light snowfall back to their rooms. They had just a few hours to prepare for the mission. "Are we going to turn the tide, or is this suicide?"

Thomas didn't answer right away. The truth was, he didn't much care if he lost his life somewhere over France, as long as he brought some Germans down with him.

But Harry, apparently reading his mind, wasn't having any of it. "Look, I know you're in a bad way right now. But you're not alone out there, you understand? I'm your brother, and so are Jarvis, Reeves, Abbott, and the rest. And I notice you didn't ask me what I think, but in my view, things are about to change. Maybe 1941 is the year we win the war, right?"

Thomas chuckled at this, for they both knew it was false optimism. The war would drag on at least until '42. The Huns weren't going to lie down at the first sniff of defeat, that was for sure.

The next morning, with a northwesterly wind at their tails and sunlight sparkling off the Channel, a dozen Blenheim bombers set off for the French coast with an armada of fighters. Thomas was just behind the right wing of the fleet as they crossed over the choppy waters, heading for a green smudge of land in the distance.

As they approached, Thomas rose above the bombing height of 12,000 feet, ducking and weaving through the clouds to check for approaching enemy aircraft. The skies were clear as the harbor of Boulogne came into view, and though there were two dozen German fighters doing practice maneuvers some fifty miles southward, no one had noticed the British incursion yet. Still, Thomas was vibrating with anticipation. Someone could spot them at any moment.

No sooner had the thought crossed Thomas's mind than the sunny afternoon exploded with whizzing black dots and puffs, anti-aircraft fire from the ground. "Damn it," Thomas cursed, expecting more. But no German planes appeared from the clouds, and none of the dark bursts hit their marks. A moment later, the Blenheims dropped their bombs into the port. It was hard to see what they'd hit, but from the percussive sounds of explosion and the belches of smoke below, Thomas guessed that they'd found the German vessels snug in the harbor. Well, then, that was something, wasn't it?

"All right, boys," the voice came over the radio. "That's a success. Let's head back now, shall we?"

Slowly, the Blenheims turned to port and the whole aerial fleet followed them back out over the Channel. In the distance, the British coast gleamed in the sunshine like a beacon welcoming them home.

SEVEN MONTHS LATER, BOMBING RUNS to the mainland were no longer a novelty; they were the pieces that made up Thomas's life. Each mission was exhilarating in its own way; there were always Huns to look out for, enemy fire to avoid, strategic sites to target. The RAF boys were dogged, determined, undefeatable.

But there were casualties too. In late June, Harry had disappeared over France on a bright, perfect afternoon. It had been a routine mission—escorting bombers in and out—but the Huns had caught them this time, and there had been a dogfight. Thomas had managed to dodge the enemy fire, but he'd heard Harry's panicked calls over the radio, and he'd seen his friend's plane corkscrewing toward the earth, its tail breathing fire.

"Harry!" he'd called back as the plane vanished beneath a blanket of clouds. "Harry! Do you read?"

But the sole reply had been a sinister static.

Thomas could only assume his friend—officially listed as missing in action—was dead. He had to be; the way his plane had burned, leaving an ominous shadow of black smoke, had shaken Thomas to the core. There was nothing he could do, and the helplessness was paralyzing.

"This one's for you, Harry," he'd said seven weeks later as he engaged in a dogfight with a 109, sending the other aircraft spinning toward the yawning earth. Sometimes, he dedicated his triumphs to Harry; other times it was Oliver; still others it was his own mother, for he was confident that she was up there somewhere, looking down on him and gracing him with a bit of extra luck. How else could he explain the way he seemed invincible?

He taxied in that night and found the flight instructor, Maxwell, waiting for him with a big grin. "You'll never guess what happened, sir," Maxwell said as Thomas unfastened his straps.

"I'm a little tired for guessing games," he said as he climbed from the cockpit.

"Oh, but this one's worth it. It's to do with Cormack."

Thomas looked up, startled. "Harry Cormack?"

"One and the same, sir. He's back, sir, alive and well. I'd suggest you get over to the mess right away."

Thomas didn't believe it until he'd laid eyes on his friend himself five minutes later, after running full tilt across the base. There, just as Maxwell had promised, Thomas found Harry in full dress uniform, gaunter than he'd been seven weeks earlier but otherwise no worse for the wear.

"Harry?" Thomas cried from across the hall, and his friend turned, smiled, and closed the distance between them, pulling Thomas into a bear hug.

"Thomas! You're a sight for sore eyes, my friend!" Harry's voice was scratchy but familiar, and Thomas felt as if he were looking at a ghost.

"I was sure you were dead!" Thomas clapped his friend on the back to reassure himself that Harry was actually composed of flesh and bones.

"I thought so too. But I went down near a farmhouse, and the farmer hid me in a storeroom beneath his barn for three days until the Nazis stopped looking."

"Who was this man?" Thomas asked in awe.

Harry shrugged. "A fellow named Jacques. I never got his surname. He sent me to a butcher in town, who hid me for another four days. And then a third chap put me in the back of his truck and took me to Paris, where they gave me directions to a safe house near a little art shop with sculptures of ballerinas in the window."

"A safe house?"

"Well, sort of." Harry chuckled. "It was more like a cupboard, really. It wasn't far from the Eiffel Tower; I had to stop for a minute and just stare, Thomas. It's like nothing you've ever seen before. The building, it had a huge red door in front, and inside, there was a man up one flight of stairs who hurried me into a sort of hole in the hall. I was there for three days, with just a little sausage and bread to eat, and on the fourth morning, a woman came to take me away.

"They gave me clothes and false papers, and I rode a train filled with Nazi soldiers all the way down to a town near Perpignan in the south. Then—and this is the most unbelievable part, Thomas—I actually walked right over the Pyrenees mountains into Spain."

Thomas stared at him. "Over the Pyrenees?"

"There's a mountain pass there, just through a commune called Banyuls-sur-Mer. We made it past the border, and then the man who took us across connected us with railway workers who saw us to Barcelona."

"I can't believe it."

"I wouldn't believe it either if it hadn't happened to me."

"Who are these people who helped you?"

Harry shrugged. "I haven't a clue. They went by code names, and it all seemed very secretive. But I'll tell you one thing. They're helping us win the war, Thomas. Before I was shot down, I rather thought the Brits were in it alone. But there are plenty of ordinary French people who are part of the effort too. They talk about Churchill like he just might be their savior."

Thomas opened his mouth to reply, to say how astonishing this all was and how glad he was that Harry was home. But he found himself too choked up, so instead, he just smiled and clapped his friend on the back again.

"I'll never forget any of it," Harry said after a minute. "And neither should you, Thomas. One of these days, you might be the one falling from the sky."

"I won't forget," Thomas said, though he had no intention of getting shot down over France. "I promise."

CHAPTER THIRTEEN

August 1941

Ruby insisted that Charlotte go home—the longer she stayed, the greater the chance that her parents would awaken and come looking for her—and then as quietly as possible, she moved Dexter into the closet in the hall. She was astonished to find not only that it was large enough to fit a man but that it had been outfitted for just that purpose. There were blankets and a pillow inside, candles and matches, a few tins of food, even some civilian clothes. Marcel had clearly been at this for some time, which made Ruby both furious and proud.

"You'll be safe here," she told Dexter. "My husband should be home soon, and he'll know what to do."

"I don't know how to thank you, miss." He was larger than he had seemed at first, a fact that became quickly apparent as he folded himself into the closet, wincing.

"You can do one thing to thank me."

"Anything, miss."

"You can stay alive. I can't have you dying on my watch, all right?" She was trying to sound confident, but she feared that he could hear the tremor in her voice. "We need you back up in the skies as soon as possible. You must promise that you'll be okay."

He smiled weakly. "I promise, miss. And I've never gone back on my word with a pretty girl."

She could feel herself blushing as she shut the hidden door. It had been a long time since anyone had called her that.

The next day was awful. It seemed to drag on forever, and though Ruby did her best to go about her normal routine—heading out with her ration tickets to stand in line, sweeping and mopping the apartment, writing to her parents yet again—her mind was on the pilot. Was he okay? There wasn't a thing she could do while it was light out. And she still had no way to reach Marcel.

She waited until midnight to venture out of her apartment, standing for a long time in the hall to listen for anyone stirring. But the building appeared to be asleep, and so she crept to the closet and opened it by pushing on the panel Charlotte had shown her the night before. When the door swung silently out, the scent of sweat and urine was so strong that it nearly choked her; she took a step back, coughing. Then she held her breath and leaned forward again, searching the darkness.

"Dexter?" she whispered.

"Miss?" The voice was weak, tremulous, but hearing it filled her with a wave of relief.

"You're okay. Oh, thank God."

"I made a promise, didn't I?" She could hear his smile in the darkness.

"Indeed you did. How are you? Can I bring you anything?"

"Oh, I'm doing just great, miss. I suppose a bit of water would be nice, if it wouldn't be too much trouble."

"Of course." Ruby shut the closet, hurried into her own apartment, and returned a moment later with a full glass. How had she not thought to bring him water earlier? She stood in the hall for a few moments again, listening for movement in the building, before quietly opening the door to the closet, holding her breath, and handing the glass into the darkness.

"Thank you," Dexter murmured weakly, and then she could hear him drinking in big, grateful gulps. When he handed the glass back seconds later, he added, "And listen, I'm quite sorry about the, er, smell in here."

"I hadn't noticed."

"That's awfully kind of you to say, miss. Only I know it's terrible."

"It's really not so bad. How's the shoulder?"

He hesitated. "Oh, healing up nicely, I think."

Ruby knew it was a lie. "Look, if my husband isn't home by tomorrow, I promise I'll find help."

"I don't want to put you in any danger, miss."

Ruby felt a surge of gratitude and shame. "Dexter, you risked your life because you knew it could make a difference in the war. What kind of a person would I be if I didn't do the same?"

"You don't owe me anything, miss. Even this, hiding me at your own risk, is more than I would have expected. You're very brave."

"Hardly." In fact, she felt like a fraud taking any sort of credit for work Marcel had clearly set in motion. "Sit tight, Dexter. You're going to be okay."

"Thank you, miss," he replied softly as she closed the door. "Good night."

MARCEL CAME HOME TWO HOURS later, just past two in the morning.

"Oh, thank God," Ruby said, rising to her feet as soon as he walked in. She'd never been so relieved to see him.

He looked startled to see her waiting for him. "Ruby, what is it? Has something happened?"

"When were you going to tell me?" she demanded, instead of answering.

"Tell you what?"

"About the pilots you've been hiding."

Marcel went entirely still for a split second, and then he was at her side, grasping her arm so tightly she knew he'd leave a bruise. "You don't know what you're talking about."

Ruby stood her ground. "The hiding space in the hall outside our apartment? The secret late-night meetings? How could you be doing something so dangerous right under my nose without telling me?"

"You can't say such things, Ruby. It's careless."

"I would have helped you, you know. You didn't give me the chance."

"Ruby, it's my job to protect you."

"*Protect* me? Marcel, I needed your protection and support

when I lost the baby, and you left me entirely alone. This would give me a purpose again. Don't you see that? If you really want to protect me, you'll trust me. After all, there's a pilot in the closet right now, and I've managed to keep him safe for a day without you, haven't I?"

He looked up in surprise. "There's a pilot in the closet *now?*"

"He came in last night. He desperately needs medical care, but he's alive."

Marcel sat down heavily in an armchair. "The more I tell you, the more danger I put you in."

"I'm hiding an RAF pilot, Marcel. I think it's a bit too late for that."

He sighed and remained silent for what felt like a long time. "I've been working with this escape line for more than a year now. We get Allied pilots out through Spain."

"Through *Spain?* Who are you working with?"

He shook his head and pressed his lips together. "Better you don't know."

Ruby gritted her teeth. "I thought you were going to trust me."

"Ruby, we only know those who come directly before us or after us on the line. It's better that way. If any of us is captured by the Nazis, it reduces the number of people we're capable of giving up."

"But surely none of you would betray the others."

"Of course that's the hope. But the Nazis use torture. Who knows who might break under that kind of pressure? And besides, there's always the possibility of the line being infiltrated by a spy."

"If it's that dangerous, why are you doing it?"

"I have to. I can't just sit back and let the Germans win."

Ruby waited until his eyes met hers. "That's exactly how I feel, Marcel. You must let me help."

"Let me take care of the pilot first, all right? We can talk in the morning."

"Is that a promise?"

He held her gaze. "It's a promise. Now go to bed."

"Fine." She had the sense he actually meant what he was saying. And he was right; the squabble between them could wait. Dexter was the priority now. "Please tell him good-bye for me. Good-bye and Godspeed."

"Who?" Marcel looked puzzled.

"The pilot. Dexter. He's a nice man, and he deserves to live."

Marcel nodded, and then he slipped back out the apartment door. Ruby watched through the peephole as he opened the closet and helped Dexter out. As they headed for the stairs, she saw Dexter look back once with the shadow of a smile on his face.

Marcel didn't look back at all.

THREE DAYS LATER, MARCEL STILL hadn't returned, and the bad feeling in the pit of Ruby's stomach was growing worse with every passing hour. He had promised they'd talk the next day, so she knew he had intended to come back. Still, she reminded herself that something could have come up. He could have been forced to hide, or perhaps to take the pilot farther along the escape line than he had anticipated. Ruby didn't know how it all worked.

When there was a knock at the door just past noon on the third

day, Ruby knew it would be about Marcel. She peered into the hallway, saw Aubert standing there, and opened the door slowly.

"Hello, Ruby." His eyes were bloodshot, his clothes dirty.

"Come in, Aubert," she said. "Marcel isn't here."

"I know." He followed her inside and waited until she locked the
door behind him. "I have some news."

"Something happened to Marcel, didn't it?"

Aubert stared at her. "Ruby, he and I were working together
on . . . something. Something important."

"You were helping him with the escape line," she said softly. It
was so obvious now.

"He mentioned he'd told you." Aubert took a deep breath. "I
can't say I approve."

"Aubert, what happened?"

"Marcel has been—" He stopped abruptly and glanced at Ruby,
then at the floor. "Marcel was captured."

"What?"

"The Germans, Ruby. They caught him escorting the British
pilot you kept here. The safe house Marcel took him to had been
compromised."

Neither of them said anything for a moment, and the only sound
was the ticking of the clock on the wall. "All right," Ruby said finally. "So we'll get him out. Surely there's a way."

"Ruby—"

"And in the meantime, I'll help. I protected this pilot, didn't I? I
can do it for others until he gets back. Ask him. He'll tell you."

"Ruby, I'm afraid you're misunderstanding me. Marcel isn't in
prison."

"Oh no. Was he put on one of those transports to the east?" Ruby had just begun to hear about political prisoners being shipped out of France to camps in Germany. It would be harder to retrieve him from there, but she had faith in the network. After all, if they managed to return pilots to Britain, surely they could rescue one of their own.

"No." Aubert twisted his cap. "They— Ruby, the Germans shot him. He's dead."

Silence fell. "Dead?" Ruby whispered. "What about the pilot?"

"What?"

"What happened to the pilot? Is he dead too?"

"Er, no. He's been sent to Germany. To a POW camp."

"But they killed Marcel?"

"There are different rules for POWs and those they view as traitors. When Marcel wouldn't give anything up, they decided to make an example of him. He was a good man, Ruby."

Ruby looked at the floor for a while, processing what Aubert was telling her. If only she'd figured out something to do with the airman herself. Could she have spared Marcel? Had it been her own inaction that cost him his life?

"Ruby?" Aubert's voice cut into her thoughts.

She looked up, breathless but suddenly as clearheaded as she'd ever been. "I must help. I must take over Marcel's work on the line."

"No, Ruby. That's impossible. I can't put you in that sort of danger."

"Marcel said he'd let me help. Before he left."

"No. Absolutely not. I couldn't put you in danger. I can't do that to Marcel."

"Marcel is *dead*," Ruby said, more sharply than she intended.

Guilt flickered across Aubert's face. "I'm still his friend. And he would want me to protect you."

"It's not Marcel's choice. Or yours."

He shook his head. "I'm sorry, Ruby. You're an American. You already stand out here. You'd only be a liability to us."

"But—"

"No." His tone was firm now. "You should try to get out. I hear there are still some ships leaving for America from the Free Zone. Contact your embassy in the south and get some help there. You can find me in the back of the bakery on the rue de la Comète if you need anything in the meantime, but there's nothing for you here anymore."

Aubert was gone before she could say anything more. Ruby stared after him before shutting the door to her apartment. She stood motionless for a few minutes, and then she crumpled to the floor and let the tears come.

Marcel was dead. Shot by the Germans. He'd been a better man than she'd given him credit for. If he'd lived, would he have let her help, as he promised? Would they have fallen back in love once he was no longer hiding from her?

She'd never have the chance to know.

TWO DAYS LATER, JUST PAST dawn, there was a sharp knock at the door.

"Marcel?" Ruby cried, springing awake, and then she was hit by a fresh wave of guilt and pain. She'd barely gotten out of bed since Aubert's visit; she'd been caught off guard by the depth of her grief.

After all, there'd been a gulf between Marcel and her for more than a year; they hadn't made love since before she'd lost the baby; and she'd had the growing sense that they would divorce at the war's end. But realizing that he had risked his life to save Allied pilots, and knowing that he had died because of it, made her look at everything differently. Certainly he hadn't been the husband she had hoped for, but would things have been different if the war hadn't come?

Maybe much of it was her fault, in fact. She should have been more prepared to give him the benefit of the doubt, to see him as the person she'd fallen in love with. Had it been her own restlessness that had made her turn away so easily?

The knock came again, and Ruby threw on a dressing gown and hurried to answer. What if it was Aubert, here to tell her he had reconsidered, that he needed her on the line? Instead, when she pulled the door open, she found herself face-to-face with two French police officers—and two Germans in full dress uniform, one fair-haired, the other darker.

She blinked at them in stunned panic before she realized that she hadn't done anything wrong. Well, except for hiding Dexter, but she doubted they knew about that. Even if they'd tortured him, surely he wouldn't have given her up; it would have been much easier to leave her out of the story altogether and explain that it had been Marcel sheltering him.

"Hello, gentlemen," she said, trying to keep the tremor out of her voice.

"You are Madame Benoit?" the shorter of the two French gendarmes asked. The buttons that ran the length of his uniform were spotless and shiny, his small hat on perfectly straight. His eyes gleamed as bright as his buttons; he was clearly pleased to be part of whatever this was.

"I am." She pulled her dressing gown a bit tighter.

"We will need to see your papers." Behind the little gendarme, the German officers were silent, their eyes boring into hers. The other French policeman looked uneasy, his eyes roving over the interior of her apartment.

"Yes, of course." She left the door ajar as she went to retrieve her papers from her handbag. The French officer inspected them first and then handed them to the Germans, who read them over. The dark-haired one snorted and handed them back.

"American?" he asked in thickly accented French. "What are you doing here?"

She explained that she'd married a Frenchman before the war, that she'd decided to stay. The German pursed his lips and muttered something to the other officer, who nodded.

"This is very suspicious, you see," he said, fixing Ruby with a steely gaze. His eyes were beady and empty, like a snake's. His French was impeccable. "Why didn't you return to the United States?"

"I wished to remain at my husband's side."

"To help him with his traitorous work on the escape line?" the little French officer sneered.

"Oh, no, but surely those accusations against him were not true." She forced her eyes wide and wrung her hands. "Surely the French police made a mistake."

"We do not make mistakes, madame," the little officer said

tightly. Behind him, the fair-haired German rolled his eyes, and the other French officer coughed.

"Oh, I'm sure *you* don't," Ruby said quickly. "I only mean that perhaps someone falsely informed on him." She batted her eyes. "It's impossible for me to believe that my husband could have been doing something so sinister right under my nose."

"We will need to search your apartment," the fair-haired German said, and Ruby nodded. She suspected that was why they had come, and she prayed that Marcel hadn't hidden anything here. If only she had used the last two days to search the place herself from top to bottom!

"Of course, gentlemen, won't you come in?" She fought to keep her tone even. "I'm certain you'll find nothing suspicious. In fact, if you had searched our home before my husband was executed, he might have been saved!"

The Germans pushed past the little Frenchman, barreling through the doorway. After a moment, the little Frenchman followed, muttering to himself. The other gendarme stayed beside her. "I'm sorry, madame," he said softly, and she nodded, understanding that some of the people collaborating with the Germans had no choice. She was surprised by the pang of sympathy she felt for him.

She watched as the Germans carefully opened every drawer and cupboard, and as the little Frenchman tore through her dresser, flinging clothing and undergarments dramatically into the air. When he reached the wardrobe, where she'd briefly hidden Dexter, she held her breath, but he passed through quickly, ripping her dresses from their hangers and throwing them to the floor.

It took them fifteen minutes to complete their search, and when they were done, they returned to the doorway.

"It appears you are telling the truth," the fair-haired German said. "But we will have our eye on you."

"Of course, sir. I understand."

"If you're hiding anything, we'll find it," the little Frenchman said, but this time, the dark-haired German placed a hand on his shoulder.

"That's enough. I'm sure she knows that no one can hide from us forever." He nodded to her crisply and turned on his heel. The others followed, and Ruby watched until they'd disappeared down the stairs. Only then did she allow herself to collapse, shaking, to the floor.

As she pulled herself up shortly thereafter, though, using the door for support, she felt a surge of hope. Marcel had spent so much time making her feel useless that it was easier than she'd expected to behave as if she was. Perhaps he had helped her after all. Perhaps the foolishness he had projected on her was the perfect cover.

Now she just had to figure out how to convince Aubert that she could use that to her advantage.

CHAPTER FOURTEEN

October 1941

It was early fall when Thomas was sent up just before dawn to fly rear cover. The bombers were to drop their loads on two German-controlled factories a hundred miles north of Paris, and then Thomas and the boys were meant to patrol the sky as their fleet returned to England, intercepting and engaging German fighters on their tail.

Missions like this had become fairly routine, the RAF in and out before the Germans had time to scramble their fighters. This morning, as they flew east, Thomas's mind was wandering. The clouds looked strange and heavenly, as if lit from within. *We're lucky*, he thought. *Most people don't get to see the sky like this.* He made a vow never to forget it as long as he lived.

"This morning's a beaut, isn't it?" a pilot named Lewis radioed, and Thomas smiled. It was just what he'd been thinking; there was something undeniably magical about seeing the birth of a new day from the heavens.

"Peaceful up here," Thomas agreed, making the turn back to the west just as ribbons of light began to filter over the eastern horizon. Sixty miles ahead lay the edge of the French coast and beyond it, a narrow strip of Channel leading to the White Cliffs of Dover, always a sight for sore eyes, even when they'd been gone for only a few hours. The cliffs meant safety, and this morning, they'd be glistening in the soft sunlight, welcoming the RAF boys home.

That's what Thomas was thinking about when a swarm of German 109s rose from the mist at the squadron's tail. Thomas's heart jumped to his throat when he spotted them. "Behind us!" he managed to shout over the radio before diving into the clouds in an evasive maneuver.

"Hold on, boys!" someone shouted back, and then there were bullets whizzing everywhere, a whole swarm of them, buzzing and hissing. Thomas struggled to turn in to the approaching 109s, so as to gain a bit of an advantage, but it was useless. His squadron was heavily outnumbered; there were at least three 109s on his tail. He pulled back on the throttle and pushed the Spit as hard as she would go, but then there was a great clanging followed by a jerking so severe that it felt as if Thomas's spine had been jarred loose from his body. He cursed, knowing he'd been hit.

He quickly evaluated the situation, trying not to panic. Could he still glide? After all, he wasn't far from the coast. If he wasn't losing much altitude, or dropping fuel, making it back over the Channel might just be possible. But the clouds below were coming closer, and a quick look at his altimeter confirmed that he was falling rapidly.

"Lewis, looks like I've been hit," he radioed, but there was no reply, only the static of empty sky. Had the others gone on and left him? Had they seen him plunge into the clouds and assumed he was done for? *All right, then, Thomas,* he said to himself as he continued to fall. *Stay calm. If Harry could survive a mess like this, you can too.*

But his forced serenity was shattered as another volley of bullets came at him, this time pinging off his engine. His windscreen was immediately black with oil, and thick smoke surrounded him on all sides. "Damn it!" he cursed. There was no saving the plane now; he had to bail out before he got any lower. And so, praying that he could make it, he ejected and found himself alone in the sky for a frozen, terrifying moment, as his Spit, belching black smoke, hurtled toward the ground without him. In the midst of his panic, he felt a surge of sadness for the plane, but there was no time to mourn a charred lump of metal. No, he was falling, and fast. He tugged the release on his chute and felt a bone-crunching jerk as it opened. Now there was nothing to do but float from the sky, feeling as if a bull's-eye had been painted on him. He braced himself for the gunshots he knew would come, but the air fight went on above him. Below, the earth was strangely silent.

Thomas took a deep breath and forced himself to focus, to survey the surroundings as he drifted. He was coming into a heavily wooded area. The nearest road was at least three quarters of a mile to the east, which meant that it would be a little while before the Germans could reach him—if anyone had seen him fall. The clouds were thick, and he had ejected right in the midst of them; it was possible that it had appeared to the Germans as if he'd gone down with the plane.

Time slowed as he glided in for a rough landing, narrowly missing a cluster of huge trees and touching down in a small clearing. The moment his feet hit the ground and he found himself in one piece, he hurried to pull his parachute down so that it wouldn't call attention to his location. He wound it into a ball, dug a hole in the dirt, and shoved it in. He kicked the dirt back over it and pulled some felled branches on top of the freshly turned earth until it appeared there was nothing there.

Next, he peeled off his Sidcot and turned it inside out, concealing the markings of the RAF. He hurriedly pulled it back on and lowered himself to his knees in the dirt. He rolled around a bit, until the flight suit was sufficiently scuffed, and then he added a bit of grime to his face for good measure. There; at a quick glance now, he might just pass for a French farmhand—at least until someone looked closely, spotted his flight boots, or tried to engage him in conversation. Though he spoke near-fluent French thanks to his schooling, his British accent would surely betray him.

Thanking God for the preparedness of the RAF, Thomas took out the escape kit that had been sewn into his uniform—a clear acetate pouch containing survival supplies such as matches, water purification tablets, and energy pills—and withdrew the tiny compass he knew he would find there. He studied it for a moment and then set off toward the south. Unless he'd drifted off course in the dogfight, he was almost due north of Paris, and though it would take a few days to get there by foot, it was the best alternative he could think of. He could still hear Harry talking about the apartment building with the red door beside the ballet-themed gallery, where there was a man ready and willing to help pilots like him. If he could make it there without getting caught, he'd have a chance of returning to England alive.

BY THAT EVENING, THOMAS WAS exhausted. He had figured that walking for a few days wouldn't be too taxing, but with his adrenaline surging earlier, he'd failed to notice that his left ankle had been twisted upon landing. It didn't bother him much at first, but as he made his way up and down hills in the direction the compass pointed, his pace grew slower and slower. Finally, just as darkness was falling, he found a stream, and he stopped to get a bit of water. He knew that soon, he'd have to find a safe place to spend the night.

He sat down on a fallen log and closed his eyes for a moment, just to catch his breath, and the next thing he knew, there was a hand on his shoulder, shaking him awake. A man with a deep voice was saying something, and Thomas jumped up, backing away. The forest was cloaked in darkness now, and he was alone in the clearing with a man holding a lantern.

"I said, Are you all right?" the man asked again, and it took a second for Thomas to register that the words were in French instead of German. A bit of relief washed over him, but he was still on guard. There was no way to know if this man was friend or foe.

"Yes, thank you," Thomas grunted in French, trying to imitate a French accent and hoping that his brevity would conceal the British edge to his words.

"You are English," the man said calmly, and Thomas's heart sank. Apparently, he hadn't been as clever as he'd hoped.

"No," he said in a clipped tone, taking another step back and considering his escape route. If the man didn't have a gun, or if he wasn't a particularly good shot, Thomas could make a break for it. But how far would his bum ankle carry him, especially in dark terrain he didn't know?

The man didn't advance though. "Relax," he said in French. "I am not one of them."

"One of who?"

"A collaborator. A Nazi lover." The man spat loudly. "I am French, and to me, anyone who is here trying to help us is a friend."

Thomas hesitated. He wasn't sure whether to believe the man, but he didn't have much of a choice. "All right. I'm trying to get to Paris."

The man didn't ask why. "Well, you are not going to get there tonight, are you? And you will be in need of a good night's rest before you continue on. Come with me."

Thomas stayed rooted to the spot. "How do I know I can trust you?"

"I suppose you do not. But the closer you get to Paris dressed like that, the more danger you will be in. So you can take your chances with me, or you can continue on dressed in an inside-out flight suit."

Thomas's stomach dropped. "You can tell what I'm wearing?"

"Your boots do not help your cause. Come, you can sleep for a bit and be on your way at first light." The man began walking without waiting for an answer. When Thomas didn't follow, the man called over his shoulder, "I am not going to beg. But this would be in your best interest."

Seconds later, Thomas followed after the man, both of them sticking to the shadows until they got to the edge of a field.

"Well, come on, then," the man said. "The longer you linger out here, the more chance you are giving the Germans to spot you, friend. And then I will have to deny that I have ever seen you."

The man began to cross the field, which was planted with what looked in the darkness like potatoes. But Thomas knew that the French were suffering from huge food shortages, just like the British, so he wondered how much of the field had been rendered fallow by Germans more concerned with starving their enemies than feeding themselves.

The man led him to a modest farmhouse and held the door open. Inside, candlelight flickered, and Thomas hesitated a moment before entering. "There now," the man said, shutting the door behind him. "Was that so hard?"

Thomas looked around him, taking in the surroundings. The place was sparsely furnished, but it looked homey and warm.

"Claude?" A woman emerged from the back of the home wearing a housecoat. She was young—perhaps in her early twenties—and pretty. In the candlelight, Thomas could finally see the face of the man who'd brought him home too, and he was surprised to realize that he was not much older than Thomas himself.

"Henriette, I have brought a guest," the man said. "Do we have any food for him?"

"Yes, of course," she murmured, studying Thomas for a few seconds before hurrying out of the room.

"That is my wife, Henriette," the man said, turning back to Thomas. "I am called Claude. And you are?"

"Thomas." He paused, considered giving his last name, and decided against it. "And thank you. You and your wife are very kind to help me."

Claude shrugged. "It is what anyone would do."

"I don't think that's true."

"Anyone with a conscience," Claude amended.

Thomas nodded. "How did you find me?"

"I was in the field when I saw you stumble toward the stream. When you sat down and did not move, I thought perhaps you were dead. But I had to wait until after dark to check, because it is impossible to tell when the German patrols are out. The lazy bastards turn in early, though. You can find them in town getting drunk on our best wine."

"Where are we?" Thomas asked.

Claude raised an eyebrow. "Near Ayette. Where are you coming from?"

"Arras. I think. My plane went down this morning in a dogfight."

"Ah, so they will be looking for you. All the better to have brought you in for the night. You covered quite a distance in a day, though. Especially with that injury." He gestured to Thomas's ankle. "Henriette can wrap it, although I do not know how much it will help."

"Thank you."

Claude nodded. "Now, why are you in such a rush to get to Paris? It is crawling with Nazis, you know."

Thomas hesitated. Claude seemed friendly enough, but what if he was a Nazi plant, fishing for information? "It seems my best bet of hooking up with an escape line."

"Yes. Yes, it does. We have seen only a few of you fellows around here, and all we can do is help you move on without getting caught."

"There have been others?"

"Yes. A fellow named Kenneth about six months ago. Went down near Arras, like you. And about four months ago, a man named Michael. Leg was so badly injured that you could see the bone. Henriette cleaned and set it. Nazis snooping around, since his plane did not go down far from here. But he made it to Paris, at least."

"How do you know?"

"My father drove him."

Thomas looked up in surprise. There was someone here giving rides to pilots? That would certainly make the next few days easier. But then Claude shook his head.

"My father died last month. Heart attack. I think that risking his life for that pilot cleansed his soul at the end, though." He didn't wait for a reply. "Now enough of that. Let us get you fed and dressed so you can sleep." Claude smiled. "You do not think you will go wandering into Paris dressed like *that*, do you? You might as well be waving a British flag."

AFTER THOMAS HAD EATEN A surprisingly delicious potato soup prepared by Henriette, who then wrapped his ankle, Claude showed him to the barn, where there was a trapdoor in the floor beneath an empty stall.

"We used to have six horses," Claude explained, his expression darkening. "The Nazis requisitioned them all."

"I'm sorry," Thomas said.

"As am I. Sorry for all of us." He handed Thomas a small stack of clothing—a shirt and some pants, it appeared, with a pair of scuffed shoes. "These were my father's. He was a tall man, so they should fit you well enough. Now get some sleep, and put these on in the morning. I will come get you at first light."

He opened the trapdoor and gestured down into the darkness. It smelled musty and stale, but Thomas realized that it was probably the best place on the property to hide.

"Not that we expect anyone to come looking," Claude said, "but if anyone arrives, they will not see the door. We will cover it with a few bales of hay for the night."

Thomas climbed down into the cellar, the bundle of clothes tucked under one arm, and within five minutes, he was fast asleep on the cold, hard floor.

In what felt like no time at all, light poured into the cellar, waking him. Thomas blinked into the sudden brightness and saw Claude's face in the opening overhead. "Hope you slept well, friend," he said. "Now put those clothes on, and fast. It is just past dawn, and you need to get into the woods before the Nazis are awake."

Thomas dressed quickly, and even though the clothes were a bit tight—he had to leave the pants half-undone and he couldn't fasten the top two buttons on his shirt—the shoes fit surprisingly well. He climbed the ladder, clutching his flight suit and boots. "I'll take these with me and bury them," he told Claude. "I don't want you to get caught with them."

Claude nodded and handed Thomas a small parcel. "Here is a bit of bread and cheese and a jug of water to get you through until you reach Paris."

"I don't know how to thank you."

"Oh, that is simple," Claude said, putting a hand on Thomas's shoulder. "You get back to England, and when you return to the skies, give those Nazis hell. We are going to win this war, and we need men like you to do it."

"And men like you," Thomas said with a smile.

Claude shrugged. "I am merely a farmer. Now, be on your way before the Nazis catch your trail. Godspeed." He pointed in the direction of the woods before turning away and walking slowly back toward the farmhouse. The lights were on inside, and Thomas could see Henriette's silhouette in the kitchen window. For a moment, he felt a strange surge of jealousy. Though Claude's life was obviously hard— it was clear in the light of day that the Nazis had razed his farm—he was still doing some good, and he had a nice home and a woman who loved him. What would it be like to have that kind of peace in one's life? Would it help make the work he did easier? For the first time in a while, Thomas felt painfully lonely. He raised a hand toward the house, just in case Henriette was watching, and then he set off into the woods. With his ankle wrapped, his belly somewhat full, and a good night's sleep behind him, he felt ready for what was to come.

THE REMAINDER OF THE JOURNEY took Thomas three days. He had to stay away from the main roads, which meant that the terrain was harder on his injured ankle. Still, Henriette's bandage helped, as did the bread and cheese she and Claude had packed. Thomas was hungry and parched by the time he reached the outskirts of Paris, but he would have been near starving without them.

Thomas spent the last day of his walk trying to perfect his French accent, repeating aloud to himself again and again, "Excuse me? Do you know where I can find an art gallery that specializes in ballet? I'm supposed to meet a friend there." By the time he'd slept and emerged from the woods the next morning, he felt he had it mostly down, but he'd need to be careful.

As he began to move through Paris's suburbs, he kept his eyes on the ground, but he was sure he could feel people staring. He must have looked odd—like a hobo, perhaps—as he trudged along in rumpled farm clothes. Still, when he dared glance around, he saw plenty of people in ill-fitting, grimy clothes, which both relieved and depressed him. It would be easier to go unnoticed, certainly, but at the same time, he had always imagined Paris as a glamorous place, and the reality was that the city was just as downtrodden as London.

It was early afternoon by the time he arrived in Paris proper. He stopped the first man who made eye contact with him and asked him, in the French accent he'd rehearsed, about the location of the gallery, but the man only shook his head and hurried on. Two more requests for information were met with the same blank looks, and Thomas was beginning to get worried. Surely pausing to find a map would draw unneeded attention to himself. And he didn't want to be wandering the streets any longer than absolutely necessary. There were German soldiers everywhere, strolling around in their uniforms, lunching at cafés, even escorting French girls, which made Thomas's skin crawl. Tour buses overflowing with laughing German soldiers rumbled down the grand boulevards, and the ball of anger in Thomas's stomach tightened.

He thought hard as he walked with purpose, doing his best to look like he belonged. Harry had mentioned the shop being close to the Eiffel Tower, hadn't he? Perhaps that was the key, then: head for the tower and simply walk the streets nearby until he stumbled upon the place. It was the best plan he could come up with anyhow, and he knew the clock was ticking. Paris surely had a curfew. He couldn't be wandering around after dark without drawing attention to himself.

"Can you direct me to the Eiffel Tower?" he asked a man who passed by. The man gave him a strange look, but he pointed behind him, explaining to Thomas that he needed to go a long way, following the main boulevard as it turned into the rue Montmartre and then the rue du Louvre. After he crossed the river, he was to turn right at the quai and follow the Seine until the Eiffel Tower loomed in front of him.

Thomas couldn't help but notice, as he continued on, how beautiful the city actually was. The Nazis had taken much of the life out of it, it seemed, for the gardens were bare and the window boxes of many apartments were filled with dying plants instead of the flowers Thomas had seen in pictures. Passersby seemed defeated, their expressions as dark and worn as their clothing. The cafés were largely empty, except those bustling with Germans.

But beyond the signs of occupation, Thomas could see why people said Paris was one of the loveliest places in the world. His parents had come here on holiday before he was born, and his mother had always talked of it with nostalgic delight. The things she had mentioned—the beautiful old buildings, the ornate lampposts, the wide avenues, the meticulous landscaping—were still evident, and Thomas could imagine how the city must look in all its glory. "I finally made it to Paris, Mum," he said softly as he crossed the river. He could see the Eiffel Tower off to the right in the distance. "Now I'm in need of a bit of luck."

Unfortunately, four hours later, the sun was inching toward the horizon, and Thomas still hadn't located the gallery, despite going up and down so many side streets that his head was beginning to spin. He had no backup plan, and he was mumbling to himself in frustration and looking down at the sidewalk when he found his path blocked.

He looked up, startled, and swallowed hard when he realized that he had nearly crashed into a Nazi soldier. The man was standing in full dress uniform in the middle of the sidewalk glowering at Thomas. He barked something in unintelligible German, and Thomas stared at him miserably, sure that he'd been caught. Was there a way to run? It seemed like the end of the line. The man said something else, seeming to wait for an answer, and finally, Thomas said in French, "I'm sorry. I don't speak German."

The man eyed him and then, surprisingly, switched to French too. "You French are imbeciles. Don't you know German will be your national language soon enough?"

Thomas was too startled to reply right away. It took a few seconds to register that the man hadn't stopped him because he believed he was an RAF pilot. He believed him to be a Parisian.

"Right," Thomas finally managed to say in French. He knew his accent was lousy, but he suspected the German wouldn't notice, since his own accent was even worse. "Excuse me."

The man snorted. "Now, as I was asking, where are you going?"

Thomas hesitated. "To an art gallery."

The man looked him up and down. "What sort of art gallery?"

"One that specializes in ballet-themed art." Thomas felt foolish.

"*You?* A laborer? What could your business there possibly be?"

"I've been, um, hired to clean it and help them hang some paintings."

"You waste your time with ballet and art in the middle of the war?" The soldier was still blocking his path. "And you call yourself a man?"

"It's only a job. I'm hungry and out of work."

The soldier looked him up and down again with an expression of disgust. "Well, you are heading in the wrong direction."

Thomas didn't say anything.

After a moment, the soldier sighed and pointed to a street two blocks behind Thomas. "La Ballerine is just there. Rue Amélie. Midway down. I'd better not catch you wandering around after curfew."

"No, you certainly won't."

"Well?" The soldier still hadn't moved. "Aren't you going to thank me for my help?"

"Thank you," Thomas muttered, hating himself a little for being cowed by the Nazi bastard.

"In *German*," the man said with a smirk.

Thomas searched his memory and managed to spit out one of the only German words he knew. "*Danke.*"

The soldier looked pleased. He smiled icily and stepped aside. Thomas hurried away without looking back, a foul taste in his mouth. That had been a narrow miss.

A few minutes later, Thomas's heart lurched in gratitude as he passed a doorway with a plaque that identified it as La Ballerine. The doors and windows were pasted over with paper, and he wondered if the place was even open, but it didn't matter. He wasn't going there anyhow. To the left of the shop was an apartment building with a huge red door, just as Harry had described.

Thomas swallowed hard and hurried past the building. He circled the block twice, just in case the Nazi soldier was following him. On his third loop, finally confident he hadn't been tailed, he ducked into the shadows and, glancing around once more, pushed the red door open. He had expected that it might be locked, but luck was seemingly on his side as he tumbled into a dimly lit hallway with a broad spiral staircase leading up at least five flights. He paused and drew a deep breath. Harry had said the man with the limp lived on the first floor, but he had never specified which apartment, and now Thomas wasn't sure what to do.

There was a discarded, rickety-looking chair in the corner near the front door, and as Thomas stood in the hall paralyzed with indecision, he suddenly realized how very exhausted he was. He hadn't eaten in more than a day, since his carefully rationed parcel from Claude and Henriette had run out, and walking for three days straight without a safe place to rest had taken its toll. His ankle was throbbing, and he felt parched and shaky. "No, Thomas," he said to himself sternly. "You've come all this way. Hold it together for a little longer, at least." But the chair in the corner looked so inviting, and after a moment, he sank gratefully down, relieved to be off his feet, if only for a moment.

"Think, Thomas," he murmured, fighting off the tide of sleep that was threatening to roll in. The encounter with the Nazi soldier had spiked his adrenaline, and now that his fear was receding, he felt more depleted than ever. "Think, lad. There's got to be a way to find Harry's man."

He was startled, a moment later, to hear the click of an apartment door opening across from where he sat. Could it be the man with the limp? But the figure who appeared in the doorway was an ancient, tiny woman bundled in a woolly sweater over a frayed dress.

"Can I help you?" she asked in French, looking Thomas up and down suspiciously.

"Oh, no, thank you, madame," he replied, speaking slowly and trying his best to speak French without a telltale British accent.

"Pardon?" The woman cupped a hand to her ear, and Thomas realized she was deaf or nearly so.

"I'm just waiting for a friend, madame." He raised his voice and then immediately felt far too exposed as it echoed through the building. She still looked skeptical.

"I am the concierge," she said. "I know everyone in this building, and none of them would have a friend in such foul clothing. Be on your way, vagrant, or I will call the authorities."

She slammed the door, and he shook his head. He'd been more conspicuous than he'd intended, and now he would have to work quickly in case her threat to report him hadn't been an empty one.

"Okay, then," he said to himself. He needed to go door to

door. His cover would be that he had just come in from the northern coast—which could help excuse an accent that didn't sound quite right—and that he was desperate to find his wife's cousin. It was the only way he could think of to explain why he didn't know the man's name. Yes, that was it; his wife had recently died, and the only relative he knew of was a man who lived here and walked with a limp, but he'd never met him. It seemed an odd story, he knew, but it was the best he could come up with. Why hadn't he used his days hiking through the woods to invent a solid cover story? Instead, he had let his mind wander to happier times, before the war came, when his mother was still alive and the future was wide open. The memories had propelled him forward, but now it felt as if he'd wasted three full days.

He walked up the flight of stairs and turned to his left. Might as well begin at the beginning. There was a door there marked 1B, and before he could second-guess himself, he took a deep breath, raised his hand, and knocked.

CHAPTER FIFTEEN

October 1941

Monsieur Benoit had been dead for two months now, and Charlotte knew there was more to the story than anyone was telling her. It was impossible for her to believe the official explanation: that he had gone out one day and gotten caught up in a police action that had nothing to do with him. She knew about the secret closet in the hall and the Allied pilots, and she felt certain that his death had been linked to them. Already, the French police, accompanied by two German officers who looked like attack dogs, had come to Ruby's door three times. Charlotte had tried her best to hear what they were asking Ruby, but she could only catch snippets here and there. It seemed that the men knew of Marcel's involvement in the escape line, but that they ultimately believed Ruby when she said she'd had no idea what her husband was up to. "He treated me like I didn't have the brains to understand anything," Charlotte had heard Ruby say on their last visit.

"Well, you *are* merely a woman," a deep French voice had replied.

"Yes, I suppose you're right," Ruby had responded, and Charlotte had felt a surge of pride that her neighbor was getting the last laugh.

Finally, the police and the Nazis stopped coming. "She clearly doesn't know anything," one of the French policemen had said on their way out of the building at the end of the last visit.

"Clearly," one of the German officers had replied with a snort. "But what a piece of ass, yes?"

His words had been followed by a nauseating stream of sexual comments, each of the men sniggering about what they'd do to Ruby if they had a chance to get her alone. And while Charlotte longed to come to Ruby's defense, she knew that in the end, what the men had said was better than their realizing that Ruby had played a role—albeit a small one—in the escape line too.

Charlotte suspected that her neighbor felt more alone than ever now; after all, she really had no one to turn to. Ruby rarely went out anymore, except to pick up her rations, and Charlotte had never seen her have a visitor.

Charlotte was still seeing Ruby once a week for English lessons—her parents were very firm on that—and while she tried to ask how Ruby was doing, most of their conversations were only about schoolwork and mundane details of daily life. Charlotte had tried to raise the subject of the British pilot more than once, for she wondered and worried about what had happened to him, but Ruby always cut her off. "You never know who's listening," she would whisper. "We mustn't speak of these things aloud, Charlotte."

But Charlotte was tired of avoiding what was obviously the

defining moment of their friendship, and so on one early autumn night, she made a decision after dinner. She would go and let Ruby know that she could be trusted and that she wasn't scared of the Nazis.

She had her hand on the door to her apartment, ready to step out into the hall, when she heard a noise that startled her. She peered through the peephole just in time to see a broad-shouldered, dark-haired man lurching toward Ruby's door. He knocked loudly, and Charlotte, suddenly paralyzed by doubt, held her breath. Was he another Nazi? Was he there to hurt Ruby? But as he knocked again, harder this time, Charlotte realized he was dressed in ill-fitting clothes caked with dirt and grime. Certainly no German soldier would wander around Paris looking like that. But he wasn't wearing a pilot's uniform either. So who was he?

Ruby's door finally opened a crack.

"Excuse me," the man said in French with an accent that sounded familiar. Where had Charlotte heard it before? "I'm just coming from the north. My wife has died, and I'm looking for her cousin. I'm sorry, but I don't know his name. I only know that he lives in this building and walks with a limp."

Ruby regarded him in silence, and in that sliver of quiet, a realization hit Charlotte: *His accent was the same as that of the pilot she and Ruby had hidden in August.* She was almost certain of it. But why was he telling such a ridiculous story? She peered back out the peephole just in time to see Ruby's expression. She looked confused, but not scared.

"A man with a limp, you say?" Ruby asked carefully, and the man nodded, although he was already backing away.

"Perhaps I have the wrong apartment. I'm very sorry," he was saying, but there was something about his voice that sounded strange
now. His words were melting together, and he sounded suddenly
weak. He seemed to rock back and forth on his feet, and then he
fell to his knees with a great crash and appeared to waver there for
a moment. "Very sorry," he said, but this time, his words were in
English, and then he toppled forward, passing out cold in Ruby's
doorway.

CHAPTER SIXTEEN

October 1941

Three facts were immediately clear to Ruby. First, the man before her was British. Second, he had come in search of Marcel, which probably meant he was a pilot in need of help. Third, she needed to get him out of the hall immediately, before the concierge or someone else saw him. As if to underscore her thoughts, the door to the Dachers' apartment cracked open, and Charlotte peeked out.

"Ruby?" she whispered.

"Go back inside!" Ruby hissed. "I don't want you involved in this!"

Charlotte looked as if Ruby had slapped her. "But I can help."

"No. Please. Forget you saw anything."

Without waiting for a reply, Ruby bent and grabbed the man under his arms, dragging his limp body into her apartment. She locked the door behind her and turned to look at him. He was large and handsome, but in a boyish sort of way. Not like the previous pilot, and not like Marcel. Or was it just that he looked innocent because he was fast asleep? She crouched down beside him, noting his pink cheeks, and placed a hand on his forehead. He was burning up.

He moaned softly, but he didn't wake, and after a moment, she made a decision. She knew she should hide him in the hall closet as she'd done with Dexter, but he needed her help immediately. She had to get his fever down before she could figure out what to do next.

She wanted to put him on the couch so that he'd be more comfortable, but he was too heavy to lift. So she settled for leaving him where he was and bringing in the pillow and blanket from her own bed. She ran cold water into a basin and spent the next two hours beside him, holding a wet cloth to his forehead and frequently dipping it back in the water to keep it cold. He stirred a few times and murmured unintelligibly, but it wasn't until nearly midnight that his eyes finally opened.

He focused on her with difficulty, his pupils dilating. Then he gasped and tried to sit up. "Where am I?" he asked in English, his voice weak. His eyelids fluttered and he shook his head. "I'm sorry," he said, switching to French. "I meant to ask where I am."

"You're in an apartment in Paris," she replied in English. "You're safe for the time being. You have a fever, though, and we need to take care of it."

"You speak English?" He looked at her in awe.

She nodded. "I'm American. And you are British?"

He hesitated, searching her face. His eyes, she noticed, were an almost translucent blue, like nothing she had ever seen. She knew he was trying to figure out whether he could trust her.

"My husband helped people like you," she said after the silence had dragged on for more than a minute.

"Your husband?"

"Yes." Ruby wondered if she was imagining the shadow of disappointment that crossed his face.

"He's here too?"

"Not right now. But I want to help you. You must tell me who you are, though."

Again he paused, his eyes locked on hers.

She could read his thoughts. "This isn't a trap," she said gently. "You've been asleep for more than two hours. If I'd wanted to hurt you—or to call the authorities—I would have done so already."

His eyes stayed on hers for a moment more, and she found herself once again thinking that they were an extraordinary color. "My name is Thomas, miss," he said at last. "Thomas Clarke. I'm an RAF pilot. My plane went down near Arras, and I've been walking for days. My friend Harry was helped by a man in this building several months ago. It was the only place I knew to go. Did you know Harry?"

Ruby shook her head. "My husband kept his work to himself."

"Your husband, he walks with a limp?"

"Yes."

"He's the man Harry told me about." His eyelids fluttered again, and Ruby could see his head bobbing a bit.

"Stay with me."

"I think I'm quite ill."

She smiled. "Yes, that's a safe guess. I'm just trying to figure out whether you're sick because you've been out in the elements for a few days, or if something more serious is wrong."

"Something more serious?"

"Like an infection. Were you hurt when your plane went down? Any wounds?"

He looked at her blankly. "I hurt my ankle, but it's not bleeding. And I might have a few scrapes on my chest."

"May I see?"

He paused, then unbuttoned his shirt slowly. His chest was muscular and taut, and just below the left side of his rib cage was an open gash at least two inches wide. It was yellowed and oozing. It didn't look right at all.

"Is there something there?" he asked weakly, trying to sit up.

"There's just a small cut." She placed a firm hand on his right shoulder. "I need to clean and dress it. It may hurt a little. Let's get you to the bed, shall we?"

He looked uncertain. "The bed? But where will you sleep? And what about your husband?"

"Don't worry. You need your rest right now more than I do. May I help you up?"

He nodded, leaning into her for support as he pulled himself shakily to his feet. She noted, as she helped him limp toward the bedroom, that her head didn't quite reach his shoulder; he was several inches taller than Marcel had been, and he was even more broadly built than she'd first noticed.

"Please, miss," he said as she settled him on the edge of her bed. "I don't want to be an inconvenience."

"You're not," she said firmly. "Now lie down, and I'll get some supplies to dress your wound."

"Miss?" he asked weakly as she headed for the doorway.

She turned. "Yes?"

"You haven't told me your name."

"It's Ruby."

"Ruby," he repeated, and there was something about the way her name sounded in his mouth that made her heart race. "Thank you, Ruby. Thank you for helping me."

"You're welcome, Thomas," she replied after a moment, but he was already asleep, his chest rising and falling with each shallow, shuddering breath.

THOMAS FLINCHED BUT DIDN'T AWAKEN as Ruby cleaned out his wound. And over the next two days, she tended to him as best she could, feeding him broth and then stale bread when he was able to keep food down. She wished she had more to share, but what she did give him seemed to help, and by the third night, his forehead was no longer burning, and some color had returned to his cheeks.

"I'm feeling much better," he told her as she brought him a small dinner of bread and weak coffee. "I should probably get out of your bed now. I'm embarrassed that I took it for so long."

"Don't be silly. You've been sick. I'm just glad you're on the mend."

"Surely my being here is putting you in danger."

Ruby avoided meeting his gaze. "You just focus on getting your strength back."

"You're an angel, you know that?" he said as she handed him a small glass of water. He drank it down gratefully. "An absolute angel, Ruby."

She could feel herself blushing. "You remembered my name. I thought you might not; you were delirious when you got here."

His eyelids were already growing heavy. "I can't imagine forgetting a single thing about you."

He drifted back to sleep before she could muster a response. And finally, for the first time in days, Ruby was sure that he would live, so she allowed herself to lie down on the floor beside the bed and close her eyes, just for a moment.

When she awoke, the first rays of dawn were streaming through the window, which meant she'd been asleep all night. She gasped and sat up, only to realize that the pilot was lying on his side, gazing down at her. "You're awake," he said. "I hope it's not out of line for me to say that you're beautiful when you sleep."

She hid an embarrassed smile. "I'm very sorry. I didn't mean to nod off."

"And I didn't mean to take over your life like this. I'm mortified that I let you sleep on the floor. I'm terribly sorry."

"You weren't in any condition to argue." She stood and put a hand on his forehead. It was cool, the fever entirely gone. She breathed a sigh of relief. "I think you've turned a corner, Thomas."

"You saved my life."

"Oh, you would have been fine with or without me."

He chuckled. He had a nice laugh, warm and strong. "Don't for a minute believe I'm going to indulge your modesty. You're a regular Florence Nightingale."

She could feel her cheeks burning again, and she quickly changed the subject. "You said when you arrived that your friend had been here?"

"Yes, miss. Harry Cormack. He described your building exactly. But I was expecting to find your husband when I got here, not you." He hesitated. "May I ask a personal question? Your husband . . . He's not here anymore, is he?"

"What makes you say that?" She hadn't told him that Marcel was dead, because she figured that it would be better if a strange man staying in her apartment had the idea that her husband could come home at any moment. But aside from his sheer size, there was nothing threatening about Thomas at all. He seemed kind and gentle, and his question appeared to come from a place of concern.

"I don't see anything that looks like it belongs to him in your room. Am I wrong?"

"No." Maybe she should have felt like he'd invaded her privacy, but he'd merely been observant. "He died a few months ago."

"I'm terribly sorry. You must miss him."

"Things between us weren't very good at the end." She couldn't believe she'd just admitted that; she couldn't explain why she'd said it. "But yes. His death was very sad. I missed him more than I expected at first."

"And now you're alone," he said softly, his eyes on hers.

"Well, yes." She felt suddenly flustered. "But I'm perfectly all right. Now let's get you changed into some clean clothes."

◆ ◆ ◆

AFTER THOMAS HAD FALLEN BACK asleep, this time on the sofa, Ruby left a note saying she was going out. It didn't feel wise to leave him alone in the apartment, but she was confident he was smart enough to hide or to climb out through the terrace if someone appeared at her door while she wasn't there.

She walked quickly to the bakery on the rue de la Comète, the one Aubert had mentioned, keeping her head down the whole way. She was certain he would chide her for sheltering a pilot in an apartment the Nazis were already aware of, but she knew she'd made the right choice. If she had tried to move Thomas, he surely would have died. That his fever had broken and he was on the mend was nothing short of a miracle. Now, she needed another one.

As she waited in the queue at the bakery, she found herself thinking more than she should have been about the pilot. Not about her mission to save him—for that was to be expected—but about the way his presence filled her apartment. The way it had made her heartbeat quicken when she came into her room and saw him asleep in her bed. It was silly, of course, surely an indication that she'd been lonelier than she realized. But the truth was, it was something more than that, something she couldn't quite put her finger on.

It took her an hour to reach the front counter. "I'm looking for Aubert Moreau," she said to the middle-aged woman with the beak nose who was standing there handing out loaves of bread.

"Never heard of him," the woman snapped. "Ration card, please."

"No, I know he's here," Ruby protested. "Or at least he was."

"There is no one by that name here."

"Please," Ruby said, softening her tone as the woman looked past her, already focusing on the next customer. "I'm Marcel Benoit's wife."

The woman's eyes snapped back to Ruby. "I have no idea who that is. But I suppose that if someone named Moreau dropped by, I could give him a message for you."

Ruby regarded her warily. "There's no message. Please just tell him I hoped to see him."

"Yes, of course. Now, would you like some bread?"

Ruby realized she'd forgotten her ration card, but the woman pressed a loaf into her hand anyhow, holding her gaze for a beat too long. Either Ruby had just left word for Aubert that she needed help, or she had alerted the authorities to the fact that they should check out her apartment once again.

Thomas was awake and out of bed when she returned. She was surprised to find him standing in the living room, looking at some of her framed photographs. "I was starting to worry about you," he said, smiling at her.

She took in the sight of him before responding. He was dressed in a pair of Marcel's pants—far too tight and short on him—and one of Marcel's old shirts, which looked like it was about to burst at the seams. He had washed his hair and he'd shaved, which made him look somehow more vulnerable too. He touched his cheeks self-consciously as she continued to stare. "I'm sorry," he said. "I found a razor in the bathroom. I hope you don't mind that I used it. I'm not accustomed to having a beard."

"No, no, it's fine," Ruby said, tearing her eyes away.

"Is everything all right? You were gone for a while."

Ruby nodded. "I was just trying to reach a man my husband worked with on the escape line. But I couldn't find him."

"I don't mean to be a burden, miss."

"First of all, you're not a burden." Ruby realized as she said the words just how true they were. "And second, you must stop calling me miss. How about just calling me Ruby?"

He laughed. "I'm sorry. Ruby it is." He turned and gestured to one of the photos he'd been looking at when she came in. It was a snapshot of her when she was around fifteen, standing amid the poppies that bloomed each spring near her parents' house in California. "This is you as a girl." It was a statement, not a question. "You were happy."

She looked up in surprise. Visitors to the apartment were often drawn to the picture, but they always commented on the vast field of flowers. Never on her. "Yes, I was."

"Do you mind me asking why you haven't gone back to the States?"

Ruby gestured to the couch, and they both sat down. "I suppose because I chose to make my world here. At first it was because I'd made a promise to my husband, but then I fell in love with Paris. And you can't just love something when it's easy, can you? That's not real love."

"Indeed." Thomas was staring at her in a way that made her feel both unsettled and understood.

She drew a deep breath and went on. "I'm glad I stayed. Maybe that sounds crazy, but in America, there would be nothing I could do to help. Here, at least I can do *something*."

"But it's risky. Especially doing what you're doing, Ruby. Hiding people like me."

She gave him a small smile. "You're the first, actually. Since my husband died."

He stood up abruptly. "Why didn't you tell me? I just thought this was something you were already involved in. I should go; I can't put you in this sort of danger."

She reached instinctively for his hand to pull him back down beside her. She realized only after his fingers closed around hers that it had been too forward of her, but suddenly, she didn't want to let go—especially when it became clear that he had no intention of releasing her either. His hand was large, callused, and warm. "Please, Thomas, sit down."

He did, looking uncertain. His fingers were still laced with hers, and he was sitting closer than he had been before, their knees touching now. "Ruby, it's not that I don't believe in you. In fact, you seem like a real ace at saving people. It's just that I would never want to be the one putting you in harm's way."

"Thomas, this is the first time in years I've felt like myself." The way he was looking at her made her think he understood. "Before I married my husband, I was a university student in New York. I was self-sufficient, and I believed in myself."

Thomas nodded and squeezed her hand gently, encouraging her to go on.

"But somehow that changed. I thought when I came here that my independence would grow. I was going on a great adventure to Paris, after all." She smiled at her own naïveté. "But somehow along the way, I went from being a brave adventurer to simply being a wife, nothing more. It would be easy to blame it on Marcel, but it was just as much my fault. I let him talk over my opinions. I let him make all the decisions. I let him push me to the side, until I wasn't myself in our marriage anymore. Maybe I never had been to start with. But regardless, I lost the person I'd been, the person I wanted to be, and I don't think I grasped it until it was too late." She felt suddenly ridiculous. "I'm very sorry. I don't know why I'm telling you all of this."

"I'm glad you are." Thomas reached for her other hand and waited for her to look up at him. When she did, he held her gaze. "I'm glad you're telling me, because you're wrong, Ruby. I'm sorry you've felt lost. But it seems to me that you've known who you were all along, even if you didn't realize it."

"You can't know that," she protested. "You don't even know me."

"Not yet anyhow. But the way you've cared for me these last few days, well, it was the work of someone who knows exactly who she is. You showed great kindness and great courage. Those things are rarer than you think."

"Thank you." She could feel her cheeks growing warm. How did he know exactly the right thing to say? "But you see, I think someone who truly knows herself is capable of helping more. And so far, I've felt very useless in this war."

"Ruby, you saved my life."

"And I'm thankful for that. But is saving one or two men enough? My husband thought I was weak and foolish. It's why he never told me about the work he was doing to help the Allies. And maybe I *was* foolish. How could I not have seen what was going on? But I want to do more. I want to be a part of this fight."

"I think you already are."

"I don't know if that's true." She looked away. "But I'm a stronger person than he ever thought I was."

"Ruby," Thomas said. He waited until she looked right at him, and then he held her gaze. "I don't doubt that for a second."

CHAPTER SEVENTEEN

October 1941

There was something about the girl—Ruby—that changed everything for Thomas. When he'd parachuted into France, eight days earlier, all he'd wanted was to get back to England as quickly as possible. Now, he was grateful for the delay. He knew that every day he stayed in Paris the danger would grow, but somehow, it didn't matter.

That was a foolish way to think, though, and he knew it. Ruby had saved him, and he had bonded to her because of that. It was what his CO would have told him, anyhow. But Thomas couldn't help thinking there was more to it.

He knew it would be wise to move on. After all, though Ruby clearly wanted to help, her husband had been the link to the escape line, not her. But he simply didn't want to go.

The day before, she had mentioned that it would be better if he slept in the small cupboard in the hall, the place where her husband had hidden the RAF pilots who had preceded him. But then darkness had fallen while they talked, losing track of the hours, and she had said it would be fine if he wanted to spend the night in her apartment instead.

"I don't want to put you in any danger," he'd said. But the truth was, he didn't want to leave. The cupboard outside her door might as well have been miles away.

"I think we're safe for now," she'd said, and he'd nodded, even though he knew better. It was just that he enjoyed talking with her—about her childhood and his, about her hopes and his dreams, about the lives they wanted to live once the war was over. He wasn't ready for the conversation to be over yet.

"You know, you remind me a little of my mother," Thomas said just before midnight, feeling like a proper fool as soon as the words were out of his mouth. "I'm sorry, that wasn't the right thing to say to a pretty girl. I only mean that she was one of the most decent people I knew, and it strikes me that you're that way too. Kind and caring and generous. I hope it's all right to tell you that."

Ruby smiled, and even in the dim light of the candles that burned between them, he was nearly certain he could see her blushing. "Thank you. It's a wonderful compliment. You remind me a bit of my father too."

"Do I?"

"He's a very good man. He always listened to me, made me feel that I was someone special, someone important. He treated my mother that way too. I've thought of him a lot over the past few years and wondered how I wound up marrying someone who wasn't like that at all."

"Sometimes that's a part of growing up, though, isn't it? We try to strike out on our own, to carve our own path, and we realize too late what we've left behind."

"Did you do that too? Leave behind a piece of your past?"

"Yes," he said after a long pause. "I believe I did. I was in such a hurry to be a hero for Britain that I raced out the door without so much as a look back. I told myself I would visit, that I would write all the time, because, you see, it was just me and my mum. My father died years ago, and we didn't have any other family. But then things became hectic, and I found myself putting it off, telling myself I would write her the next day or visit her the next week. That wasn't who she raised me to be, you see. I was supposed to be a better son than that, and I always thought I would be when the war was over, after I'd helped save Britain. But then, I ran out of days and weeks." He was embarrassed to feel moisture in his eyes, and he turned away quickly before Ruby noticed.

"She died?" Ruby asked.

"Yes. In the Blitz. I—I couldn't save her."

"I'm so sorry, Thomas." Ruby moved closer to him on the couch and put her arms around him, pulling him into a hug. Her touch was electric. "I know just what it feels like to lose someone you love deeply, to feel as if you failed because you couldn't save them."

And just like that, the moment was over. "Yes, of course, your husband." He pulled away, hating the pang of jealousy he felt. Of course she'd loved the man she'd married; it shouldn't bother him to hear that.

Ruby looked startled. "No, that's not who I meant."

Thomas thought she might elaborate, but instead, she went silent, her eyes filling with tears. She folded inward, and she suddenly looked haunted, broken. He wanted to ask who she was talking about, who had shattered her this way, but he knew better than to press. Instead, he put his arm around her and murmured, "I'm very sorry, Ruby."

"I don't think I've ever talked to anyone like this before," she said after a while.

"Neither have I." They looked into each other's eyes, and for a moment, he thought he might try to kiss her, but then he lost his courage.

"I feel as if I could talk with you forever, without running out of things to say," she said at last.

And so they stayed up hours more, talking about everything, although she never told him whose death had broken her heart. He got up just past three in the morning to get them a couple of glasses of water, and when he returned to the living room, he found her asleep on the couch, her head tilted to the left as her hair spilled over her shoulders. He gently pulled a blanket over her and settled onto the hard-backed chair across from her. Then he simply watched her sleep until he himself drifted off, just before dawn.

When he awoke, her eyes were open and she was studying him. She quickly glanced away as he came to. "You're up," she said.

He smiled at her. "What time is it?"

"Just past nine. I never sleep this late."

"Me neither."

The silence between them felt loaded.

"You covered me with the blanket last night?" she asked finally. "After I fell asleep?"

"You looked so peaceful. I didn't want to disturb you."

He could see her swallow hard. "Thank you. That was very kind. I haven't slept that well in ages." She cleared her throat. "Anyhow, I promise I'll try again today to find Aubert. I really am very sorry about the delay. You must be eager to move on."

"No," Thomas said carefully. He waited until she looked up at him. "The truth is, I'm not sure I want to leave."

He loved the way her cheeks turned pink before she replied. "I just wish I had more food to give you. But with the rations . . ."

"Ruby, I have everything I need." He looked her in the eye and wondered if there was any chance at all that she was feeling the same way.

SHE LEFT AN HOUR LATER, over Thomas's objections that she was putting herself in danger. "We're all in danger all the time," she said with a sad smile as she paused in the doorway. "The only way to change that is to fight back."

She was gone before he could reply. Thomas spent the next hour staring at Ruby's framed photos, feeling helpless. She was risking her life for him, and there wasn't a damned thing he could do about it.

He hadn't expected this. He hadn't expected *her*. She was different from the girls who hung around the air bases, batting their eyes at the pilots. She was different from the girls he'd gone to school with too, and not just because she was American. There was a strength to her, a fearlessness, and the strangest thing was that she didn't seem to see it in herself. She wasn't tough and standoffish like one might expect from a courageous girl. Someone had made her put her defenses up, though, and he thought it might have been her husband. But that didn't explain whom she was grieving for. Had there been someone else, another man she'd loved?

A sharp knock at the door pulled him out of his thoughts and he froze. What if it was the Germans? Should he flee via the terrace? Hide in Ruby's wardrobe? Stand here like a man and try to fight them off? Then again, if he was caught in Ruby's apartment, she would be on the hook for it. He couldn't do that to her.

"Damn it," he cursed, paralyzed by indecision, just as the knocking came again, more insistent this time. He took a careful step toward the door. Ruby had a peephole; perhaps he could assess the situation in the hall before deciding what to do. If there were only two soldiers there, he had a chance to take them.

He was just about to lean in toward the door when he heard someone crying. It sounded like a child. He peered out and realized he was looking at a dark-haired little girl, maybe twelve or thirteen.

"Please, Madame Benoit!" the girl said in French through sobs. "It's my maman! She needs your help!"

Thomas held his breath. Could it be some sort of trap? Had the Nazis put the child up to this so that he'd open the door?

When he didn't answer, the girl seemed to pull herself together a bit. She knocked once more, more softly this time. "Monsieur Pilot?" she said more softly, and he was so startled that he took a step back from the door. "I know you're in there. Please, my mother has fallen. I need your help. I can be trusted. I'm Ruby's friend."

Thomas stood stock-still, and after a moment, the girl whispered "Please?" in such a pitiful tone that he could feel his heart breaking a little. "I don't know what else to do," she added, backing away from the door. He watched her through the peephole as she disappeared into the apartment in the elbow of the building.

He hesitated only a moment longer before slipping quietly out of Ruby's apartment into the dim hall. He felt exposed, but he couldn't go back now. It would be unconscionable to turn his back on a child who needed his help. Drawing a deep breath and hoping for the best, he knocked lightly on the door of the girl's apartment.

CHAPTER EIGHTEEN

October 1941

Charlotte was in a panic. She and Maman had been in the kitchen, chopping a few precious potatoes to make a soup, when her mother suddenly collapsed in a heap, striking the counter on her way down. Now, Charlotte couldn't wake her, and the blood pouring from her forehead was forming a small, frightening pool. She had tried everything she could think of—shaking her mother, talking loudly to her, placing a cool cloth on her forehead—but Maman hadn't even stirred. And her father likely wouldn't be home for hours; he had disappeared early this morning for a meeting with a few other men Charlotte knew from the synagogue.

Charlotte had tried Ruby's apartment, but no one had come to the door. The other neighbors, well, some of them had made clear their feelings about Jews. And she certainly didn't want to enlist the help of anyone who hated her family. Who knew what could happen? She couldn't call a doctor for help either; the one who had delivered Ruby's stillborn baby had left for the Free Zone weeks ago, and she didn't know another. Her father had spoken sternly to her several times about how there was no way to know whom to trust anymore.

Charlotte bent to her mother's side again. "Please wake up, Maman. *Please!* I don't know what to do!" But her mother still didn't stir.

Just then, there was a light knock at the door. Heart thudding, Charlotte crept to the peephole and looked out. There was a man she didn't know in the hallway, dressed in pants and a shirt too small for him. "I'm the pilot, mademoiselle," he said softly in accented French. "I'm here to help."

She recognized him now, though he was clean-shaven and looked much different than he had the day he arrived. She took a deep breath and opened the door. "Hello, monsieur." She looked him up and down. He had broad shoulders, dark hair, and bright blue eyes, the kind that looked like they would crinkle at the corners when he smiled. "Please, come in."

"Something happened to your mother?" He was already moving into her apartment.

"Yes." Charlotte swallowed hard, scrambling after him. She could see him looking around quickly, and she wondered fleetingly what he was seeing. Did he notice the Star of David quilt her grandmother had sewn, now lying folded over a chair? Did he see the threadbare sofa, the worn rug, the things Maman was ashamed of? "She fell while we were chopping potatoes. I—I can't wake her up."

Charlotte could feel tears streaming down her face, and she was embarrassed. She wasn't a baby; why was she crying? But the pilot didn't seem to notice. He was already kneeling beside her mother, placing two fingers on her neck, and bending his ear toward her mouth.

"Is she breathing?" Charlotte asked, trying not to sound as frantic as she felt.

"She is. Do you have a clean towel you can bring me?" he asked without turning around. "And a jug of cool water, please?"

"Of course." Charlotte raced into the bathroom, where she grabbed a fresh towel. She handed it to the pilot, who was still bent over her mother, then she quickly got him a large pitcher of water. "Is she going to be all right?"

"Yes. I think she just fainted. Look, she's already regaining consciousness."

Charlotte peered over his shoulder at her mother, whose eyelids were indeed beginning to flutter. "Oh, thank God. Maman? Maman? Are you all right?"

Her mother mumbled something unintelligible and closed her eyes again.

"She'll be okay," the pilot said. "We'll just need to check and see how badly she hit her head. Had she been ill?"

"Not that I know of." Charlotte felt like a terrible daughter. How could she not have noticed that there was something wrong with her mother?

"Don't worry," the pilot said, apparently reading her thoughts. "Sometimes these things just happen. And you acted quickly to get her help. You showed great presence of mind."

"But I risked exposing you." She realized suddenly how foolish she'd been. "If someone had seen—"

"But no one did. Besides, when one's mother is ill, it's impossible to think clearly, isn't it?"

Charlotte nodded. "Do you—do you have a mother?" She knew the question was silly as soon as it was out of her mouth. Of course he had a mother!

"Yes, I did. She was a wonderful woman." He hesitated. "Now, let's get your mum over to the couch so that we can prop her head up a bit, shall we?"

Charlotte nodded, and as the pilot scooped her mother effortlessly into his arms, she grabbed the bloodied towel and the water and followed him to where he laid her down gently. Maman's eyelids were fluttering again, and she was trying to say something. "What is it, Maman?" Charlotte asked, leaning in.

"The man," her mother rasped weakly. "Who is the man?"

The pilot smiled and stepped back as Charlotte squeezed Maman's hand. "A friend, Maman. He's a friend."

AN HOUR LATER, MAMAN WAS resting comfortably in her own bed, her head bandaged after the pilot had determined that the wound wasn't deep. "It might be a good idea to have a doctor take a look, just to ensure it doesn't get infected," he said. "But it's nothing to worry about for now. As for the fainting, I think perhaps your mother isn't getting enough to eat."

"None of us are."

The pilot nodded. "Rations are very tight, aren't they?"

"I sometimes think the damned Nazis are trying to starve us all to death."

"I certainly wouldn't put it past them." If the pilot was shocked by her language, he didn't show it. "Let's say we let your mother rest for a while. She should feel better after a bit of a sleep."

Charlotte hesitated, nodded to herself, and led the airman out of the room. "Can I make you some coffee to thank you?" she asked.

He smiled again. He really did have a very nice smile, and she'd been right about his eyes crinkling at the edges. "But you've just told me that things are strictly rationed."

"We have a bit of real coffee saved for special occasions."

"Oh, but I don't think this is a special occasion. Your mother would surely have woken on her own. How about a simple glass of water, and you and I can have a chat?"

Charlotte suddenly felt shy. "Okay." She got him a glass of water from the kitchen and returned to the living room to find him sitting in the chair that her father normally used. She hesitated before handing him the glass.

He leaned forward. "Do you know Ruby very well?"

"Yes. We're very good friends." Charlotte knew she was boasting, overselling her friendship with her neighbor, but Ruby really *was* her closest friend these days.

"Perhaps you can answer a question for me, then."

Charlotte paused. "Maybe."

"Do you think there's anything I can do to help her? She seems sad, and I wish I knew how to fix it."

Charlotte was startled; it wasn't at all what she'd expected him to ask. "I—I don't know." Was he fishing for information? He didn't look like a gossip. In fact, he appeared genuinely concerned. "It's not because of her husband, you know. I think she misses him sometimes, but he wasn't very kind to her. Not as kind as someone should be to someone like Ruby, anyhow."

"It's hard to imagine being unkind to a woman like her."

Charlotte felt guilty. She knew she'd said too much. But the pilot didn't look like he was judging Ruby. He just looked sort of sad himself. "Not to speak ill of the dead. But I think—I think Monsieur Benoit made her feel useless."

"She's anything but useless, isn't she?"

"She's very strong."

"And yet there's a sadness to her." The pilot looked lost in thought.

"It's because of the baby, I think."

"The baby?" He leaned back like she'd knocked the wind out of him.

She swallowed hard. Now she'd definitely gone too far. "I shouldn't have said anything. She—she doesn't like to talk about it. But she was pregnant, you see, a while ago. And the baby was born too early, without breathing. She hasn't been the same since it happened."

The pilot's gaze was still on Charlotte, but she had the sense that his mind was somewhere far away. "I'm very sorry to hear that," he said softly. "Very sorry indeed."

"Me too," Charlotte agreed. They were silent for so long that Charlotte began to grow uneasy. "Can I ask you something?"

"Of course." He seemed to snap back to reality.

"What are you doing in Paris?"

He told her of being shot down and hiking to the city in search of the man who lived in the building with the red door. "And I should probably move on now," he concluded. "But I can't bring myself to."

"Why not?"

He sighed. "I don't exactly know."

"Is it because of Ruby?"

"Maybe." He refocused his gaze on her. "Charlotte, would you do something for me?"

"Yes, anything." She was relieved to think she might be able to pay him back for helping her.

"Will you promise to look out for her after I leave? Make sure that she has some happiness in her days?"

Charlotte swelled with pride. "Yes, sir, I will." She paused. "You care about her."

"I do." The pilot stood up and smiled once more. "Let me check on your mother again, and then I should be heading back."

"Of course." Charlotte led him down the hall to her parents' bedroom once again, where he felt her mother's pulse, put a hand on her forehead, and watched her sleep for a moment.

"She should be fine," he said. "But come back and get me if there's any problem, all right?"

"Yes. Thank you again." Charlotte led him out of the room, already feeling sad that their time together was up. He'd been a welcome distraction, and much like Ruby, he had talked to her as if she were an adult. "Can I give you some bread and cheese to thank you?"

"Oh, that's not necessary."

But Charlotte was already packing a small bundle. She knew Ruby's ration cards were for only one person, and that surely wasn't enough to feed this man. She thrust the package at him and said, "Please. It's the least I can do. If not for you, then for Ruby. The cheese is from the countryside. A friend of my papa brought it. But I know Papa would want you to have it, for helping my maman."

He hesitated, then nodded, accepting the food as she walked him toward the front hall. "May I ask you another question?" The pilot paused with his hand on the door. "Are you Jewish? Is that why you couldn't go for help?"

Charlotte stared at him. Her father had said she wasn't supposed to volunteer her Judaism to anyone who might hurt her. But she knew that this man would never do that. "Yes."

"One day, things will be different," he said after a very long pause. "We're going to win this war, Charlotte. In the meantime, just hold on. Don't lose sight of who you are."

And then, before she could reply, he had slipped into the hallway. She watched him from her doorway until he was safely inside Ruby's apartment.

CHAPTER NINETEEN

October 1941

"Ruby?" Aubert's eyes were wide with alarm as Ruby entered Café Michel on the rue de Bourgogne just past noon. She had racked her brain all night trying to think where she might find him, and finally, she had remembered Marcel mentioning the place in passing, back when the Nazis first entered Paris. Aubert sometimes stopped there, Marcel had said once before abruptly falling silent, as if he'd said something wrong. Ruby had barely noticed it at the time, but in retrospect, she was sure he'd revealed something he wasn't supposed to. In any case, here Aubert sat, in the back of the café. There were Nazi soldiers dining nearby, talking, laughing, their plates piled with meat, bread, and vegetables, their glasses full of wine. She hated them with a ferocity that surprised her.

"Hello, Aubert," she said, impressing herself with how calm she sounded.

His eyes widened further. "It's Philippe," he corrected. "Surely you have me confused with someone else."

She stared at him for a moment before she understood. He was using an alias. Had Marcel had one too? There were so many things she didn't know. "Yes, of course. Philippe. My mistake."

"Not a problem." His smile was unnaturally stiff. "Would you like to take a stroll?" He was already placing a few coins on the table before she could respond. He grabbed her arm and led her out of the café.

"What in the hell are you doing here?" he demanded in a whisper as soon as they were on the street.

"Trying to find you."

"Ruby." He sighed and withdrew a handkerchief from his pocket, blotting at the sweat that had beaded on his forehead. "Your husband was executed for aiding Allied fugitives, in case you've forgotten. You could have led the Nazis straight to me!"

"I wasn't followed."

"You approached me in a café right under the Germans' noses!"

"You were *sitting* in a café right under the Germans' noses," Ruby pointed out.

"Part of my cover. I'm a collaborator, as far as they know. You can't just put that in peril."

"You need to listen to me." She was sick of being chided. "I'm sheltering an RAF pilot."

All at once, he went very still. "Pardon?"

"He showed up five days ago, looking for Marcel. He had a bad infection and a high fever. He's on the mend, but he needs to get back to England." There was a lump in her throat as she said the words.

"He just appeared at your door?"

Ruby nodded. She tried not to think of how vulnerable Thomas had looked when he collapsed in the hall. "He'd heard about the escape line from another pilot who made it home safely."

"Damn it!" Aubert's face turned red. "They're not supposed to talk about the details."

Ruby remained silent until Aubert calmed down. "I need to connect Thomas—the pilot—to someone who can help him get out of Paris. And after that, I want to help. I want to help on the escape line."

"That's ridiculous, Ruby. You can't help."

She flinched. "How can you say that? I'm *already* helping."

"Marcel said you meant well, but that's not enough, Ruby."

"There's much more to me than good intentions."

Aubert stared at her for a moment. "Marcel also said you were careless. I'm sorry."

The words hit their mark. "Yes, well, Marcel was wrong about a lot of things. You know that as well as I do. He was hot-tempered and rash, and I'm not."

Aubert didn't say anything for a long time. "It's dangerous work, Ruby."

"You think I don't know the risks?"

Aubert sighed and put his hands up in a gesture of defeat. "I'll send someone to pick up your pilot tomorrow. If all goes well, we can talk. But I make no promises."

She nodded, struggling to keep a straight face. "How will I know that the person who arrives tomorrow to retrieve the pilot is legitimate?"

"She will address you with a code name."

She? So there were other women working on the line. Had Marcel worked side by side with them, treating them with respect while he belittled her? "A code name?"

"We all have one. It's helpful not to know one another's true identity." He paused and studied her. "From now on, you'll be Fleur."

"Fleur?"

He smiled slightly. "Marcel said you were always talking about the poppy fields back home. *Alors,* now you have a chance to be your own flower."

He whirled around and walked back into the café before she could say another word. She wasn't sure whether the name was meant to mock her, but she liked it regardless. She allowed herself a tiny smile before turning in the opposite direction.

Fleur, she thought as she headed back toward her apartment. *She who blooms in the midst of the darkness.* She felt invincible as she walked past a cluster of Nazi soldiers at the corner of the rue de l'Université. One of them whistled at her, but she ignored him. She finally had a purpose, a reason for being here, but there was also a part of her that was full of regret.

Thomas. Sending him on his way was the right thing. There was no doubt about it, but Ruby knew her apartment would feel empty without him. How was that possible? She'd only just met him.

You can't think that way, she reminded herself as she hurried along, keeping her eyes straight ahead. *You can't get emotionally involved.* But there was something different about Thomas, something she couldn't quite put a finger on. And now perhaps she'd never know why she felt the way she did.

It was nearing dusk when she arrived home. "Hello?" she called when it seemed she was alone in the apartment. For a moment, her heart was in her throat. Had the authorities come for Thomas? Had something happened? But a moment later, he emerged from her wardrobe, looking sheepish.

"I heard someone and hid," he said, running his right hand through his hair. "Sorry."

"No. You did the right thing."

"Where were you?" He paused and shook his head. "I'm sorry. That came out wrong. Not that I have any right to know. What I mean is, I was worried. Are you all right?"

"Actually, I went to meet with the man I told you about, the one my husband knew. And good news; he's sending someone from the escape line to pick you up tomorrow."

"Oh."

"I thought you'd be excited."

Thomas looked away. "I am. And I'm glad I won't be a danger to you anymore. But—"

"But what?"

"But who will protect you if I'm not here?"

Ruby could feel her cheeks heating up. "You're worried about me?"

He looked surprised. "Well, of course."

"It's been an awfully long time since anyone cared what happened to me."

"It shouldn't be that way, Ruby. I know I'll always care, now that I've met you."

Something inside of her felt like it was breaking open. "I'll always care about what happens to you too."

They held each other's gaze for a long moment, and Ruby could almost hear her own heart beating.

Thomas was the one to speak first. "I should tell you that your friend Charlotte came to the door today."

"Charlotte? From next door?"

He nodded. "Her mother fell."

"Oh, no! Is Madame Dacher all right?"

Thomas nodded. "She's fine, I believe. If I had to hazard a guess, she hadn't been eating enough and simply fainted. She hit her head on the way down, so there was some blood, which must have been frightening to Charlotte."

"You went to their apartment?"

"It was the right thing to do. She was looking for you. She sounded scared."

"You risked being spotted in order to help her."

He shrugged and looked away.

"I should go check on her," Ruby murmured after a pause. But she couldn't move. Thomas was staring at her again, and it made her wish, somehow, that she could linger in this moment for a while more. "You're a good man, Thomas," she said. "A very good man." She didn't wait for a response before slipping out the door.

"I THINK THE PILOT LOVES you," Charlotte said gravely to Ruby thirty minutes later, after Ruby had checked on Madame Dacher, who was awake, though still woozy.

"He's only been here a few days, Charlotte! People don't fall in love that quickly."

"Sometimes a few days is all it takes," Charlotte said confidently, and Ruby had to hide a smile. Charlotte might be wise beyond her years, but she was still a child. She couldn't possibly understand such things.

"He'll be gone very soon anyhow, back to England."

"The war will end someday, you know. And then you can see him again."

If we both survive, Ruby thought. But she mustered a smile and said, "Let's not make this into something it's not. I'm just helping him for a few days, that's all. Now, you're sure you and your mother are all right?"

Charlotte nodded.

"Please don't hesitate to come get me if anything goes wrong."

"Okay. Please tell your pilot I'm grateful."

Ruby slipped out of the Dachers' apartment with Charlotte's words ringing in her ears. *Your pilot.* The mere thought of him belonging to her was enough to make her light-headed. But she was being foolish, and she knew it.

She drew a deep breath and forced herself back to reality before opening the door to her own apartment. Inside, it smelled like someone was cooking, but that was impossible. "Thomas?"

"In here."

She rounded the corner to the kitchen to find two candles lit on the table and Thomas standing at the stove. "What are you doing?" she asked.

He turned and smiled. "I hope you don't mind. I'm making us a meal. Charlotte gave me a bit of bread and cheese. It's not much, but my mother always said I had a special talent with cheese on toast. I thought we might bring half to the Dachers and share the rest between us."

She just stared at him, sure this was some kind of a mirage. Never in all the time she'd spent with Marcel had he ever offered to cook for her. No man had done that. She knew the bread was likely stale and the cheese was probably old, but somehow, it smelled like the most delicious thing in the world.

"Sit down," Thomas said, turning back to the stove. "Make yourself comfortable. I wish I could offer you a glass of wine, but alas, all I have is water."

"Wait, I have some wine," Ruby said. She'd been saving the last of Marcel's collection for a special occasion, but this was just that, wasn't it? She went to the cupboard in the parlor and rummaged in the back until she found a bottle of 1937 Bordeaux. "Will this do?" she asked, returning to the kitchen.

Thomas raised his eyebrows and grinned. "If you're sure you want to open it, I think it would elevate the meal to a proper feast."

THE OPEN-FACED SANDWICH THAT THOMAS prepared was one of the best things Ruby had ever eaten, and by the time they'd made it through the bottle of wine, they were sitting on the couch side by side, sharing stories of their childhoods. Ruby told him about the time she got lost in the poppy fields the year she was five and how frightened she'd been, and Thomas chuckled and told her about how he'd been the same age when he wandered off one afternoon in London, scaring his poor parents half to death. They talked about school and their childhood dreams; Ruby had wanted to be a teacher, and Thomas had hoped to be a doctor.

"I always loved science," he explained. "And I like taking care of people. It seemed like a logical path to follow. In fact, I had already taken several courses in anticipation of continuing on to medical school."

"So why didn't you?"

He sighed. "The war happened. I wanted a chance to help. I had just finished university when I decided to enlist."

"Do you think you'll go back to school? Become a doctor someday?"

"Honestly, I don't know. A doctor is supposed to save lives, but I've had to take them. I'm not sure how that has changed who I am."

"Things are different in wartime. And you're fighting for a greater good."

"But there must be Germans who feel that way too. If there's one thing I've learned in the sky, Ruby, it's that absolutely nothing is black and white. And as a doctor, I think you're supposed to see the world a bit more scientifically. I'm just not sure that's the person I am anymore."

"But maybe, in a way, you've become a better person. After all, it's the nuances that make the world beautiful, isn't it?" Her cheeks warmed as Thomas held her gaze.

"And how about you?" he asked. "Do you still want to be a schoolteacher?"

"A year ago, I would have said no. But I've been working with

Charlotte, helping her to learn English, and it has reminded me how much I love education. Knowledge is power, especially in times like these."

Thomas nodded. "Talking of Charlotte, she mentioned something to me when I was in her apartment earlier," he said. "It's my fault; I was asking about you, and I'm afraid I pried more than I intended."

Ruby blinked a few times. "What did she say?"

"She told me about the baby. I'm so very sorry, Ruby."

Ruby felt suddenly numb, cold. She was glad, in a way, that Thomas knew. She had wanted to tell him the night before, but she hadn't known how to say the words.

When she didn't say anything, he went on. "He's who you were talking about last night, isn't he? You said that you felt as if you'd failed because you couldn't save him."

The tears were falling now, and she didn't bother to pretend otherwise. "He came too early. I wasn't strong enough."

"Ruby." He reached for her hands and waited until she looked at him. "I can't even imagine the pain of a loss like that. But you must know that it wasn't your fault."

"But a mother's most important job is to protect her child."

"Sometimes that's impossible, though. I know you well enough now to know that you did everything you could to keep that baby safe, didn't you?"

Ruby nodded, feeling miserable.

"Sometimes, God's plans are different from ours, and it's impossible to know why," Thomas said. "I need to ask something of you, Ruby."

She looked up, startled. He was asking her a favor in the midst of a conversation like this? "All right."

"I need you to forgive yourself."

"Thomas—"

"Please, let me finish. You can carry the sadness with you, but not the guilt. Guilt will eat you alive, and in this case, there's no reason for it. It's not my business, Ruby, but if there's one thing I hope for you, it's that you'll try to let go of the feeling that you failed, because you didn't. I want the best for you. I want you to be happy. And I don't think you will be, not entirely, until you lay this burden down."

When he was done speaking, she stared at him for a long time. "I'll try," she whispered at last. "But why do you care? We'll probably never see each other again."

"The war will end someday, Ruby," Thomas replied. "And Paris isn't so far away from London."

Ruby let herself imagine a future where they could have all the time in the world to get to know each other. But that simply wasn't realistic. What were the chances that an RAF pilot and an American girl in Paris would find their way back to each other? She settled for saying, "It's a nice thought, Thomas. A very nice thought."

They talked long into the night, until Ruby's eyelids grew heavy. Finally, she glanced at the clock on the mantel and stood up. "You have a long journey ahead of you tomorrow. You must get some sleep."

He stood too, and she was struck anew by the sheer size of him, the way her head would fit perfectly against his solid chest. He took a step closer, and she held her breath. In a split second, his lips were on hers, soft and tender. He laced a large hand through her hair, cradling the back of her head as he pulled her toward him, and she kissed him back, although she knew it was foolish. But it felt perfect and right, and she didn't want the moment to end.

When he finally backed away, he looked dazed. "I shouldn't have done that. I'm sorry."

Ruby looked into his eyes. "I'm very glad you did."

"Well then." He kissed her again, more intensely, and this time, it was Ruby who broke away.

"Thomas, we must get some sleep," she said.

"Yes, yes, of course."

Ruby hesitated. "Good night, then. And thank you for a lovely dinner." She walked into her bedroom without looking back, but after she closed the door behind her, she stayed there, listening. She yearned to go to him, and she wondered if on the other side of the wall, he was feeling the same way. If he came to her door, she would let him in, even if it was against her better judgment.

But he didn't. And after a while, her heart heavy with longing for something she knew she could never have, she crawled into bed and stared at the ceiling until dawn arrived.

CHAPTER TWENTY

October 1941

"Fleur?" The dark-haired woman standing outside Ruby's door was early. Too early. She was also too beautiful. Ruby knew that was a ridiculous thing to think, especially since the woman's voluptuous curves, bee-stung lips, and large green eyes probably made her an asset to the Resistance, keeping the German soldiers distracted. But Ruby hated the idea of handing Thomas off to her, especially after the kiss they'd shared last night.

"I'm sorry, you are Fleur?" the woman repeated more uncertainly. Ruby could tell from her accent that she was French, but her beauty seemed foreign somehow, exotic.

"Yes. And you must be . . . ?"

"Laure. I'm here for the package." The woman smiled slightly, which unfortunately made her look even lovelier. "Philippe sent me," she added when Ruby still hadn't said anything.

"Oh yes, of course." Ruby forced a smile. Aubert's cover name.

"And you have the package?" Laure was regarding Ruby warily now.

"One moment, please." Ruby shut the door on Laure, knowing it was rude, but not particularly caring. She wanted a few seconds alone with Thomas.

"That's her?" His voice came from behind her, where he stood wearing Marcel's clothes. "The woman who will take me to the next stop on the line?"

"That's her," Ruby confirmed flatly.

Thomas closed the distance between them in three long steps. He pulled Ruby into his arms and kissed her once more before pulling away. "I don't want to leave you."

The words made Ruby's heart ache. "But you must."

"I'll be back one day," Thomas said. "I swear it."

Ruby doubted that the words could ever be true. But she wanted to believe.

There was a knock at the door again, and Ruby held Thomas's gaze for one more long moment before opening it. Laure was standing with her hands on her hips, looking perturbed.

"We really must go," she said. "May I come in?"

Ruby nodded, stepping aside and closing the door behind her. Laure introduced herself to Thomas; then, acting as if Ruby wasn't there at all, she plunged into a rapid-fire set of instructions in English.

"You're to walk behind me," she said. "No contact. No acknowledgment. If someone stops me, you keep walking. If someone stops you, I keep walking. There's no way we can be seen together. If all goes well, I'll lead you to the train station, where I'll board first and you'll board a few minutes later in the same car. Again, we do not know each other. Here are your ticket and your identity papers, as well as your German travel document, all flawless forgeries." She withdrew a few papers from her purse and handed them to Thomas. "You are a French farmworker who is deaf and mute. Do you understand?"

"But I can speak French."

"With an English accent. Under no circumstances will you speak when spoken to."

Thomas nodded.

"You will change into the clothes I have here." She held up the bag she was carrying. "And you will carry this sign." She withdrew a sloppily hand-lettered sign that read in French, DEAF AND MUTE. CAN YOU SPARE A COIN? "We will exit the train at Bordeaux, and you will follow me to another train. Understand?"

"Yes." Thomas was all business. "Thank you. I understand you're taking a great risk."

Laure seemed to soften a little. "We all are, including you. The important thing is to return you to combat." She turned to Ruby. "Philippe says you did well nursing this pilot back to health. You're to meet him on Monday at ten in the Tuileries if you're still interested in discussing things."

"I am." Ruby felt stiff and awkward. "Thank you."

Laure nodded. "Well then. We must be on our way."

Thomas stepped forward and took Ruby's hand. "I don't know how to thank you," he said softly. Then he leaned in and kissed her quickly on the cheek—the most either of them dared to do in front of Laure—and moved away.

"You can thank me by staying safe, Thomas."

He was heading for the door, already too far away from her.

"You must change what you're wearing." Laure's voice was sharp.

Thomas blinked a few times. "Of course." She handed him the bag and he disappeared into Ruby's bedroom. Laure and Ruby regarded each other silently in the long minute it took him to change. When he emerged, he looked like a different man. The clothing Laure had given him was worn and stained. He would easily pass for a French farmer.

"I've left your husband's clothes on your bed," he said, locking eyes with Ruby. "Thank you again. For everything."

"You're welcome."

He moved toward the door with Laure, and Ruby was afraid those were the last words they'd ever say to each other. They felt strangely impersonal. But as he passed her, he stopped and touched her cheek gently. "I will never, ever forget what you did for me."

"Helping you is what any decent person would have done," Ruby said.

"I'm not talking about that." He studied her face for another second, as if memorizing her features, and then he let his hand fall and was gone. Laure glanced back at Ruby once before pulling the door closed behind her.

After that, there was only silence.

Ruby stood in place for a long time before making her way to the couch and sitting down in a daze. Had last night really happened? Had the last few days been real? Now what? There was a part of her that wished she'd asked Aubert about the percentage of pilots who made it safely back to England, and a part of her that was glad she hadn't.

There was a knock at the door some time later, and Ruby jumped up to answer. What if something had happened to Thomas? But it was only Charlotte standing there, a single red rose in her hands. She held it out to Ruby.

"This bloomed on our terrace this morning," she said. "Can you believe it? In October? Maman wanted you to have it."

"Thank you, Charlotte." Ruby took the rose and inhaled. It smelled strong and sweet, and its color reminded her of the poppies that flourished near her parents' house in California, the ones she'd told Thomas about. It was enough to make her eyes fill with tears.

"Your pilot is gone," Charlotte said bluntly.

"Yes. Yes, he is." Ruby drew a deep breath. "How is your mother feeling, Charlotte?"

"A little better, thank you."

"I'm very glad."

Charlotte nodded, but she made no move to go. Ruby had the sense there was something the girl wanted to say.

"Is everything okay, Charlotte?"

"I can hear my parents at night," she blurted out. "Arguing. They don't sleep anymore. I don't know what I should do. They just stay up and fight about the situation in Paris. They talk about whether we should try to leave."

Ruby felt a surge of pity for the Dachers. She knew things were only getting worse for Jews; there were frequent reports of arrests and deportations across the city. "Maybe you should," she said gently.

"This is our city, Ruby. It's the only home I've ever known. Why should we have to go?"

"Because it's getting dangerous."

"But *you've* decided to stay! Why should things be any different for us?"

Ruby could tell just by looking that the girl knew the answer to her own question.

FOR THE NEXT FEW DAYS, Ruby could barely sleep. Each time she closed her eyes, she saw something terrible happening to Thomas. She imagined him caught by a Nazi soldier on a train, betrayed by Laure, picked off the street in southwest France, shot on sight as he tried to cross into Spain. She knew she had to keep telling herself to forget him. Her mother had once told her that some people you meet are meant to be a part of your world forever, but some are meant only to change the course of your life and then move on. Thomas had shown her that she could be useful in the escape line, restored her faith in herself, given her back a purpose. He had even helped her to begin letting go of her guilt over the baby. Maybe that was all he was meant to do. Maybe in time, she would stop thinking of him, stop remembering the feel of his lips against hers.

On Monday, Ruby went to the Tuileries gardens to meet Aubert. As she strolled through the flower-lined pathways, she was struck by how normal things seemed. There were little boys racing white-sailed boats in the pond, giggling girls chasing each other, contented mothers pushing prams and chatting. It was like none of them knew a war was going on. Ruby wasn't sure whether she should be grateful for the normalcy or horrified by it.

"Act casual," Aubert said quietly as he approached quickly from the west entrance to the park. He kissed her on both cheeks and put an arm around her. "Behave as if we're old friends, just meeting up for a chat."

"But we *are* old friends," Ruby said. "Aren't we?"

She drew her answer from his silence. He had never been her friend. He had merely tolerated her. Was that what he was doing now? Putting on a friendly face to keep her happy?

They settled onto a bench together facing the pond. It was the perfect cover for a clandestine meeting. There were thousands of witnesses, so no one could accuse them of conspiring, and yet they could talk without being overheard. "Always hide in plain sight," Aubert murmured. "It's the last place the Nazis look."

"Is the pilot safe?" Ruby couldn't help but ask. "The one I was sheltering?"

"I don't know. Once they leave Paris, I have no idea what happens. It's better that way; the less each of us knows, the less we can reveal if we're captured."

"But he got out of Paris, at least?"

"Yes." Aubert was silent for a moment. "You know, it's our job to send them on to the next stop in the line, not to befriend them."

Ruby looked away, but she was sure Aubert could feel her shoulders tensing under his arm. "I nursed him back to health, Aubert, so obviously I care what becomes of him."

"Laure seemed to feel there was something more between the two of you. Of course I told her she must be wrong. Surely you're still mourning your husband."

"Of course I am," Ruby said quickly, swallowing a hard lump of guilt.

"In any case, I know you want to help us. I appreciate that, Ruby, but I've considered it and I don't think you're the right fit. You already stand out."

"And yet I harbored a pilot for days."

"Still, I'm not sure you're capable—"

She didn't wait for him to finish. "You didn't think I'd be capable of something like this in the first place, though, did you? And I have already proven you wrong."

"Ruby—"

"And truly, Aubert, why would anyone suspect me?" she asked, interrupting him again. "Because of Marcel, people think I'm nothing, a nobody."

From the sheepish look Aubert gave her, Ruby knew he'd thought it too. Perhaps he still did.

"See?" she continued. "Marcel laid the perfect groundwork. If the Nazis ever have a suspicion, they'll only have to ask around, and they'll be informed of just how useless I am." Her laugh sounded more bitter than she intended it to. "He created the perfect cover."

"This is very dangerous work, Ruby."

"I'm aware of the risks."

"But they torture people. You can't possibly know how you'd stand up to that."

"I *do* know that I would sooner die than risk endangering any of the pilots I'd be helping."

"And under no circumstances could you tell the Nazis about me or Laure or anyone else you meet on the line. As an American, you might survive, but those of us who are French would be executed immediately. We'd be putting our lives in your hands, Ruby."

"Aubert, I'm involved already, which means your life is in my hands now. I suppose it's up to you what happens next." She held her breath.

His hand on her shoulder flexed and released. "Very well. But from now on, I'm Philippe. You must remember that. The code names are for our protection, and you mustn't be careless. I'll send you your first pilot within a week's time, as long as the Brits agree, and I'll work on getting you extra ration cards. Laure or a man with the code name Jean-Louis will do the pickups from your apartment. Unless something goes wrong, you should have the men for forty-eight hours at most."

Ruby took a deep breath. "Thank you."

"Those are the wrong words for a situation like this. You think that you're embarking on a great adventure, Ruby. But I fear you've just started down a road that will ultimately end in your death."

SIX DAYS LATER, THERE WAS a soft knock at Ruby's door, and she opened it to find a man with small, dark eyes dressed in dungarees and a faded shirt. There was a deep gash down the right side of his face, and he looked exhausted. "Fleur?" he asked, glancing around nervously. He reminded Ruby of a skittish deer.

"Yes," Ruby said in English, realizing immediately that he was the first of the men Aubert had promised to send her way. "Please, won't you come in?"

He didn't move at first. "You speak English."

"I'm American."

His eyes filled with tears. "God, you have no idea how nice it is to hear my own language." He stepped inside, and she shut the door behind him. "What on earth are you doing here, so far from home?"

"I might ask you the same."

He laughed, which turned into a hacking cough. "I was shot out of the sky over Abbeville. A farmer saw my plane go down and reached me before the Germans did. Hid me in his barn for two days before passing me along to a chap who drove me to another town. I slept three nights there in the basement of an inn, then I was picked up by a member of the Resistance, who gave me a bicycle and had me follow him to the suburbs of Paris. I was given instructions to come to you. I'm told this is my last stop before I head for Spain."

Ruby was sure he wasn't supposed to have filled her in in such detail. "Each of us only knows the next step in the line," she said gently. "But please take care not to tell anyone else where you stayed at each step of the way. It could endanger the operation."

He narrowed his eyes, and she could tell in an instant he wasn't accustomed to being chided. "I didn't give you any details. Besides, surely you know all of this already."

"Actually, I didn't."

"If you say so."

She didn't like the way he was looking at her now.

"Anyhow," he said, "I suppose Fleur isn't your real name."

"I suppose not." She left it at that.

"Well, then. My name is Lawrence. Not an assumed name, mind you. Lawrence Bartholomew Fischer. I fly Spitfires."

"Well, it's nice to meet you, Mr. Fischer. And I think you'll find the accommodations here quite suitable. I'll show you to the closet."

"The . . . closet?"

FISCHER WAS WITH RUBY FOR a day and a half, followed less than a week later by a bomber pilot named Harley Holt and then a gunner named Stephen Orlando. They ran together after that; one or two a week would show up at her door, and each time, she would welcome them, feed them, and sneak them into the hall closet, where they waited for Laure to pick them up.

There were a few close calls—neighbors who happened to see the men coming or going, the infrequent appearances of the concierge, Madame Lefèvre, in the hall downstairs—but Ruby knew from their pursed lips that they assumed she was entertaining various gentleman callers. Just as well.

Charlotte, however, was well aware of what was going on, and this concerned Ruby. She knew she could trust her young neighbor, but in the end, Charlotte was only a girl. What if she let something slip? Or what if Ruby was found out and someone believed that Charlotte and her family had been involved?

Still, Ruby couldn't turn her back on the men.

In her third month working with the escape line, she was surprised to welcome an Air Force pilot on loan to the RAF who'd been raised in Palmdale, just ten miles from her own hometown.

"Golly, miss, of course I know Lancaster!" he'd exclaimed when she told him where she was from. She knew she shouldn't be handing out details like that, and normally, she was much more discreet, but she couldn't help jumping at the opportunity to reminisce about Southern California with a stranger who had somehow found his way to her door on the other side of the world. "Your parents must be mighty worried about you. You hear from them often?"

She shook her head. "It's been months now."

"Damned war. Well, if you want, I can get a message to them on your behalf when I get home."

She hesitated. For a second, it sounded like a dream come true. But telling him her real name or who her parents were came with too many complications. She'd already said too much. "Just help the Allies win the war, will you?"

"Yes, miss." His expression was grave. "I will do my absolute best. It's why I'm so eager to get out of this damned city. No offense intended, of course."

"None taken. It does feel a bit like Paris is damned, doesn't it?"

He nodded and looked toward her window. "I imagine this must have been a pretty beautiful place before the war."

"It truly was."

"You think you'll move back to the States when this is all done?"

"I honestly don't know. I have trouble thinking beyond tomorrow."

"Strange how war changes things, isn't it? I was supposed to be taking over my father's tax business. Instead, I'm hiding out in a pretty stranger's apartment in Paris. Never thought I'd wind up here."

"Neither did I," Ruby said, and like the pilot, she wasn't just talking about Paris. She was talking about the way life had twisted, the way she no longer recognized the ground she was standing on. "But the war can't last forever, can it? Maybe it's not too late to find our way back to the lives we're supposed to have."

"Or maybe this is it." The pilot smiled sadly. "Maybe this is exactly who we were meant to be all along."

CHAPTER TWENTY-ONE

October 1941

After Thomas left Ruby's apartment, Laure led him to a train station in Paris, where there were three other British pilots waiting, each with his own guide. Thomas had been given strict orders not to acknowledge any of them—and certainly not to talk to them—but it was a comfort just to know they were there. He was no longer in this alone, which made him feel like he had a legitimate chance of survival.

They boarded a night train to Bordeaux, and though Laure was in his compartment, he was not to look at her or attempt to communicate in any way. The value of a night train was that he could feign sleep each time a train official or German officer walked by, and that was exactly what he did, cracking his eyes open slightly only after their footfalls had disappeared. In the morning, they switched to a train to Bayonne, and he caught glimpses of the other pilots boarding cars along with their guides too. So far, so good;

they were in southern France now, which seemed less perilous than Paris.

In Bayonne, their guides left them with terse good luck wishes and handed them off to another man, who gave them each a ticket and put them on a smaller train to the tiny town of Dax. This, Thomas understood, was to be another dangerous part of the journey; the new man wouldn't be accompanying them because of the risk of capture. They were to get off the train and try to appear inconspicuous as they waited to be picked up outside the station by another contact. "Rely on your false papers," the man said quietly in French, which Thomas quickly translated for the others. "Say nothing, even if questioned."

On the train, Thomas watched with growing trepidation as a German soldier boarded the first compartment and began asking passengers for their papers. One of the other three RAF pilots seemed younger than the rest—nineteen, maybe twenty—and he was the first one the Nazi soldier reached. Thomas sat paralyzed as the young pilot looked blankly at the soldier who was barking an order at him. *Give him your papers,* Thomas thought, wishing he could come to the boy's rescue without arousing suspicion. *Damn it, just do what the guides told you to!*

After a few long seconds, Thomas watched as the boy reached into his pocket with hands that were clearly shaking and handed over his identity papers. The Nazi soldier looked at them for a moment and asked in French what the purpose of his travel was. The boy continued to stare, and the soldier, his eyes blazing with suspicion, repeated the question more loudly. *Oh God,* Thomas thought. *He's about to be caught.*

But then an elderly woman sitting across the row from the pilot spoke up, explaining to the German soldier that the boy was her grandson, that they were going to visit a distant aunt, and that the boy was deaf. "How dare you ridicule him?" the woman asked. The Nazi soldier looked uncertain, but the woman moved next to the young pilot and put an arm around his shoulder. "There, there, my boy. He didn't mean any offense." The soldier narrowed his eyes, but after a moment, he grunted in disgust and moved on.

Thomas exhaled a huge sigh of relief, and although he dared not make eye contact with any of the other pilots, he did lock gazes with the elderly woman, who smiled slightly at him, nodded, and left to find a seat in another car. *Thank God for Good Samaritans.*

When the train arrived in Dax, the four pilots got off and tried to blend into the small crowd as they handed their tickets in and left the station. Outside, a pair of men were waiting for them.

"Welcome," the taller one greeted them in English. He sported a mustache and a faded cap. Thomas didn't think he sounded French, but he couldn't place his strong accent. "We're here to take the group of you to the mountains." He lifted his chin at the six bicycles leaning against the wall beside them.

There was no time to ask questions as they mounted up and pedaled out of the train yard into a quaint French village. Thomas could feel sweat beading on his brow as they passed a café with a few Germans at tables out front, but none of the soldiers gave them a second glance, and once they were around the corner, Thomas relaxed a little. They just might make it after all. There seemed to be far less of a German presence here than there had been in Paris, which boded well.

They cycled all day in silence. The man who'd spoken to them rode ahead, and the man with him, who had yet to say a word, brought up the rear. Just before nightfall, with the Pyrenees looming in front of them, they pulled off the main road into a village, where they made their way down winding lanes to a small, isolated bungalow at the edge of the forest. "You will spend the night here," the man in the faded cap said, looking at each of them in turn. "They are very nice hosts, very brave to shelter you. In the morning, we go."

"Go where?" asked the youngest pilot.

The man jerked his thumb toward the jagged mountains, which cast a shadow over the town. "South. To Spain."

That night, over a hot dinner of lamb and beans, the pilots spoke to each other for the first time. Their hosts were a middle-aged couple who retreated to their own bedroom after dinner, leaving the men alone after explaining in French that their location far from the town center was perfect for concealing guests; the handful of Nazi soldiers stationed nearby didn't make the effort to venture out this way.

Thomas learned that the youngest pilot was named Norman Wimbley, and that he was two months shy of turning twenty. He was cocky, but as he related his story of being shot down over southern Belgium and encountering a farmer who was part of an escape line, Thomas could hear the tremor in his voice. The others—Scott Pace and Walter Caldwell—were closer to his own age and had known each other in flight school; Scott had been shot down just outside Paris, and Walter had gone down on the French side of the German border. Like Norman, they had both been assisted by locals with connections to the escape line. Thomas found himself wondering just how extensive the network was. It was amazing to think of all the French and Belgian civilians who were risking their own lives to return men to war.

"Are we really supposed to climb over the mountains?" Norman asked, gesturing out the window into the darkness. "It sounds insane."

"We don't have a choice," Scott pointed out. "It's the only way out of France right now."

"But climbing a *mountain?*" Norman persisted. "Have any of you done that before?"

"No," Walter said. "But do you want to get back into the cockpit or not? If you're uncertain, you may as well stay behind."

"That's not what I'm saying," Norman grumbled. "Only that it'll be hard."

"Life is hard," Walter snapped.

"Look," Thomas said after a moment, "there's no doubt this will be difficult. And we can't let down our guard. But we're going to stick together and do what the guides tell us, and we'll make it through."

Scott and Walter nodded, and though Norman muttered something to himself, he eventually shrugged and said, "Fine."

The two men who'd picked them up at the station materialized again before dawn, waking the pilots after just a few hours of sleep. They introduced themselves as Florentino and Alesander and explained that they had been helping pilots over the mountains to Spain for the past few months. "Alesander speaks very little English and also little French," Florentino said. "We both grew up with the Basque language. If you have questions, you ask me."

"How do you propose we make it over the mountain when none

of us even has hiking boots?" Norman asked, earning him a hard look from Florentino.

"With courage," Florentino said, "and these." He held up a burlap bag and dumped the contents on the floor of the bungalow. Inside were several pairs of shoes with soles made from thick rope. "They will help you with the mountain terrain. Put them on quickly, then we go."

"Espadrilles?" Norman snorted. "Surely you're joking. They're for women."

Florentino glared. "We've been using these shoes for hundreds of years. The soles mold to you, they help your feet to have air, and they help with the steep inclines. You wear your own shoes if you'd prefer. Just don't expect me to help you when your feet bleed and you fall off a cliff."

Five minutes later, with the strange rope shoes tied on, the pilots were walking quickly toward the mountains with bags of bread and sausage over their shoulders. Each had also been given a goat-skin bag of wine, which was to be consumed sparingly during the crossing. "We go," Alesander grunted, the first words he'd said since meeting the pilots. He pointed to a narrow road that seemed carved out of the steep side of the mountain ahead. "Follow."

Thomas took a deep breath and fell into line. If this was the way home, he was determined to walk it.

THREE DAYS LATER, THE GROUP arrived on the other side of the Spanish border, freezing and exhausted, having waded across the icy

Bidassoa River separating France from Spain. Sometimes, Florentino said, he was able to take pilots over a bridge that spanned the water, but Alesander had gone ahead on this trip and had returned to report that the bridge was being heavily patrolled by Spanish police. Drenched below the waist and standing in an icy field, Thomas was sure he'd never been so cold in all his life.

They had to stick to the shadows for the remainder of their descent, but they made it undetected. In a small town below, Florentino and Alesander led them to a barn, where they spent the night shivering under thick blankets. They hiked the next day to another town, where they slept in a farmhouse and had a hot meal of potatoes and mutton, and then on their third day in Spain, Florentino and Alesander brought them to a road, where they were picked up by a black car and driven to the coastal town of San Sebastián. From there, a car with Union Jacks drove them to the British embassy in Madrid, where they were heartily welcomed by the vice-consul, given new clothing, and lodged for two days. Thomas slept and ate well, but now that his journey was almost over, he found himself thinking not of how close he was to England but how far he was from Paris.

Eventually, the pilots were driven to a port in Seville, where a Norwegian ship was waiting to take them to Gibraltar, on the southern coast of the Iberian Peninsula. There was an RAF base there, and Thomas and the others were given new uniforms before being sent on the final leg of their journey: a flight home to Britain. After a few days of questioning in London, Thomas was sent back to Northolt, where not even the sight of Harry was enough to pull him from the depression he'd slipped into.

"But you're home, my friend!" Harry said, pulling him into a bear hug. "Do you know the odds that were stacked against you?"

"I had to make it here," Thomas replied. "It's the only way to get back to Paris."

"Back to Paris?" Harry chuckled. "I'd have thought you'd want to stick to this side of the Channel for a while. After I was shot down, I was in no great hurry to return to France."

Thomas shook his head. "It's not France I'm eager to return to." He left it at that, because he'd received very strict instructions that he was never to talk about any piece of the escape line. It was the one condition under which he'd been allowed to resume fighting over French territory, although he knew many returned pilots were now being redeployed to Africa.

That vow of silence included Ruby, he knew. And so he tucked his memories of her away and vowed never to speak of the time he'd spent in her apartment. What would Harry or the others say, anyhow?

But it had been real. He was sure of it. And as he was cleared to return to the skies and he began once again escorting bombers into France, he vowed that no matter what, he'd see her again.

CHAPTER TWENTY-TWO

May 1942

Charlotte was very proud of Ruby, but it wasn't as if she could say that. Thirteen-year-olds didn't go around telling adults that they were proud of them; it sounded condescending.

Though Maman and Papa had some idea of what had happened in Ruby's apartment—how could they not after Maman's fall?—they didn't know that the situation was ongoing. Charlotte spent far too much time watching through the peephole as strange men arrived at night and left a day or two later, but she made a habit of distracting her parents if they ever appeared ready to go out into the hall when it was occupied by Ruby's visitors. It wasn't that Charlotte thought she couldn't trust her parents; it was that she didn't want one more thing weighing on them. They were already drowning in their worries.

Papa seemed to grow more frantic by the day, racing out to secret meetings with other men from their synagogue. Charlotte couldn't decide whether he was taking the Nazi threat seriously or burying his head in the sand. He continuously swore to her that mass deportations couldn't possibly happen here. Not to them. "Even in the east, the word is that they're taking away only the riffraff, not the productive members of society. I'm still working, Charlotte. We're contributing. Everything will be okay."

But she didn't believe him. And what was more, she knew Maman didn't either. Once strong and solid, Maman had become somebody different since the war started, and that was even more troubling to Charlotte than her father's increased anxiety. While Papa seemed constantly wound up, her mother was wasting away. She was always sick with worry and malnutrition, and whenever Charlotte tried to comfort her, Maman's eyes would fog over. "It'll all be okay, dear," Maman repeated over and over, a broken record.

They were treating Charlotte like a child, and she was tired of it. Couldn't they see that she was just as concerned as they were? That their soothing words felt flimsy? If only she could do something brave to help out in the war effort, the way Ruby was. Then her parents would have to take her seriously. Instead, she was mostly confined to the apartment, a prisoner to her parents' fears that she could be picked up off the street and taken away without them knowing. Maman had given up on Charlotte's lessons too. Her only links to the outside world were occasional trips out with Papa, the books in their apartment, and her weekly English lesson with Ruby.

And then, in the final days of May 1942, everything became worse. The order came down that all Jews in France were obligated to wear a yellow star on the left side of their coats. They had just a few days to pick up the cotton insignias from their local police stations, and by the second week of June, there would be stiff penalties for those caught on the streets without them.

Papa retrieved the stars for the family, and Maman dutifully sewed them onto the coats and sweaters they wore most frequently. "It's just a Star of David," Papa said, his tone strangely flat. "Nothing to be ashamed of. After all, we're proud to be Jewish."

"But people will laugh at us," Charlotte said softly, slipping into her own coat with the hateful yellow blemish.

"Those who treat us poorly because of the star are the same ones who have hated us all along." Papa didn't meet her gaze. "Just hold your head high." But Charlotte could see the pain in Papa's face, and she knew that the new law was wounding him as much as it was wounding her.

The first time she wore the star during a walk with Papa, a bearded man spat on her, his saliva landing on her right cheek. She blinked back tears and refrained from reacting until she'd turned the corner, out of his sight. A group of teenage boys yelled from a doorstep, calling her a dirty Jew, and a German soldier sneered at her with a look of such disgust that she had to stop herself from physically recoiling. By the time she and Papa made it back inside their own building, she was shaking.

"It's not fair," she murmured, trying to stop crying. Papa embraced her quickly and went into the apartment ahead of her, his face dark with worry, telling her to take all the time she needed to settle herself, but that she mustn't upset Maman.

She was still trying to calm down when Ruby's door opened. "Charlotte?" Ruby asked, stepping into the hall. "What is it?"

"It's the star," Charlotte managed, and despite her best intentions, she began to sob harder.

Ruby pulled Charlotte into her arms. "What's happened?"

"I don't understand why people hate us so much."

"Why don't you come in for a little while? Let's talk about this."

"But you're busy." Charlotte pulled away. "I don't want to interrupt if you have a . . . guest."

Ruby smiled. "The place is all ours today, Charlotte. Please. Join me."

Charlotte followed Ruby in, marveling at how different the apartment felt to her now, although it looked virtually the same as it always had. Most weeks, Ruby came to Charlotte's apartment for her English lesson, so Charlotte hadn't been here in a while. And while the décor had changed only minimally after Marcel's death, there was something about knowing that it was a haven for heroes that transformed everything.

Ruby fetched them each a small cup of ersatz coffee, and Charlotte felt very adult as she stirred a lump of sugar into hers and took a sip.

"So tell me," Ruby said, sitting on the couch beside her. "Are you different today than you were yesterday?"

Charlotte paused with her cup halfway to her mouth. "Well . . . no."

"Well then, the only thing that has changed is what you're wearing. Am I correct?"

Charlotte glanced down at the yellow star. "Yes. But—"

"But nothing," Ruby interrupted firmly. "You should be proud of who you are, what you are. You don't think I stick out here every day because of my terrible French accent? I know people are mocking me."

Charlotte allowed herself a tiny smile. Ruby's accent *was* pretty awful, though her vocabulary was nearly perfect. "Yes," she said after a long pause, "but no one spits at you in the streets for being American."

Ruby put an arm around her and squeezed hard. "Charlotte, you know as well as I do that it's what's inside a person that counts. And sometimes, you have to walk through fire in order to find your true self. Maybe this is your fire."

"What do you mean?"

"I mean that sometimes, we only discover our calling in life when things are darkest." Ruby grasped Charlotte's shoulders and looked into her eyes. "Use this experience to make you stronger."

Charlotte stared at her lap for a long time as she thought about what Ruby was saying. She knew the advice was sound, but taking it was easier said than done. Finally, she looked up. "I think it's bothering my father very much too."

Ruby's expression softened. "That's very good of you to worry about him, Charlotte. But your papa's a very religious man, isn't he?"

"Yes."

"Then trust that he will find solace in that. That's one thing faith is especially good for: giving us strength in times of crisis."

"How do you know?" Charlotte didn't mean to sound rude. "You're not Jewish."

"No, I'm Catholic. And in the end, Catholicism isn't really so different. Believing in God is at the core of our faith, just like yours, and as things have gotten more difficult for me, Charlotte, I've learned to pray harder. It's brought me comfort."

"How? Prayers are just words."

"But they're words that remind us that there's something out there greater than ourselves. And they're words that lead us to be the best versions of ourselves."

Charlotte looked at Ruby for a long time before nodding. "Okay."

Ruby pulled the girl into a hug. "Things are always darkest before the dawn, my friend."

"I know." But what Charlotte didn't say was that sometimes, the dawn never came at all.

CHAPTER TWENTY-THREE

July 1942

The pilot who came to Ruby's door in mid-July, a twenty-three-year-old American from Boston named Samuel Sullivan, arrived after the curfew, which Ruby knew was dangerous. The French police had been cracking down on violators, and if Samuel had been picked up near her apartment, he might very well have given her away. Ruby welcomed him anyhow and made a mental note to speak with Aubert about it later. They'd taken to meeting every two weeks in the back of an abandoned dance studio on the rue d'Estrées, and sometimes, Laure would join them. Ruby had never asked her about the journey south with Thomas because she knew the rules; they weren't to speak of the pilots after they'd departed. Ever. But she was still envious of the time the beautiful raven-haired guide had spent with the kind, charming pilot. Ruby had assumed at the beginning that she would forget about him as the months went on, but he was still the first thing on her mind each day when she awoke.

"Something's going on out there tonight, you know," Samuel said after Ruby had given him some bread, cheese, water, and fresh clothes.

"What do you mean?"

He shook his head. "I'm not sure, honestly. But there's a lot of police activity on the streets. You don't think they're gearing up for a raid, do you?"

Ruby felt a ripple of fear. "Where were they? Only in this neighborhood?"

"No, miss. It's what took me so long. There were police out all across Paris tonight."

"German?"

"French, I think."

"Hmm." What Samuel was describing sounded unusual. After all, the French police rarely did things on their own; they were the Germans' puppets. If they were out in force, there was no question that the Germans were behind it. But was Samuel exaggerating? Ruby didn't know him at all, so it was impossible to tell. "I'm sure things are fine," she said after a long pause. "None of them spotted you, did they?"

"No. I was very careful."

"Good. Now, let's get you settled for the night, shall we? I'll come get you in the morning once the building is quiet, and we can talk about the next step."

"It's very kind of you to help me."

"It's not kindness. It's my duty." It had become her line lately, and she meant it. She really wasn't doing anything extraordinary. In fact, if anything, she feared her role on the line was selfish, for it filled her days so she didn't have time to worry about whether Thomas was still alive. Nor did she have time to wonder why she cared so much.

She stepped outside her front door, listening to the silence of the building. When she was sure the coast was clear, she hurried Samuel into the hall closet, which she had filled with freshly laundered blankets just that afternoon. He'd be comfortable there for the night.

After she'd gotten him settled, she went down the stairs and opened the door to the outside, but all was quiet. She could hear trucks clattering by in the distance, but on the rue Amélie, things were peaceful. A quick look to both ends of the shadow-cloaked street confirmed only the usual traffic.

Still, Ruby went to bed just past midnight feeling unsettled. She tossed and turned for a long while before sleep came, and she had just drifted off when a rumbling sound jolted her awake. She grabbed her watch from the nightstand as she flicked on a light. It was 4:25 in the morning, and something was going on outside.

She crept into the hall outside her apartment and peered out the building's large front window, which was visible from the landing. The street was filled with two police lorries and a small transport bus already teeming with people. Four French policemen were entering the building just across the way, illuminated by the headlights of the lorries, and soon, two others emerged from the building next door, escorting a family of four, all of whom wore yellow stars on their overcoats. The mother and father looked sleep-tousled and worried; the children, two girls who couldn't have been more than three and five, were crying.

A moment later, the first policemen she'd seen emerged from the building across the way with a sobbing mother and three young children. One of the policemen was screaming something at the woman, and she was shaking her head vigorously. This family, too, had yellow stars on their overcoats, which they were wearing on top of their pajamas. Ruby stifled a gasp as the policeman slapped the woman hard across her face, snapping her neck back. She quieted down after that, her cries now muffled sobs. She and her children were quickly shepherded onto the waiting bus, their suitcases shoved into the police lorry.

Ruby had seen enough.

She turned and ran to the Dachers' apartment, where she pounded hard on the door. "Wake up, Monsieur Dacher! Madame Dacher! Charlotte! It's an emergency!" The seconds ticked by, and Ruby knocked more insistently, knowing that she was probably waking half the building in the process. She prayed that people would stay in their apartments and the hidden pilot would have the good sense to remain quiet. Finally, Monsieur Dacher came to the door clutching a poker. His expression softened when he saw that it was Ruby.

"Madame Benoit," he said, "what is it?"

"The police are rounding up Jews," she said quickly. "They're just outside. You must get out."

She expected him to alert his wife, to grab the family's things quickly, to flee; but instead, he shook his head. "No, no, that's impossible, Madame Benoit."

"Monsieur Dacher, I just watched two families, including children, dragged from their homes and loaded onto buses."

"They must be foreigners," Monsieur Dacher said, although his face had paled. "Not good French citizens like my wife and me."

"I have no idea, but is that a chance you want to take? Besides, you were born elsewhere, weren't you?"

He looked surprised. "Yes, but—"

He was interrupted by Madame Dacher appearing in the hall behind him, her face white. She looked younger without her makeup, more vulnerable than Ruby had ever seen her. "Reuven, do you really believe that they will leave us alone simply because you used to run a successful business?" She glanced at Ruby, her eyes wide and mournful, before looking back at her husband. "Madame Benoit is right. We are better safe than sorry."

"But, Sarah, surely you don't think—"

"Reuven!" Madame Dacher cut him off. "Now is not the time for your pride to get in the way."

"But they're rounding up stateless Jews, Sarah. They must be."

"You don't think they consider us that? The Nazis don't care about your contributions to the French economy. They want to see us all removed."

There was a moment of tense silence. "No," Monsieur Dacher finally said, his tone resolute. "I won't be driven from my home."

"But—" Madame Dacher began.

"No," he said firmly.

"Papa?" Charlotte said, emerging from behind her mother. She was wearing a pink nightgown, and her hair was plaited. She looked scared. "I think it's true what Ruby is saying. I told you the butcher had heard rumors, and I—"

"And I told you that rumors are hardly ever true. You can't believe everything you hear, my dear. We'll be fine. If the police come here, we'll simply explain that—"

"Stop, Reuven!" Madame Dacher said sharply, stepping forward. "I'm not willing to take this risk with Charlotte." She turned to Ruby. "Will you take her? Protect our baby? If nothing happens tonight, she will come back in the morning."

"But, Maman!"

Madame Dacher grasped Ruby's hand, her eyes full of tears. "Please, Madame Benoit. I know you are brave and strong. And I know you care for Charlotte. Can you keep her if the Germans come for us? Just until we are able to get back safely."

"Of course."

"No, Maman!" Charlotte tried again. "If they come, I will go with you."

"No, darling, you won't." Madame Dacher took her daughter's hands. "Now there isn't much time, and you mustn't argue. You must be strong, Charlotte. And you must be brave. Don't be afraid to be who you are. Promise you'll never forget us."

"But, Maman!" Charlotte was sobbing now, but Madame Dacher kissed her on the forehead and backed away.

"You must go, before it's too late." Madame Dacher looked at Ruby with tears coursing down her cheeks and mouthed *Thank you* before turning back to Monsieur Dacher. "Say good-bye to Charlotte, Reuven."

He knelt before his daughter. "Your mother is overreacting, dear. If the police come for us, it's just a misunderstanding that we'll have cleared up soon. But in the meantime, be good for Madame Benoit."

"We must go." Ruby felt as if her heart were shattering as she took Charlotte's hand and pulled the girl away. "Before the police arrive." She paused at the doorway and turned back to Monsieur Dacher once more. "You are sure you don't want to try to get away while there's still time? I could hide you too."

He met her gaze and smiled. "This is France, Madame Benoit. We are French citizens. I feel very certain we will see you in the morning."

Ruby knew that there wasn't enough time to change Monsieur Dacher's mind, so she nodded at him, locked eyes with Madame Dacher for a few awful seconds, and led a sobbing Charlotte down the hall and into her own apartment.

"You must climb into the wardrobe, sweetheart," she said quickly, as soon as she had shut and locked the door behind her.

"No!" Charlotte said, beginning to cry harder. "Maybe I can convince my parents to leave."

"There's no time, honey."

"But what if they're taken away?"

"Then we hope and pray that your father is right," Ruby said, wiping away Charlotte's tears.

"But you don't believe he is, do you?"

Ruby didn't know how to reply. Being honest with Charlotte would only make the girl feel worse, but she didn't want to lie to her either. She settled for saying gently, "Perhaps the police won't come for your parents at all. But just to be on the safe side, Charlotte, let's get you hidden. You mustn't make a sound, no matter what. Understand?" Ruby pulled the girl into a tight hug and then took her hand and led her quickly into the bedroom, where she arranged some blankets on the floor of the wardrobe in which she'd once hidden Thomas.

"I'll come get you as soon as I'm sure the police are gone," she promised.

Charlotte nodded, and Ruby quickly closed the wardrobe. No sooner had she done so than she heard noises in the hall. She made her way to her door as quietly as possible and peered out the peephole, terrified for both her hidden pilot and Charlotte's parents.

The police were here, just as Ruby had feared.

There were four of them—the same four who had dragged the woman and her children from the building across the way—and they made a beeline for the Dachers' door, knocking loudly. After a moment, Monsieur Dacher answered, already dressed in crisp gray slacks, a button-down shirt, and suspenders. He looked like he was headed out for a business meeting. "We are here for Reuven Dacher and his family," one of the policemen, the one who had slapped the crying woman across the street, said.

"I am Reuven Dacher." His voice was shaky but strong. "But there is some mistake. I am a French citizen, a war veteran. I am a furrier. I have many ties to the community, and I—"

"You will come with us. I'm sure if there is a mistake, it will be sorted out in the morning." The police officer consulted the papers in his hands. "Your wife, Sarah, and your daughter, Charlotte, must also come."

Ruby could feel herself shudder. This was no ordinary arrest if they had children on their list. She could see the same realization cross Monsieur Dacher's face.

"My wife, I will get her." His voice was trembling now. "But Charlotte—our daughter—is with friends in Aubergenville."

The policeman smirked at him. "You expect us to believe that?"

"You can come in and search all you like, but she is not here." Monsieur Dacher cleared his throat and added, "Besides, she was born here in France. She is as French as anyone else in this building."

"And yet you and your wife are not. You were born in"—the policeman consulted his list again—"Poland."

"I've lived here nearly all my life, as has my wife."

The policeman laughed. "And you think that makes you French like us?" He didn't wait for an answer before shoving past Monsieur Dacher. "We will find where your daughter is hiding."

Monsieur Dacher stood rigid in the doorway as two other officers followed the first into the apartment. The fourth policeman stayed outside, looking uncomfortable. Ruby watched him as he glanced between Monsieur Dacher's white face and the floor several times. She prayed the pilot, who was hidden just a few feet away, wouldn't make a sound. She had the feeling that this particular officer was distressed to be a part of these roundups, but that didn't mean he wouldn't do his job if it came down to it.

After a moment, Monsieur Dacher turned and went into the apartment, and Ruby could hear him saying something. He emerged a few minutes later, clutching Madame Dacher's hand. Each of them held a suitcase as the four policemen escorted them out of the building. Neither of the Dachers looked back, and Ruby knew it must have been tearing Madame Dacher apart to leave Charlotte behind. Ruby wished she had said more to reassure the Dachers that she would protect their daughter with her life, but there simply hadn't been time.

Ruby waited until the policemen were long gone before she slipped into the hall outside the apartment. She said a silent prayer of thanks that the pilot hadn't been discovered, and then she moved to the front windows of the building and looked out. The street outside was deserted again. If she hadn't witnessed it herself, she never would have known anything had happened here at all.

She took a deep breath. She had to get ahold of herself before going back inside and facing Charlotte. She'd do that before tending to the pilot, because the girl was probably beside herself by now.

A few minutes later, she opened the door to the wardrobe to find Charlotte staring at her. "What happened?" the girl asked, her voice flat.

"The police took them away." Ruby was trying to sound as unconcerned as possible, although her insides were screaming.

"Well, we have to go after them."

"Honey, we can't. They had you on their list too. There's no way I'd risk anything happening to you. Your parents told them you were in Aubergenville, and they must have believed it."

"But . . . we have to do something."

"I'm certain things will be sorted out in a few days," Ruby said, trying to project a confidence she didn't feel. "Surely there's been a mistake. In the meantime, let's get you out of this wardrobe, shall we?"

Charlotte's hand was ice-cold as she slipped it into Ruby's. Ruby could feel the girl shaking as she led her to the sofa in the living room.

"Papa is so sure that being French will save him," Charlotte said softly once she sat down.

"Yes."

"But there is no French anymore, Ruby. There are just Jews, those who hate us, and people who are too scared for their own lives to fight back."

"But there are also people like you and me, Charlotte, people who are doing what they can to help. We'll win in the end."

"It will be too late for my parents by then."

"No," Ruby said firmly. "When morning comes, I'll see what I can find out, all right? I don't know what these raids were about, but your parents must have been included by mistake. I'll fix this."

Charlotte shook her head. "But what if you can't, Ruby? What if you can't?"

CHAPTER TWENTY-FOUR

July 1942

It took Ruby more than an hour to get Charlotte settled down, but finally the girl fell asleep on the couch. Just before dawn, Ruby slipped into the hallway and rapped lightly on the door to the hidden closet. "It's Fleur," she whispered. "You can come out." She slid the panel back to find Samuel crouched in the crawl space, clutching a knife.

"What in God's name was that?" he demanded. "Those voices in the hall . . . I was right, wasn't I? Something terrible has happened."

Ruby put a hand on his arm. "It was a raid," she said calmly. "To take Jews away." And then, somehow, she was crying, and she couldn't stop. The pilot quietly climbed out and wrapped his arms around her.

"It's okay," he murmured. "It's all going to be okay."

His words of comfort just made her cry harder, because he didn't really understand. He only knew the war from the sky.

"We need to get into my apartment before someone sees you," Ruby said, drying her tears and suddenly realizing how stupid it was to be embracing a fugitive in plain sight. She suspected that the building's residents were still battened down for the night, but she couldn't take that chance. "We need to be quiet, because Charlotte is finally asleep," she added in a whisper as she opened her front door.

"Charlotte?"

"The daughter of the couple next door who were taken away."

"Dear God," Samuel murmured, glancing at the girl asleep on the couch as Ruby ushered him inside, shut the door quietly, and locked it behind them.

Ruby gestured for him to follow her to the bedroom, and once they were inside, she left the door ajar and sat down on the edge of the bed, indicating that he should join her.

"What happened?" Samuel asked. "To the girl's parents?"

Ruby recounted the events of the past several hours, explaining that Madame Dacher had asked her to keep Charlotte safe. "Charlotte's father is convinced that they'll be returning soon. But I fear he's wrong."

"But what could the police possibly be doing with the Jews?"

Ruby shook her head. "I only know the rumors of what's happening in eastern Europe. They're putting Jews in camps. There are rumors that they're putting some to death."

"Jesus Christ." Samuel crossed himself and looked heavenward. "So what are you going to do about the girl?"

Ruby was silent for a moment. She'd been thinking about it all night. "I don't think she's safe here. What if the police come for her again?"

Samuel nodded slowly. "What if I take her with me? To the Pyrenees? I could help her get out of the country."

Ruby could feel her eyes filling with tears. "Samuel, that's a very kind offer. But that's not what the line is designed for, and I'm afraid it would put all of you, especially Charlotte, in danger. It's perilous enough for grown men. She's just a girl."

"I'm not just a girl." Charlotte's voice from the doorway interrupted them, startling Ruby.

"Charlotte." Ruby jumped up from the bed. "I thought you were asleep."

Charlotte glanced at Samuel and then back at Ruby. "I'm not just a girl," she repeated. "I want to do something. And I'm not leaving France."

Ruby could feel her chest tightening. "How much of that did you hear?"

"Enough."

Ruby prayed she hadn't heard her repeat the rumors of putting Jews to death. Besides, there was no reason to think that would happen to Charlotte's parents. Surely the French police wouldn't be complicit in doing that to their own people. "Charlotte, we need to do everything we can to keep you safe."

Charlotte shook her head. "This is my country too. I want to help. I want to do *something*, just like you are. Saving these pilots has given you a life back. It's made you feel that you're making a difference. I want to make a difference too. I want to make sure Maman and Papa come home safely."

"And they will." Ruby regretted the words as soon as she'd said them because it wasn't a promise she could keep. It was all out of her hands. "But, Charlotte, I won't put you in harm's way. You're a child."

Charlotte stared at her, and in the silence, Ruby heard the words the girl hadn't spoken. She wasn't a child anymore. She hadn't been for a long time; the war had changed them all. "I need to know what's happened to them," Charlotte said at last.

"I will see what I can find out. But for now, you must get some rest. All of us must. If we're going to fight, we need to keep our strength." Ruby glanced at Samuel. "You can return to the closet in the hall if you'd like, but I don't think the police are coming back tonight. Why don't you take the couch? You can hide in the wardrobe if anyone comes. And, Charlotte, why don't you sleep here with me?" Ruby gestured to the other side of her bed. "We'll figure everything out in a few hours."

JUST PAST TEN IN THE morning, Ruby left the apartment to find Aubert, who would surely know what was going on. Samuel had promised he'd stay to protect Charlotte. "I'll be fine alone," Charlotte had protested, but he'd been unwavering.

"This is what the war is about," he'd said solemnly in English. Charlotte's eyes had filled with tears as Ruby translated the words for her. "I'm here to fight for you and your parents. I'll keep you safe. I swear it on my life."

The streets were eerily quiet, save for the police lorries and buses that rumbled by every few minutes. Ruby felt sick as she looked at the faces of the people staring out from the bus windows; there were at least as many women and children as there were men, and they all looked terrified. It seemed that the roundups were continuing and that most people had stayed inside their apartments to avoid it all. Ruby felt conspicuous as she hurried along, head down, toward the dance studio.

"You shouldn't have come." Aubert's face was drawn and pale as he answered the studio door after five minutes of Ruby's insistent pounding. "If you'd been followed . . ."

"I wasn't followed. They're too busy arresting innocent Jews to pay attention to me."

"Quickly, come inside." Aubert put a hand on her arm and led her into the back room. She was surprised to find Laure already standing there.

"Hello, Fleur," Laure said, kissing Ruby on both cheeks. Ruby reciprocated stiffly.

"Laure here was just telling me what she's been able to find out about the roundups," Aubert said, taking a seat and gesturing for Ruby to sit down too.

Laure nodded, and Ruby realized the other woman looked rattled. She'd never seen Laure in anything less than total control. "The roundups aren't over," Laure said solemnly. "They're continuing through many parts of the city, although thank God, many people have gotten word now and have gone into hiding. So there will be at least a few saved."

"Saved from what?" Ruby asked, afraid to know the answer.

"Word is they're being sent out of the country from Drancy."

"Drancy?" Ruby knew the place only as a suburb of Paris.

"It's the location of a new internment camp," Aubert explained.

"The French police control it, and people are shipped east by rail from there."

"To Germany. And Poland. To work camps." Laure glanced at Aubert. "And death camps."

"No." Ruby's reply was instant. "The French police wouldn't do that. They couldn't."

Laure sighed. "Don't be naïve. It's happening. You saw it with your own eyes last night, didn't you? That's why you're here?"

"Yes. But they're taking children. They couldn't possibly be sending them east to work." Ruby felt nauseated as she heard the truth in her own words. They were being sent east to die.

Laure and Aubert exchanged looks, but neither of them said anything for a long while. "It's why the things we're doing are so important." It was Aubert who finally broke the silence. "We have to put a stop to this, and helping the Allies is the best way we know how."

"My neighbors were taken," Ruby said softly. "The Dachers."

"Foreign-born Jews?" Laure asked.

Ruby nodded. "The parents are from Poland, but they've been French for years. The husband fought in the Great War, for goodness' sake."

"That might help them," Laure said. "I understand they're not deporting veterans for now."

"I'm sorry," Aubert interrupted. "Did you say your neighbors were taken?"

Ruby nodded. "They live just next door."

"So the French police have been in your building? But you have a pilot staying with you at the moment, don't you?"

"Yes. But he remained well hidden. I think we're all right."

Aubert rubbed his temples. "It's impossible to know for sure."

The three of them were silent for a moment.

"I took their daughter in," Ruby blurted out.

Aubert and Laure both snapped their heads up to stare at her. "You . . . what?" Aubert asked.

"The Dachers' daughter. Charlotte. I've been tutoring her in English. She's thirteen; she has become like a sister to me. When her parents heard that the police were on their way, they asked me to take her."

Aubert gaped at her. "What have you done? You could be jeopardizing the line!"

"No, I don't think they'll come back for her."

"You can't know that!" Aubert's face was turning red. "You've put us all at risk."

"No, she did what was right," Laure cut in, surprising Ruby. "That's what our mission is—protecting innocent people from falling into the hands of the Germans. Who is more innocent than a child? Now we must decide how to proceed."

"Is there any way to find out where Charlotte's parents have gone?" Ruby ventured. "Maybe we can get them out."

"They're almost certainly in the Vel' d'Hiv right now," Laure said.

"The cycling stadium?" Ruby asked. "In the fifteenth?"

Aubert cleared his throat. "It has apparently been rented by the French police as a sort of holding site."

"But for how many people?" Ruby asked. "It's not that large." She'd been there only once for a boxing match with Marcel, just after they'd moved to Paris. She'd found it stuffy and outdated.

"There are rumors," Laure said slowly, "that the French police have a list of nearly thirty thousand Jews."

"Thirty *thousand?*"

"Not that we believe they've rounded up nearly that many," Laure hurried to say. "But even if the number is half that, it's quite a lot of people."

"They can't possibly keep them all in the stadium," Ruby protested. "They'd have to stand on top of each other."

"And you think that would bother the Germans?" Aubert asked.

"I'll go later today and see what I can find out," Laure said, her tone soothing. "I will ask around about Charlotte's parents too. The Dachers, you say?"

"Yes. Reuven and Sarah. This won't put them in more danger?"

"I'll be very discreet. I promise."

"Thank you." Ruby turned to Aubert. "Perhaps I should stop taking pilots for now. I mustn't do anything to put Charlotte in danger."

"No." His reply was instant. "Please, you're too important to the line."

"I thought I was useless. Isn't that what you said? That you didn't need me?" Ruby could see Laure hiding a smile, and she had the feeling it was an expression of solidarity. Perhaps Aubert had behaved the same way toward her at first.

"Yes, well, I was mistaken," he said crisply. "Please, you must continue to help."

"But I also must keep Charlotte safe," Ruby said. "That has to be my priority now. I could help save a thousand pilots, but if I let the Germans come take a little girl I've promised to protect, I could never forgive myself."

Aubert stared at her for a moment. "If her parents aren't returned in the next few days, we'll forge some identity papers for her. It will help."

"How?"

"We forge them for the pilots all the time. We'll invent a cousin of Marcel's in Brittany. This girl will be their daughter. You can tell people her parents have died, and you have adopted her."

"Will that actually work?"

"It's a plausible story. As long as she's bright enough to play along."

"She's one of the smartest people I've ever met."

"If her parents haven't returned by Sunday, I'll send someone with papers to your apartment." Aubert paused. "In the meantime, you'll need to keep your current pilot for a few days more, until life returns to normal in Paris."

"Normal?" Ruby asked. "I don't think any of us knows what that is anymore."

BY THE TIME RUBY HAD stood in line for rations and made her way home in the early evening, the streets were quiet again. It appeared that the roundups were over, but had the police managed to arrest most of the Jews they were after, or was this merely the quiet eye of the storm? Was Charlotte still in danger? And what would happen to the girl's parents? Ruby could still see Madame Dacher's woeful, frightened expression as she said good-bye to her daughter. It was as if she knew it would be the last time.

I must stop being a pessimist, Ruby reminded herself as she walked down the rue Amélie. *Surely the Dachers will be back soon.* But she'd been thinking all day about Laure's reports of the Vel' d'Hiv. Ten, twenty, thirty thousand people packed into the tiny stadium; it was horrific. And a government that would preside over that kind of inhumanity wasn't the type that would make exceptions for people who didn't really belong there. *None* of them belonged there, but that didn't seem to be stopping anyone.

Ruby turned the key to her apartment door and entered quietly. She almost screamed when a large figure emerged from the shadows and rushed toward her.

"Oh, it's just you," Samuel said in his deep, Boston-accented voice as Ruby recoiled, clutching her chest.

"Samuel! You scared the daylights out of me!" As Ruby's eyes adjusted to the darkness, she could see that he was holding the same knife he'd been clutching in the hall closet the night before.

"I swore I would protect the girl," he said weakly. "She's in the bedroom. She's been crying a lot today. I couldn't comfort her without knowing any French. I'm sorry."

"I'm sure it helped just to know you were here."

"Did you find out anything about her parents?"

She shook her head and lowered her voice. "Nothing. But the news in general isn't good."

"I was afraid of that." He jerked his head toward the bedroom. "Why don't you go talk to her? I'll listen for anything suspicious in the hall. When you're done, I'll head back to the closet."

Ruby nodded. "Thank you."

"No, thank *you*. If I'd been on the streets last night, I surely would have been rounded up too."

Tomorrow, Ruby would do more to find out what she could about Charlotte's parents. But for now, all she could do was try to bring a bit of comfort to a girl who was far too wise to be soothed by empty promises of a future Ruby couldn't guarantee.

CHAPTER TWENTY-FIVE

July 1942

By Sunday, Charlotte knew her parents wouldn't be coming home anytime soon.

"They've already been sent to Drancy," Ruby told her gently that morning. "Laure has spoken with a few people who saw them just yesterday. They're in decent spirits, sweetheart."

Charlotte nodded, trying hard not to cry. She wanted Ruby to confide things like this in her; and she was afraid that if she broke down, Ruby would revert to treating her like a child. "Where will they go from Drancy?"

Ruby hesitated. "There's still a chance they'll be released. But I don't want to get your hopes up. Realistically, they may be headed east, to a work camp."

"A work camp," Charlotte repeated flatly.

"Your parents are both healthy. It will be difficult for them, but there's every reason to expect that they'll be fine."

But nothing was fine anymore, and Charlotte was certain Ruby knew that as well as she did. The world had changed overnight.

When Ruby had explained the idea of drawing up false papers to identify her as Ruby's adopted daughter, Charlotte had begun to cry. Ruby had pulled the girl into her arms, explaining over and over again that it was only a ruse, that it was just to protect her until her parents came home, which would surely be soon. But Ruby had taken it wrong—that wasn't what Charlotte was crying about. She was sobbing because she knew it was a dire measure, one that Ruby wouldn't take unless she truly believed Charlotte was here to stay. And there was a part of her that was crying because she knew how lucky she was to have found a home—even under such strange and terrible circumstances—with the bravest woman she'd ever known.

"I won't be replacing your parents," Ruby had said firmly as she embraced Charlotte. "Not at all. I would never try to do that. But from now on, Charlotte, I hope you know I'm your family too."

"But won't I be putting you at risk by staying?"

"No." Ruby's answer had been firm.

"What about the escape line? Can I help you with it now?"

"Absolutely not. I don't want you involved."

"But—"

"No, Charlotte. It's too dangerous."

Samuel had departed a day earlier, leaving just past dawn with Laure. And Ruby had left at noon for a meeting with some of the others on the escape line, leaving Charlotte at home by herself for the first time since the roundups.

She was walking around the apartment in a daze, trying to imagine how this place could ever feel like home, when there was a knock at the door. She froze. What if it was the police? Then again, perhaps it was a pilot seeking refuge. Maybe she could prove to Ruby that she was capable of helping after all. She tiptoed across the room and peered through the peephole.

She saw a boy around her age, maybe a year or two older, standing in the hall. He had black hair and wore ragged clothes, and despite the fact that his face looked young, he had the broad shoulders of a man a decade older.

Charlotte took a step back, unsure of what to do. He didn't look like he could be working with the police, but he wasn't a pilot either; he appeared too young—and too comfortable in his grimy outfit. She was about to turn away when he knocked again.

"I can hear you in there, you know," he said through the door. His accent was most definitely French, and his voice was deeper than she'd expected. "I mean you no harm. I have a delivery for Fleur."

Ruby's code name. Charlotte knew that much from the eavesdropping she'd shamelessly done on her neighbor over the last several months. So was this boy a part of the escape line?

"Please just let me deliver my package, and I'll be on my way," he said when she hadn't moved.

Charlotte still wasn't certain that it was the right thing to do, but she suddenly had a desperate urge to be face-to-face with this stranger. She took a deep breath and opened the door.

For a moment, they just stared at each other. She could see the questions in his green eyes. He was wondering who she was and what she was doing here. But was he searching for something else in her face too? She found that once she had locked gazes with him, she couldn't look away; he had the kind of eyes that looked too bright for his face—for any face, in fact.

"Good day," he said, breaking the silence. "I'm looking for Madame Fleur."

"She's not here. But she's my cousin." Charlotte could scarcely believe she'd just said that. It was part of her new cover, of course, but it felt like a betrayal of Maman and Papa. "I can take a message, if you like."

The boy studied her, one corner of his mouth curling up slightly. "I see. Well, then, please tell *your cousin* that I've delivered your papers. Forged them myself." He held up an envelope.

Charlotte's cheeks grew hot. He knew she'd just lied to him. "*You* forged them?" she asked.

He shrugged. "It was nothing."

"But how old are you?" Charlotte realized right away that it hadn't been a polite question.

"Fifteen."

"Oh." She felt silly for asking and didn't know what to say next.

"I learned to forge from my dad," he said finally. "But he's dead now, so I had to take over. I'm pretty good. Take a look."

Charlotte took the envelope from him and slipped the papers out. She didn't know what birth certificates and adoption papers were supposed to look like, but these appeared very official, with stamps and seals and everything. "Nice work," she said, trying to sound like she knew what she was talking about.

His smile widened a bit. "Thank you."

"Maybe—maybe I could help too."

He looked confused. "You want to forge papers?"

"No. I mean, maybe, though I don't know that I'd be any good at it. But I want to do something. I'm tired of just watching things get worse and worse and not doing anything." If Ruby wouldn't let her help, maybe this mysterious boy would.

He studied her for a minute. "How old are you?"

She drew herself up to her full height. "Nearly fourteen."

"Are you brave?"

"Oh yes." She wanted to believe it was true. After all, she hadn't broken yet.

The boy searched her face again. "Well, I suppose you could be useful. Let me talk to some of the people I work with. I'll be in touch."

"Really?" She could scarcely believe it.

"Why not?" He shrugged, then turned to go.

"Wait!" she called after him. "You didn't tell me your name."

"It's Lucien." He held her gaze for a moment. "The papers say you're named Hélène. But who are you really?"

She hesitated. "Charlotte. But I'm not sure I'll ever be her again."

"Charlotte's a beautiful name. But so is Hélène. Whoever you decide to be, I'm glad to know you. I'll see you again."

And then he was gone. Charlotte stared after him as he disappeared down the stairs of their building, confused by the way her heart was still pounding and the fact that her face felt like it was on fire.

CHAPTER TWENTY-SIX

July 1942

News of the massive roundups in Paris had reached England, and Thomas was worried. He knew how much Ruby cared for the girl who lived next door, and every time he closed his eyes, he imagined Ruby throwing herself between the child and the barrel of a Nazi soldier's gun. Ruby wouldn't let something happen to Charlotte without putting up a fight, but what did that mean? And what guarantee was there that either of them was still alive anyhow?

He knew he should be worrying only about his own missions, but each spare minute somehow belonged to her. He had signed up for this fight, had even derived some enjoyment from his time in the cockpit. Ruby, on the other hand, hadn't asked for any of this; she'd fallen in love with the wrong person and had found herself in the middle of a war. He wondered if she had continued to harbor pilots after he'd gone, but no other pilots from his squadron had returned after being shot down, so there was no one to ask.

Today, he was returning from a mission over eastern France after escorting a fleet of bombers. He let down his guard for a second, just as they passed Dunkirk, and thought about how Paris lay almost directly to the south, just over 150 miles away. It was a distance he could cover quickly in his Spitfire. What would happen if he made a ninety-degree turn to the south and simply disappeared over the horizon? It was a nice fantasy, but of course he knew exactly how it would end; he'd get shot at as he approached Paris and probably die in a fiery explosion in the sky. No thank you.

And so he forced himself to refocus. He had to survive if there was to be any hope of seeing her again. And he wouldn't live through the war if he was daydreaming every time he flew over the Continent.

The cliffs of Dover came into view, white and gleaming, as Thomas made his way back across the Channel, and when he turned toward his home airfield, he tried hard to focus on what lay immediately ahead instead of on a future he couldn't control. For all he knew, she hadn't given him a second thought after he left her apartment.

As the landing strip came into view, Thomas opened the cockpit hood, reduced his airspeed to 140 miles an hour, and prepared for landing. Undercarriage locked. Propeller functioning normally. Flaps down. He made a wide turn, reducing his speed further, and then he brought her down safely, easing the long nose in and bumping a few times along the runway before bringing the plane to a stop. He taxied off quickly to leave room for others to land behind him, and once back in dispersal, he cut the engine and turned the instruments and radio off. Another successful flight under his belt.

He had just returned to his room and was about to get dressed for an evening at the pub with Harry, who'd promised to buy the first round, when there was a knock at his door. He answered quickly, but instead of Harry standing there, it was the squadron adjutant, a man named Fred Horn. "Clarke? I'm afraid something has happened."

"Sir?" Thomas's mind immediately went to Ruby, but that was crazy. He certainly wouldn't be notified if anything happened to her. But who else was there? He was a man without a family. "What is it?"

"It's Harry Cormack, I'm afraid," Horn said, his eyes downcast. "He didn't come back today."

Thomas felt his heart drop to his knees. *Harry? Again?* "Do you know his status? Where did he land?"

"I'm afraid I'm not being clear enough. Some 109s caught up with him over the Channel."

Thomas felt a heavy weight settle on his chest. "Did anyone see him go down?"

Horn nodded. "There was a whole mess of 109s out there, complete chaos. But Wellesley and Newton both saw him go into the water on fire. Had a couple of boats out in the area after the crash, but no sign of survivors, I'm afraid."

Thomas felt a wave of hopelessness wash over him. Harry was one of the best pilots he knew. A swarm of German 109s shouldn't have been too much to handle, unless he was severely outnumbered or one of them got very, very lucky. Even then, wouldn't Harry have tried to bail out? "Any evidence of ejection?" Thomas asked.

"It seems his plane went into the water intact." Horn looked away. "No indication of attempted escape."

"Damn it." Thomas pounded his fist against the door.

Horn was already backing away. "Anyhow, Clarke, I just thought you should know."

"Yes. Right. Thank you." Thomas closed the door and crossed the room to his bed. He sat down heavily, dazed by the news. *Could Harry really be dead? Just like that?* He couldn't understand why he was so shocked. After all, this was the sort of thing that happened nearly every day. No pilot was guaranteed a safe return. Hell, no civilian was either. Just look what had happened to his mother.

It was so senseless. There were days that Thomas felt on top of the world as he soared above the clouds, but other days, especially as he crossed over France, he wondered what it was all for. Someone would win the war one day, whether it was the Allies or the Krauts, and then all those lives lost would feel as if they'd been taken in vain. And what if Britain wasn't triumphant in the end? Would that mean that Harry and Oliver and Thomas's mother had died for nothing? What if Ruby was lost in the end too, swallowed into the gaping hole of German aggression?

And so, just before he sat down to write yet another letter—this one to Harry's parents—Thomas found himself on his knees, praying for his friend's soul, for his own mother's soul, for an end to the fighting, and for the strength to play a role in bringing this war to an end. But most of all, Thomas found himself pleading with God that Ruby would stay safe and that one day, fate would deliver him back to her door.

CHAPTER TWENTY-SEVEN

August 1942

"I'm afraid I have some bad news." Aubert was standing outside Ruby's apartment, which was, in and of itself, alarming. He wasn't someone who just stopped by.

"Are you sure you should be here?" Ruby quickly hustled him inside before anyone saw him.

"I'm an old friend of your husband's, coming to check on you, if anyone asks. But this couldn't wait."

"What's the news?" For a fleeting second, Ruby imagined that he was going to tell her Thomas had been shot down. But that was crazy, wasn't it? How would Aubert know such a thing? And even if something had happened to the British pilot, why would anyone inform her? He probably hadn't given her a second thought after returning to England.

"It's about Charlotte's parents," Aubert said, lowering his voice.

Ruby closed her eyes for a moment. She didn't want to hear what he had to say. She couldn't. But she had to. "What is it?"

"They've both been sent to a camp in Poland."

"Already?"

"Drancy is overrun. They're moving people out as quickly as they can."

"But I thought we were working on getting them out."

"The best we can hope for now is that they're treated humanely wherever they go."

"What will I tell Charlotte?"

"I think she's stronger than you're giving her credit for."

Ruby stared at him. "How would you know that? You've barely spoken with her."

"The boy who delivered her papers? I've known him since he was very small, and though he's only fifteen, he's an integral part of our operation. He met Charlotte, and he spoke very highly of her resolve to help us."

"Aubert, she's just a child."

"So is Lucien. But war makes us all into something different. It has changed you, hasn't it?"

She looked away. "I won't allow it, Aubert. I'm responsible for her."

He glanced over her right shoulder. "Perhaps it won't be up to you."

Ruby turned, following his gaze, and saw Charlotte standing there, staring at them. "Are you here about my parents? What's happened to them?"

"They've been deported," Aubert said, watching her face. "To a camp in Poland."

"Charlotte—" Ruby began, taking a step toward the girl.

But Charlotte held up a hand to stop her. "How can I be sure they're alive?" she asked. "How do I know you're not just trying to give me false hope?"

Aubert looked her in the eye. "Because, my dear, war is no time to deceive the people we are supposed to trust."

"You hardly know me. You can't possibly trust me."

"Lucien said you were brave."

Ruby could see color rising to the girl's cheeks. "He doesn't really know me either."

"But he's a very good observer of people," Aubert said. "And he told me he felt you were strong and bold."

"He said that?" Charlotte looked startled.

Aubert nodded. "Look, Charlotte, we have a few sources inside Drancy. By all accounts, your parents have been treated relatively well so far."

"You're certain?" Charlotte asked.

Ruby hated to hear how hopeful Charlotte sounded, because for all his posturing about honesty, what if Aubert was just saying what he knew the girl needed to hear? There was a part of her that wanted to believe him, but there were too many questions. What were the Germans doing with all the people they were shipping east?

"As certain as possible. Now," Aubert said. "The next order of business. The two of you must move to a new apartment."

Ruby and Charlotte exchanged looks. "What?" Ruby asked.

"We feel that Charlotte staying here with you creates a serious problem. The neighbors know who she is; you won't be able to pass her off as a cousin if you stay. All it takes is one person to report her in exchange for a few ration cards. You would likely be arrested; and heaven forbid you have a pilot staying with you at the time. The line would be exposed. We can't risk that."

"But . . . what if pilots can't find me at my new address?"

Aubert looked confused. "Of course the contacts who send them to Paris will simply direct them to your new home."

"Yes, of course," Ruby mumbled, her eyes stinging with tears she knew she couldn't cry. How would Thomas find her if he ever made his way back? But protecting Charlotte was a thousand times more important, and Ruby knew that she didn't have a choice.

Aubert was watching her carefully, as if he suspected what she was thinking. But he couldn't possibly. "We've found you a place near the Arc de Triomphe, across the river."

"Already?"

"It has a space to hide pilots inside the apartment. The landlord is one of us. He'll be able to help if you ever need assistance. You have to go as soon as possible."

"Well." Ruby forced a smile. "I suppose we'd better pack, then."

"I'll leave you to it. I'll send some fellows to help you with your things the day after tomorrow, if that's agreeable."

"Yes, fine," Ruby said. "Thank you."

He disappeared out the door before she could say anything else.

"You're worried about him finding you," Charlotte said softly when Aubert was gone. Ruby had been standing in the center of the living room, staring off into space, for at least a minute.

"Who?"

"Thomas. The pilot."

Ruby began to protest, but Charlotte merely shook her head.

"I think he felt that way about you too," she said. "And he'll come back. My parents will too. You just have to believe."

Ruby forced a smile, but instead of the words making her feel better, they made her feel worse. She had her doubts that Charlotte's parents were coming back at all—and of course the chances she'd see Thomas again were slim. But she could deal with only so much heartbreak in one day, so she put an arm around the girl and said brightly, "What do you say we begin packing? We have a lot of work ahead of us."

TWO DAYS LATER, THE CONTENTS of Ruby's life in Paris were stuffed into boxes, the old apartment stripped bare. The surge of grief Ruby felt looking around at the emptiness was unexpected; her life in Paris had begun here, and it had been Marcel's family home for generations. But the Benoit family was gone now, and she wasn't meant to be a part of it anymore. It was time to go.

"How will my parents find us when they get out?" Charlotte asked as they waited for the men Aubert had promised to send.

"I will stop back a few times a week," Ruby promised, "and Aubert will have people checking too. Don't worry, Charlotte. We'll know when they return."

"I can go back to check on the apartment too."

"No. We can't risk anyone seeing you."

Charlotte hung her head. "So that's it? I have to just disappear and become someone else?"

"In order to survive, yes."

Charlotte sighed. "We can't even go to my apartment now to get some of my things?"

Ruby was about to say no, but she hesitated. Charlotte couldn't be seen entering or leaving the apartment. But what if Ruby went in? If anyone tried to stop her, it would be easy to explain; she could just sheepishly say she was checking for valuables; she would look like someone trying to take advantage of the poor Dachers' misfortune. She knew such things had happened across Paris, though she hadn't heard anyone entering the Dachers' apartment. "I'll try, Charlotte. What would you want, if I can only retrieve a few things?"

Charlotte brightened. "My blue dress, please. The one with the yellow ribbon. It's hanging in my wardrobe. One of my father's sweaters, please, and my mother's silk gloves, which she always keeps in the third drawer of their dresser, tucked toward the back. And my mother's anniversary ring too; it's gold with a few small diamonds. It should be on the dressing table, in a small blue box." Charlotte paused, and Ruby's heart ached at the realization that the poor girl had been thinking about this for days. "And one or two of the framed photographs from the living room, if it's not too much to ask."

"I'll do my best." Ruby slipped out into the hallway, said a cheerful hello to Madame Colin from the second floor, who was just leaving the building, and then used Charlotte's key to unlock the Dachers' door. She was so intent on making it into the apartment undiscovered that it took her several seconds to register what she was seeing once she was inside.

"Oh no." She gazed around in dismay. The place had been torn apart from top to bottom. The beautiful velvet sofa and chairs were slashed open. Pale spaces on the wall loomed ugly and empty. Books had been pulled from the shelves and destroyed, and all of Madame Dacher's china was missing from the ornate cabinet in the corner.

Ruby's eyes filled with tears. She and Charlotte hadn't heard anyone breaking into the apartment, and the door was intact, so the thieves must have had access to a key—most likely from the landlord or the concierge. It made Ruby nauseated to think of neighbors lying in wait to take advantage of the family. Had one of them reported the Dachers to the police in the first place? Was there someone in this building who was directly responsible for their deportation?

Pulse pounding, Ruby slipped into the kitchen, which was equally destroyed, and then into the bedroom of Madame and Monsieur Dacher. The bed was stripped bare, and all that remained on the dresser top were rings of dust. Still, there were some clothes dangling from hangers in the closet, so she quickly rifled through until she found a scratchy wool sweater that had belonged to Monsieur Dacher. She couldn't imagine why someone would have left it when winter clothes were at a premium, but perhaps their hands had already been full of other valuables.

Madame Dacher's silk gloves and anniversary ring were gone, of course, though Ruby dutifully searched for them. In the end, she settled for a silk blouse that had been hidden between two plain cotton dresses. In Charlotte's small room, she found more destruction, and it appeared that the blue dress the girl had asked for was missing as well. Ruby hastily chose two cotton dresses instead; she suspected they'd been hand-sewn by Madame Dacher, and she could make the argument to Charlotte that they had more sentimental value. There were no family pictures anywhere; they'd surely been taken for the value of the silver frames that held them.

She grabbed a couple of Charlotte's books and then headed back to her own apartment, closing the door forever to a sad piece of the past.

"Did you get the things I asked for?" Charlotte asked.

"You know," Ruby said carefully, "I think your mother must have taken her anniversary ring and gloves with her. And that blue dress you mentioned? The more I thought about it, the more I realized how impractical it would be. You'll need everyday dresses. I got one of your papa's sweaters, though!" She handed the armful of belongings to Charlotte, who looked disappointed. "I also brought a few of your books."

"And a family photo?" Charlotte asked quietly.

"Oh, I thought perhaps that wasn't a good idea," Ruby replied. "What if someone searches our new apartment and finds it? Besides, I feel sure that your parents will be back in no time. You won't need a photo to remember them by."

Charlotte bit her lip. "The apartment was looted, wasn't it?"

Ruby hesitated. "Yes. I'm so sorry."

"There are truly terrible people in this world."

Ruby pulled Charlotte into a hug. "But there are good people too. And I like to think that in the end, the good ones outnumber the bad."

Charlotte let herself be held for a moment before pulling away. She moved to the window and looked out for a long time without saying a word. Ruby didn't interrupt her; she knew that the girl needed to say good-bye in her own way.

THE NEW APARTMENT WAS IN a nice building on the rue de Lasteyrie in the Passy district, a thirty-minute walk across the river. The neighborhood, though close to both the busy Avenue Foch and the bustling Avenue des Champs-Élysées, was quiet and residential. In fact, the street had much the same feel as the rue Amélie.

The landlord, a man named Georges Savatier, was there to greet them when they arrived. "You must be our new tenants, Fleur and her cousin Hélène," he said, smiling brightly. "Come, come, we must get you settled." He was perhaps a decade older than Ruby, with a deep voice, a substantial waistline, and a big, bushy black mustache, which seemed at odds with his very bald head. His smile was wide and jolly, and Ruby liked him immediately.

He showed them to an apartment two flights up, explaining, as they walked, that the building didn't have a lift but that he knew they were young and healthy and hoped they'd be comfortable. "Our second floor is also our quietest," he said, giving Ruby a meaningful look. "You have no neighbors." He stopped in front of apartment C and smiled. "This will be you. Apartments A, B, and D are vacant."

"What happened to the people who used to live there?" Charlotte asked.

Monsieur Savatier frowned as he turned the key and opened the door. "They left some months ago in the middle of the night. Perhaps to the countryside." He gave Ruby a quick look. Had the previous owners been rounded up in the recent raids too?

Ruby and Charlotte followed him inside. It was immediately obvious that the apartment was half the size of the place they'd come from, but it had a nice terrace that overlooked a private courtyard.

"My favorite part of the apartment," Monsieur Savatier said, beckoning toward one of the two doors in the back. "Come, I will show you." He led them into a tiny room with one small window. "This, I think, will be the master bedroom," he said.

Ruby was about to protest that it would hardly fit a bed when his smile widened and he pointed toward the wall on the left. "I understand that you are in need of some discreet storage space."

He put his hand on a panel of the wall just above waist level. He pushed gently up and in, and the wall slid open, revealing a crawl space large enough for a man to sit up comfortably. "Voilà," Monsieur Savatier said. "In case you need to store anything here."

"It's perfect," Ruby said, exchanging looks with Charlotte. It was larger than the hall closet in the old building, and it was also a more secure hiding spot, concealed within their own apartment. It would be much easier to slip pilots in and out without being observed. The wall space above it was filled with cupboards and cabinets; it was designed in a way that made it appear the entire wall was used for storage.

"Yes, I thought so," Monsieur Savatier said. "I built it myself. I cannot do much to help; I manage several buildings, and I'm sure there are eyes on me. But this, in a small way, is my contribution." He pointed up and added, "I live just two floors above with my wife. We are both here to help if you ever need us. Below you, the apartments are mostly deserted too, so you won't have to worry about prying eyes. And of course there's no concierge."

"I don't know how to thank you," Ruby said.

"Don't thank me yet. I haven't told you the bad news. The building next door, which I also manage, has several Nazi officers as tenants. So you are living very close to them. But I think they do not suspect a thing."

BY LATE EVENING, AUBERT'S FRIENDS had delivered their furniture and belongings, and Charlotte and Ruby had begun to make the cramped new apartment feel like home. There were more boxes to unpack, but Ruby could see Charlotte's eyelids drooping. "Why don't you go to bed?"

Charlotte yawned. "But there's still so much to do."

"It will all be here in the morning. It's been a long day."

Charlotte nodded and headed into the larger bedroom. They had determined it would be hers; having her stay in such close proximity to young pilots wouldn't be appropriate.

"Thank you," Charlotte said, pausing at her doorway and looking back to the living room, where Ruby sat at the small table in the corner.

"You don't need to thank me for anything."

"But I do. You didn't have to bring me with you."

"Charlotte, you're my family now," Ruby said firmly. "I wouldn't have it any other way. Now get some sleep. Everything will look better in the morning."

CHAPTER TWENTY-EIGHT

January 1943

By the beginning of 1943, food was scarcer than ever, but Ruby and Charlotte were surviving. They had helped eight pilots since moving into the new apartment, and though there was still no word about Charlotte's parents, the girl seemed to have reached some kind of peace within herself.

At night, Charlotte and Ruby would sit together with an oil lamp burning between them and talk about the pilots they'd saved, wondering how many had made it back to England or America, how many had returned to the skies. They made up vivid stories of the men they'd known only briefly. An American fighter named Earl Johnson, for example, had stayed with them in August, and now they imagined him flying missions over western Germany, shooting Nazi aces out of the sky. A British bomber named Jay Cash had been their guest for almost a week in October, and they had convinced themselves that he was now the one dropping bombs on Nazi-run factories in the Paris suburbs.

In the first week of the new year, they hosted an RAF pilot named Jon Payne, who stared long and hard at Ruby on his first night with them. "I'm sorry," he said when she caught him looking for the third time. "You just remind me of someone."

"Who?"

He cleared his throat. "It's rather foolish, but there's a fellow in my squadron who was shot down a little over a year ago and helped by an escape line through Paris. He and I roomed together for a little while. He'd have these nightmares, and he'd yell out a name over and over again. When I finally asked him about it, he said he couldn't talk about the specifics of the escape line—of course that's one of the rules—but that there was a woman in Paris who had helped him. He told me a bit about her; he thought she was extraordinary. He didn't realize he was calling out her name, of course. But the way he described her, she sounded just like you."

"Like me?"

The pilot nodded. "Yes. She was American too, just like you are, and beautiful. But of course you go by Fleur."

"And what name was he calling out?"

"I'm not sure I should say."

Ruby nodded and waited. Surely there were other women around Paris helping on the line. And wasn't it far more likely that the pilot in question was calling out the name of the gorgeous Laure?

"Well," Jon said after a moment, "all of you go by code names anyhow, don't you?"

"You're right, of course."

"It was Ruby," Jon said. "The name he said over and over was Ruby."

Ruby felt her whole body go numb. She reminded herself that the pilot could have been anyone, but she hadn't used her real name with anyone else, with the exception of Dexter, the first refugee to show up at her door. "Who was the pilot?"

"I suppose I'd better not tell you his surname. But no harm in telling you his first name. It was Thomas. Do you know a Thomas?"

Ruby swallowed hard. "Perhaps."

That night, Ruby lay in bed, wide awake and staring at the ceiling. The man Jon had mentioned *had* to be Thomas, *her* Thomas. But did this really mean he was thinking of her the way she was thinking of him? Or merely that she'd played a role in the most terrifying ordeal of his life? Still, the fact that he'd described her as extraordinary and beautiful, well, that was something.

The next morning, before Laure was due to arrive, Ruby pulled Jon aside. "This Thomas friend of yours," she said. "He's all right?"

"He's just fine, miss. The nightmares are gone, and he's returned to flying missions over France." He paused and leaned in conspiratorially. "Though I think he still has a soft spot for the girl he was dreaming about."

Ruby blinked a few times. "Well, when you get home, would you tell him that Ruby is fine? And that perhaps she thinks of him from time to time as well?"

Jon grinned. "I'd be happy to pass along the message, Fleur."

Laure came to retrieve Jon just before noon. After he'd gone, Ruby kicked herself for not asking more. Had Thomas been injured in his escape from France? Had he run into any trouble? But to have appeared too interested would only have invited questions she couldn't have answered. She'd have to rest assured in the knowledge that Jon would make it back to Britain safely and would pass along her message. He'd known who she was, and Thomas would too. Furthermore, now Thomas would know that she had moved and that he should be looking for someone named Fleur if he ever returned.

But then, two weeks later, Ruby and Charlotte received some terrible news. "Philippe asked me to tell you that several pilots and one of the leaders of the escape line were arrested in Urrugne last week," Monsieur Savatier told them grimly. "They're all being questioned now. One of them was the pilot who was here just a couple of weeks ago, Payne. There's a real worry that one or all of them will talk and that the line will be blown."

"What will happen to them?" Ruby managed, although she was reeling from the news.

"The pilots will be sent to POW camps in the east. As for the French and Belgians accused of helping them? Tortured for information, most likely. Then executed."

Ruby nodded. Of course she'd known; after all, it had been Marcel's fate too. It just reminded her anew of the stakes—and of the danger she was putting Charlotte in.

"Philippe wanted me also to tell you that you won't hear from him for a while," Monsieur Savatier said. "Nor will you receive any pilots. Just try to live normally. There's no reason to think that this portion of the line has been compromised yet."

"But if it has?"

Monsieur Savatier frowned. "I will do what I can to protect you and your cousin. But you need to be ready to run at a moment's notice."

FOR DAYS, RUBY AND CHARLOTTE waited. What was happening to the pilots who were shot down over Belgium and northern France in the meantime? Were they wandering around in the freezing wilderness, wondering why no one was coming to their aid? Or had they found refuge with sympathetic farmers and villagers who knew better than to send them on to Paris until they'd received an all-clear?

Despite herself, Ruby worried constantly about Thomas too. Jon Payne had said that Thomas had returned to the skies over France, but what if he was shot down again? What if he tried to get to Paris to find her? What if he made it to her old apartment building only to realize she was gone?

And so three weeks after her work on the line had ground to a halt, Ruby roused Charlotte early on a Saturday morning. "Would you like to go for a walk?"

Charlotte rubbed the sleep out of her eyes. "A walk?"

"Past the old apartment. Just to see."

"But I thought you said it was too dangerous for me to come with you."

"It's cold out. You'll wear a hat and a scarf, and we won't get close enough to encounter old neighbors. Besides, I can't leave you alone." In fact, since news of the arrests had come down, Ruby had barely let Charlotte out of her sight. She knew she was probably driving the poor girl crazy, but what choice did she have?

"Do you think it's very cold where my parents are?" Charlotte asked as they walked briskly south through Passy a half hour later. German transport vehicles full of soldiers rumbled down the avenues, and Nazi flags stained the city red, like a bad rash.

Ruby hesitated. "Yes. But I think they are all right."

"You can't know that."

"Sometimes you have to believe in things you cannot see."

Their breaths were clouds of air. "Like religion," Charlotte said at last. "Like the way we must believe in God even when we can't see Him."

Ruby glanced at her. They hadn't spoken of God much; it seemed a dangerous topic in these times, and Ruby herself wasn't exactly a dedicated churchgoer. But she agreed with what Charlotte was saying. "Yes. Much like that, Charlotte. Faith."

"Faith that in the end, we'll all be okay."

Ruby nodded, but she was suddenly too choked up to reply. She *did* believe in God—she always had—but she'd been struggling lately to understand how He was letting this war happen.

They reached the rue Amélie more quickly than Ruby had expected. As they rounded the corner onto the street where their lives had first intertwined, Ruby reached for Charlotte's hand. The girl was trembling, and Ruby had the feeling it wasn't just from the cold. "Are you all right?" she asked.

"Yes," Charlotte said, her voice strong and clear. "It's just that living across the river makes me feel as if we've reinvented ourselves. But here, you are still you and I am still me, even if we're pretending to be something different. It means we have to face what we've left behind."

Ruby squeezed Charlotte's hand. "I couldn't have said it better myself."

They slowed as they walked by the building, but they couldn't stop; they couldn't make themselves stand out. The tip of the Eiffel Tower appeared ahead of them, grand and beautiful, and Ruby was reminded of the early days of her marriage, when she'd sat on her tiny terrace, rejoicing in the knowledge that she was really here, really in Paris. But the tower no longer meant what it used to, and the view also triggered memories of staring out the window after the baby died. This apartment had been the site of much sadness, but it had also been the place where she'd met Charlotte and Thomas. The bitter always came with the sweet.

"Are you thinking about Thomas?" Charlotte asked as they reached the end of the block. "I know you think of him often."

"I suppose I'm thinking of all the things that happened here. I was lucky to have lived here. I was lucky to have met you."

This time, it was Charlotte who squeezed Ruby's hand comfortingly. "And I, you."

They circled the block twice more, but there was no movement in or near the old building. It was merely a ghost of another time and place.

They were mostly silent as they made their way back across the Seine. "Do you really believe they'll find us if they come back?" Charlotte asked as they turned left onto the rue Boissière. "My parents? Thomas? The people from our old lives?"

"Yes, I do."

Charlotte looked at her. "But how can you be so sure?"

"Because fate isn't so cruel that it would return them to Paris and keep them from us," Ruby said. She just wished she could believe her own words.

When they rounded the corner of the stairs on the second floor of their new building some twenty minutes later, Ruby was startled to see a young man waiting for them on the doorstep. For a moment, she thought it might be a pilot. But then he turned, and she realized he was at least a few years too young. He was fifteen, maybe sixteen, with a curly mop of dark hair and piercing, hooded green eyes.

"Where have you been?" Charlotte asked, quickening her pace and embracing him. His eyes met Ruby's over the top of Charlotte's head.

"Hello," he said calmly. "I'm Lucien."

Charlotte pulled away, her face red, and glanced at Ruby.

Ruby raised an eyebrow. "You're the forger. The one Char—Hélène—told me about?"

His smile widened a bit. "Ah, so she speaks of me? This is good news." They both glanced at Charlotte, whose face had turned an even deeper shade of red as she was studying the floor. "Yes, I am the forger. Among other things. Today, though, I am a messenger. May I come in?"

Ruby hesitated. The boy seemed nice enough, but there was something about him that made her uneasy. Or was she just reacting to the way Charlotte was behaving? This was no time for idle crushes. Especially not for a child. Ruby shook the thought off quickly. She wasn't being fair. "Yes, of course. Come in."

Lucien held out his hand and gestured for Charlotte and Ruby to enter the apartment first, then he followed them in.

"What is it?" Charlotte asked once they were inside. "What's wrong, Lucien?"

He hesitated, and in the silence, Charlotte and Ruby exchanged worried looks.

"Is it my parents?" Charlotte asked, her voice small.

"What? No. No, I have no word about your parents."

"Oh." Charlotte's shoulders slumped in relief.

"It's about Philippe."

Aubert's code name. Ruby could feel the tension crackling in the air, and from Lucien's suddenly downcast eyes, she knew that something was terribly wrong. "What's happened?"

Lucien looked up to meet her gaze. "He was arrested." His voice was flat, but Ruby could see the storm in his eyes. "Several days ago. One of the men in Urrugne gave him up, along with several others who were part of the operation."

"Oh, no," Ruby breathed. Charlotte looked as if she was about to cry, so Ruby put an arm around her shoulder and tried not to break down.

"Is he okay?" Charlotte asked.

Lucien hesitated, and before he spoke, Ruby knew what he was going to say. "I'm afraid he's gone," he said softly. "Firing squad. He refused to talk, and they didn't have any leverage against him. He doesn't have any family; there was no one they could threaten to arrest. He'd covered his tracks well."

"He's dead?" Charlotte asked.

"Yes."

"My God." Ruby hung her head and said a silent prayer. "Laure is all right?" She was surprised how concerned she felt for her.

"Yes, as far as I know. But I'm afraid the line has been compromised too greatly. There won't be any more pilots sent to us for now."

Ruby let the words sink in. "Should we relocate? Is there a chance the Nazis know about us?"

"No." Lucien's answer was firm. "You're safer here; you haven't lived here for long. Monsieur Savatier will help protect you." His gaze lingered on Charlotte. "I will too. I will be nearby. I won't let anything happen to you." His last words were spoken directly to the girl.

"Perhaps it's better if Charlotte and I leave the city," Ruby said.

"No," Charlotte replied immediately. "If we leave, how will my parents find us when they return?"

Lucien glanced at Ruby, and she could see in his eyes that he shared her fear about the Dachers' fate.

"I can't put your life in any more danger than I already have," Ruby said after a long pause.

"I don't think either of us will feel complete if we're not doing something," Charlotte said. "But what can we do? Our part of the line is dead."

Lucien cleared his throat. "There are others trying to establish a new escape route. The British are behind it."

Ruby closed her eyes for a moment. How easy it would be to simply remove herself and Charlotte from danger by taking a step back. But then she'd be letting the Nazis win, wouldn't she? Aubert's death would be in vain. Everything she'd worked for would be in vain. "Please," she said at last, glancing at Charlotte, "keep us informed."

"I will." Lucien nodded at her and held Charlotte's gaze for a long time before making his way to the door. "I'll be in touch. I'm very sorry to be the bearer of such bad news."

CHAPTER TWENTY-NINE

February 1943

"I'm afraid Ruby no longer believes that we'll be able to help," Charlotte said to Lucien one cold winter night two weeks later. Ruby had gone to bed early, and Lucien, seeing her bedroom light go out, had stopped by. It had become a habit of his: waiting thirty minutes or so after Ruby had turned in and then tapping lightly on their front door. Ruby hadn't caught them yet, but then again, they weren't really doing anything wrong. Lucien hadn't even kissed her; they merely sat and talked for hours. But Charlotte had never had a boy look at her the way he did, and she'd never felt her heart race like it did when they locked eyes.

"Why do you say that?" Lucien asked. He was sitting just inches from Charlotte on the couch, close enough that she could feel his breath on her cheek.

"She talks now about how useless she feels. How she fears that by doing nothing, she's letting the Germans win."

Lucien scooted a bit closer. "You understand, though, don't you, that I'm reluctant to place you in harm's way?"

"Why?"

Lucien looked into her eyes before looking down. "Because I've come to care for you very much."

Her heart skipped. "And I for you. But there is no future for us if the Germans are allowed to remain here."

"Charlotte . . ." Lucien didn't complete his thought.

"You know I'm right. I'm Jewish, Lucien. The Germans wouldn't even let us be friends." She summoned her courage and added, "Never mind more than friends."

"More than friends?" The corner of his mouth turned up into a half smile. "What did you have in mind?"

"Does it matter? As long as the Germans are here, it is impossible. *Everything* is impossible."

"Don't talk like that, Charlotte," he said softly. She loved it when he called her by her real name. He and Ruby were the only ones who did; the handful of others who knew her, including Monsieur Savatier and his wife, knew her only as Hélène.

"Lucien, I can't help it. There's no place in this society for people like me."

"Well," he said after a moment, "I have no desire to be part of a society that would turn its back on you. So that makes two of us who would find it impossible to make a home here."

She blinked back tears. The strange thing was that she knew he was telling her the truth. Lucien was complicated, but he never lied. Not to her, anyhow. "Thank you," she said. "But there's no point in us talking about that now. We need to talk about how we can make things better. Ruby and I need to help." She had abandoned calling Ruby by her code name when speaking with Lucien. Charlotte had discovered a few weeks ago that Lucien's father had been the one to forge Ruby's new identity papers when she started working with the line, so he'd known her name all along.

Lucien didn't say anything. After a moment, he got up and began to pace. "Charlotte," he said at last, "it is very dangerous. The Nazis don't have morals. Do you know they sent the police to arrest children at an orphanage this week? Children, Charlotte, some as young as five!"

Charlotte went still. "That can't be. What reason did they give?"

Lucien laughed bitterly. "They needed some more Jews to fill up their train cars."

Charlotte looked at her hands. Reports like that terrified her; she'd been mostly sheltered from the news about the Jewish arrests because her main link to the outside world was Ruby. And of course it made sense that Ruby would try to protect her, but Charlotte wanted to know the truth. She wanted to be aware of the horrors. "I need to help." Her tone was resolute this time, and she hoped that Lucien could hear that she wasn't frightened. "The Allies have to win, Lucien. They have to. I can't do nothing while the Germans take everything."

He sighed and sat down beside her again. This time, their knees were touching. "I've heard rumors of a new escape line, but it's not operational yet. They're still trying to work out the details. In the meantime, some of the pilots are simply being held in place, mostly in the countryside. If someone were to be sent here, he might be with you for a very long time."

"We could handle that."

"And we don't have extra ration cards now."

"That's fine." Charlotte smiled at him. "I know a forger who might be able to help us with that."

Lucien smiled. "Sounds like he's a good person to know."

Charlotte held his gaze. "He's the best."

The air around them seemed to freeze. Then he leaned in and his lips landed softly on hers. When he pulled away—too soon—his cheeks were splotched with red. "I'm sorry."

"I'm not."

"I—I have to go." Lucien stood up. His face was still flushed, and he looked nervous. "I'll see what I can do." He kissed her once more, on the cheek, and then he was gone, shutting the door quietly behind him.

Charlotte sat in the living room long after Lucien had departed, thinking about a future that would quite possibly never come. She knew she couldn't tell Ruby; Ruby would say she was too young to be having these feelings for a boy. Ruby still saw Charlotte as a child, no matter what Charlotte did to prove otherwise—and she was wary of Lucien. "How would your parents feel about you getting involved with a forger like him?" Ruby had said once.

"I'd like to think they'd be proud," Charlotte had replied.

But the truth was, Charlotte didn't know what her parents would think. Lucien wasn't Jewish, and she knew that both Maman and Papa had always imagined she would follow in their footsteps, marry a good Jewish boy, raise good Jewish children.

Then again, the world Maman and Papa had dreamed of was long gone. Maybe the only thing to do was to follow her heart.

◆ ◆ ◆

ONE NIGHT IN LATE JULY, Charlotte and Ruby were sitting on the
small terrace of the apartment on the rue de Lasteyrie. Charlotte's
parents had been gone for a year, and there'd been no word of their
whereabouts since they departed from Drancy. The roundups in
Paris had slowed, and the city had fallen into a strange rhythm of
false normalcy. Parisians went about their daily business, heads
down, while the Nazis lounged in cafés and strolled the grand avenues as if the city had been theirs all along. Just last week, though,
Lucien had brought news that twenty-one Jewish families had been
arrested on the Boulevard Beaumarchais for no reason at all; the police had simply swept in and carted them away, sobbing and screaming, children and all. Charlotte knew such things would continue to
happen, and that even with her cover as Ruby's Christian cousin,
she was always in danger.

The risks had made Ruby into a bit of an oppressor, actually.
Charlotte knew that her friend was just worried about her, but it
was difficult living with someone whose protection felt so burden-
some. Ruby forbade her from going out at all now, insisting that
Charlotte was much safer in the apartment, where no one could see
her and get suspicious. But it was summertime in Paris, and Charlotte longed to stroll the streets, smell the flowers, feel the grass
beneath her feet. Then again, it wasn't the Paris of Charlotte's childhood anymore. And as long as Ruby was protecting her—and as
long as Ruby herself seemed so miserable—Charlotte felt she had
no choice but to respect her wishes, even if the confinement filled
her with loneliness and longing.

"Do you think of your parents often?" Charlotte asked abruptly as twilight fell over the city. The sky in Paris turned an almost magical shade of blue most nights, especially in the summer. The French had always called it *l'heure bleue,* and Charlotte had been startled to learn from Ruby that across the Atlantic, Americans didn't feel the same way about the final hour of daylight. Perhaps the sky was more beautiful here than it was anywhere else, but Charlotte had begun to doubt that. Surely there was something better out there. Besides, *the blue hour* had also come to mean something else; it was what the French called the end of innocence at the dawn of the Great War. Charlotte hadn't been alive then, but she thought she understood now what France had lost.

"My parents?" Ruby asked. "Why yes. I do. Very often."

"But you never speak of them."

Ruby didn't say anything for a moment. "It is painful for me, Charlotte," she said at last. "I think often of how cruel I was to simply leave them behind."

"You weren't cruel to leave, Ruby. You were living your life. I'm certain your parents would have wanted that for you. You couldn't have foreseen what was to come."

"But I should have. My father always spoke of the instability in Europe. I thought he was just being overly cautious."

Charlotte didn't reply. She was thinking about her own parents, who had so steadfastly refused to leave Paris. If her father had listened, she might be with them in the Unoccupied Zone right now. Or perhaps they would have secured safe passage out of the country, to Spain or the United States. "Sometimes, though, our parents are wrong. That is why it is up to us to forge our own paths."

Ruby turned to look at her. "Do you think of your parents often too, Charlotte?"

"Every day." The sky was turning darker now, and Charlotte wondered what it looked like in the east, in the place her parents had been sent. "But I think they are dead by now."

"Charlotte! What would make you say such a thing?"

"Lucien has told me what goes on in the concentration camps." She wouldn't repeat it aloud. She couldn't. "My mother has always had a weak constitution. I can't imagine she could tolerate the conditions Lucien has described. And my father, he has such a firm sense of right and wrong. I can't believe so much time could have gone by without him standing up for someone at the risk of his own life."

"But there's still a chance."

"I haven't heard anything from them in a year. I must brace for the worst." There was no official word from the east of course. It wasn't as if the Nazis politely sent back death notices. But sometimes, loss could be felt in one's bones.

"You can't lose hope, Charlotte."

"But *you* have, haven't you?" Charlotte spoke before thinking, and Ruby flinched. "I can see it. You feel like you don't matter anymore."

Ruby rose slowly and crossed to the edge of the terrace, where she gazed into the distance. "Even after I lost the baby, I was able to find a purpose to my life. But who am I now? I don't know anymore."

"You're my family," Charlotte said. Ruby turned and looked at her, and Charlotte went on. "You're my family, Ruby," she repeated more firmly. "I wouldn't have survived without you. Don't you see that?"

"But there will come a time when you won't need me anymore," Ruby said. "And then what?"

That night, Charlotte couldn't sleep. To say aloud that she believed her parents were dead felt like a betrayal. But now that she had, well, it was all she could think about. Every time she closed her eyes, she saw Maman's face, or Papa's. They reached out to her, begging her to save them, but there was nothing she could do. She'd had her chance, and she'd failed. She began to cry, and once she started, she found she couldn't stop.

Just past midnight, something pinged off the frame of her open window. She slid out of bed, peered into the dark courtyard, and blinked a few times as her eyes adjusted to the darkness.

"Charlotte?" The voice from below was a whisper, but she recognized it immediately.

"Lucien?"

"You are crying," he replied.

She could barely see him in the darkness, and she was glad, for it meant he couldn't see the way her cheeks were flaming. "I'm fine. What are you doing here?"

He didn't answer her question. "Meet me at your door."

She heard a rustling below, and then he was gone. She stayed paralyzed for a moment. He had never called on her this late before, and certainly never once she was in her nightgown. Ruby would be furious if she found out. But Charlotte had to see him. She crept quietly to the front door of the apartment.

Lucien was already there, and as she stepped aside to let him in, he pulled her into his arms. He kissed her on both cheeks, tenderly. "You taste like salt," he murmured.

"What are you doing here, Lucien?"

"I heard you. You sounded sad."

"But why were you in the courtyard in the first place?"

Instead of answering right away, he took her hand and led her quietly into her bedroom. Her heart was nearly pounding out of her chest. "I'm in the courtyard often, Charlotte," he said as he shut the door behind them. "To make sure that you and Ruby are safe. But I've never heard you cry before."

"I'm okay," she mumbled.

He pulled her into his arms. "It's all right not to be."

"I want to be strong," she whispered. But pressed against his solid chest now, breathing in the impossibly woodsy scent of him, all she could think about was what she'd lost.

"You *are* strong," he said gently, pulling her even closer. "What is it?"

"I shouldn't be here."

"With me?" he asked, beginning to push away a little.

"No," she said, holding on. "No. That's not what I meant. I meant that my parents are probably dead. And somehow, I've survived. I don't know how to live with that."

He sighed and eased her onto the bed. For a moment, she was sure that he was about to kiss her. But instead, he simply lay down beside her, his body pressed against hers. "You *have* to live with it," he said after a while. "Because if you're not alive, I don't want to be alive."

"But I let them take my parents . . ." She was sobbing again, and she was grateful for the darkness in the room, because she knew her tears weren't pretty.

"There's nothing you could have done."

"How can I ever forgive myself?"

"There's nothing to forgive. Surely your parents' greatest wish would have been to know that you were free."

After that, there were no more words to say. Charlotte didn't know how to believe what Lucien was telling her, but she wanted to. She wanted to forgive herself. She wanted to hope. And maybe someday, she could. But for now, the warm comfort of his body was enough. He held her and stroked her hair as she faded into sleep. The last thing she was aware of was his kiss on her forehead, lingering, comforting, telling her silently that despite everything, it was all going to be okay in the end.

CHAPTER THIRTY

November 1943

It was a brisk fall morning, and Thomas's mission was to help escort twelve Douglas A-20 Boston bombers to their target forty miles south of Dunkirk, France. What was unusual about the mission was that in addition to escorting the bombers, Thomas and the other Spitfire pilots were tasked with flying close to enemy fighter bases in Saint-Omer for the purpose of eliciting a response that would draw attention away from the bombers' mission. The idea was that the Huns would be so busy chasing down the fighters they'd miss the bombs being dropped on German-run munitions factories in northern France until it was too late.

"It's dangerous, lads," the briefing officer had told them in no uncertain terms. "Chances are that at least one of you will be shot down today. If you are, it is your duty to try to evade capture."

Thomas knew all this, of course. And in fact, it didn't need to be stated; it was basic self-preservation. But he also knew the escape line that had once shepherded him safely out of the country and across the Pyrenees was no longer operating as efficiently; the British embassy in Spain had sent word months ago about the breach of the network. He worried every day that Ruby had been caught up in the stings that had followed the arrests in Urrugne.

But what could he do beyond continuing to fight for the Allies? The sooner they could weaken the Nazi stranglehold on France, the safer she would be. Would it be too late, though? He couldn't let himself consider that option.

He stood in line upon leaving the briefing room to get his standard-issue survival pack, which was more advanced than the one he'd had when he parachuted into the French wilderness. It contained a map of France printed on a silk handkerchief, some francs, some food tablets and water purification tablets, and two trouser buttons that could be assembled into a compass.

The pack was supposed to make the pilots feel prepared, but Thomas knew that once you were on the ground, if you were lucky enough to survive your plane going down in the first place, all bets were off.

They set out at midday in formations of three, joining up with three other squadrons over Britain and then climbing above 11,000 feet once they had cleared the Dover coast. Over Calais, Thomas and a few others broke away from the main group to head toward Saint-Omer. Thomas was just preparing for possible air combat—unlocking the catches on the armament, tightening his safety harness, going through a mental checklist of evasive maneuvers—when a terse voice came over the VHF. "Bandits three o'clock below."

Thomas cursed as at least a dozen Nazi 109s materialized from the clouds.

"Attack in sections!" yelled the CO over the radio.

Thomas took a deep breath and peeled off to the right, initiating a dive. It should have been routine, but suddenly, his cockpit was on fire. He hadn't even realized he'd been hit, but there was the attacking plane behind him, lining up to come at him again.

It turned out that wasn't necessary. The flames were advancing quickly; the fuel tanks were less than a minute away from igniting and blowing up the plane in midair. Thomas had to get out.

He ripped off his oxygen mask and radio plug and pulled back the canopy hood. "Please, God," he found himself murmuring as he detached his safety harness and pulled the cord to open his parachute. In an instant, he was watching his flaming jet peel away from him, trailing smoke, a Nazi fighter still on its tail.

The drift to the ground seemed to take forever. He came down in the middle of an empty field, not a soul around. Quickly, he bundled his parachute, his life jacket, his helmet, his goggles, and his gloves and buried them in the dirt, then he struggled out of his flight suit, turning it inside out like he did last time. There was still no sign he'd been noticed, so he pulled out the silk map and determined that Paris was some 140 miles away. A three-day journey if he could keep up a brisk pace. He took a deep breath, snapped his compass together, and began to walk south. To Paris. To Ruby. To the future.

CHAPTER THIRTY-ONE

November 1943

By the time the air had turned crisp in the autumn of 1943, Ruby knew there was something going on between Charlotte and Lucien. She supposed it should have bothered her more, especially since she was the girl's guardian, but Charlotte had sworn that she hadn't had relations with Lucien and certainly wouldn't, and Ruby believed her.

It wasn't just the blossoming relationship that scared Ruby, though. It was the danger that seemed to swirl around all of them like a gathering storm. And with her role in the escape line finished, Ruby felt powerless to do anything about it. Every time she passed a Nazi soldier on the street, guilt coursed through her. She should be doing more, but how? Her only mission now was to protect Charlotte, and she had thought she was doing that to the best of her ability. But she'd forgotten, somewhere along the way, that Charlotte might not want to be protected anymore.

"You're stifling me," Charlotte blurted out over dinner one night.

Ruby paused with her fork halfway to her mouth. "Stifling you?"

"I know it's because you care for me, but I can't keep living my days confined in this apartment while the world goes on without me."

"It's my duty to keep you safe, Charlotte. I promised your parents."

"I know. And you've been marvelous, Ruby. But it's time you begin letting me make my own choices. I'm not a child anymore."

"But you are! You're just a girl."

Charlotte's cheeks turned red, and she stood abruptly from the table. "I'm *not*! Don't you see that you're doing the same thing Monsieur Benoit did to you?"

Ruby stared. "What?"

"He refused to see you for what you were. And you're doing the same. You think you're protecting me, but you're taking away my right to be who I am."

"Charlotte—"

"No, please let me finish. I can be doing something, Ruby. I can help Lucien; he has offered to teach me to forge documents. I feel like I can't survive this war by merely being a prisoner in this apartment. I've tried to respect your wishes so far, but you must let me go. You must let me help. It's what I'm meant to do; I know it."

"But you can't think I'm like Marcel. He refused to see me as an equal. He thought I was nothing."

Charlotte didn't say anything, although Ruby could hear the accusation in her silence. It stung, not least of all because there was some truth to it.

"I've never for a moment believed that you're nothing, Charlotte," Ruby said after a moment. "I know you're resourceful and smart. It's that I can't bear the thought of something happening to you. I love you, and I'm just trying to keep you safe."

"And you have. You've given me a home. You've given me a life." Charlotte paused and leaned forward. "And I'll owe you forever for that. But if we want to defeat darkness, we must find our own way to the light. We have to follow our hearts and accept the danger. It's my turn to fight, Ruby. Please try to see that."

Ruby stared at the girl for a long time. She could already see her slipping away, but it was no longer in her hands. She knew that now. She saw herself in Charlotte, and it scared her. "You must promise me that you won't do anything foolish. You must never let your guard down. The danger is so much greater for you than it is for me."

Something changed in Charlotte's face, and Ruby knew the girl understood she was letting her go. "I know," she whispered. "But don't you see? That's why I need to help. France has turned its back on people like me, but I can't turn my back on France. I still believe in the goodness of mankind. I believe that things will change, but only if we're brave enough to stand up."

"And Lucien will be with you? He will be there to look out for you when I'm not?"

"Lucien will be with me always."

And so Ruby did her best to leave Charlotte be, and in the next few weeks, it became a bit easier. Charlotte disappeared with Lucien every few days for several hours at a time, and although Ruby's stomach was always in knots as she waited for the girl to come home, she also knew it was the right thing. There was a lightness to Charlotte that hadn't been there before, and Ruby recognized it as a sense of purpose. Charlotte was finally playing a role in saving herself. It was just how Ruby had felt when she began work on the escape line.

And although Ruby worried too about Charlotte getting her heart broken in the midst of everything else, she also had the feeling that Lucien wasn't planning to hurt her. More than once, Ruby had seen Charlotte's eyes fill with tears over something—most often a mention of her parents—and Lucien was immediately at her side, comforting her, before Ruby herself could react. He was in tune with her in the most rare and wonderful way.

Ruby had been wrong about him, and the realization taught her a lesson. When she'd first seen Lucien, he had seemed dangerous, the kind of boy her own parents would have warned her to stay away from when she was Charlotte's age. But if there was one thing she had learned, it was that you could never judge a book by its cover. Lucien was a much better person than Marcel had been, certainly, and Ruby had dropped everything and flown across the ocean to be with him. What if there had been a Lucien right under her nose all along, and she had simply neglected to see him? Would her life have turned out differently?

But she couldn't think like that. If she'd followed a different path, she wouldn't have known Charlotte. Or Thomas. Or any of the people here in Paris who'd made her proud to be fighting for something bigger than herself.

AUTUMN HAD PAINTED THE TREES in the brilliant hues of sunset, and as Ruby strolled toward the Seine on a sunny November afternoon, she could almost believe that life was normal. It was a trick of the light, but on days like this, when the neighborhoods bustled and the Germans weren't filling the streets, Ruby could imagine that this was the Paris she had dreamed of. This was the Paris that Hemingway had written about a generation ago, the Paris that had tantalized her from afar.

She crossed the river at the Pont de l'Alma, marveling as she always did at the way the Eiffel Tower sliced into the bright blue sky off to the right, and made her way down the Avenue Bosquet. She turned left on the rue Saint-Dominique and right on the rue Amélie, intending to walk by the old building just once, as she did every Monday. She had mostly lost hope that she'd ever see Charlotte's parents or Thomas or any of the other pilots again, but to cease trying would be to admit defeat. So it had become part of her weekly routine to walk briskly along the narrow street that had once been her home, pausing only briefly outside the old building to look for signs that someone was trying to find her. She never knew quite what she was searching for: a note? A handkerchief tied to a terrace? It was a fool's errand, but it soothed her somehow. As she passed, she always said a prayer for Charlotte's parents, for her own lost baby, and for the safety of all the pilots she had helped, and this day was no different. In fact, she was so lost in her own thoughts that she almost didn't hear her name being hissed from across the street.

"Ruby!" There it was again, an urgent whisper coming from the shadows of a doorway on the other side of the narrow lane. She turned in the direction of the voice, cursing herself for being careless enough to come here like this. She could be putting everything in jeopardy. She took a few steps backward, prepared to make a hasty retreat.

But then the figure in the doorway emerged into the crisp afternoon light, and she froze. The man in the shadows was thinner than he had been two years before, his face darker, his eyes more intense. But she would have known him anywhere. "*Thomas?*"

He began to walk toward her, and for a moment, she couldn't move. It felt like an impossible mirage. Surely, the handsome pilot wasn't once again standing in front of her, smiling that perfect smile, looking at her with relief and tenderness written across his face. "It's you," she whispered, a warm glow spreading over her whole body.

But then, common sense kicked in and unfroze her, reminding her of where they were—*who* they were. Quickly, she motioned him back into the shadows. He paused and retreated toward the doorway he'd been standing in. She scanned the street for passersby. They were alone, but for how long? She crossed the street quickly, and then, she was just inches from him. *This couldn't be happening.* She knew she'd have to get him someplace safe, but for now, time stood still. She reached out to touch his face, her fingertips grazing the stubble along his jaw. She longed to kiss him, to fall into his arms, but she couldn't do it here, not in public.

"Ruby," he murmured, and it was his deep, familiar voice—the one she'd never really expected to hear again—that finally snapped her back to reality. What if he didn't feel the same way she did? After all, it had been two years. Anything could have happened in that time. The fact that he'd returned wasn't necessarily an indication of his feelings; it could just as easily have been that he knew nowhere else to go. Suddenly self-conscious, she dropped her hand back to her side. "Thomas, what are you doing here?"

"I was shot down over Saint-Omer a few days ago. I came as quickly as I could."

"But the escape line has been compromised. Didn't you hear?"

"Yes, but I had to see you. I had to make sure you were all right." His smile faltered. "But no one answered at your apartment, and I began to fear the worst."

"You were worried about me?"

He reached for her hands, pulling her closer. He was cold, and she had the sudden, strange thought that she'd like to draw him a warm bath. "Ruby, of course."

"But why?"

He looked startled. "I've thought of you every single day. Have you thought of me?"

"Yes," she whispered.

They stared at each other for another long moment, and finally, she believed. The impossible had happened; he had come back to her. But she was being careless; an old neighbor could recognize her, or worse, a collaborator or a Nazi could spot Thomas in his uniform. "Come," she said, abruptly breaking the loaded silence between them and pulling her hands from his. "I must get you somewhere safe. Are you injured?"

"Nothing like last time."

"Very well." She forced herself to be practical, to push her feelings aside. What mattered now was getting him to safety. "We'll need to walk a bit. To get to my new apartment, we must cross the Seine, which means you'll be out in the open, and I'm afraid your disguise isn't very foolproof. So instead of crossing at the Pont de l'Alma, we'll work our way south and then west on side streets, and we'll cross at the Pont de Passy. There's a lower likelihood of Nazi presence there, and it'll be easier to stick to the shadows. All right?"

He nodded and listened carefully as she explained the route she had in mind. It would take an extra thirty minutes, which would expose him for longer, but she couldn't simply march him through a neighborhood swarming with Germans.

"Once we get there, you must stay in our courtyard until nightfall. I can't bring you inside in broad daylight, just in case we're followed. I can't put Charlotte in danger."

"Your neighbor? The one whose mother I helped?"

"Yes. She lives with me now."

He looked grim. "Her parents are gone?"

"Deported more than a year ago. We've had no word."

"Ruby, I'm so sorry."

"I am too." She reached for his hand, lingering longer than she should have. What if she was just a woman standing on the beautiful streets of Paris with a man she loved? It was a wonderful fantasy, but it could never be true, not as long as the war raged around them. She let go. "We must go now before someone sees us."

She was acutely aware of Thomas several paces behind her as she headed west along the rue de Grenelle. She wound her way southeast down smaller side streets until they'd cleared the Champ-de-Mars and the École Militaire, two places that were often bustling with Nazis. Then she turned right and right again as she wove back toward the river. She looked back a few times and was relieved to see Thomas hugging the shadows, his head down. A few people stopped and stared, but they passed very few German soldiers, and the ones they did see were too preoccupied with their own conversations to give them a second glance.

When they finally turned onto the rue de Lasteyrie, Ruby nodded toward the entrance to the courtyard and let herself into the building through the front door. She watched from her window as Thomas sat down in the shade, his back against the building. He was here; he was really here. Now there was nothing to do but wait.

CHARLOTTE HAD LEFT A NOTE saying that she'd be spending a few hours with Lucien that afternoon, so Ruby was alone in the apartment. As she waited for night to fall, she felt like a giddy schoolgirl, changing into a cotton dress she hadn't worn in more than a year and rummaging through a small box of odds and ends until she found a stubby red lipstick that she'd put away after Marcel had died.

Daylight had vanished by five-thirty, and there was a soft knock at the door. Ruby opened it to find Thomas standing there, his cheeks pink from the evening chill. For a moment, they just stared at each other, and then his arms were around her, and his mouth was on hers. Ruby pulled him into the apartment and fumbled with the lock, and then she found herself pressed against the door, her whole body on fire.

"I've missed you, Ruby," he murmured, drawing back to gaze into her eyes.

"I've missed you too."

"I thought of you every time I flew over France."

"But why? I'm just a woman who helped you long ago. Aren't I?"

He kissed her again. "You're the person I think of each time I take off. You're my good luck charm. I've spent the last two years not knowing if you were dead or alive. Standing here in front of you now feels like a miracle."

"I think of you all the time too, Thomas." She wanted to lead him to her bedroom, to feel his body against hers the way she'd hardly dared imagine, but Charlotte would be home soon. Besides, Thomas had been walking for days and was covered in grime; surely he'd want to feel like himself again. "Why don't you freshen up? I've drawn you a bath and laid out a fresh set of clothes for you."

"Your husband's?"

"No, I don't have any of his things anymore. I keep spare clothes on hand now in case pilots are sent my way."

His smile faltered, and he took a small step back. "So there have been others you've helped? Others like me?"

"Thomas," she said softly, holding his gaze, "there is no one like you."

CHAPTER THIRTY-TWO

November 1943

While Thomas bathed, Ruby paced the apartment. She couldn't stop thinking about the feel of his body, the way his mouth had lingered on hers.

When he emerged thirty minutes later, freshly shaven and dressed in gray slacks and a white shirt, he looked like a different person. His dark hair was still damp and curled at the ends, framing his chiseled face perfectly.

"You're staring," he said softly, smiling at her.

She looked away, embarrassed. "I was just thinking that it must feel nice to be clean after your long journey."

"Oh, is that all you were thinking?" His tone was light, teasing.

"I might also have been thinking that you are even more handsome than I remember."

His smile widened. "So you *have* been thinking of me."

"All the time." She took a deep breath. "We had a pilot here in January who said he knew you. Jon Payne. He was captured in Urrugne soon after."

"I heard about Urrugne. Poor Payne. He was here?"

"I—I couldn't believe how relieved I felt when he told me you were still alive, Thomas. I had no way of knowing, although I had the strangest feeling that I would have sensed it if you were gone."

He took a few steps closer to her until they were standing just inches apart. He grazed her cheek with his thumb, as if he couldn't quite believe she was real. "And you've continued to work on the escape line, Ruby?"

"Until the arrests in Urrugne. We've been inactive since the winter. I'm very sorry, Thomas; I don't have any way to get you out of France right now."

"I know."

"And you still came to me?"

"I had to."

They stared at each other for a moment. "I—I suppose you could try to venture out on your own, since you've made it out of France before. Or—" She paused and glanced up at him before returning her gaze to the floor. "Or you could stay here until we can find you a safe way out."

"But won't I be putting you in danger?"

She took a deep breath and looked into his eyes. "Any risk would be worth it, just to have you here."

"You mean that?"

"But perhaps it's foolish of me to suggest—"

He didn't wait for her to finish. He pulled her into his arms, covering her mouth with his. When their lips met, she had the sudden, strange sensation that she was floating. He folded her in closer, and she could feel his body pressing against hers as his tongue softly parted her lips. She let out a small, unintentional moan, and he started to back away, but she grabbed his collar and drew him closer. She didn't want this to stop. Ever.

But then there was the sound of the front door opening and closing, and they both pulled away, startled.

"Thomas?" Charlotte was framed in the doorway, her mouth hanging open as she stared at them. Lucien was behind her, his eyebrows arched in surprise.

"Um, yes, hello, Charlotte," Thomas said, taking a step back from Ruby. "Lovely to see you again."

"What are you doing here?" Charlotte asked.

"Don't you think we'd better go inside before someone sees us?" Lucien hurried her into the living room and shut the door. "Hello," he said to Thomas. "I'm Lucien, Charlotte's friend. And you, it appears, are Ruby's friend."

"Yes, ah," Thomas said in French, clearly still struggling to regain his composure. "Nice to meet you. I'm Thomas."

"*The* Thomas?" Lucien asked. "The pilot?"

Thomas raised an eyebrow at Ruby and smiled. "Indeed."

Lucien grinned. "Well then! Welcome back."

OVER THE NEXT SEVERAL WEEKS, life changed for everyone inside the apartment on the rue de Lasteyrie. Ruby was happier than she'd ever been. She was in love, and she couldn't bear the thought that she'd have to let Thomas go once again. But she knew that Lucien was making inquiries about escape routes, and that as soon as they found one, Thomas would be on his way. Each day together could be the last.

They'd fallen into a routine; in the mornings, Charlotte, Ruby, and Thomas would drink their weak grain coffee and eat small slices of stale bread together, and then Ruby would head out with ration cards, and Charlotte would leave with Lucien. She was officially his assistant now; she came home with ink-stained hands late each afternoon having spent the day forging papers for Jews in hiding and people who were part of the Resistance.

When Ruby returned from standing in hours-long ration lines each day, she'd knock three times on the sliding wall in her bedroom. Thomas would unfold himself from the closet, stretch his hands over his head as he climbed out, and smile that dimpled, crooked smile that always made Ruby's heart melt. "What's for dinner?" he would ask, winking at her, and she'd answer with something ridiculous, such as "Chateaubriand and caviar, of course."

They'd spend the next hour or two holding hands and talking until Charlotte arrived home. Ruby couldn't ask Thomas enough questions; she wanted to know everything about him. She delighted in answering his endless questions about her life too. She told him about her parents, what it had been like to grow up in Southern California, what New York was like in the springtime. He knew now that she hated mushrooms and loved baked pears, that she preferred big band music to jazz, that her favorite movie was *Camille*, and that she sometimes had nightmares about falling from the edge of a cliff into a black abyss. He, in turn, talked of his childhood in London, the games he used to play with his schoolmates, and the way he missed his mother every day. He told her what it felt like to be 14,000 feet in the air in the tiny cockpit of a Spitfire, how frightened he'd felt the first time he stalled in midair, how he sometimes felt racked with guilt over the German lives he'd taken.

Sometimes, they didn't talk at all; they would sit on the couch and then his lips would be on hers, and they'd kiss until Charlotte came home. It never went further than that, though. Ruby had learned to be careful with her heart, and even though she knew she was already deeply in love with him, she worried what would happen once he was gone. Now wasn't the time to be foolhardy about anything. His life was in her hands, as was Charlotte's, and she couldn't do anything to put either of them in jeopardy. She loved them both too much.

But everything changed on the fourth Thursday in November. At home in the States, it was Thanksgiving, and Ruby felt dejected all day thinking of her parents, aunts, uncles, and cousins gathered around the dinner table without her, holding hands and probably praying for her. Did they believe she was dead? Now that the United States was involved in the war, were the American papers filled with news of what was happening here? Could they imagine what her life had become? On a holiday like this, she couldn't help but feel terribly homesick.

The lines at the butcher and baker were shorter than usual, and Ruby returned to the apartment more than an hour earlier than she had expected. Charlotte was out for the day, and Thomas looked surprised to see Ruby when she knocked on the hidden closet door. "Did you not make it to the shops?" he asked as he climbed out and followed her into the kitchen.

"No, I did." She gestured to the small amount of food she'd placed on the dining table. "I thought perhaps I'd try to prepare something special for us tonight. It's a special holiday back in the United States." She told him about how her family would get together for roast turkey, cranberry sauce, and sweet potatoes. "I miss my family terribly. Of course I also miss roast turkey. Wouldn't that taste amazing right now?"

Thomas drew her into his arms. "We could use our imaginations. We'll have a feast!"

"I *do* have a few bottles of wine left. Perhaps we can open one tonight."

"That sounds wonderful." He kissed her, long and hard. "We'll have potatoes for turkey. And this bread for the cranberry sauce."

"Someday, when this war is over, you can come to my parents' house for a real Thanksgiving meal."

"I would love that." Thomas was watching her closely and she could feel her cheeks turning warm.

"I'm sorry," she said. "I—I shouldn't have said that. I know we don't talk about the future."

"I'm very glad you did," Thomas said after a moment. He pulled her closer. "I hope you know, Ruby, that it has always been my plan to come back for you after the war ends. It has been since we first met. I will come for you." He paused and waited for her to meet his gaze. "If you want me to."

"Of course I do," she whispered. "But I don't want you to feel obligated."

He looked surprised. "Obligated? Ruby, I love you."

"You do?"

"Can't you see that?"

And then, at once, she could. She'd known it all along, she supposed, but it was easier not to acknowledge it, not to open her eyes. "I love you too," she whispered.

"Good."

This time, when his lips touched hers, his kiss felt different than it had before. It was tentative but urgent, and she could taste the question on his tongue. Her answer was to burrow against him, making sure that she wasn't holding back.

In a moment, his hands were under her dress, coarse and warm against her skin. "Ruby?" he murmured, and she understood that he was asking for her permission to go further.

"Yes," she breathed, and then her dress was in a pool on the kitchen floor, followed by his shirt. His hands were all over her body, and her hands on his, and it was like nothing she had ever experienced before. It had certainly never felt like this with Marcel, who relied on the same rapid series of caresses each time, a dance that had clearly been choreographed long before she arrived.

With Thomas, though, everything felt new; there was nothing rushed or planned about it. When he picked her up and carried her into the bedroom, she'd never felt more alive.

They made love twice, the first time urgently, the second time slowly and tenderly, gazing into each other's eyes. And for the first time in more than three years, the war slipped away. It didn't matter that Europe was being torn apart, that Paris was bleeding. The only thing that meant anything was this.

Afterward, as she lay in his arms listening to his heartbeat, reality began to crash back in. Charlotte would be home soon, bringing the outside world with her. Thomas would leave one day—maybe even one day soon—and they were all in danger all the time. How she wished she could take his hand and stroll out into the open with him, walk across the bridges of Paris, stroll through the gardens and museums, kiss him for everyone to see. But it was impossible, and soon, she would have to leave the cocoon of his arms and resume living in the real world.

For now, though, she nestled closer, breathing in the scent of him, allowing herself to dream, just for a moment, of a future in which this could be their reality.

CHAPTER THIRTY-THREE

December 1943

Hanukkah began on December 22 that year, and although it was too risky to have a menorah, Ruby, Thomas, and Lucien joined Charlotte in lighting a single white candle on the first night of the Festival of Lights.

"Blessed are you, Lord our God, king of the universe, who sanctified us with His commandments and commanded us to kindle the Hanukkah light," Charlotte recited solemnly, her eyes closed, while the four of them held hands. "Blessed are you, Lord our God, king of the universe, who performed miracles for our forefathers in those days, at this time. Blessed are you, Lord our God, king of the universe, who has granted us life, sustained us, and enabled us to reach this occasion." She opened her eyes and looked up with a half smile. "I might have gotten some of the words wrong. It was my papa who used to say the blessings."

"It sounded beautiful, Charlotte," Lucien assured her. "Should we say a prayer for your parents too?"

Her eyes filled with tears, and she nodded. Ruby waited for her to speak, but instead, the girl closed her eyes and remained silent. When she opened them again, she looked somber. "My prayers for them were in my heart. God knows what I was asking."

"Amen," Thomas murmured, and Ruby and Lucien followed suit.

They gathered each night to light the same candle again, and on the twenty-fifth, they celebrated Christmas together too. There were no presents, no tree, no feast, but the four of them were together, and that felt, to Ruby, like the greatest gift she could ask for. They had become a family, somehow, and though she'd never been a very religious person, she couldn't help but feel that God was with them. *God is present wherever love can be found*, her mother used to say.

She didn't have a doubt that Thomas loved her, and she him, but what had surprised her over the past few months was that she could see the same feelings reflected strongly in Lucien and Charlotte. Before the war, she would have said that they were too young to know what love was. But they'd both lost so much and had managed to find each other. It gave Ruby a feeling of hope, because she knew that if anything happened to her, Lucien would protect Charlotte with his life. He was a survivor, and he would make sure Charlotte lived too.

THE YEAR 1944 ARRIVED UNDER a dark shadow, although there was the sense throughout Paris that the tide was turning. The Americans were involved heavily in the war now, and Lucien often brought news of illicit BBC broadcasts that spoke of Allied victories against the Germans and Italians. Berlin was being bombed regularly, he informed them, and the Germans were surely growing weary. "It's just a matter of time now," he said again and again, grinning at Charlotte, and Ruby and Thomas would exchange concerned looks. Believing that the end of the war was on the horizon was certainly tantalizing, but it didn't feel realistic. Not yet. And Ruby hated to think of Charlotte harboring the false hope that within a few months, her parents could be home.

Thomas continued to spend his days hidden in the closet and his nights in Ruby's bed, but it was clear he was growing restless. He hadn't been outside the apartment in more than two months for fear of drawing attention, but Ruby had caught him staring longingly out the window more than once. As much as he loved her, part of him must have yearned to return to the skies.

A few days after the new year, Lucien arrived at their door just past dawn, wearing a grim expression. "I'm not just here for Charlotte," he said right away when Ruby opened the door, pulling a bathrobe around herself.

A shiver ran down Ruby's spine as she stepped aside to let him in, closing the door behind him. "What is it?"

Lucien cleared his throat again, as if the words he needed to say were lodged there. "There's word of a new escape line, Ruby. This one goes west, to the coast. It's put together by MI9, British intelligence. It's—it's a way to get Thomas out. If you want."

Ruby didn't respond right away. Of course she wanted to get Thomas out. Didn't she? After all, the sooner he left, the safer they all were. Yes, there would be risks involved in his escape, but she had to believe that a line established by MI9 would be as secure as possible. He wouldn't have to sleep in a hidden closet or stay confined to a small apartment while the world went on without him. And he could once again try to make a difference in the war effort. She knew those things would make him happy.

But he would also be gone from her life, a thought that made her feel as if her heart were splitting in two. Though she'd known that the euphoria she'd felt over the past weeks couldn't last, she still wasn't prepared for it to end so abruptly. He'd promised to come back for her at the war's end, but what if he didn't survive the escape? What if he was killed in air combat a few months from now? What if someone came for Charlotte, and Ruby died protecting her? What if the arrests of last January finally led back to her door? If they parted now, there was no guarantee that she'd ever see him again. But she had no choice, and neither did he.

"Ruby?" Lucien asked into the silence.

"I'm sorry." She refocused on the boy. His eyes were full of sympathy, and suddenly, she wanted to cry. But she had to be stronger than that. "Of course. I'll tell him. Thank you."

"If you're not ready . . ." Lucien's voice trailed off.

"But I must be. This is for the best, isn't it?"

"Yes."

They stared at each other for a moment. "Let me go see if Charlotte is dressed yet. And I'll tell Thomas you're here."

When Lucien's knock had come, Thomas had hurried into the hidden closet, just in case. So when Ruby arrived back in her bedroom, it seemed, for a moment, like he was already gone. She could still see the imprint of his head on the pillow on the right side of the bed, still see the spot where the sheets had wrapped around him as he held her tight the night before. She sighed and shook her head before rapping lightly on the wall. "Thomas, Lucien is here. You can come out. He's found you a way home."

"YOU'LL HAVE TO LEAVE TONIGHT," Lucien said ten minutes later as the four of them sat in the living room, their expressions somber. "There's a bistro not far from here where one of the men who runs the escape line will interrogate you to ensure that you're really an RAF pilot."

Thomas looked confused. "Who else would I be?"

"A few of the escape lines have been infiltrated by German spies. They need to be absolutely sure that you are who you say you are before they take you to the next stop on the line."

"And where is that?"

"I don't know. I only know you'll be heading west. The escape is by water rather than by land."

Thomas looked surprised. "By water?"

"Across the Channel. From what I've heard, this plan was months in the making. But you'll be among the first to test it. I've vouched for you, but the men involved in this escape line don't really know me. So they'll need to evaluate you for themselves."

"Of course," Thomas murmured.

"I, um, was hoping that you wouldn't mind if Charlotte spends the day with me today," Lucien said, glancing first at Charlotte and then at Ruby. "I have a lot of work to get done, and I could really use her help."

Ruby smiled at him sadly. Charlotte left with him every day; there was no need to ask her permission anymore. But she understood what he was saying: he was promising that Ruby and Thomas would have the apartment to themselves. "Of course," Ruby said.

"Good." Lucien smiled encouragingly at her. "We'll be back at five so I can bring Thomas to the bistro."

"Thank you, Lucien." Thomas stood and shook the boy's hand. Lucien stood too, and Ruby had the strange, fleeting thought that they could almost be father and son—or at the very least, brothers.

Charlotte stood and hugged Thomas tightly. "I'll be very sorry to see you go. We will miss you very much."

"I'll miss you too. All of you." Ruby could see tears in Thomas's eyes, and that ripped the hole in her heart even wider.

Charlotte gave Ruby a quick peck on the cheek. "Are you all right?" she whispered.

Ruby could manage only to nod; to speak would have been to open the dam.

After saying good-bye to Lucien and Charlotte and closing the door behind them, Ruby turned slowly and found Thomas gazing at her with a sad smile. "What is it?" she asked.

"I was just thinking about what a beautiful future we're going to have," he said. "You and me."

All at once, there were tears streaming down her face. "Thomas, we're barely guaranteed tomorrow."

He took a few steps toward her and pulled her into his arms.

"We just have to believe, Ruby. We have to believe that things will work out just the way they're meant to."

"But how?"

He was silent for a moment. "Let's talk about the life we'll have," he said. "Tell me about what it will be like for us in California."

She pulled back to look at his face. "You're saying you'll come to California with me?"

"Unless you'd prefer to stay in Paris."

She thought about that and shook her head. Everything she'd come for was gone. The only thing that mattered here was Charlotte, and she was confident that if Charlotte's parents didn't return, she would be able to officially adopt the girl and move her to America after the war. "No. But what about England?"

"We can go there too, if you'd like. Buy a farm, maybe, move to the countryside. But wouldn't you rather go somewhere that hasn't been ravaged by the war?"

"Yes," Ruby whispered.

"Will your parents like me?"

Ruby laughed, wiping a tear away. "They'll love you, Thomas. You're exactly the kind of person they've always wanted for a son."

"So tell me." He touched her cheek gently. "Where will we live?"

She hesitated, because to speak her dreams aloud would surely be to jinx them. But what if, instead, giving them voice made them come true? "My parents have a big piece of land near Lancaster," she said. "It's about sixty miles north of Los Angeles."

"So we'll be rubbing elbows with all the movie stars? Cary Grant and Humphrey Bogart will be around for dinner a few times a month?"

"Hardly! It's worlds away from Hollywood. But it's the most beautiful place you've ever seen. My parents live on the edge of a huge poppy field."

"I remember. The photo in your old apartment. The one of you in the field when you were a girl."

"Yes. The poppies bloom every spring, and it's like the whole world has come completely alive. Sometimes, when I see sunsets here, I think of home, because the colors are the same: reds, oranges, yellows in every shade you can think of. It's truly like nothing you've ever seen."

"Poppies," Thomas said, holding her gaze. "You know what they mean, don't you?"

"Yes. Remembrance." In Europe, after the Great War, poppies had become a symbol to honor soldiers who had lost their lives in battle. It wasn't something she wanted to think about now.

"'In Flanders fields the poppies blow,'" Thomas said softly, reciting the words to the famous John McCrae poem. "'Between the crosses, row on row.'"

"My father used to read me that poem when I was small," Ruby said. "He fought in the war, and he said once that he liked to look out at our fields and imagine a parade of his fallen brothers in arms. But the poppies always meant something else to me. When I was a little girl, I imagined fairies living among them, and even when I was older, I believed somehow in the flowers' magic. I still do. It's a very special place. My parents always said that if I wanted to come home, they'd give me a piece of their land to build my own house on. I think they were very disappointed when I moved here instead. But it's not too late to fix that."

"We could build a house together."

"With a porch and rocking chairs."

"And a fireplace with a big chimney for the nights when it gets cold." Thomas paused. "Does it actually get cold in California?"

"It does sometimes." Ruby smiled. "And we'd have big windows in our bedroom that overlook the poppy fields."

"And plenty of room for our children to play in the yard."

Ruby reached up and touched his face. "Children?"

"I want to have children with you someday, Ruby. If you want that too."

"Of course I do." She wasn't sure she'd ever felt happier than she did in that moment.

"And if Charlotte's parents don't come home," Thomas said carefully, "we'll adopt her."

"You'd do that?"

"In a heartbeat."

Ruby smiled. "Of course that means we'd probably have to bring Lucien too. We'll all live happily ever after."

Thomas pulled her to him and kissed her. "We'll all live happily after."

They made love three times that day, staring into each other's eyes, whispering about the future, making promises that they both knew they might be powerless to keep.

They fell asleep in the early afternoon, and Ruby woke a few minutes before four. Thomas still had his arms around her, and his chest was rising and falling in an easy rhythm. For a long time, she just watched, committing to memory the shape of his jaw, the color of his eyelashes, the constellation of freckles that dotted his collarbone. "I'll see you again," she whispered. "I know I will."

She woke him at four-thirty, knowing that Charlotte and Lucien would be home soon. Already, the light that streamed in through the bedroom window was turning apricot. Evening was on its way, and there wasn't enough time to say all the things she wanted to, but she knew there never would be. Perhaps that was what it was like to love someone deeply: to feel that no matter how many moments together you were granted, there would never be enough.

Thomas blinked at her a few times upon awakening, as if reminding himself that he wasn't in a dream, and then he kissed her once more, softly, tenderly. "I was thinking," he said, "that we should also have a white picket fence. Isn't that very American?"

She laughed. "And maybe an American flag flying in the breeze."

"And a British flag."

"But of course."

They smiled at each other. "Tell me more about the poppies," he said.

And as they rose reluctantly from the bed and got dressed, Ruby did just that. She described the way the poppies soaked in the desert sunshine, blooming the color of clementines as far as the eye could see. She told him about the soft purple owl's clover, the deep purple lupine, the tiny yellow wildflowers, and the buttery white cream cups that grew there too, a rolling field of watercolors stretching into the horizon. She told him about the mountains in the distance, the way everything looked carved out of the brilliant blue sky. "It's like heaven on earth," she concluded. "I can't wait to be there again. With you."

They heard Charlotte's key in the lock, and Thomas pulled her to him once more. "Thank you," he said. "Thank you for painting me a picture of the future. It will sustain me until the day I see you again."

And as Charlotte came inside, followed by Lucien, both of them wearing expressions of regret, Ruby thought with a strange surge of hope that perhaps this wasn't so senseless after all. Maybe this was the reason for the hell they'd all been going through. Maybe this was the life she was supposed to find all along.

CHAPTER THIRTY-FOUR

January 1944

Seeing the pain on Ruby's face that evening as she said good-bye to Thomas was wrenching for Charlotte. After all, she was in love too, and she couldn't imagine being forced to let Lucien go. Now that she had realized what it was to feel that way, she had the clarity to see just how deeply Ruby's feelings for Thomas—and his for her—ran. In fact, Charlotte wondered now if Ruby had ever really loved Marcel, or if she'd simply mistaken a desire to escape the mundane and a need to be wanted, for the real thing.

Sometimes, two people are just meant for each other. It was as simple as that. And so Charlotte's heart broke a little as she watched Thomas whisper something in Ruby's ear, and Ruby whisper something back. Charlotte couldn't hear their words, and she supposed she didn't need to; she knew they were saying "I love you" in their own way.

"It's time," Lucien said after the hands on the clock had ticked past five. Charlotte watched as Ruby and Thomas exchanged one last pained glance and finally pulled away from each other.

"Thank you," Ruby said simply, looking at Lucien, "for finding Thomas a way out. Please promise me that you'll do your best to keep him safe."

"I swear it on my life," Lucien said solemnly, which made Charlotte love him even more.

Thomas turned to Charlotte. "You take care of Ruby for me, all right? I know I asked you that once before, but I need to ask it again now."

Charlotte reached out and grasped Thomas's hands in her own. "You don't have to worry. Just concentrate on getting home safely. We look forward to seeing you again."

He kissed her gently on both cheeks, then turned back to Ruby. They didn't say anything; they just held each other's gaze for a long moment and then leaned in for one more kiss.

"Be well, my love," Thomas said. "I will see you again soon."

Ruby smiled through her tears. "Remember the poppies."

And then, far too soon, he was disappearing out the front door with Lucien, a hat pulled low over his eyes. He looked back, just once, and then he was gone down the stairs. Ruby and Charlotte held their breath until they heard the front door of the building open and close.

Ruby choked back a sob. "He'll be back," she said, wiping her eyes. And then, in the smallest of voices, she asked, "Won't he?"

"I know he won't rest until he's with you again," Charlotte said over the lump in her own throat.

Still, as Ruby retreated into her bedroom and shut the door behind her, Charlotte's heart was heavy. Only Thomas's return would bring Ruby back to life.

CHARLOTTE WAS STILL AWAKE ON the couch four hours later, when Lucien came back. He knocked lightly on the door and slipped into the apartment without another sound.

"She is asleep?" he asked, nodding toward Ruby's door.

"I think so."

Lucien sighed. "It is done. He's in the hands of MI9 and their associates now."

"Do you think he'll get home?"

Lucien looked away. "I don't know. This will be the very first run of the new line. There hasn't been time to work out any problems."

"Don't say that. Losing Thomas would destroy Ruby."

"This has been months in the making. I think it should be all right."

"Thank you, Lucien, for doing this."

"I'd like to think I'm your family, Charlotte," Lucien said gently. "And that makes Ruby my family too. I'd do anything for you."

Charlotte nodded, too choked up to reply.

"You know, I will protect you always. No matter what."

"And I will protect you." Charlotte had come to believe in her own power. No longer was she a little girl who had to wait for others to chart her course. She had transformed into someone else, someone she thought her parents might be very proud of.

"Charlotte?" Lucien said after a moment. "There's something I must ask you. But I swore to myself that I wouldn't put you in danger."

"What is it?"

"The new escape line. They need more people they can trust. I told them about you and Ruby, how you'd worked on a line in the past, how you have the perfect apartment for harboring pilots." He looked at the floor and then back up at Charlotte. "They want to know if you and Ruby would consider providing a safe house for the new line too."

"Yes," Charlotte said without hesitation. Lucien's expression was concerned, and Charlotte knew he was already regretting asking. But helping out on the line would give Ruby a reason to get out of bed each day.

"Are you sure? This could be more dangerous than last time. The Nazis are cracking down."

"It's a risk I'm willing to take. And I know Ruby will feel the same way."

CHAPTER THIRTY-FIVE

January 1944

There were fifteen other pilots—most American, a few British—along for the journey west to Saint-Brieuc, a commune in Brittany situated on a bay that opened into the English Channel. As had been the case on his last journey out of Paris, Thomas was given a fake ID and a forged Ausweis travel permit as well as a change of clothes to make him look like a poor French farmworker. Giving up the garments he'd worn at Ruby's was more wrenching than he'd expected; handing them over felt like giving away his last piece of her. But he was doing that anyhow by fleeing Paris, wasn't he?

The men were divided randomly into groups of two or three and instructed not to speak with one another. They traveled separately to the Gare Montparnasse, not far from Ruby's old apartment, and were warned to avoid eye contact, to stay silent, and to pretend to be asleep if officials passed through their compartment. The 250-mile journey through the French countryside was uneventful, and several hours later, all sixteen men exited the train and were met by couriers. Some of the pilots were lodged in Saint-Brieuc, but some, including Thomas, were sent on via a small local train to Plouha, an even smaller town just up the coast. Thomas found himself with two American pilots in the tiny attic of a farmhouse a mile inland.

Storms pounded Brittany for a week, and Thomas spent many hours sitting silently at the small attic window, which happened to look east to Paris, wondering about Ruby. Was she safe? Did she miss him? Had she meant the things she'd said about the future they'd share after the war? Each day, he made small talk with the other pilots and with their hosts; he was the only one among the refugees who spoke French, so he slipped once again into the role of translator. Each night, he lay awake, staring at the low-beamed ceiling as wind whistled by the house, and thought about Ruby's field of poppies.

They'd been in the cottage for nearly two weeks when their hostess, a young woman named Marie, climbed into the attic late one afternoon and said in English, "It is time." She turned to Thomas and, asking him to translate, quickly relayed the plan. They'd wait for full dark, then she'd take the pilots to another safe house. Later in the evening, they would be led down a steep cliff to a cove tucked against the rocks. From there, they'd be picked up by small British boats to take them across the Channel. "Godspeed," Marie concluded in English, making eye contact with each of the men in turn.

An hour later, she brought them through the darkness across muddy fields and country lanes to a small cottage that overlooked the moonlit water. There were six pilots there already, and the others who had been on the train from Paris arrived shortly thereafter.

They were joined by a Russian and two Frenchmen, all of whom were running from the Germans and would make the journey with them. The man who had interrogated Thomas in the bistro in Paris—who had introduced himself as Captain Hamilton—arrived just past ten-thirty to explain the plan. By morning, he said, if all went well, the men would be back home. "I'll need your IDs and anything personal that could identify you," he concluded.

Thomas lined up with the others to hand over the last of his effects, and then he waited. When Hamilton was done collecting everything, he went on to explain in a clipped tone exactly what would happen next. There would be six guides to lead the men to the cliff Marie had mentioned, and then they'd have to proceed, one by one, down the hundred-foot drop to the beach while making as little sound as possible.

"On the way there, we have to cross through fields patrolled regularly by the enemy," he added. "Be prepared to fight them off if it comes to that. We can't compromise the mission."

Just before midnight, they made their way across the road and into a field filled with thorny bushes. The men had been told to remain completely quiet and to hold hands, forming a silent human chain. They broke apart as they reached the cliff, and for a moment, standing on the edge of France, Thomas felt nauseated as he looked down into the blackness. The surf crashed below, loud and hungry, frothy white waves glowing in the moonlight. It was a long way down, and once he'd made the plunge, there would be no going back.

The man in front of Thomas stepped to the edge of the cliff and disappeared in a rumble of falling rocks. Then it was Thomas's turn. The man behind him nudged him forward and Thomas took a deep breath. This was it. He closed his eyes, and as Captain Hamilton had instructed, he lay on his back, extended his legs with his feet flexed, and pushed off. His body slammed down the cliff, and as rocks ripped through his clothes and tore his skin, he held a fist in his mouth to keep from crying out. He hit the beach with a thud, and with an aching back, he stood and moved into the shadows. Reid, one of the Americans who'd been sheltered with him at Marie's house, put a hand on his shoulder and squeezed once, a reassurance.

Once they were all huddled in the hollow by the sea, there was nothing to do but wait. Captain Hamilton had been vague about the events that were meant to unfold, but Thomas had assumed there would be boats along to retrieve them shortly. Instead, the moon ascended higher and the tide continued to rise. One of the guides flashed a Morse code signal into the blackness at one-minute intervals, indicating that they were ready for pickup, but no one came, and Thomas began to worry that something had gone wrong. In the distance to the west, the pillboxes of the Pointe de la Tour, a coastal guard post manned by the Germans, were just visible against the night sky. Thomas began to wonder about the logic of this plan.

But then, after they'd waited for more than two hours, three pale dots appeared on the horizon, moving toward them at a rapid clip. As they drew closer, Thomas realized they were wooden surfboats, each manned by three fellows with oars. As they slid silently into the cove, the men aboard the boats exchanged greetings with Captain Hamilton and the guides, and they put away the submachine guns they were carrying. Quickly, they unloaded a large gasoline tank and six suitcases. "Now," Hamilton whispered to the airmen, gesturing for the one closest to the water to come forward. Quickly, the escapees boarded the boats, and by the time Thomas turned back around to watch the beach slip away, Hamilton and the others were gone, as if they'd simply melted into the night.

Soon, they were approaching a wooden-hulled motor gunboat, an MGB, that seemed to materialize out of nowhere. Quickly, the men were pulled aboard and escorted belowdecks, and the surfboats were secured. A single engine purred to life, and they headed north, toward England, the cliffs of France vanishing into the blackness behind them.

The small cabin exploded in a cacophony of voices as soon as the last man descended. There were cheers, expressions of disbelief, jolly complaints about the gashes many of them had sustained on their backs and legs from sliding down the cliff to the beach. But Thomas stayed silent; he knew he should have felt overjoyed to be heading home, but all he could think was that with each passing moment, he was farther and farther away from France, farther away from Ruby, farther away from the future he so badly wanted. He knew he didn't have a choice, that the only way back to Ruby was to return to England and rejoin the war, but right now, it felt like he was making the biggest mistake of his life.

Six hours later, as they pulled into Dartmouth Harbor, the rest of the pilots filed toward the front of the boat to watch as they approached land. Only Thomas turned the other way, looking southeast toward the country that was no longer visible across the Channel. "I'll come back for you," he whispered into the morning mist. "I promise."

CHAPTER THIRTY-SIX

February 1944

The days without Thomas felt empty at first, but within a week, after several interviews with stern-faced MI9 men, Ruby began to host pilots once again. The new work kept her occupied and prevented her from dwelling on all the terrible things that could have befallen the man she loved. She cried herself to sleep, but during the day, she put on a cheerful face for Charlotte and Lucien. In the mornings, she pretended not to see the concerned glances of pilots who, hidden in the wall overnight, must have heard her sobs.

The changes in Paris as the winter dragged on were unmistakable. The impeccably dressed Nazi soldiers and ingratiatingly polite officers were beginning to disappear, replaced by scruffy, ill-mannered German troops. "They're sending the decent ones to the front now," Lucien commented one day. "It's a good sign. It means the Allies are winning the war, you see. They need all the best men to fight."

And while Ruby believed Lucien, the presence of the less civilized soldiers also made things more difficult. The Germans grew crueler and more violent in their reprisals. More and more frequently, French people were picked up on suspicion of being part of the Resistance and were shot to death within hours, without any sort of due process. The Germans were nervous, Lucien said, because they were slowly losing their hold on France. But all Ruby could see was that they were tightening their grip.

On the first Tuesday in February, she stepped out into the frigid cold to queue, as she always did, for her rations. She was armed with her own tickets plus some of Lucien's forgeries, the only way she could provide enough food for Charlotte and the pilots. It was risky to use the fake ones, of course, but it was a necessity she had grown accustomed to.

There was something different about this day, though, something ominous, and Ruby sensed it moments after she'd taken her place in the line. As the women around her rubbed their hands together, trying to get warm, and breathed out puffs of air, two German soldiers approached from the rear and two from the front. The mundane chatter—about the icy weather, about naughty children, about the punishing shortages of coal—died out as the Germans began walking the length of the line, looking at each woman's face. Ruby held her breath and studied the ground with great interest. What if they were here for her? What if her work on the line had finally caught up to her?

One of the Germans stopped in front of her and reached out to tilt her chin up. His leather glove felt oddly warm against her chilled skin as he turned her head from side to side, as if he was inspecting cattle. He had beady blue eyes, bushy black eyebrows, a mouth that looked too small for his face. "You," he said in deeply accented French. "Your identity card."

Ruby could feel the eyes of the other women on her, and for a moment, she was frozen.

"*Schneller!*" the German shouted after only a few seconds.

Ruby fumbled in her handbag and withdrew her card, the real one that identified her as Ruby Benoit. The German stared at it for a moment and then looked up at her with narrowed eyes. "Do not move."

He took a few steps to where the other Germans were standing, and as they conferred in hushed tones, examining her papers, she could feel her knees quaking. The others in line had scooted away from her, as if whatever was happening to her was contagious. A few left the line altogether, disappearing down alleys when the Germans' backs were turned.

Finally, the beady-eyed German returned and thrust her papers at her. "What is your business here?"

"Queuing for barley flour," she managed.

"Do you know Adèle Beauvais?"

The name didn't ring a bell at all. Was it someone attached to the escape line, or was this purely a case of mistaken identity? "N-no."

"She is not your sister?"

"No. I've never heard of her. I swear."

He grabbed her chin again and held it firmly as he looked into her eyes. She refused to blink, to show him any weakness.

"Very well," he said at last. He turned and barked something at the other Germans, and then he turned back to her. "If I find that you are lying, I will happily shoot you in the head myself."

And then he turned sharply on his heel, followed by the other three. They got into a car a half block away, and then they were gone. Ruby collapsed to the sidewalk, breathing hard. Only one of the other women in line, a woman old enough to be Ruby's mother, came to her aid.

"Perhaps if you know this Adèle Beauvais, you should tell her to get out while she still can," the woman said as she helped Ruby up.

"But I've never heard of her."

"Dear," the woman said gently, "I can read on your face that you are not as innocent as you would have the Germans believe."

Ruby opened her mouth to deny it, but then the woman pressed a package into her hand. "Here. My eggs and meat. Go home now before the day gets any worse for you. That was a narrow escape."

"But—"

"Take it. And if you're doing something to undermine the Germans," she added in a whisper, "then thank you. Vive la France." She turned her back on Ruby, pulling her wool coat more tightly around her. Finally, Ruby stepped out of line and began the walk back to her apartment, haunted by the fate that could have found her by accident.

"PERHAPS WE SHOULD STOP," RUBY said that night as she and Charlotte ate dinner alone in the kitchen. They were between pilots, and Lucien was out at a meeting, so it was just the two of them. Ruby had told her what had happened that day and how much it had shaken her. "Things are getting more dangerous."

"But if we stop fighting, we've already begun to lose. We have to keep at it until the very end."

"Yes, I know. But today terrified me, Charlotte. The next time the Germans come, it could be for us. Your parents didn't leave you with me thinking that I would insert you into the fight for France."

"You didn't insert me anywhere. With or without you, I would have found my way into the Resistance. Anyhow, my parents couldn't have imagined how the world would change. My father left our apartment a year and a half ago thinking that the police would let him go because it was the right thing to do. He didn't get to stay here long enough to change his mind. But he would have, Ruby. He would have seen the need to fight back. He just didn't realize yet what would happen to the city he loved."

"But the risk—" Ruby began.

"The risk is part of it," Charlotte said firmly. "Nothing great happens without risk."

"I know. I just can't help feeling as if our luck is running out."

Over the next several weeks, the arrivals and departures of pilots flowed like a steady tide. There were Refilwe and Poloko, two pilots from South Africa who arrived together, conspicuous in both their accents and their appearances. They were two of the most polite pilots Ruby took in, but she was glad when they departed after only two days, for they would have been harder to pass off as Frenchmen if the authorities came looking. There was a pilot named Travis from New Zealand, whose charming accent made Charlotte giggle, and there was a pilot named Raymond from Worthington, Ohio, whose sister had gone to university in New York at the same time Ruby had. Howie from Topeka was with them for almost a week, and he spent evenings patiently helping Charlotte practice her English verb conjugations and mornings sipping watery ersatz coffee with Ruby in companionable silence. Terence from Liverpool was worried about whether his fiancée, Elizabeth, would stay faithful to him when he was gone. "She has legs that go on for miles," he said more than once, "and don't think that the other men don't notice. She's always flirting, but she swears she loves me. Do you think she's telling the truth?"

Marcus from Arlington, Texas, was disturbed that Ruby and Charlotte were involved in the escape line. "But you're women," he said, looking baffled. "This is dangerous work, which means it should be done by men." Still, he thanked them profusely for their hospitality and was never rude, but Ruby was happy to see him go when Laure—whom they had recruited for the new escape line— came to pick him up. Ernest from Spring Gully, South Carolina, had such a thick southern accent that Ruby could hardly understand him, and Joseph from Brockton, Massachusetts, came down with a fever and murmured for two days straight about someone named Catherine, whom he called the love of his life. Fortunately, he came out of the fog on the third day and was in traveling shape by the fourth, having sweated out the illness under Ruby's concerned supervision.

All the pilots brought welcome news of Allied victories and spoke of the hope that the war would be over soon. The Germans were being pushed back on every front. "France will be liberated any day now," a pilot from St. Louis named Tom Trouba told Ruby confidently in late February. "You wait and see. The war'll be over by the end of 'forty-four."

He departed with Laure the next day, leaving Charlotte and Ruby alone once again. Charlotte went out in the late morning to meet Lucien, and after Ruby returned from exchanging the day's ration tickets, she sat down in the living room, basking in the rare silence. She hadn't been feeling well for the past few weeks, which she attributed to the doldrums of winter and the constant pit of worry in her stomach over Thomas's safety. But today, alone for the first time in weeks, she had time to truly think about how she'd been feeling and when the symptoms had first appeared. As she sat on the couch in silence, her stomach swimming, something suddenly occurred to her: she hadn't had her time of the month since December. More than two months ago. "Oh my God," she said aloud.

And all at once, she knew. The pit in her stomach. The lack of appetite even when she should have been starving. The swelling in her breasts even as her belly grew flatter. It was exactly what had happened last time.

She was pregnant. The realization hit her like a lightning bolt, and she didn't know whether to be ecstatic or terrified. It was what she and Thomas had spoken of, the life they had planned together, but she wasn't ready for the future to come yet. At the same time, though, what if the pilots were right and the war would be over soon?

She was carrying Thomas's baby. The thought echoed in her head again and again like a favorite song, soothing and thrilling her. This meant that a piece of him was still here. But she'd lost the first baby—what if she was fated to miscarry again? Losing this baby too might just destroy her. She felt a sudden, desperate need to protect the life in her womb at any cost. But how could she bring a healthy child into the world when she could scarcely survive herself?

She sat with her hands on her belly for the next few hours, imagining a future with Thomas and the child they now shared. She knew—with the same certainty that she'd known her first baby would be a boy—that this child would be a little girl. She could see Thomas laughing and chasing a pigtailed daughter through the poppy fields with the sky clear and blue and perfect above them. Ruby would watch from the porch, her heart filled with joy, as she thought about how far they'd come. The war would be over, the world would be right again, and everyone she loved would be safe. Charlotte would be there too, sitting beside her on a rocking chair, finally protected from all the forces that could hurt her.

"Are you okay?" Charlotte's voice jarred Ruby awake sometime later. Ruby didn't remember falling asleep, but darkness had fallen.

"Oh, yes," Ruby said, struggling upright. "I must have been more tired than I realized."

Charlotte frowned. "You're feeling all right?"

"Yes."

Ruby was suddenly aware of how much older Charlotte looked lately. She was fifteen now. The innocent girl Ruby had first met nearly five years ago had vanished, replaced by a young woman.

Would Charlotte's own parents recognize the person their daughter had become?

"Is there anything you'd like to talk about?" Charlotte asked, sitting down beside Ruby.

Ruby lowered her eyes and shook her head. When she looked up again, the girl was still staring at her knowingly. Charlotte's gaze moved to Ruby's belly, and Ruby was startled to realize that her own hands had returned there, apparently of their own accord, as if she could shield the baby against all the evil in the world.

"You're pregnant, aren't you?" Charlotte's tone was gentle.

"What?"

"You're pregnant."

"I—I didn't even realize it myself until a few hours ago," Ruby said, her voice shaking. "How did you know?"

Charlotte looked sad. "Because you're peaceful. Just like you were the last time. It's like—" She paused, searching for words. "It's like it doesn't matter what's going on around you. You're just calm."

"Calm," Ruby repeated. And as implausible as it sounded, she understood what Charlotte meant. Over the past month, she'd felt her energy turn inward. She had worried less about the pilots and the state of the war, and had concentrated more on the memories that she carried with her, as if they would provide her a means of survival. Now she recognized what Charlotte had already seen— that she'd been nesting before she even knew there was a need. "I'm very frightened, Charlotte," she said after a moment. "What if I lose this baby too?"

"You won't."

"How can you know that?"

"I just do. This is what's meant to be, Ruby. You're meant to raise a child with Thomas."

Ruby half-smiled. "You don't judge me for having . . . relations with him?"

"Of course not! You would marry him right now if you could, wouldn't you?"

Ruby could see in her mind's eye a church somewhere—maybe in England, maybe in California—a white dress, and Thomas standing handsome and tall at the altar in an RAF dress uniform, waiting for her. Her favorite love song, "Cheek to Cheek," would play afterward as all their loved ones celebrated, and they'd hold each other and dance long into the night. "Yes, I would."

"Then God knows how you feel. This war, it has changed everything about the world. But our most important lives are still on the inside, aren't they? What matters is what's in your heart."

"When did you get so wise?" Ruby's eyes were suddenly wet.

Charlotte leaned forward and kissed Ruby on her cheek, then she placed a hand gently on Ruby's belly. "Someone I love very much set a good example for me."

"You mustn't tell anyone, Charlotte. Not even Lucien. I—I don't want anyone to know until I've told Thomas."

"Your secret is safe—at least until your belly begins to grow. But maybe the war will be over by that time, and Thomas will have returned."

There was a knock at the door then, and Charlotte went to peer out the peephole. "Another pilot," she said, and Ruby nodded, wiping her tears away.

She took a deep breath and stood, ready to greet the newest fugitive. Their work had to go on. It was her duty to do everything she could to build a better world for the child she already loved with all her heart and soul.

THE NEW ARRESTS BEGAN IN March.

At first, there was the rumor that a man who had worked on Aubert's original escape line had been arrested and executed for trying to smuggle pilots out of France. Soon after, Laure was picked up, questioned, and released, but she got word to Ruby through a friend of Lucien's that she wouldn't be working as a courier for the new line anymore, because she was certain the Germans were following her. She could think of no other reason why they would have let her out so quickly.

Ruby, whose belly was just beginning to blossom, grew increasingly nervous. She knew Laure hadn't talked, but what if the authorities had been following her long before they picked her up? What if they'd seen her coming and going from Ruby's apartment? The risks seemed enormous, but after a few weeks passed and no more arrests were carried out, Ruby began to relax. Perhaps the first arrest had been a terrible fluke and Laure's had been a mistake. Besides, by early April, there was buzz about a possible Allied invasion in the next few weeks. Surely the Germans would be more worried about that.

"We still need to lie low," Ruby said to Charlotte and Lucien over dinner one night. "Even if things seem to be turning in favor of the Allies."

"You mean stop taking in pilots?" Charlotte asked.

Ruby hesitated. Her gut was telling her yes, but what would happen to the men who needed refuge? She couldn't simply abandon them. "We just need to be more careful, I think."

Lucien and Charlotte exchanged uneasy looks. "Ruby," Lucien said after a moment, "I can take in pilots in my apartment for a while, just until things blow over. In case your apartment has been compromised."

"No," Ruby said firmly. "We have the perfect setup here with Monsieur Savatier looking out for us and with the hidden closet in my bedroom wall. We just need to hang on a little longer, and the Allies will be here. We're nearly at the end. I can feel it."

Within a few weeks, Ruby was escorting pilots on foot to the Montparnasse station. Though it put her out in the open, it just made sense now that Laure was unavailable; it lessened the traffic in and out of her apartment, nearly eliminated her contact with others on the escape line, and allowed her to see the pilots safely off on the next step of their journey.

In fact, Ruby wondered why she hadn't started doing this sooner. Fewer people involved in the line meant fewer chances for something to go wrong. And now that the threat of Allied invasion was looming, the German troops in Paris seemed distracted anyhow. Surely they wouldn't notice a woman who was simply out for a stroll on a spring afternoon.

Her charge the second week of April was an American pilot named Christopher. He had graduated from the University of Florida before joining the Army, and he was as clever as he was friendly. When he'd first shown up at her door, two days earlier,

Ruby had assumed that he was French, because he had somehow managed to acquire a set of worn clothes that fit perfectly, as well as a Frenchman's particular way of holding a cigarette. He'd even greeted her in French, and it had taken several seconds for her to notice his American accent. Perhaps that was why, as she strolled down the rue Letellier on a bright morning, trailed by Christopher a half block behind, she hadn't thought to worry. Some pilots were more foolhardy than others; some resisted listening to a woman's counsel; some were simply clumsy and nervous. But Christopher was a model guest, and Ruby was sure she'd have him to his train in no time.

She was so confident, in fact, that when a large black car drew to an abrupt halt beside her, she hardly noticed. But then three men jumped out, all dressed in the uniform of the German police, and Ruby's heart shot into her throat. Surely they weren't here for Christopher. She reminded herself to continue walking, to keep her head down. But two of the men stepped directly into her path, and the other cut off her only potential route of escape by coming up behind her. "Identity papers," said the broader of the two men in front of her. He had a nasty scar across his cheek and a short, dark mustache that made him look like Hitler.

"Yes, of course," Ruby said, trying to sound calm. From the corner of her eye, she could see Christopher turn down a side street behind her. The police didn't seem to notice him, which filled her with some relief—but it was short-lived. Why were they stopping her if it wasn't because of the pilot?

She rummaged in her purse and withdrew her papers—she carried only her real ones now, the ones that identified her as Ruby

Benoit. She was sure that even if the Germans had something on her, they wouldn't execute her for fear of reprisal from the U.S. government. It was her trump card, but perhaps she was being overly optimistic.

"This says you were born in the United States," the mustached officer said, glaring at her. "What are you doing here?"

"I am French by marriage."

"Where are you going?"

"Just out for a stroll." She could tell by the look on his face that it was the wrong answer. "I needed to stretch my legs."

He frowned. "What is your address?"

"Twenty-four, rue Amélie." She gave him the old address without hesitation, because she didn't want anything to lead to the new apartment. Charlotte was there, and Ruby wouldn't put her in danger.

"Most people out for a stroll would walk *toward* the river," the officer said.

"I wanted to be alone," she replied. "There are crowds near the river on a beautiful day like today."

"So you were not going to the Montparnasse station," he said with a smirk, "to aid in the escape of Allied pilots."

Ruby could feel her mouth go dry, but she forced a neutral expression. "What? Of course not."

"And you're certain that's the story you want to stick with?"

"I'm sure I don't know what you mean."

He grabbed her handbag and began to rifle through. Her mind spun as she wondered whether she'd mistakenly left anything incriminating in it. She didn't think so, but a moment later, he withdrew a bundle of ration tickets.

"You live with your husband?" His expression told her he already knew that Marcel was dead.

"No. He died in 1941."

"Yes. I am aware. The traitor Marcel Benoit."

Ruby swallowed hard. So she hadn't been stopped on a whim. They had sought her out. This was much worse. "My husband wasn't a traitor. The evidence against him was false."

The officer guffawed. "Madame, we do not make mistakes. But *you*, it seems, have made a serious one. Why do you have so many ration tickets if you live alone?"

She thought quickly. "I offered to pick up some supplies for neighbors."

"Ah. And these neighbors—as you call them—are not Allied pilots trying to escape from France?"

"Of course not!" Ruby tried to appear indignant.

"Ah yes, I'd nearly forgotten. You're merely out for a walk." He grabbed her by the arm and shoved her toward the car. The other officer, who'd been in front of her, took her other arm, while the man who'd been behind her walked around to the driver's seat.

"What are you doing?" Ruby demanded. "I have rights!"

The men laughed as they shoved her roughly into the back of the car. The mustached man climbed in beside her. "Unfortunately for you, madame, that isn't true at all."

AT THE POLICE HEADQUARTERS, RUBY was thrown into a small cell by herself and told to wait. She spent the day worrying about Charlotte. What if the police found out where Ruby lived now? What if Charlotte was arrested? Ruby still felt confident that her own American citizenship would spare her from execution. But if they found Charlotte, it would be only a matter of time until they realized she was Jewish. How had Ruby allowed her to participate in something so dangerous? The guilt overwhelmed her, and she sat on the floor sobbing until nightfall, when a guard came to retrieve her, yanking her to her feet and hauling her into a room that looked like an office.

Inside, she found two uniformed guards waiting for her. "Tell us everything you know," one of them said without preamble. "If you lie to us, you'll be shot first thing in the morning."

Ruby struggled to keep a neutral face. Her hands went to her belly. *Breathe*, she reminded herself. *Stay calm. They have nothing on you, or you'd already be dead.* "I haven't done anything," she said evenly. "You have made a mistake. I am American. You can't execute me."

The guard shrugged. "Have it your way."

A female guard entered a moment later with a bologna sandwich and a cup of water, and though Ruby worried that the food had been drugged, she wolfed it down; she was starving. Soon after, another guard came in and dragged her to a cold, damp cell with a straw mattress on a dirt floor. "Get some sleep," he said, not unkindly, and then he closed and locked the door behind her.

CHAPTER THIRTY-SEVEN

April 1944

"Ruby has been arrested." Lucien's face was pale when he arrived at Charlotte's door that night, far later than she'd expected him. She had been pacing the apartment, worried sick that Ruby hadn't come home. The last Charlotte had heard, Ruby was on her way to deliver Christopher, the American pilot, to the Montparnasse station. Had he been careless? Followed her too closely? Drawn unwanted attention to both of them? Charlotte had been bracing for the worst as the hours rolled by with no sign of Ruby, but Lucien's words still broke her.

"No, no, no." Charlotte was suddenly unable to breathe. "There must be a mistake. Lucien, tell me there's a mistake."

He shook his head slowly. "There is no mistake, my dear. The Feldgendarmerie picked her up hours ago. She's to be turned over to the Gestapo in the morning."

"No. Lucien, how did this happen?"

Lucien didn't reply until after he'd stepped into the apartment and she'd closed the door behind them. "Someone must have betrayed her. They knew exactly who she was when they stopped her. From what I understand, they didn't even notice the pilot tailing her. He made it to his rendezvous point at the station; he's the one who told us of her arrest."

"Did they hurt her?"

"I don't know." He took her hands. "But, Charlotte, Ruby is strong. She will survive whatever they throw at her, and they won't dare execute her, because she is an American. She will survive."

"But she's pregnant," Charlotte whispered.

All the remaining color seemed to drain from Lucien's face. "What?"

Charlotte began to cry; she had promised Ruby that she'd keep her secret, but things were very different now. "If the Germans find out . . ."

"Thomas is the father?"

"Yes."

"The pregnancy isn't visible yet?"

"Not really." Ruby's belly had begun to swell, but not enough that someone who didn't know her would take notice.

"That's good. But if she's sent east . . ." Lucien's voice trailed off, and he and Charlotte exchanged horrified looks.

"They kill the pregnant ones first," Charlotte said, her voice hollow. "That's what I've heard."

"Let's just hope for now that it does not come to that. I will try tomorrow to find out everything I can about her situation." He paused. "In the meantime, I think you should stay with me.

If they've arrested Ruby, it's only a matter of time before the trail leads to this apartment. I will speak with Monsieur Savatier about removing anything incriminating, but for now, Charlotte, we must go. Quickly."

Charlotte wiped her eyes and nodded. It was only a place, after all. What was important was that they all found a way to survive.

"I will do everything in my power to make sure she's okay," Lucien said, as if reading her mind.

"Thank you," Charlotte replied. But the words felt hollow, because she knew he could do only so much. For now, Ruby was on her own, and her fate rested in the hands of the increasingly hostile German authorities.

CHARLOTTE COULDN'T SLEEP THAT NIGHT, but she dozed off after dawn, falling into an abyss of nightmares. At first, she could see Ruby at the bottom of a dark hole, crying out for help. And then she was on a crowded train car headed east. In the third dream, she saw Ruby delivering a stillborn baby in a dirty jail cell. When Charlotte awoke, sweaty and panting, Lucien was gone and she was alone.

He returned late that afternoon, his expression grim. "I've spoken with Monsieur Savatier," he said. "We cleared out the hidden closet. If the Germans come, they won't find anything out of the ordinary. Monsieur Savatier will contact me if Ruby returns or if anyone comes looking for her."

"Thank you." Charlotte hesitated. "Is there any word about what has happened to her?"

Lucien cleared his throat. "She has been moved to the prison at Fresnes."

"Fresnes?"

"I'm afraid so."

They didn't say anything for a moment, but Charlotte knew that Lucien was thinking the same thing she was. This was a bad sign. The conditions were reportedly horrific; people passing by could hear the screams of tortured prisoners.

"Have you learned anything else?" Charlotte asked.

"Just that a man named Léo Huet disappeared at the same time and hasn't turned up in any of the prisons, as far as we can tell. He was working on the escape line, and the suspicion is that he betrayed Ruby and a few others. Laure has also been apprehended, as has another man who ran a safe house just outside Paris."

"And have any of them talked yet?"

"Not as far as I know. But the Nazis have their techniques."

"Will they torture her?"

"I don't know."

But from the way Lucien averted his eyes, Charlotte guessed that the answer was probably yes. She felt suddenly sick to her stomach. "Surely the fact that she is American will help her."

"Yes. I hope so," Lucien said. But his tone was flat and unconvincing. "Charlotte, if there's a way to survive, Ruby will. I know she will."

"Yes," Charlotte agreed. But she also knew that survival might not be a possibility. There was no reason to say it aloud.

CHAPTER THIRTY-EIGHT

June 1944

From Dartmouth, Thomas and the other two British pilots who'd made their escape from Plouha in January had been escorted to London by two MPs, who took them first to the movements office and then to the Ministry of Defence. There, Thomas had been grilled for hours by an MI9 man who was evidently trying to confirm that Thomas was who he said he was. "You never know," the man said at the end, when he was assured that Thomas was telling the truth. "It wouldn't be the first time the Germans had tried to infiltrate us. Welcome back, son."

The interrogation was followed by fourteen days of mandatory leave, which Thomas was supposed to use to "get his head straight," according to the MI9 man. But he didn't want to straighten out his head. He wanted to return to the skies. He wanted to defend Britain. He wanted to drive those damned Nazis out of France. He wanted to get back to Ruby.

It was clear, however, that none of that was going to happen immediately, so he accepted an invitation to visit Harry's family for a week, although he left after just four days because Harry's mother hovered over him, staring as if he were a ghost. He knew she could see shadows of her son in him, in the way he carried himself, the way he spoke, the way he walked, and he realized how difficult his visit was for her. So he made his excuses and spent the rest of his leave alone in a small hotel room in London, dreaming of the day he'd make it back to Ruby. Sometimes, when he closed his eyes, he could see poppies. It was the only time he felt a sense of peace.

Thomas received word on the last day of his leave that instead of returning to Northolt, he was to report to RAF Headquarters for a new posting.

"Won't I go back to my old squadron?" Thomas asked the movements officer, whose office he was shown into upon arrival.

"No," said the man, who introduced himself as Roscoe Vincent. "I'm afraid you can no longer take part in ops over Europe."

"Pardon?" Thomas's stomach was suddenly in free fall.

"The regulations have changed," Vincent continued as he studied Thomas's file, which was open on the desk in front of him. "You see, if you were to be shot down and captured by the Germans, you'd be in a position to give them information about the escape line. We can't risk that."

"But I would never do that. I swear it!"

Vincent was unmoved. "Of course you don't *think* you would. But no one really knows how they'd hold up under torture, eh? In any case, those are the rules, and there's nothing I can do about that. Now, shall we talk about where to post you? Perhaps you might like to fly Lysanders in a unit that handles air-to-air firing practices?"

"No." Thomas resisted the urge to squirm in his chair. "I need to be back in combat."

"Then Malta."

"I wouldn't really be making an impact in the war effort there, now would I?"

Vincent sighed and made a note in Thomas's file. "The RAF base in Drem, then. You can fly missions in North Africa."

"With all due respect, sir, I'd like to be as involved in the campaign in Europe as possible."

Vincent peered at Thomas over the top rim of his glasses. "Why?"

Thomas hesitated. "The people of France saved my life. I vowed to myself that if I got out alive, I would do all I could to protect them."

Vincent studied him for a long time. "So you met a girl."

Thomas didn't say anything. He didn't want to hurt his cause.

"Europe isn't an option." Vincent marked something in Thomas's file and then flipped it closed with finality. "We'll start you at Ras El Ma in Morocco. It's being used as a staging post for now. From there, I suspect, you'll be heading to"—he checked his notes—"Oujda. Also in Morocco. Rest assured, you'll be a very important part of the war effort. That will be all."

He stood and waited until Thomas, the breath knocked out of him, rose and made his way to the door. The poppy fields felt farther away than ever, but he was powerless to change that. If he needed to help win the war from the edge of Africa, that's what he would do. After all, the base in Morocco wasn't far from the European coast. And that was something.

IT TURNED OUT THAT INSTEAD of flying combat missions, Thomas's assignment was to deliver Spitfires to airfields in Corsica through the heat of the summer. The aircrafts would be used in the upcoming liberation of France, so Thomas was able to rationalize to himself that in a way, he was protecting Ruby after all, even if he wasn't doing so directly. But he longed to fly missions, and as the weeks rolled into months, he began to feel as if he would be stranded in Morocco forever.

On June 6, Thomas was on another continent as more than 160,000 Allied troops landed on the beaches of Normandy to fight the Nazis head-on. The men storming through northern France were a mere 170 miles from Ruby, and he wasn't there.

Thomas took a short assignment in midsummer training other RAF pilots to evade capture if they went down behind enemy lines. The tide of the war had changed after D-Day, and it was becoming clear that the Nazis wouldn't be able to hold on. Still, they seemed to be hunting downed pilots ruthlessly. It was more important than ever for pilots flying over the Continent to know what to do if they had to eject over land.

"There are good people on the ground there," Thomas said to a group of fresh-faced young men in late June. "People who rise above the danger and risk their own lives to help us. It's why we will win the war, because the things we stand for are rooted in that sort of goodness."

"How do you maintain your faith in humanity, sir?" asked a young pilot. "How should we go about believing that we will get home safely when the odds are against us from the moment we hit the ground?"

"You must think of the people you love the most," Thomas said, "and remember that you're fighting the war to make the world safe for them. Whatever becomes of you—whether you live or die— you'll know that you are doing things for the right reasons. That's how you maintain your faith."

CHAPTER THIRTY-NINE

June 1944

Ruby was still imprisoned at Fresnes when she heard the news of the Allied invasion of Normandy. The end of the war, it seemed, was at hand. But how long would it take for the Allies to reach Paris? Would she survive that long?

Five and a half months into her pregnancy, her belly was growing, but the guards hadn't noticed yet. In fact, they hardly seemed to notice her at all anymore. They'd tried to force the names of her associates out of her when they first captured her, but she'd maintained a steadfast denial, repeating that they were wrong, that she'd never worked for the Resistance, that she had no idea what they were talking about. She suspected the only reason she hadn't been tortured or executed was that she was American.

Home was now a whitewashed cell ten feet long and six feet across with an iron cot attached to the wall and an open toilet in the corner. Every day, weak coffee was handed out in the morning, and just before noon, the soup cart came by. The same bland potage was served at dinner along with a small piece of bread. The prisoners were given minuscule amounts of cheese or meat twice a week, and sometimes, there were Red Cross food parcels filled with treats like chocolate, jam, and crackers. Some prisoners received clothing or food from relatives, but of course Charlotte couldn't come forward with a delivery without revealing herself. Ruby received packages just twice, from her "cousin" Lucien, who wrote that his wife was fine and in good spirits. She knew it was his way of telling her that Charlotte was alive and well, and that knowledge brought her far more comfort and warmth than the wool socks and bread he sent.

Twice a week, the prisoners were taken into the courtyard for twenty minutes of exercise. Communication with prisoners from other cellblocks was forbidden, but Ruby was heartened to catch glimpses of Laure twice during the first few weeks. After that, the raven-haired courier was gone, and Ruby had no way of knowing whether she'd been released, sent east, or executed. She prayed for the first but knew the last was far more likely.

Ruby found she could communicate with the prisoners in the adjoining cells by speaking close to the faucets; somehow, the pipes went through the walls and carried sound next door. She learned that the woman to her right was a twenty-three-year-old named Angelique, accused of helping to distribute a Resistance newsletter. To her left was Jacqueline, who was forty-two and suspected only of being the girlfriend of a man who worked on one of the escape lines. Both women refused to admit any wrongdoing, and they were beaten regularly for it. Ruby found strength in their steadfast resistance, and she tried to draw upon that inspiration in her darkest hours.

And there were many dark hours. She was by herself for most of the day, but she wasn't really alone, for she had the baby in her belly. Thomas's baby, her source of strength. And if she was grateful to the Germans for anything, it was that they never tried to starve her as a tactic to make her talk. They took away every other freedom they could, but the fact that she was still able to feed herself meant that her baby was able to grow. At night, when she couldn't sleep, she sang softly to her belly and hoped that the baby wasn't somehow absorbing her fears. She prayed for a better life for her child, and she begged God each night to continue to conceal the pregnancy.

There were four women who had babies with them and had been allowed to remain at Fresnes, but still, Ruby hesitated to give up her secret. She didn't know what the other women had been accused of, but she suspected their alleged transgressions were more minor than hers, for the guards left them alone.

In mid-June, she was moved to the prison at Romainville, on the edge of Paris, which sent chills down her spine. She knew that this was the place where prisoners were taken before being deported to Germany. On the way into the prison, she had to sit down with one of the commanders, a hulking Nazi soldier who looked blank and unsympathetic as he quickly skimmed her file.

"I'm American," she said, trying to sound confident. "You can't send me east. I have rights."

He merely laughed and said, "None of you have rights. Haven't you worked that out by now?"

For a week and a half, she languished in a cell with nine other women, all of whom were just as worried as she was about what was coming next. Romainville should have seemed a pleasure after Fresnes—after all, they were allowed to socialize with each other, and their cells even had windows, which looked out on the prison yard—but the 4:00 A.M. roll call each day ruined any chance Ruby had at happiness. Every morning, the prisoners were marched into the prison yard, and thirty or forty names were read out. These women were on the list to be deported east, and most of them stepped forward with heads held high. Some shouted "Vive la France!" and others simply smiled bravely and waved good-bye. All of them seemed to be facing the future with courage. Ruby didn't know how they did it.

And then, on June 25, her name was called. She didn't dare look back at the others, for fear of crying. She felt so much weaker than they were; she wanted to scream and rage and cry out that this wasn't fair, that this was France, that the Germans had no right to take her away. But there would be no point in any of that, and she knew it. She was on her own.

Ruby was loaded onto a bus full of other women, all of whom were silent as they made their way through the familiar streets of Paris. Ruby stared out the window and searched the faces of passersby, hoping against hope to see Charlotte or Lucien or even Monsieur Savatier, but of course it was only a sea of strangers, many of them staring with detachment as if the same couldn't possibly happen to them.

At the Gare de Pantin, on the northeast edge of the city, the SS shoved the women into trains, sixty to a car. There was straw on the floors and very little ventilation from the tiny slit windows above.

There was an air of fear as they pulled out of the station, and soon that fear was tinged with the pungent scent of urine from the over-flowing tin toilet in the corner.

For the next few days, the train stopped frequently, sometimes for hours at a time, as it chugged slowly east. Twice a day, the prisoners were let out briefly, with armed guards standing by, to relieve themselves in fields. A few tried to flee, but they were shot dead on the spot. Ruby simply tried to blend in with the others, hiding her belly as the transport drew closer to the German border. There were rumors that children and pregnant women were being shot upon arrival at the concentration camps. She didn't know if this was true, but she couldn't risk anyone noticing her condition. As long as she was still in France, as long as she could hear bombs dropping in the distance, Ruby held on to the hope that they could be rescued.

Then, on June 30, her mother's birthday, the train passed through the eastern French city of Nancy and finally, inevitably, into Germany. Once the French border had disappeared behind them, Ruby's heart sank. They were in Hitler's land now. And as they rolled farther into Nazi territory, Ruby felt a heavy sense of certainty. There would be no reprieve. She had to do all she could to protect herself and her child until the Allies came.

RAVENSBRÜCK—THE CAMP WHERE RUBY AND the other prisoners were taken—was hot. Blisteringly hot. On the day of their arrival, Ruby and the other women were marched through a town called Fürstenberg, some fifty miles north of Berlin, up and down dusty hills and winding roads until they finally reached the enormous green gates of an expansive prison camp. Barracks seemed to stretch as far as the eye could see, and the women who were already imprisoned there walked back and forth, pushing carts and pulling wagons with hollow eyes, sunken cheeks, and emaciated limbs. It was like something out of a Bela Lugosi horror movie, and Ruby had to pinch herself as a reminder that in fact this was real life. *Her* life. Her stomach lurched, and she had to bite her tongue to avoid vomiting in the dirt.

Ruby was horrified when the arriving prisoners were ordered into a huge building and told to undress. What if someone noticed her belly? But a heavy woman who had been near her on the train moved toward her as they entered the building and took her arm. "You are pregnant?" the woman whispered in French.

Ruby hesitated. "Is it obvious?" Tears clouded her vision. Had she been fooling herself to think she could get away with concealing it?

"Stand behind me," the woman said firmly. "We will not let them see. We *cannot* let them see."

"Thank you," Ruby whispered. She held her breath as she cowered, naked and terrified, behind the woman.

"I have two daughters of my own," the woman said softly as they inched forward. "They are around your age. I pray every day for their survival; as a mother, it is the most important thing in the world, is it not?"

"Yes," Ruby managed. "Yes, it is."

Ruby shuffled with the rest of the prisoners through several stations, where they were ordered to hand over their clothes, their jewelry, and all their belongings to the guards. In another room, she was forcibly separated from the kind woman and told to climb onto a table. She wanted to scream as a hawk-faced female guard probed between her legs. But the exam was a cursory one, and as Ruby was ushered on, quaking with relief, she realized that every woman who came into the room was being subjected to the same indignity. The guards were checking to make sure they hadn't hidden any valuables inside their bodies.

Next, Ruby fell into a line to have her head shaved, and she sobbed as her auburn hair fell in glossy ringlets to the floor. The tears earned her a slap across the face, and then, nearly bald and shivering, she was sent into another room, where she was shoved under a shower, handed a tiny towel, and given a pair of dirty underpants and a thin cotton dress with an *X* sewn onto both the back and the front.

She saw the kind woman again as the prisoners were herded into the huge barrack that would become their home. There were dirty straw mattresses, roughly five feet wide, arranged in bunk formations three high, and the women were told they would be sleeping three to a bed. The older woman sidled over to a dazed Ruby and took her hand. "You are all right?" she asked.

Ruby could only nod; she still couldn't understand how the physical examination had failed to reveal her condition.

"Thank God for that," the woman said. "He must have heard our prayers."

But as the days turned into weeks, Ruby began to wonder whether God could hear them at all here or whether all of Germany was somehow a void from which no prayers could escape.

She was sent to work at first on a crew that leveled sand dunes. It was hard, grueling labor under the watchful gaze of a female guard with a face like a bulldog's. They worked for nearly twelve hours each day, with very few breaks, and Ruby worried constantly that the food she was given wouldn't be enough to keep the baby alive. Every day, she inhaled a small amount of rutabaga or beet soup, a tiny portion of bread, and some watery grain coffee. Once a week, the meager rations were supplemented with a slice of sausage or an ounce of cheese. Ruby knew she was losing weight quickly. Her belly was still growing, and she was relieved to know that the baby, at least, was receiving some nourishment. But it came at Ruby's expense. The only saving grace was that with the near starvation, Ruby's pregnancy wasn't readily apparent, although it should have been by now.

On her second week at Ravensbrück, Ruby's dorm was flooded with two dozen new arrivals, women from Russia who came in with their freshly shorn heads held high. At first, the French women Ruby had arrived with bristled at the intrusion, and Ruby was afraid that there would be an argument. But one of the Russians—a young woman named Nadia, whose high cheekbones and clear green eyes distinguished her as beautiful even in this hellhole—spoke French and managed to defuse any misunderstanding. "We are all in the same situation," she said in a tone that was impossibly soothing. "We are friends, all of us, united against a common enemy. Let us work together."

On the third day after the Russians arrived, Nadia approached Ruby. "You are not French. Yet you are with the French prisoners. Why?"

"I'm American," Ruby said. "But I've lived in France for several years now."

"Why?" Nadia asked again, her gaze sharp and penetrating.

"I married a Frenchman. And when the war started, I couldn't bear to leave. I—I didn't realize that things would get so bad."

"If you were to do it over again, would you go home? Before the war began?"

"No. I think perhaps I did some good before I was arrested." Ruby also knew that if she'd gone home, she would never have helped save Charlotte. Or met Lucien or Thomas. And she wouldn't be carrying Thomas's baby right now. The way things had unfolded felt predestined somehow, even if she couldn't imagine the reason.

"And you are here why?" Nadia's questions were unrelenting, but her eyes had turned kinder.

"I was arrested on suspicion of being part of an underground escape line for Allied pilots."

"And are the accusations true?"

Ruby smiled slightly. "Of course not."

But the look they exchanged told a different story, and Ruby knew that Nadia understood. Ruby had put her neck out and had been caught, something she could never admit aloud.

"I see," Nadia said.

"And you? Why are you here?"

The woman smiled. "I, too, was accused of helping people to escape. Of course I confess nothing, but there are perhaps five hundred men who might tell a different story."

Ruby stared at her. Was she saying she had helped five hundred men escape the Nazis? "Well," Ruby said at last, "it is good we are both so honest and obedient. Just think what would have happened if we'd actually been involved in undermining the enemy."

Nadia grinned. "Yes, just think."

The next morning, when they were given their rations for the day, Nadia sidled up beside Ruby and pressed half of her bread into Ruby's hand.

"Why?" Ruby asked, trying to hand the bread back. "You need your strength too."

But Nadia turned away, smiling at Ruby over her shoulder. "There are two of you," she said, glancing at Ruby's belly, "and only one of me."

She had disappeared into a swarm of other prisoners by the time Ruby recovered enough to respond. Was her pregnancy really that obvious by now? And if so, why hadn't the guards noticed? She wasn't sure if she could, in good conscience, accept another woman's bread. But she was hungry, so hungry. Nadia was already gone. And surely, just this once, it would be okay.

Ruby stuffed the bread into her mouth before she could change her mind, and as she set off for the dunes with the rest of her work crew, she touched her belly and hoped her baby was getting the nourishment she needed to survive.

IN LATE JULY, RUBY, NADIA, and sixteen other women were taken out of the camp to the nearby Siemens factory, beyond the south wall, to interview for temporary jobs. "They are taking women who are clever," Nadia whispered to Ruby on the way. "The rumor is that these are skilled labor positions. Pay attention, Ruby, for this will be much better than the work we've been doing."

Ruby knew that Nadia's concern came from the fact that Ruby's belly was swelling more obviously beneath the loose cotton of her dress now, though she still managed to conceal her condition from the guards by rounding her shoulders and leaning forward slightly during roll call. She was nearly seven months along, and there would come a time soon when her body could no longer rise to the demands of the daily physical labor. Factory work would be much less taxing. It was, she realized with a surge of panic, the only chance she had of saving herself and her baby.

"Do you know what we'll be making?" Ruby ventured.

"Does it matter?" Nadia asked.

"But what if they have us making weapons that will be used against the Allies?"

Nadia was silent for a moment. "There are a thousand women waiting behind us. If we don't take the jobs, someone else will. At least you and I will have a chance of sabotaging the work."

Ruby looked up sharply. "Sabotage? I thought you were talking about saving my baby."

"I am," Nadia said, her eyes sparkling. "But we do what we can to fight the war."

Their interviews were with a man called Herr Hartmann, a German civilian who oversaw part of the assembly line. He was about the age of Ruby's father, and Ruby thought it strange that her first reaction to him was that he had kind eyes. She had come to despise the Germans, but there was something different about Herr Hartmann.

"Why do you want to work here?" he asked stiffly in French as Ruby sat down with an SS guard lurking in the corner.

"I—I think I have the ability to do a more skilled job than I've been doing at Ravensbrück so far," she said. "I have a university degree and a bit of technical experience." The last part was a lie, but she knew he wouldn't be able to check the veracity of her words.

"A university degree? From where?"

"Barnard College in New York."

"Are you American?"

She nodded. "I married a Frenchman before the war and moved to Paris. But yes. I was born in California."

He leaned forward, switching to English. "I would very much like to go to America someday." They exchanged a look before Herr Hartmann blinked and glanced at the guard. "In any case, the job here is on an assembly line. Do you think you can handle taking orders and working with machinery?"

"Yes, sir." She paused. "Your English is quite good."

"Thank you," he said. He gave her a sad smile. "I took courses in English literature long ago. I was a university professor, once upon a time."

"The war has changed us all," Ruby said softly.

Herr Hartmann nodded. "Yes, I look in the mirror and feel I hardly know myself anymore."

She knew as she left the interview that she would get the job.

CHAPTER FORTY

July 1944

Nadia and Ruby began work at the Siemens factory the following Monday. Though the job was somewhat easier than the physical labor of the dunes had been, it was still grueling. The women sat at their stations for twelve hours a day, hands numb and bleeding, eyes bloodshot and raw.

Ruby realized quickly that they didn't need the specialized technical skills Herr Hartmann had claimed. They were assembling electrical parts to be used in rockets, and they needed only to be able to follow basic instructions. Ruby imagined, as she worked, that she might be building an electrical component for a weapon that would be fired at Thomas's base in England, that somehow, she would be responsible for both saving him and destroying him in the same lifetime. So when Nadia showed her how to solder the parts loosely, so that there was a chance the circuits would short out, she was an eager pupil. "You must insert everything properly so that the

Germans don't notice," Nadia explained patiently, "but there's still room to tinker."

Ruby could have sworn that Herr Hartmann knew what they were doing, but the man never said anything. On the contrary, in front of the guards, he treated the prisoners like the slaves they had become, ignoring them almost entirely except to coldly correct the construction of a part here and there. But there were corners in the factory where the guards rarely ventured, and Ruby soon learned that if she carried her electrical components there as if on an errand, Herr Hartmann would often be waiting, eager to have a chat. It turned out that he was horrified at the lack of humanity being shown to Ruby and the others. He would whisper questions—*Why did they shave your heads? What happens to the women who are too frail to work? How much do they feed you?*—and his face would grow paler with each answer.

In her third week at the factory, Herr Hartmann pulled Ruby aside and asked if she'd like him to send a letter for her. "Your family must be very worried about you," he said. She wondered, for a split second, if it was a trap, a false invitation designed to bait her into breaking the rules. But his eyes were as kind as ever, and after a moment, she whispered, "Yes," her heart soaring. To know that there was at least a chance she'd be able to get word to her parents would be worth the risk. "But I don't have any paper or a pen."

He assured her he would provide both the following day. True to his word, he slipped her two sheets of paper and a pen on her visit to the corner the next morning, and that night, while her two bunkmates slept, she wrote by the light of the moon. She kept the letter light and devoid of most personal information and negative commentary, because there was always the chance that it would be confiscated.

Dearest Mother and Father,

Words cannot express how much I miss the both of you. I think of you all the time, and I dream of the day I'll be able to see you again. In the interim, please know I'm all right. I am in a prison camp in Germany at the moment, but you mustn't worry. Marcel died in 1941, but my cousin is in good health. She's fifteen years old now, in fact. She can explain everything to you. Please do all you can to bring her to the States and to look after her if something should happen to me. Until we meet again, please know that it is my thoughts of you and of home that sustain me.

My deepest love always,
Ruby

She knew she couldn't mention the baby, and she debated for at least an hour before deciding to include the verbiage about a cousin. She knew it would baffle her parents, but she hoped that if she were to perish in Germany, Charlotte would somehow find her way to them, and that they would understand who the girl was and how much Ruby had loved her. To mention any more, though, would be to put Charlotte in danger.

Thinking of Charlotte was painful. At least Ruby could fight to the death to protect the baby in her womb. Charlotte, by contrast, was hundreds of miles away. For all Ruby knew, Charlotte could have been picked up already, shot to death. Ruby gagged and heaved at the thought and tried to push it away, but she couldn't sleep that night without seeing Charlotte being tortured.

"Are you all right?" Nadia asked her the next day after their contingent of prisoners had been marched from Ravensbrück to the factory in the hazy light of early morning. They settled next to each other on the assembly line and whispered, as they often did, when the guards' backs were turned.

"I'm just thinking of someone I left behind," Ruby replied. The letter to her parents was folded and pressed into her underclothes, just in case she was searched on the way in, but the guards seemed distracted this morning.

"Your beau?"

Ruby smiled. "No. There is a man, but . . ." She trailed off and shook her head. How could she explain Thomas to anyone? It all still felt like a dream to her, like he'd never been real at all. "No, Nadia, I was thinking of a girl who's very important to me. Her parents left her with me two years ago, when they were taken, and she's become like a sister to me. Maybe a daughter, even. I worry about her every day."

"And there is someone hiding her?"

"There is a boy looking out for her. He's only sixteen, but he loves her."

Nadia's expression softened. "How extraordinary to find love in the midst of war."

Ruby nodded, again thinking of Thomas. "Extraordinary indeed."

"She will be all right, then."

Ruby had to laugh at the certainty in her friend's voice. "I wish I had your optimism. You seem so sure about the future."

A guard passed by then, glaring at them, and Ruby pretended to be deeply absorbed in her work. When he was gone, Nadia nudged her. "I am not sure of anything. But if we don't have hope, we don't have anything."

"I wish I had your hope, then."

"You do," Nadia said. At Ruby's confused expression, she smiled. "That is what my name means. Hope. So as long as you have Nadia, you have hope."

Ruby smiled. It was a nice thought, the idea that hope itself could be embodied in a person. She was silent for a moment as another guard passed by. "Herr Hartmann has offered to send a letter home to my parents for me. You don't think it's a trap, do you?"

Nadia bit her lip. "No, I do not. I think he is a good man who feels terrible about the things that are happening to us."

"Then why doesn't he do something to stop it?"

"You don't think he wants to? You don't think there are many Germans who want to? I think that in a place like this, the system itself has grown so huge that it's impossible to stop. Like a snowball that starts at the top of a mountain and has turned into a boulder by the time it reaches the bottom. I think, though, that there are people like Herr Hartmann trying to make a difference on a smaller level, with people like us. I think you can trust him."

"So do I."

Later that afternoon, Ruby passed by Herr Hartmann in the corner of the factory and slipped him the letter. "Thank you," she whispered.

"It is the least I can do, Ruby," he said gravely. "None of you should have to endure this."

"But how can you stand to work for the Gestapo? To run an assembly line that produces weapons for the Nazis?"

He frowned, and for a moment, she was sure she had overstepped her bounds. But after a pause, he shook his head. "I manage just enough breakdowns in the assembly line that I slow the production of weapons. It's not much, Ruby, but it's something. We all must do what we can, don't you think? It is the only way good has a chance of winning in the end."

BY MID-AUGUST, RUBY HAD HEARD that prisoners who could no longer pull their weight were being killed immediately, their bodies cremated in enormous furnaces that sent cruel clouds of black smoke belching into the sky. The smell of burning flesh lingered in the air.

Ruby was nearly eight months pregnant, but she didn't look that way. Her belly was half the size it had been during her first pregnancy. She was only five or six weeks away from being full-term, and yet if she stood just the right way, the cotton of her loose dress skimmed the air, keeping her secret safe. The guards at the factory were distracted much of the time anyhow, and they didn't seem to be as focused on abusing the prisoners as the guards inside the camp had been.

Death no longer lurked around the corner quite as hungrily as it had when Ruby had worked inside the main camp. But at the same time, falling ill would land a prisoner back inside the gates, and if you remained in the hospital block for too long, the rumor was that you were sent directly to your death. That's what had happened to Denise, a young, quiet French girl who worked several stations down from Ruby on the assembly line. One day, she'd been coughing; the next, she was gone. It had taken a week before word came back that she'd been diagnosed with rheumatic fever and condemned to die. The factory workers had held a secret moment of silence for her on Tuesday, and by the end of that day, Ruby was horrified to realize that she, too, had a nagging tickle in her throat.

"I think I might be getting ill," she said to Nadia that night as they settled down to sleep. Her throat was raw and scratchy, and she could feel herself beginning to perspire.

Nadia put a cool hand on her forehead. "Ruby, you're burning up."

"Fever?"

Nadia nodded, her expression grave.

Ruby struggled upright. "But I can't be sick. My illness could hurt the baby."

Nadia frowned. "I am more concerned about what will happen if they bring you to the hospital block. They certainly won't miss your pregnancy this time." She was silent for a moment. "You must tell Herr Hartmann."

"What?"

"You must tell him," Nadia said more insistently. "He has helped you before, Ruby. He will not let you die."

"But what can he do?" Ruby was crying now. She'd been strong for such a long time, but she was suddenly so tired. She felt the heat of her fever surge within her.

"I don't know. But I think it is your only chance."

The next morning, Ruby felt even worse. Her face was hot, and the world seemed to be spinning. Before she left the barracks, she put her hands on her belly and whispered a prayer. "I don't know if you can hear me, God, but please, save my baby." She bit back tears, splashed water on her face, and headed out to roll call, praying that the guards wouldn't notice her illness.

Fortunately, they didn't, but that meant only a brief reprieve. Ruby could tell, as the morning wore on, that she was getting worse. Her hands shook as she tried to piece together electrical parts, and she could feel sweat dripping from her brow. Her mouth was dry, so dry, and she thought that if she dared close her eyes, she might never open them again.

"You must go to Herr Hartmann now," Nadia whispered as midday approached. "You have no choice, Ruby. The guards will notice your condition very soon if you do not."

"It is my only option?" Ruby asked.

Nadia nodded. "I think so, yes."

And so Ruby rose shakily after the next time the guard walked by, and she made her way toward the back corner of the building, where she'd seen Herr Hartmann heading a few minutes earlier. It was a struggle to walk straight without leaning into the wall. She had to concentrate hard so that the floor in front of her didn't reach up to drag her down. By some miracle, she found Herr Hartmann alone, going over several pages of notes with a furrowed brow. He looked up when she approached. "Ruby!" he said, smiling. But his expression quickly turned as she stumbled forward. "My God," he said, reaching out a hand to steady her. "What's wrong?"

"I'm ill," she whispered.

"Yes, that much is clear. The guards haven't noticed yet?"

"No. But I'm afraid I might not have much time."

He was still holding her arm. "And what will happen? They will send you to the hospital block?"

She took a deep breath, which made her cough. It was time to tell him the truth. "Herr Hartmann, I am pregnant."

He glanced at her belly and then up at her face again, a deep well of sympathy in his eyes. "Yes, I know."

"You do?"

"I could see it the day I hired you, Ruby. How far along are you?"

She coughed again. "Nearly eight months."

His eyes widened. "I thought perhaps four or five."

She shook her head. "We are starving, Herr Hartmann. It's a miracle my baby is still alive."

"A miracle indeed." He studied her. "And if you go to the hospital block and they realize you're pregnant . . . ?"

"Death, I think."

"Dear God," he murmured, raking a hand through his hair. She could see a storm of indecision in his eyes, and for the first time, she realized how unfair this was. She was asking him to do something that would put his own life in danger. And what obligation did he have to help her? "Ruby," he said at long last, "you must leave today. There's no other choice."

His tone was so firm that she almost wanted to laugh. As if it were that easy to simply walk away! "But how?" she whispered.

He thought for a moment. "Meet me here at four o'clock. I'll have an answer then." He strode away before Ruby could reply.

The next few hours ticked by, and as Ruby had told Nadia about Herr Hartmann's words, they were both wondering about what he could be planning. It wasn't as if a woman in prison could simply stroll out into the afternoon sunshine and make a home for herself in the German countryside. And while the primary concern was getting out of the factory unnoticed, Ruby would still have to deal with her raging fever.

"I will come with you to talk to him," Nadia said firmly as the hands on the wall clock inched toward four. "Someone must protect you. Let us see what Herr Hartmann is planning, and I will do what I can to help."

Ruby was too weak to protest, although she was terribly afraid that Nadia would be putting herself in unnecessary danger. She hoped, of course, that Herr Hartmann would talk Nadia into going back to work. After all, Ruby had nothing to lose; death was a certainty if she stayed. But surely the camp would be liberated soon, and Nadia was strong, brave. She would survive. *Hope*, Ruby thought.

Together, just before four, the two women slipped away when the guards' backs were turned and headed toward the corner. Herr Hartmann was already there, and he looked surprised to see Nadia. "You must return to your station," he said.

"Ruby is my friend." Her reply was immediate and firm. "I must do all that I can to help her."

Herr Hartmann looked at her for a moment, as if trying to decide something. "Yes. All right."

Nadia nodded. "What is the plan?"

He held up a cloth sack. "You will take this with you, Ruby. It is some clothing from my twelve-year-old daughter."

"You have a daughter?" Ruby asked.

"And a wife and a son."

Ruby stared at the cloth sack and then shook her head. "No. No, I can't do anything that would endanger you or your family."

"My mind is made up. As is my family's. We all know the risks. Here. Gisela's clothes should fit you; you're so very small. They'll help you to blend in. There is a place to the southeast corner of the complex where a gap is being repaired, just large enough perhaps for a prisoner to make her way out if no one is watching. You must head to the woods to the east and move as quickly as you can. You won't be safe until you're far away from Ravensbrück. Once you've walked for a few miles, begin looking for Red Cross trucks on the roads. It's impossible to know which Germans you can trust, but you should be able to trust the Red Cross to nurse you back to health without turning you over to the Gestapo."

"But . . . what if I don't find one?"

"You will. I know you will. They are everywhere. You will find the Red Cross, and they will help with your fever, and they will safely deliver your baby. We have to believe in that, because there's no other way." He handed her the sack. "There are a few potatoes and some bread in there, as well as an empty bottle. There are plenty of creeks in the woods where you can stop for water. Now, quickly, Ruby, you must go before the guards notice us talking."

"Why are you helping me?"

Herr Hartmann sighed. "Because everyone deserves a chance to live, Ruby. And because this is not the Germany I know and love. There are good German people too, you know."

"I know," Ruby whispered. Of course she knew. In every place evil dwelled, good could also be found. It was a truth that kept the world moving forward, through all the wars, through all the terrible machinations of mankind. "Thank you."

"You must go now."

"How will I get out without the guards seeing me?"

Herr Hartmann glanced at Nadia. "We will create a distraction. I will reprimand her loudly, which should make the guards pay attention to us."

Ruby glanced over at Nadia, who nodded and took her hands. "Yes. It is a good idea. But you must run as fast as you can, Ruby. Your life depends on it."

"Thank you," Ruby whispered, looking into her friend's eyes.

Nadia smiled. "No matter what happens, Ruby, remember I am with you. As long as you have Nadia, you have hope."

Ruby blinked a few times. "Nadia—"

"Go," Nadia said firmly, glancing at Ruby's belly. "If we cannot make the world a better place for the next generation, what is the point?"

She kissed Ruby on the cheek, and before Ruby could respond, Nadia had begun to scream, hurling a string of Russian obscenities at Herr Hartmann.

"Nadia!" Ruby exclaimed, knowing that her friend wasn't just creating a diversion; she was initiating a situation for which she would surely be beaten.

"Go!" Nadia hissed. "I accept the risk. Go and be free, Ruby!"

"Go," Herr Hartmann echoed before grabbing Nadia by the arm and barking orders at her in German. As several guards began trotting in their direction, Ruby took one last look at the two brave people risking their lives for her and slipped out the back door.

She sucked in a huge breath of air—brilliantly, gloriously fresh air—and began to make her way toward the edge of the complex. But a guard appeared from around the corner of the building, drew his gun, and bellowed, "Halt!"

No. Ruby couldn't stop. Not now. Not when she was so close to freedom. Not when Nadia was inside risking so much for her. So she began to run, praying that the guard would miss if he tried to shoot. From the corner of her eye, she saw Nadia's face framed in the factory's window. *Ignore me*, Ruby thought even as she watched Nadia register the danger Ruby was in. *Don't make things worse for yourself.*

But it was too late. Still yelling Russian obscenities, Nadia burst from the same factory door Ruby had just exited and hurled herself at the guard with the gun.

"No!" Ruby screamed, but everything was already in motion.

"I said go, Ruby!" Nadia cried, clawing at the guard's face as he cried out in surprised pain.

Ruby hesitated for a split second, knowing she should go back, wanting to do all she could to save Nadia's life. But then the baby kicked inside her, once, sharply, directly into her rib cage, and she remembered in a flash all that she was fighting for.

And so she ran. She ran for the nearly invisible gap, which was just where Herr Hartmann had said it would be, then for the woods, even as shots rang out behind her. She ran even as she heard Nadia's strangled cry. She ran as her friend's body hit the ground, riddled with bullets. She ran and ran and ran until the factory vanished, until the canopy of trees overhead obscured the blue of the sky, until she was alone in the middle of a silent forest, certain that there were no footsteps behind her.

And in the quiet, she began to sob. *No matter what happens, Ruby, remember I am with you,* Nadia's voice echoed in her head. *As long as you have Nadia, you have hope.*

CHAPTER FORTY-ONE

August 1944

After the initial adrenaline of her flight had worn off, Ruby's pace slowed. There was no one following her, and the underbrush grew trickier to navigate as she moved deeper into the forest. She couldn't see the sun, and she was no longer certain of which direction she was going. Her body burned, her head throbbed, and her vision was blurry with tears. "Nadia," she repeated over and over as new tears spilled. What had her friend done? Had she known, when she encouraged Ruby to flee, that this could happen? Was that what Nadia was trying to tell her, that she was prepared to die to protect her?

By the time night fell, the world was spinning. Ruby stopped near a creek, filled the bottle Herr Hartmann had given her, and drank it all down. She ate half a potato but vomited it back up almost immediately. She sat and leaned against a fallen tree and told herself she would rest for just a few minutes before moving on. But before she knew it, the night had closed in. Sleep overtook her, and her slumber was rich with nightmares about Nadia's blood spattering the foggy German afternoon.

When she awoke, daylight was streaming through the trees, and Ruby sat up with a start. How long had she been out? There was no way to know; she had no watch, and she couldn't see the position of the sun in the sky. She struggled to her feet, made her way back to the creek, and drank more water, followed by another half potato. This time, the food stayed down, but she knew she was still feverish. Her stomach swam; her forehead burned. But at least some of the dizziness had receded, which had to mean she was getting better.

She changed into the dress and shoes Herr Hartmann had given her, and she was surprised to realize just how well a child's garments fit her. Had she really lost that much weight? She knew, as she looked down at her body, that the answer was yes. She was skin, bones, and belly. Herr Hartmann had also included a kerchief, which she tied around her head, knowing that her short hair might give her away as an escaped prisoner.

Ruby sat for a few minutes to gather her strength and to talk to the baby, then she stood and began heading in the direction she thought was west. It was possible, she realized, that she might even be trudging back in the direction of the camp, right into the arms of a search party. Then again, did they know she was missing? Perhaps the guard who had shot Nadia was humiliated that he let Ruby go. Maybe he didn't say a word to anyone. She would have been missed at roll call this morning, but by then, surely they would have considered it too late to hunt for her. She only hoped that Herr Hartmann's complicity in her escape hadn't been discovered.

As she walked, Ruby begged God to deliver her safely into the hands of someone who would help her rather than turn her over to the authorities. After all, she knew that Ravensbrück wasn't near anything but the Polish border, and heading east seemed foolish; the Germans still had a stranglehold on Poland, and there were, in fact, more horrific concentration camps located there. Before she'd fled, the camp had started receiving shipments of prisoners from Auschwitz, and those women looked even more skeletal than the women at Ravensbrück. They died by the hundreds each day, some dropping dead right in the middle of their forced labor, some simply failing to wake up in the morning.

"Hush, little baby, don't say a word," Ruby began to sing shakily as she walked, her hands protectively around her belly. "Mama's gonna buy you a mockingbird. And if that mockingbird don't sing, Mama's gonna buy you a diamond ring." Ruby couldn't remember any more of the lyrics, so she sang the ones she knew again and again.

Eventually, hours later, Ruby came to a broad road on the edge of the forest. She stopped in her tracks, unprepared for the risks that came with a return to civilization. But she might pass as a local laborer instead of a prisoner. The problem was that she knew very little German—only a few words. She certainly couldn't pass herself off as a German civilian, but perhaps she could make someone believe that she was a refugee from somewhere else. The other alternative was to melt back into the forest and press on in a different direction, but already, Ruby felt wildly lost, and she had the feeling she would starve to death or succumb to her fever long before she found her way to safety. No, her best bet was to try to hitch a ride with someone heading west and to hope that whoever picked her up would take pity on her. It was her only chance.

She began to walk along the road, head down, heart thudding. She wasn't sure she was doing the right thing, but she was certain she had no choice. Several cars whizzed by, their drivers ignoring her entirely, and then, in the distance, she saw a small truck whose hood featured a white square emblazoned with a red cross. She blinked a few times as it drew closer, sure at first that she was imagining things. Could it be a German Red Cross vehicle?

She stepped into the middle of the road and began waving her arms over her head. "*Bitte stoppen!*" she cried in German. "Please, stop!"

To her relief, the truck slowed and came to a halt beside her. The man in the driver's seat looked barely older than Charlotte, and she could see that his gaze was concerned rather than angry. It was a good sign. He said something to Ruby in German. She shook her head and murmured, "*Ich verstehen nicht.*" I don't understand. He tried again, repeating his words more slowly, but still she shook her head. "I'm sorry," she said in French. "I don't understand."

Something in his expression changed, and he looked her up and down. "Prisoner?" he asked in French.

"No," she said quickly. "Laborer. Er, *Arbeiter.*"

The man looked skeptical, but he turned to confer in German with the other two men in the truck. Finally, nodding, he turned back to her. "Get in," he said in French, nodding to the back of the truck. "We take you as far as we go. Then you exit."

"Yes, yes, of course," Ruby said, a wave of relief sweeping over her. "Thank you so much. *Vielen Dank!*"

"*Bitte,*" the man said with a small smile. He paused and asked in French, "You are sick? Ill?"

Ruby's mouth went dry. Yes, the truck likely had medical supplies, but what would she do if they refused to transport her because they didn't want to be exposed to her fever? No, it was more important that she get as far away from Ravensbrück as possible. "Just very tired," she said as firmly as she could. "And hungry."

"Yes," the man said. He turned and said something to the man in the passenger seat, who rummaged in a bag and withdrew an apple, a piece of bread, and a piece of cheese. "Here. You eat." He nodded again to the back of the truck, and Ruby, momentarily stunned by the bounty of the feast, mumbled a thank-you before grabbing the food and climbing in. She ate greedily as the truck began to pull away, and although she felt nauseated, she closed her eyes and willed the food to stay down. Her baby needed it. Soon, lulled by the truck's movement, she fell into a deep sleep.

It was dark by the time she awoke to a man shaking her shoulder. It was the driver of the Red Cross truck, she realized, and he was saying something to her. "I—I don't understand," she managed to say as she struggled upright.

"You go here," he said in French. "We go that way." He pointed down the road, and although she wasn't sure why she couldn't continue with him, she knew better than to talk back.

"Thank you very much for the ride," she said. "Where are we?"

He took a moment to process her question. "Very near to Swiss border. Swiss is that way." He pointed down the road in the darkness.

"Switzerland?" She sat up straight now, her heart thudding. It wasn't the direction she had intended to go, but wasn't this better? Switzerland was neutral, and she'd be more likely to find help there than she would have if she'd headed north to occupied Denmark. Switzerland adjoined France too, which meant she wasn't so far from home. "Thank you," she said to the man, who was glancing not so subtly at his watch. "*Danke*. Thank you very much."

"*Bitte*," he said. "*Viel Glück*. Good luck."

He helped her down, and before she had a chance to say anything else, he was already climbing back into the driver's seat, already pulling away. It wasn't until he'd gone that she realized he'd handed her another apple and another piece of cheese before he left.

She wolfed down the food as she stood in the grass, trying to decide what to do. This was a smaller road than the one they'd picked her up on that morning; it was made of dirt and appeared to wind through an unpopulated rural area. If she was near the Swiss border, as the Red Cross man had said, she could feel a bit safer. Perhaps she didn't need to melt back into the forest and risk getting lost. If she stayed along the main road, maybe she'd find a safe place to sleep.

Her body ached, and she sang to the baby again as she walked. Her fever, she realized, wasn't burning quite as fiercely. The sleep on the truck had been restorative, but she knew that if she let her body get depleted again, the illness could come storming back. She had to find a safe place to stop for the night.

Without a watch, and without guards barking orders about where she needed to be, it was impossible to keep track of time, so it might have been thirty minutes later, or it might have been ninety, but eventually, Ruby saw a farmhouse on a hill just off the road a quarter mile ahead, backlit by the glow of the moon. She picked up her pace, her mind spinning. It was late; she couldn't just knock and ask for refuge, could she? Besides, what if the people who lived there called the authorities? But there was a small barn next to the main house, and Ruby reasoned that at the very least, she could sleep for a few hours in the hay before moving on prior to daybreak.

But as she approached a few minutes later, walking across what appeared to be a cornfield, the front door of the house opened, and a man emerged, holding a lantern. "*Wer ist da?*" he called into the night. Ruby cowered in the darkness, hoping he wouldn't see her, but her clothing must have caught the moonlight, for a moment later, he came striding directly toward her, barking a string of threats. Or she thought they were threats, anyhow; they sounded just like the tirades the guards went on at Ravensbrück just before they pulled prisoners out of line to beat them.

Ruby considered running, but she was so weak, and she knew the man would overtake her quickly. So she stumbled backward a few steps and then began to cry, her hands raised. "I mean no harm!" she said in English, switching to German to add, "*Ich werde dich nicht verletzen,*" which she thought meant roughly the same thing.

And then, before she could say another word, the man was standing a foot away, shining his lantern in her eyes. She shielded her face from the light.

He asked her something in German, and although she couldn't understand the words, she realized he sounded less aggressive now. He had a head of bushy red hair and a full beard and mustache to match, and he was huge—easily more than six feet tall with broad shoulders and a thick neck. He asked her another question in German, more gently this time, and she answered in English, "I don't speak German," and then repeated the same words in French.

The man stared at her for a moment more before replying. "You speak French?" he asked in French.

She blinked, weak with relief, and replied in French, "Yes. I live in France. You speak French too?"

"Yes. We are not so far from the French border here." He paused and looked her up and down. "Who are you? What are you doing here?"

"I'm . . ." She trailed off, unsure of how to answer. What if he was in collusion with the Nazis?

"Don't worry," he said a moment later, as if reading her mind. His tone was gentle, and there was something about him that reminded her of Herr Hartmann. "I will not hurt you. Are you running from the Nazis?"

"Yes," she whispered.

"You will come inside, then. You must rest. I think perhaps you have come a very long way."

"Yes." But she hesitated, not sure if she could trust him.

"Come." He placed his hand on her arm. The motion was gentle, supportive. "My name is Fritz. My wife is just inside."

Ruby finally relented, letting the farmer lead her toward the house.

Inside, she found a fire blazing in the hearth and a woman about her age with long, dark hair and big, brown eyes cutting a piece of meat in the kitchen. The woman turned as she entered and said something in German, but Fritz spoke quickly, and the woman changed effortlessly to French.

"You are an escapee, no?" the woman asked, and Ruby glanced at the man and then back at the woman. Was this a trap after all? But before she could reply, the woman added, "Don't be frightened. We want to help you. We do not believe in the same things the Nazis believe in." The woman exchanged looks with her husband. "We are, how do you say, fighters for freedom."

Ruby blinked back unexpected tears. She didn't know whether the woman was telling the truth, but her instinct was to believe the words.

"And you, the Nazis have done much to hurt you?" the woman asked.

Ruby nodded, wordless.

The woman's eyes filled. "We are so very sorry. Please, have some food, and get some rest here. We will figure out tomorrow how to help get you to safety."

"Why?" Ruby whispered. "Why would you help me?"

"Because no one deserves what has happened to you. Now come. Sit. Eat. Tonight, you worry about nothing."

AFTER FEEDING RUBY A SMALL dinner of sausage, bread, and ale, Fritz's wife, who introduced herself as Eva, showed Ruby to a small bedroom that looked as if it had belonged to a child. Ruby awoke some time later with a sharp pain in her abdomen. When she blinked into the unexpected daylight, she realized Eva was there beside her, holding her hand.

"You are pregnant?" the woman asked gently, and Ruby struggled to sit up. Doing that made her hurt even more, and her heart thudded. What had she gotten herself into by coming here?

"Why do you say that?" Ruby wanted to get up, to run away, but the sharp pain in her abdomen was back, and she cried out, inadvertently squeezing Eva's hand. The woman held tight to her.

"Because you are in labor," Eva said gently. "The baby is coming now."

Ruby blinked up at her. "No. No, that cannot be. I must keep the baby inside." Images of her tiny dead son in the Dachers' apartment flooded back, and she was terrified. The urge to protect the child in her womb was the only thing that had gotten her this far. If she failed now too, how would she go on? What was there to live for?

"Relax," Eva said calmly. "Your baby is strong. I will help you. I have helped deliver many babies in this town."

Ruby blinked a few times, losing herself to another contraction. "Please, you must make sure my baby stays safe," she murmured when she could speak again. "Please, promise me."

"I promise. Now, will you tell me your name? And the name of the baby's father?"

Ruby could feel her own expression freezing in horror.

"Don't worry," Eva said quickly. "I will never betray you. But in case something happens to you, I need to know where the baby should go."

Ruby thought about this for a few seconds and nodded. Of course. She didn't want her child to wind up in an orphanage in Germany. "My name is Ruby Benoit." She didn't mention Thomas, because she didn't want to endanger him. "If something happens to me, you must contact my parents. They are in America."

"America?" Eva's eyebrows shot up in surprise. She beckoned to her husband and said something in German. He appeared by her side a moment later with a piece of paper and a pen, which Eva handed to Ruby. "Here. Please write their information here. But this is only in case of an emergency, Ruby. I know you will be fine."

Ruby still wasn't entirely sure she was doing the right thing, but what harm could there be in giving this woman her parents' address? She scribbled it out and then looked Eva in the eye. "Make sure the baby stays safe," Ruby said as another contraction overtook her. "Please. It's the only thing that matters."

Eva squeezed Ruby's hands tightly. "Ruby, you can make sure of that yourself. Now relax. Breathe with me. The baby is coming."

The last thing Ruby was aware of before drifting off into a dreamless sleep was the feeling of a great weight slipping from her body, followed by the most beautiful sound she'd ever heard: a baby's piercing wail. Ruby began to sob, and as she looked up, Eva entered her blurry field of vision cradling a tiny, squirming bundle.

"It's a girl," Eva said, smiling. "A beautiful baby girl."

CHAPTER FORTY-TWO

August 1944

"Do you think Ruby knows?" Charlotte asked as she and Lucien pushed through a crowd of people singing "La Marseillaise" on the Champs-Élysées on the last Tuesday in August. The world had changed once again, and after a week of fighting, of tanks rolling through the streets, of gunfire ringing out in the night, Paris was free. The Allies had arrived, and now, a victory parade was moving toward the Place de la Concorde. The French flag flew from the Arc de Triomphe, and American flags snapped in the breeze as U.S. servicemen grinned and blew kisses to French girls from their procession of military trucks. Parisians rushed forward with bottles of wine for the soldiers, who swigged from them, laughing.

"About the liberation?" Lucien kept his eyes on the parade, as if he couldn't quite believe it, as if he expected something terrible to happen at any moment now. After all, just a few days earlier, the day after de Gaulle had moved into the war ministry, German snipers had fired on a celebrating crowd just like this. Lucien's shoulders were tense, his jaw set. "I hope so. Any little piece of faith will help sustain her."

"It won't be long until the camps are liberated too, right? Ruby will be home soon."

Lucien squeezed her hand. "I don't know. There is still a lot of fighting to be done, Charlotte. It will take the Allies a while to move farther into Germany, I think. And if we're right about her being sent to Ravensbrück, she's very far east."

Charlotte didn't reply. He wasn't saying anything she didn't already know, of course. It was just that she needed words of hope and inspiration today. "I would know if she was dead, wouldn't I?"

Lucien looked down at her. "Why do you say that?"

"Because I believe it of my parents. I feel it in a way I can't explain. But I don't believe it of Ruby. She's still alive. She must be. I just know."

"Then we will believe in that. She is strong and brave, and I believe she would do anything in the world to get home to you."

"And the baby?"

Lucien shook his head. "My love, I can't imagine the baby has survived. It's better for Ruby, in fact, if it hasn't."

Charlotte nodded. They had talked of this before. And while she knew Ruby's chances of survival would be much higher if the pregnancy had ended, she also knew that losing a second child might just destroy her.

"But chin up," Lucien said after a moment, giving Charlotte a sad smile. "This is the beginning of the war's end. Can't you see? If the Germans have surrendered Paris, it's only a matter of time until we take Berlin too."

Looking around at the jubilant crowd, and at the weary, smiling soldiers, Charlotte knew he was speaking the truth.

"This is a big day for us, for France, for the war." Lucien leaned down and gave her a kiss. "It's not a day for sadness, my love."

"I know." Of course he was right. But the sun looked brightest when it was emerging from the darkest clouds. And today, Charlotte feared, the storm wasn't quite over.

"I love you," Lucien said.

"I love you too, Lucien."

And together, with all the voices of Paris, they joined in the singing of the national anthem.

Arise, children of the homeland.
The day of glory has arrived!

THE NEXT MORNING, CHARLOTTE AWOKE shortly after dawn to a beautiful sunrise just outside the window of the apartment she shared now with Lucien. She had been living with him since the day the police picked Ruby up in April, and although Lucien had been back to the old building a handful of times to check on things and to meet with Monsieur Savatier, Charlotte couldn't bring herself to go. This was her life now—until Ruby returned, at least—and looking forward was easier than looking back. It was just that the past had a strange way of haunting you, even when you didn't want to think about it.

If someone had told Charlotte three years ago that she'd be living with a boy she loved, she would have laughed out loud and then turned bright red. It simply wasn't what proper young ladies did. But things were different in wartime, and although Charlotte was only fifteen, she might as well have been twenty-five. She and Lucien had seen too much, done too much to ever go back to childhood. Even after Ruby had been arrested, they had continued to work for the Resistance, and that was the kind of thing that changed a person forever. Now that Paris was liberated, that work was done, and there was nothing left to do but wait.

Lucien rolled over and wrapped his arms around Charlotte, pulling her closer and burrowing his face into the warm space between her neck and shoulder. He was most affectionate when he was sleeping, when his guard wasn't up, when he wasn't worrying about the things that could go wrong. She loved these moments before the world was awake, when she could pretend for a short while that she was nothing more than a girl in love with a boy.

As she gazed out at the coming morning, she wondered whether Ruby could see the same sky. Were the colors of dawn—pinks, oranges, blues—as brilliant where she was as they were in Paris? Or was the sky here celebrating the liberation along with the rest of the city while the sky to the east remained stubbornly gray?

Beside her, Lucien stirred, murmuring her name as he often did upon waking. She turned and kissed his cheek and then looked out the window again.

"What are you thinking about?" he asked softly, burying his face in her hair.

"Just that maybe somewhere out there, Ruby can see the same sky," Charlotte said, closing her eyes. "Maybe one of these days, the sun will rise, and as it makes its way west, she will follow it home."

CHAPTER FORTY-THREE

August 1944

On the same morning, some twelve hundred miles farther south, Thomas was watching the sunrise too. He was in the cockpit of a Spitfire, his heart pounding as he waited for takeoff.

He was heading back to France. To the land where Ruby lived. To the country the Allies were in the midst of reclaiming. Now that the good guys were in control again, it no longer mattered to his superiors if he returned to France; there was no escape line to betray, no danger of being shot from the sky.

His job was simply to deliver the Spit to an airfield near Ramatuelle that had, until a month ago, been an olive grove. When the Allies had arrived, the U.S. Army had bulldozed the area to create a makeshift landing strip for deliveries. This was to be a staging spot from which to wage the remainder of the war to the east.

Thomas took off just past dawn, marveling, as he often did, at the glorious colors of the world at both ends of the day. Dawn and dusk were like beautiful bookends, and though the color often leached from the sky as noon approached, the day always began and ended with the same magnificent hues. Thomas smiled to himself that morning, thinking of how, when the war was over, he would take Ruby for a flight through the sunrise sky. Would the colors near the horizon—the oranges, the reds, the yellows—remind her of the poppies she'd told him about? Did the sunrises look the same over California?

He thought of Ruby as he flew, wondered what she was doing right now. He'd seen the newsreel footage of the liberation of Paris, and he'd searched the jubilant crowds for her face, knowing that the odds of seeing her were slim. Still, he imagined her—with Charlotte and Lucien by her side—dancing victorious down the Avenue des Champs-Élysées. He felt a great sense of relief; she would no longer have to put herself in danger by sheltering pilots. If Paris was free, then so was Ruby. The end of the war was in sight, and one day soon, he'd be able to return to her. As he flew north, he imagined that he could see all the way to the French capital, could see the French flags flying triumphant over the city once again.

In what felt like no time, the French coast was upon him. Beneath the Spit, the water gleamed a perfect topaz blue. Ramatuelle, a fingernail of a village carved out beneath Saint-Tropez, seemed to rise from the edge of the sea, its rooftops glowing sherbet orange in the morning light as they crawled up the cliffs away from the water. He could make out a church tower, a forest beyond that, a few boats bobbing serenely in the water. He could see the airstrip in the distance, and he began to prepare for landing.

And then, everything went wrong.

It started with a shudder, an abrupt *rat-tat-tat* in the engine that felt unfamiliar and strange. Frowning, Thomas checked his instrument controls, but he didn't need them to tell him the most pressing problem: he was losing altitude, and fast. Had he been hit? Had something happened to the fuel line? Was there an electrical problem? He was usually an ace at diagnosing problems and reacting calmly, but right now, he was at a loss. Everything had been fine one moment, and the next, his plane had gone haywire for no apparent reason at all.

He radioed Ramatuelle with a distress call. "Can you hear me? I'm losing altitude. Need to attempt emergency landing." The only response was a faint crackle. He could see the coastline, but he wouldn't reach it, not at the rate he was falling. His mind spun as the plane continued to descend. Could he save the aircraft? To lose a Spitfire now, on an errand like this, seemed foolish.

On the other hand, if he couldn't bring her in closer to the coast, he was out of luck. Spits weren't designed to float, and neither were the pilots enclosed in their cockpits. So that was it. He'd have to eject. The Spit was headed for the sea, and he didn't want to go with her.

Quickly, fighting a wave of disappointment, he went into survival mode, ripping off his oxygen mask and radio plug and detaching his safety harness. For a frozen second, he thought of the last time he'd gone down over France, when he'd parachuted in over Saint-Omer. He thought of the things that had happened after that, the way Ruby had felt in his arms, the sense that he was living his destiny, the feeling that his life was forever tied to hers.

And then, he reached for the release toggle, but nothing happened. The canopy hood didn't open. He tried again, desperately, and when the switch remained stuck, he began to claw at the hood, doing his best to force it open.

But the hood was jammed, and as the sickening realization hit, Thomas's heart sank. His only option was reaching the small strip of sandy, rocky beach that he could see in the distance, but he knew that it was impossible. He'd been flying Spitfires for years now, and he understood exactly what this plane was capable of—and what she couldn't do.

He slammed his hands against the canopy again and again, knowing that his only chance of survival now would be to break the seal and pray that the plane's plunge into the water was gentle enough not to knock him unconscious. But the Spit was descending too quickly. As the sea rose up to meet him, he knew with a terrible certainty that this was the end.

Thomas closed his eyes, and the world Ruby had painted with her words came alive. In the distance, he could see the house with the white picket fence, the one where they would raise their children together. But before he could get there, he had to make it through the brilliant sea of poppies. The flowers gleamed beautiful, magical, just like the sunrise, and as they danced in the breeze all around him, he could feel himself smiling. They were welcoming him home.

"Ruby!" he cried out just as his Spit plunged into the shallow sea a few hundred yards from the French coast. Just beyond the poppies, there she was, smiling and beckoning, letting him know that at long last, it was all right to rest.

CHAPTER FORTY-FOUR

August 1944

Ruby was vaguely aware of murmurs, quiet voices, whispered questions, and then, something like music. She strained to listen, and it was only after a few moments that she realized what the sound was. A baby cooing. *Her* baby cooing. "My baby!" she managed to whisper, though the world felt hazy and untenable. Where was she? How long had she been sleeping? Why couldn't she see more than foggy shapes?

Eva, the farmer's wife, appeared in her field of vision, carrying a small, perfect bundle. "You're awake, Ruby. Would you like to say hello to your daughter?"

Ruby's throat constricted as Eva brought the baby closer and placed her gently on Ruby's chest. Her vision cleared enough that she could see the baby's face in all its perfect detail. She was beautiful, healthy against all the odds. She had Thomas's brilliant blue eyes, and for a few seconds, as Ruby gazed into them, she had the feeling that Thomas was right here with her. She could hardly wait until they were together again. Soon, they'd all go home. Not home to Paris, but home to the United States, the place they'd spend the rest of forever together. She knew her parents would love Thomas and their new granddaughter with all their hearts, and they'd welcome Charlotte with open arms too. Ruby would show them the world of poppies, the way that each new day exploded in a symphony of colors and hope. She could see the future, and it was glorious.

Although Ruby felt weak, she was still able to hold her baby, who was rooting around for her mother's breast. Tears came to Ruby's eyes, for she wasn't producing milk; it was impossible after Ravensbrück.

"We have some milk for her," Eva said, seeming to read Ruby's mind. "She'll be all right."

"Thank you," Ruby rasped, still astonished at her good fortune to have ended up here. She swore to herself that she would repay Eva and Fritz one day.

"What is her name?" Eva asked. "Your daughter?"

Ruby smiled down at the baby in her arms for a moment without replying. She had hair the color of midnight and the tiniest fingers and toes Ruby had ever seen. Her skin was pale and her cheeks were pink. She was far smaller than she should have been, maybe only five pounds, but she was healthy and whole, which seemed impossible. She was, Ruby knew, the very definition of a miracle. And that gave her hope for the future, for if miracles could happen within her own body, they could happen anywhere. It meant that Thomas would come back to her, that Charlotte would be waiting for her in Paris.

"Nadia," Ruby murmured with a smile, thinking of her Russian friend who had given her this gift, this chance of survival, at the cost of her own life. The child she had saved would forever bear her name. "Her name is Nadia. It means *hope*."

Eva had tears in her eyes as she smiled down at Ruby and the baby. "Nadia," she said softly. "A beautiful name."

"Yes." Ruby gazed down at her daughter, who looked up at her mother's face, searching. "My sweet little girl. You will have a good life, my darling. I promise you."

"Ruby," Eva said after a few minutes. "I have some news for you. Paris was liberated a few days ago. The Allies are headed east. It is only a matter of time."

"Paris was liberated?" Ruby felt breathless, and she imagined joy flooding through the capital, people dancing in the streets, the French flag flying once again. Charlotte would be safe now, and that alone was enough to bring tears of joy to Ruby's eyes. "Thank God." She drew a ragged breath. "May I ask one more thing of you? There are three letters I'd like to write, just in case something happens to me."

"Of course." Eva went to retrieve a few pieces of paper and a pen, and when she returned, she offered to hold Nadia while Ruby wrote. But Ruby didn't want to let go, and so she cradled her daughter in the crook of her left arm while writing shakily with her right hand. When she was done, she addressed the letters—one to her parents, one to Thomas in care of the RAF, and one to Charlotte in care of Lucien—and handed them to Eva. "Thank you," she whispered.

"There's no need to thank me."

Eva eventually took Nadia and fed her milk from a bottle as Ruby drifted off. When she awoke, it was morning, and she could have sworn she'd heard an explosion somewhere in the distance. "Has something happened?" she asked, struggling to the surface.

Eva was there beside her, cradling Nadia, and she looked startled by Ruby's abrupt question. "I don't think so."

"I thought I heard a noise," Ruby murmured, focusing on her daughter's face. Eva rose and placed Nadia on Ruby's chest once more, and Ruby touched her lips to the top of her daughter's head, feeling her soft, downy hair. Ruby was hot, so hot, but the baby's skin was cool, and Ruby knew she would be okay. "My sweet little girl," she murmured. "One day soon, you will meet your father, and your aunt Charlotte and uncle Lucien, and your grandmother and grandfather. They'll all love you so much, my sweet angel, just like I do."

Eva left the room as Ruby cooed to the baby, and she returned a moment later with a wet cloth, which she put on Ruby's forehead. "You're burning up, my dear," she said. She reached for Nadia, but Ruby held on tightly, shaking her head.

"Please," she whispered. "Not yet."

Eva nodded, backing away, but Ruby could see concern in her eyes.

"What day is today?" Ruby asked, because she wanted to remember everything about the start of her child's life.

"Wednesday, August thirtieth," Eva replied.

Ruby's eyes filled with tears. She tried to take a deep breath, but there was pressure on her lungs, and she couldn't quite inhale. "I know I have no right to ask anything else of you," she began, "but please promise me again that you will protect my baby."

"I swear it on my life," Eva said firmly, and Ruby believed her. "Sleep now, Ruby. It's okay. You've saved your daughter."

"I did. I really did. And now, I'll see Thomas very soon."

"Yes," Eva agreed. She had moved to Ruby's side and was stroking her forehead.

"And Charlotte. And my parents."

"Yes."

Eva's words and the cool touch of her hand were so soothing. Against her brittle, hollowed chest, Ruby could feel her baby's heartbeat, and she smiled, relaxing into the rhythm. For the first time in years, she knew in the depths of her soul that everything would be okay. "Nadia," she whispered as the world faded away once again. "Thomas."

And then she closed her eyes, and the poppy fields were there, their vibrant, familiar colors bright against the crisp blue sky. It had to be a dream, didn't it? But there was her house, the one she'd grown up in, and beside it, impossibly, was the home she had talked of building one day: a whitewashed cottage with a white picket fence, exactly as she'd imagined it. She could feel the fresh desert air; she could feel the grass whispering beneath her feet; she could smell the fragrance of her mother's apple pie wafting from the open window of her parents' kitchen. Somewhere in the distance, Fred Astaire sang "Cheek to Cheek."

Ruby began to walk toward the house, and that's when she saw Thomas emerging from the poppies. He looked just as he had when she'd last seen him, handsome and strong and full of hope. "Ruby!" he called, and all at once, his arms were open, and she was running toward him. She had always known, somewhere deep inside, that she would see him again, but this still felt like a miracle.

"Thomas!" she cried as she fell into him, and that's when she knew for sure this wasn't a dream. He was warm and solid and real.

Soon, she would tell him about Nadia, about the way her blue eyes sparkled, about the way her hair was feather-soft, about the way she looked just like him. She would tell him that she had saved their daughter, but that it was he who had saved her all those years before by giving her a reason to live. She would tell him that she loved him, that she intended to spend the rest of eternity by his side, if he'd have her. There would be time for all of that, but for now, she only wanted to feel his arms around her, to hear his heartbeat, to breathe him in.

She looked down and realized she looked just as she had that day in 1941 when Thomas had first arrived at her door on the rue Amélie. Her curves were once again ample, her skin glowing. Her dress was white, silky as a feather, billowy as a cloud. The poppy fields were familiar and unfamiliar at the same time, but their brilliant colors, more brilliant than she'd ever seen, soothed her.

She knew she was exactly where she was meant to be, and as she found her home at last in Thomas's arms, she could see the future stretching before them, beautiful and bright.

CHAPTER FORTY-FIVE

March 2002

We reach the top of the hill just as the sun is nearing the horizon. I'd tried, at first, to push my darling girl through the fields in her wheelchair, but it had been too much; the wheels lodged in the mud. So I'd scooped her into my arms and carried her—like a bride over the threshold—the rest of the way. My whole body hurts, but I don't care. Being able to hold her one last time, to feel her heartbeat against mine, is worth the pain.

Spreading below us now is the vast swath of poppy fields we inherited from Ruby's parents when they died in 1947. My wife has always said that she feels Ruby's presence here, especially when the poppies are in bloom. For a long time, I never felt it, but I do now. Now I believe.

After the war, the Red Cross was able to get word to Ruby's parents about Nadia, and when they came for her, the farmer and his wife gave them the letter Ruby had written just before she died. In it, she told them all about how Charlotte had become her family, and so when it became clear that Charlotte's parents had perished in Auschwitz, Ruby's parents insisted upon adopting her and bringing her to California as well. They understood how much Ruby had loved her, and so they loved her too, right from the start. But both of them died before Nadia was two, leaving sole custody of their granddaughter to Charlotte, who had just turned eighteen. After waiting for a visa, I married my darling girl amid the poppies that March and became Nadia's adopted father.

We were never able to have biological children ourselves, but Nadia is ours in every way that matters, and I can't imagine loving a child more than we love her. As Ruby and Charlotte discovered so long ago, family is about so much more than blood.

"Do you think I'll see Ruby, Lucien?" my darling girl asks me now as I set her gently down at the crest of the hill, my arms aching nearly as much as my heart. "And Thomas? And my parents?"

"I think," I say slowly, my eyes filling with tears, "that they're with us every day. I think they have been all along."

Nowhere is that more evident than on this spot. Ruby's body came home in February 1946, and the month after her parents buried her here, with a silver statue of a poppy to mark her grave, the hill bloomed only in ruby red. Every year since, although the rest of the valley blossoms in a sunset rainbow, this place remains drenched only in crimson. I believe with every cell in my being that it's a sign that Ruby watches over us from the other side.

My darling girl nods and gazes off toward the east, where the horizon is beginning to melt into the late-afternoon mist. "I imagine sometimes that I can see all the way to Paris from here," she murmurs. "That I can see into the past. That Ruby is still alive, and Thomas has just shown up at our door, and my parents are coming home any moment now."

I close my eyes, too choked up to reply. I never knew my wife's parents, but I love them for raising such a wonderful woman—and for having the foresight to protect her. As for Ruby, well, she was always Charlotte's, but I love her too. I love her for saving my wife and for the way she fought until the end to save Nadia. There's not a piece of my world today that would exist if she hadn't come into Charlotte's life all those years ago.

I slip my arm around my darling girl and pull her close. "From up here, it sometimes feels like the past and the present collide," I say. "I feel it too." We stay that way for a long time, until the poppies begin to glow in the waning evening light.

"You said once that I was brave," Charlotte says, breaking the long and lovely silence between us.

I smile. "I'm sure I've said that many times, my darling."

"But the first time. When you said it to Philippe."

I sigh and look off into the distant east once more. "I remember." It is the fault of those words that Charlotte became part of the Resistance, that Ruby became more involved than she should have been. It's a black mark on my conscience that I've never been able to erase.

"You told Philippe that I was strong and bold."

"Did I?" I kiss her on the cheek. "I always was a good judge of character."

I'm teasing her, but the half smile falls from my face as she looks up at me with eyes full of sadness. "What if you were wrong, Lucien?" she asks in a small voice. "What if I'm none of those things?"

"Oh, but you are, my darling. You're the strongest person I know."

When I lean in to kiss her once more on the cheek, I can taste her tears. "I'm scared, Lucien," she says. "I'm frightened of what comes next."

And that's when I know for sure. She's telling me she's ready to go. For a moment, I don't say anything, because I can't. But it's time for her to find peace, and it's up to me to help her.

Slowly and with great effort, I get down on one knee and offer her my hand. I did this fifty-five years ago when I asked her to marry me, and I know she realizes I'm asking her to trust me one last time. I guide her down beside me, gently, until we're lying side by side among Ruby's poppies, staring up at the sky, which is just turning the deep cornflower blue of early twilight. I can see the first star of the evening flickering above us.

"Remember the first time I held you in my arms this way?" I ask.

She sighs. "I was fourteen. Ruby was asleep, and you appeared in the courtyard outside my window on the rue de Lasteyrie."

I smile into the darkness and wipe away a tear. "You were crying. You insisted you were all right, and I reminded you that it was okay not to be."

"I remember." Her voice is fading, and it takes all my resolve not to beg her to stay with me a little while longer. But that would be for me, not for her.

"It's okay now too." I nuzzle her neck and pull her close to me, curling my body around hers just like I did on that night. "I told you then that you had to hold on to hope, my darling girl."

"And I did. For all these years, Lucien."

"Good." I breathe into her hair, inhaling the scent of her. "Then just hold on a little longer. Hope will carry you home."

"I love you," she murmurs, so softly that I can barely hear her.

"I love you too." And just like that night so many years ago, I know that the comfort of my body against hers has soothed her. She melts into me, and as I stroke her hair and murmur *"Je t'aime,"* again and again, the night closes in, and I can feel her slipping away.

"Ruby," she murmurs, her voice full of hope and love, and then she smiles softly, and she's not breathing anymore. I know she's already made the crossing, and that somehow, Ruby is there to take her home. Peace settles over me as tears fill my eyes.

"Good-bye, my love," I whisper. I know that one day soon, I'll see her again.

I struggle to my feet, and in the waning light, I gently lift my sweet Charlotte into my arms for the last time and begin the long walk down the hill, across the fields of poppies.

Author's Note

While researching World War II connections to Florida for my 2016 novel, *When We Meet Again*, which is set partially in the Sunshine State, I came across the extraordinary story of Virginia d'Albert-Lake, a Florida woman who married a Frenchman in 1937, moved to Paris, and ultimately worked with the Comet escape line in 1943 and 1944 before her arrest and imprisonment at the infamous Ravensbrück concentration camp. Like Ruby, the heroine of *The Room on Rue Amélie*, Virginia initially had the option to return to the States and decided against it. She felt compelled to help.

From the start, I felt a kinship with Virginia, who died in 1997 at the age of eighty-seven. I never knew her, but the paths of our lives overlapped many times, albeit decades apart. Like me, she moved with her family from the middle of Ohio to St. Petersburg, Florida, when she was a child. Like me, she was published for the very first time in the *St. Petersburg Times*. Like me, she lived in the Orlando area as a young woman and then fell head over heels in love with Paris. She even lived in the same Paris arrondissement where I once lived, just over a mile from my old address. I was drawn to her story and fascinated by the idea of an American woman choosing to stay in Paris during the war so that she could help save lives. The idea for the character of Ruby was born.

Virginia's diary survived the war and was published in 2006 as *An American Heroine in the French Resistance* (Fordham University Press), providing me with a wonderful jumping-off point for the story of the fictional Ruby Henderson Benoit, who, like Virginia, couldn't sit idly by with the world at war. In a 1993 interview in the *St. Petersburg Times*, Thomas Yankus, a pilot shot down over France in 1944, said of Virginia, "There we were, walking into this apartment after some pretty hairy experiences and being greeted by this beautiful woman who said, 'Hi, fellas, how're you doing?' She had no fear whatsoever." I envisioned Ruby as that kind of woman too.

Creating Thomas, Charlotte, Lucien, and the other characters who populate *The Room on Rue Amélie* took a lot of research too, and I'm indebted to many authors who chronicled the war years in Paris so well. The heartrending *Journal of Hélène Berr*—often compared to Anne Frank's diary—was very useful in helping me to understand the sentiments of Jews in Paris as the war dragged on, as was *Jews in France During World War II* by Renée Poznanski. Caroline Moorehead's *A Train in Winter*, Ronald C. Rosbottom's *When Paris Went Dark*, and Alan Riding's *And the Show Went On* were great resources for understanding life in Paris in the 1940s. *First Light* by Geoffrey Wellum and *Survival Against All Odds* by John Misseldine were fascinating firsthand accounts of what the war was like for RAF pilots who flew missions over the Continent. And *The Freedom Line* by Peter Eisner, *Little Cyclone* by Airey Neave, and *The Shelburne Escape Line* by Réanne Hemingway-Douglass, and many newspaper features, helped me to understand the Allied escape lines through France and how they operated. It's important to note, however, that while based heavily on the Comet, Shelburne, and Pat O'Leary escape lines, the escape routes in this book are fictionalized.

I'm also indebted to the kind folks at the Holocaust Memorial Resource and Education Center of Florida and the Mémorial de la Shoah in Paris, as well as to Sarah Helm for her illuminative book about Ravensbrück.

Ultimately, Ruby's story takes a much different course than Virginia's real life did. But I'd like to think that there's a little piece of the heroic Virginia in this book. In fact, I'd like to think there's a little piece of Virginia in all of us—and that when we see injustice, we might just have the courage to stand up and fight against it.

Kristin Harmel

Acknowledgments

I can't say enough about all the wonderful people who have helped me with this book—and with my career in general. To Holly Root: You are the best agent on the planet, and I'm so fortunate to be your client—and your friend. Thanks for all your hard work and wonderful advice, and for always being in my corner. I'm so excited to see what the future holds for Root Literary. To Abby Zidle: Lady, how do you *do* it? You are juggling about five million responsibilities, and you somehow execute all of them perfectly. Thanks for being a wonderful editor and a great advocate for me and my novels. To Kristin Dwyer: Striking out on your own is such an act of bravery, and I'm so glad to see you finding your happiness. Woo-hoo for LEO PR!

Heather Baror-Shapiro, you are a goddess of foreign rights, and I'm so glad to be working with you. Dana Spector, you are a rock star for so many reasons. Andy Cohen, I'm so happy to see you having such "Gifted" success. And Farley Chase, I will never forget the way you changed my life by first bringing my novels to a large, worldwide audience.

To Eva Schubert: I miss working with you, but I'm so glad that our friendship continues to flourish. We need a red velvet cupcake date soon, my dear! (Thanks for correcting my German in this book too!) And to Elisabetta Migliavada: Thank you for both your friendship and your continued support of me and my books. Hope to see you again soon—and to meet Giulia! Thank you also to Julia Fronhoefer, Nicola Bartels, Jorid Mathiassen, Hilit Hamour-Meir, and all my wonderful editors and publishers all over the world. I'm beyond grateful that you've shared my novels with so many wonderful readers.

Big thanks to all the other wonderful people I've had the opportunity to work with at Gallery Books, Root Literary, and Waxman Leavell Literary, especially Meagan Harris, Nancy Tonik, Diana Velasquez, Mackenzie Hickey, Chelsea McGuckin, Jen Long and the whole Gallery sales team, Taylor Haggerty, and Ashley Lopez. An extra-special thank-you to Jen Bergstrom, Louise Burke, and Carolyn Reidy.

Huge love and gratitude to my Swan Valley sisters (and brother), some of the kindest, most talented people I have the pleasure to know: Wendy Toliver, Linda Gerber, Allison van Diepen, Emily Wing Smith, Alyson Noël, Jay Asher, and Aprilynne Pike. Everyone should read *everything* these talented souls write! I'm a better writer and a better person for knowing them.

To those of you in the book blogging/reviewing community who are so vocal and supportive about the books and authors you enjoy: THANK YOU. You help share our books with readers, which is such a gift. Thanks especially to Jenny O'Regan, Melissa Amster, Amy Bromberg, Aestas, Brenda Janowitz, Liz Fenton and Lisa Steinke, Kristy Barrett, Hailey Fish, and Lorelei—and

I know I'm just scratching the surface. And thank you to all the readers who take the time to give me feedback on my novels—whether by email, social media, or review sites. It means a lot to hear from you.

Thanks, as always, to all my wonderful family members and friends, who are too numerous to name—but you know who you are (I hope!). I love you all.

A special thanks to Lauren Boulanger for being so wonderful with Noah.

And of course a very deep and special thank-you to Jason and Noah. You two are the center of my world, and every day you teach me more about the depths of my heart. As long as there are stars in the sky, I will love you.